A Call to Courage

Holly Green writes historical sagas about love and war, and her books are inspired by the stories she heard from her parents when she was a child. Holly is from Liverpool and is a trained actress and teacher. She is married and enjoys spending time with her two delightful grandchildren.

D0238439

**Causeway Books,
Bushmills.**
07776075176

A Call to Courage

HOLLY GREEN

First published in the United Kingdom in 2023 by

Hera Books
Unit 9 (Canelo), 5th Floor
Cargo Works, 1–2 Hatfields
London SE1 9PG
United Kingdom

Print ISBN 978 1 80436 372 0
Ebook ISBN 978 1 80436 371 3

Look for more great books at www.herabooks.com

Printed and bound in Great Britain by Clays Ltd, Elcograf S.p.A.

I

Chapter One

Paris

August 1939

Chez Michel, a cafe-bar in the Latin Quarter, was loud with the noise of young voices discussing and disputing and hazy with the smoke from Gitanes cigarettes.

A man banged his fist on the table and declared, 'It's a betrayal of everything we stand for! How can we, as communists, support a pact with the fascist dictator Hitler?'

'You're wrong!' another voice shouted. 'By signing the pact with Ribbentrop, Comrade Molotov has made a great contribution to safeguarding the peace.'

'I don't agree...'

The argument had raged among students at the prestigious Sorbonne University ever since the Treaty of Non-Aggression between Germany and the Union of Soviet Socialist Republics had been announced.

From a nearby table came the sound of a glass being smashed and a voice exclaimed, *'Jebiga!'* The flame-haired girl sitting next to the last speaker turned her head sharply to look for the source of the oath. A young man was trying, rather ineffectually, to mop up a pool of red wine with a paper napkin.

'Gee, fellers, I'm sorry! Excuse me! *Je m'excuse…*'

Whether in English or French the accent was indisputably American, but the oath had been in neither language. She craned her neck, but all she could see of the man was a head of dark, rather unruly hair set above broad shoulders.

'Alix!' her companion tugged at her sleeve. 'You agree with me, don't you?'

She turned back to him. 'Yes, of course I do. This non-aggression pact just leaves Hitler free to do whatever he likes in Europe.'

The argument continued until Michel, the owner, began pointedly clearing glasses and stacking chairs on empty tables. As the gathering broke up and the crowd jostled to get out of the door, Alix managed to get close to the young American. For a moment she hesitated, searching for a way to start the conversation. In the end she said, 'Your mother would smack your hand if she heard you use that word.'

He looked round at her in surprise. 'I'm sorry. I didn't mean to offend anyone. I didn't think anyone would understand a Serbian swear word.'

Now that she could see him properly she discovered dark, deep-set eyes under strongly marked brows in a face that looked as though he spent a lot of time outdoors in the sun.

'Most people wouldn't,' she replied, in Serbocroat. 'As they say, it takes one to know one.'

'You speak Serbian?'

'I am Serbian. Well, half Serbian. My mother is English. But you're American. Right?'

'Serbian American. My folks came from Macedonia.' He held out his hand, with a little formal bow. 'Stefan Popovic, at your service. But call me Steve.'

She shook his hand. 'Alexandra Malkovic. Call me Alix.'

The man she had been sitting next to turned away from concluding his argument and caught her arm. 'Alix! Come on.' He eyed the other man suspiciously. 'Who's this?'

'This is Stefan,' she said. 'He's American, but his parents are Serbian. Steve, this is Raoul.'

Steve stuck out his hand and said in French. '*Enchanté*. Pleased to meet you, Raoul.'

Raoul simply nodded and ignored the offered hand. 'Come on, Alix. We need to get back.'

He took her arm and drew her away. She looked back with a shrug and a half-smile of apology and Steve raised his hand in farewell.

'That was very rude!' she said as they walked. 'What's the matter with you?'

'I don't like to see you chatting away with a strange man like that.'

'Don't be silly. It was just nice to speak my own language for a few minutes. There's no need for you to be jealous.' She shook off the hand on her arm. Really, since they had become a couple Raoul had become increasingly possessive.

'I'm not jealous! We don't know anything about him. He could be trying to infiltrate the group.'

'Oh, grow up, Raoul! Anybody would think we were in some kind of secret society.'

'There's a war coming. We all know that. A lot of people are suspicious of anyone with communist sympathies. I don't trust the Americans. He could be a spy.'

'Oh, rubbish!' she exclaimed, but with less conviction in her voice.

If pushed to describe their relationship, Alix would not have chosen to call him her lover. He was a friend with whom she occasionally had sex, but there had never been real love on either side. It was true to say that for both of them the act was more political than romantic. She was beginning to realise, however, that for him it was about something else. It was about control. From the start there had been very little tenderness and over the last weeks his behaviour had become more demanding, asserting his dominance over her. She had accepted it at first, telling herself that his impatience was a sign of his overpowering desire for her. She had even found it exciting. But recently it had begun to frighten her.

–

The following evening, Alix was with Raoul in the same cafe and she saw Steve come in. He was on his own and his gaze moved from table to table until he found her and raised his hand in greeting. On an impulse, she waved him over.

'This is Steve,' she said to her friends. 'He's American. You don't mind if he joins us, do you?'

People moved up, a spare chair was found, wine was offered, and very soon Steve was the centre of an eager enquiry into American attitudes to the situation in Europe.

'If it comes to war, will the Americans join in?' was the question asked most urgently.

Steve shook his head apologetically. 'I'm sorry. I don't think so. Most people seem to think it's nothing to do with us and don't want to get involved.'

As the discussion became more animated, Raoul remained silent, glowering at the American. After a while, he pushed back his chair and got up. 'I'm going. Alix, are you coming with me?'

She frowned up at him. 'No, it's early yet. I'll stay.'

'Suit yourself,' he said, and left.

As the focus of the conversation moved elsewhere, Steve leaned across to Alix. 'I hope your friend didn't leave because of me.'

She smiled at him. 'Oh, don't take any notice of Raoul. He gets these moods sometimes.'

'I'm glad I found you here. I wasn't sure if we'd ever meet again.'

She looked at him. There was something about his face that seemed familiar, although she knew they had never met before. It awoke memories of her childhood growing up on her father's estate outside Belgrade. The thought that he had come to the cafe expressly to look for her gave her a small thrill of pleasure.

'Oh,' she made her tone casual, 'we're here most nights.'

When the cafe closed and they all left, he asked if he could walk her back to wherever she was staying. There was no sign of Raoul so she agreed, feeling again that little internal quiver of delight.

'I'm staying at the College Franco-Britannique; it's for foreign students studying at the Sorbonne,' she told him. 'It's a bit of a trek.'

'I don't mind,' he said. 'The walk will do me good.'

They left the bar and, turning their backs on the Seine with the dome of the Sacré Coeur floating above it in the moonlight, headed down a long boulevard into the 13th arrondissement.

'So,' he said as they walked, 'what are you doing in Paris?'

She gave him a sideways look. 'Not getting married.' It seemed natural to answer him in Serbocroat and they continued in that language.

'Ah.' He thought about this for a moment. 'Does that mean that if you were not in Paris you would be getting married?'

'Put it this way: I'd be finding it very hard not to.'

'Someone pressuring you?'

'My father.'

'Why would that be?'

She caught his eye. He was looking at her as if her answer really mattered to him. She sighed. 'My father belongs to a very old, aristocratic family. He's Count Malkovic. And he has very firm ideas about where a woman belongs and what she should do. He's made up his mind that I ought to marry the son of another old, aristocratic family, to cement an alliance.'

He whistled softly. 'Gee, that sounds positively Victorian.'

'I'd say medieval was closer to the mark,' she replied. 'That's the trouble with Serbia. They – the older gener-ation, I mean – are all still fighting the battle of Kosovo when the Serbian army was wiped out by the Turks. They are still trying to restore their honour and avenge the defeat.'

'That's going back a bit, isn't it?' he said.

'1389,' she agreed with a grin. 'We got rid of the Turks sixty years ago, but we seem to have been fighting someone or other ever since. I suppose it's not surprising that people feel – I don't know – embattled?

Maybe because of that, social attitudes haven't changed in centuries.'

'So, how did you manage to escape?' he asked.

'That was down to my brilliant mother. She's English. She persuaded my father that I ought to see a bit of the world before I settled down, so we went on a sort of Grand Tour. We went to Venice and Rome and Florence, and then, when we got here to Paris, she enrolled me at the Sorbonne. I've been here since May.'

'What are you studying?'

'European history. But I'm not a very good student, I'm afraid. I'm just not the academic type. It's just an excuse to stay here.'

'So how has your father taken that?'

'I don't know. I haven't been home. I'm scared he won't let me come back. And I can't expect my mother to rescue me again. I'm afraid he hasn't forgiven her for getting me in here in the first place. She's back in England now, keeping out of the way until he has time to simmer down.' For a moment she wondered why she was telling him all this, but he was easy to talk to and he seemed genuinely interested. In that way he was very different from Raoul, who never wanted to talk about anything but politics.

'She sounds like a pretty strong lady,' he said.

'Oh, she's a free spirit. She goes her own way, whatever anyone else says.'

'Doesn't sound like the sort of woman your father would want to marry,' he remarked.

'You would think so, wouldn't you? But he makes an exception for her. They adore each other. I don't know the whole story, but they fought through the last war together. She was a nurse and very brave. I think they met even before that, back in 1912 when we were fighting to get the Turks out of Macedonia.'

'Ah-ha!' he exclaimed. 'I knew we had something in common. That's part of my history, too.' He looked genuinely delighted, and she found herself smiling back at him.

'How?'

'That's how my parents met. My Pa volunteered to fight in that war. He met my Ma and took her back with him to Fairbanks.'

'Fairbanks? Where's that?'

'Alaska. It's about as far north as you can go in the USA.'

'Why was he living there?'

'There are a lot of people of Serb extraction there. Most of them came out at the time of the gold rush. You've probably heard of the Klondike and the Yukon? My grandpappy was one of them. He never struck it rich, but he realised that the soil in the Tanana Valley was very rich and although the winters were very cold and the summers were short, the fact that it hardly gets dark in mid-summer meant that crops could ripen fast. He'd been a peasant farmer back home and he'd made a little money from the gold, so he bought a few acres and started growing things... strawberries, mostly. The farm went well, so he went back to Macedonia and found himself a wife and they had five kids. My pa was the second son.'

'So does your father grow strawberries?'

'No. There wasn't enough income from the farm to support several families, but my ma is an excellent cook. They opened a restaurant serving traditional Serbian food, and it's doing very well. They have three now, in different parts of the city.'

'So, are you here to study French cuisine?'

He gave a short, embarrassed laugh. 'No, 'fraid not. Nothing as useful as that.'

'Why, then?'

'You'll think I'm a crazy dreamer.'

'Try me.' She smiled at him.

'I want to be a writer.'

'There's nothing crazy about that. What sort of writer?'

'I'm not sure. Novels, probably – or perhaps journalism.'

'And why Paris?'

'That's the really mad bit. I knew I'd never have anything to write about if I stayed in Fairbanks, but Ernest Hemingway's a sort of idol of mine. I'd read about his time in Paris. I just wanted to be here, walk in his footsteps, eat in the cafes he ate in, drink in the bars… oh, you know the sort of thing. And I was really lucky. I was studying at the University of Alaska and I got a few things published in the local rag, and when I talked to my professor about it, he said I ought to travel, to broaden my experience. He managed to convince the university to give me a grant for a year. I only got here a month ago.'

Alix looked at him. He was unlike any man she had ever met, prepared to take a chance, trust to luck. And when he spoke he ran a hand through his thick, slightly curly hair with a rueful, self-deprecating smile that made her want to reach out and touch him.

'So are you enrolled here, at the Sorbonne?' she asked, pushing the impulse to the back of her mind.

'No. I'm just, you know, bumming around, soaking up the atmosphere. I've got a part-time job in a bookshop on the Left Bank. I keep hoping someone really famous will come in for a book, but no luck so far.'

They walked in silence for a few minutes. He made no attempt to take her arm, but Alix was very aware of his physical presence, as if there was an electric current between them. After a while, he said, 'I hope you don't mind me saying it, but you don't look Serbian, with your red hair and your blue eyes.'

'I know,' she said. 'I take after my mother. When I was a kid I used to wish I did look more like the others. It was quite a relief when I was sent to school in England and found that I wasn't so different after all.'

'You went to school in England?'

'Yes, from when I was twelve. Well, education for women isn't a top priority in Yugoslavia. My parents decided I'd do better there.'

'How did you feel about that?'

'I was homesick at first, of course. But I enjoyed it once I'd settled in.'

They cut across the Parc Montsouris, where the night breeze whispered in the trees, and arrived outside the imposing frontage of the College Franco-Britannique. Alix stopped. 'This is where I live. Thank you so much for walking me back.'

'It's been my pleasure,' he said with a flourish of gallantry.

For a moment they were both silent. Alix was wondering if he would try to kiss her, and how she would react if he did, but in the end, he only said, 'Will I see you again?'

'Well, as I said, we're at the cafe most nights. But we don't have anyone famous calling in.'

'That doesn't matter, as long as you're there. But...'

'What?'

'What about your… what about Raoul? I wouldn't want to cause trouble between you.'

She tossed her head. 'Raoul can go boil his head if he's going to be difficult. I don't let any man tell me who I may or may not talk to.'

He laughed. 'That sounds to me like your mother talking. A chip off the old maternal block, eh?'

She smiled. 'I can't think of a bigger compliment.'

—

That night Alix found it hard to sleep. Speaking the language of her own country had brought a sudden wave of homesickness. She thought of the estate where she had grown up; the long, low house with its elegant pillared portico, its beautifully laid out grounds, the vineyards that surrounded it and the fields where she had ridden her first pony and then the splendid horses that had taken its place. She pictured her father, the teasing smile in his deep-set dark eyes when she asked for something extravagant and the rueful laugh with which he admitted he could refuse her nothing. That was why it had come as such a shock when he had introduced Nikola and told her that this was the young man she was going to marry. She had thought it a joke at first, but he had made it clear that he regarded it as her duty, and when she refused, he had declared that she was no daughter of his and would henceforth have to fend for herself. She had sobbed and pleaded and then stormed at him as a heartless tyrant, but to no avail, until her mother had intervened with the suggestion that she was still too young to make such a commitment and must be given more time.

Next evening, the usual group congregated in the cafe. The pact between Ribbentrop and Molotov was still the main item of discussion and the same arguments were being aired. Usually, Alix would have listened avidly, but tonight she found it impossible to concentrate, and her eyes kept turning towards the door. Would Steve join them again?

He arrived twenty minutes later and was made welcome. As before, people moved up to make space for him, and his glass was filled from one of the communal bottles of *vin ordinaire*. He looked across at Alix and said, in Serbian, 'So, you see? Here I am again.'

She replied in the same language and for a few moments they chatted, ignoring the conversation going on around them. She was brought back sharply to the present by Raoul slamming his hand on the table.

'Stop that! I won't have you jabbering away in a language no one else can understand.'

She was about to make an angry response when Steve cut in, speaking his heavily accented French, his tone apologetic.

'I'm sorry. It was my fault. It was rude of us to talk like that when we're part of a group. Please,' – he looked around the table, making it clear that he was apologising to everyone present – 'do forgive us.' He gave a small laugh. 'To be quite honest, between French and English and Serbian, I sometimes don't know which language I'm speaking.'

There was a general murmur of acquiescence from the rest of the group, with comments that made it clear no one else had been offended. Raoul glared from Steve to

Alix for a moment, but he was left with no option but to resume his seat in resentful silence. Alix threw Steve a quick look of gratitude and then turned her attention to the general conversation. There was a question at the back of everybody's mind. Was war inevitable? Since the spring the city had been disturbed by preparations. Miles of trenches had been dug; gas masks had been distributed and signs put up pointing the way to the nearest air raid shelter. It was still possible, however, to cling to the hope that it might all come to nothing.

Alix made a point of listening to Raoul's contributions and backing him up wherever possible and slowly his resentful mood softened. As they prepared to leave, he said, 'Come back to the apartment tonight. I'll tell the other two to make themselves scarce.'

Raoul lived in a small flat, which he shared with two other students, under the eaves of one of the tall grey houses off the Avenue Rockefeller. That night he was rougher than usual, pushing her down on the bed and holding her wrists together above her head with one hand. When she protested, he said, 'Shut up! You need to learn who you belong to.'

She tried to twist away from him. 'I don't belong to you. I don't belong to anyone.'

He grabbed her hair with his free hand. 'You little whore! You can't play me off against another man. You're mine! You'd better remember that.'

She stopped struggling, afraid of what he might do if she continued, and he pushed himself into her. When it was over and he rolled off her, she slid off the bed and gathered up her clothes.

He looked at her. 'What are you doing? We've got all night. The others won't be back.'

'I'm going,' she said quietly, trying to keep the tremor out of her voice as she pulled on her underwear. 'I don't want to stay if it's going to be like that.'

He sat up and reached for her, but she avoided his grasp.

'Alix!' His tone was different, almost pleading. 'Don't be like that. I didn't mean to hurt you. Come back to bed, please!'

'No.' She pushed her feet into her shoes. 'I'm sorry, Raoul. It's finished.'

'Don't!' he cried. 'Alix, I'm sorry. It's only because I can't bear the thought of you being with anyone else. Don't you understand? I love you.'

She hesitated, with her hand on the door. He looked almost desperate.

'I'm sorry,' she said again.

'Don't leave me! I can't bear it! It won't happen again. I swear it.'

She drew a long, shaky breath. 'I'll see you tomorrow. We'll talk then. Now, I'm going home.'

She was still shaking when she reached her own room. She sat on the bed and put her head in her hands. How had she allowed herself to be caught up in this relationship? It had begun soon after she arrived in Paris. She had been lonely, and Raoul, a fellow student, had been attentive. She had been excited by his radical views and had enjoyed being part of the group to which he had introduced her. It was only later that she had begun to discover the violent and jealous side of Raoul's nature.

Next day he was humble and more loving than she had ever known him. It reminded her of their first days together when she had been grateful for his companion-ship, and she was reluctant to lose that. But when he suggested she should come back to the apartment that night, she refused, giving the excuse that it was not reasonable to expect his flatmates to move out again. In the cafe that evening she was careful not to give Steve too much of her attention and not to speak Serbian, and for the next few days, her relationship with Raoul seemed to be back on an even keel.

–

At the end of the month, news spread that children were being evacuated from Paris and sent to the provinces. The reports spoke of thirty thousand being involved. That night, all the streetlights were turned off in expectation of a bombing raid. It was still the summer recess, so there were no lectures, and the next morning Alix was sitting on the grass in the Parc Montsouris with her friends when a fellow student, a boy named Eric, came running over, red-faced from the heat and wild-eyed with excitement.

'It's happened. Hitler's invaded Poland!'

There was a brief moment of silence while they took in the implications of the news. Then Raoul said, 'So we're at war, then.'

'I'm not sure,' Eric said. 'That wasn't on the wireless.'

'It's inevitable, though, isn't it?' someone said. 'I mean, we shall have to honour our treaty with Poland.'

'Oh yes, it's inevitable,' Raoul agreed. 'Which means some of us can look forward to being called up within days.'

'But what about the treaty between Germany and Russia?' someone else asked. 'Is it right for us, as communists, to fight a country that has a non-aggression pact with our comrades in the Soviet Union?'

There was an instant babble of argument, which was brought to an end by Raoul. 'Most of us won't have a choice. Those of us who have done our military service will be the first to go, but it won't be long before the rest of you get your papers.'

'But what about the girls?' Eric asked. 'What about our families? Will they be safe in Paris?'

'No need to worry about that,' Raoul said. 'The Huns will never get past the Maginot Line. There's no question of France being invaded.'

Alix was only half listening. Her thoughts had gone at once to Steve. If all Europe was going to be caught up in the chaos of war, what would his position be? If America remained neutral, it would be invidious, to say the least. She got to her feet.

'I've got a terrible headache. I'm going to the pharmacy for some aspirin.'

Caught up in intense discussion of the implications of the news, no one took any notice of her departure. She headed for the Left Bank. Steve had said he had a part time job in a bookshop there, but he had never told her which one. She mentally berated herself for not asking him. The Left Bank was lined with bookshops. It could take hours to find him.

As it happened, she struck lucky on her fifth attempt. The shop was empty and Steve was sitting behind the counter scribbling in a notebook. He looked up as she entered and jumped to his feet, his dark eyes lighting up with pleasure.

'Alix! How good to see you!' Then, a little less exuberantly, 'Were you looking for me, or did you come for a book?'

'Looking for you,' she said breathlessly. 'Have you heard the news?'

'News?'

'Hitler has invaded Poland.'

'Oh, gee! I guess that means France will be at war with Germany very soon.'

'I can't see how we can avoid it. And Britain will be in the same position. Steve, you should go home, while you still can. Once the war starts it may not be possible for you to get a passage on a ship crossing the Atlantic – and it could be dangerous, too.'

He ran his hand through his hair. 'I don't think I want to do that.'

'Why not?'

'It feels too much like running away. I want to be involved, help in some way, if I can.'

'You said you didn't think America will join in.'

'No, I don't think we will. But that doesn't mean I can't do my bit, somehow. What about you? Will you go home now?'

'No. I feel like you. I don't want to be one of the rats leaving the sinking ship. Not that it will sink, of course. Everyone says there's no chance of the Germans invading. But all the same, things are bound to get difficult. There may be air raids, for one thing.'

'God, I hope not! Surely even a maniac like Hitler wouldn't bomb a beautiful city like Paris.'

'Let's hope not. But there are bound to be casualties, if not civilians, then among the fighting men. Raoul expects to be called up immediately. Maybe I could volunteer to be a nurse, like my mother in the last war.'

She spoke almost without considering the import of what she was saying. As soon as the words were out of her mouth, the full significance struck her. Nothing in her vision of her future had included a war, but now all her hopes and plans were being overturned.

Steve chewed his lip before continuing, 'Will Yugoslavia come in on the side of the Allies?'

Alix shook her head. 'No, there's no chance of that.'

'So,' he said, 'as non-combatants, where does that leave us?'

'Who knows? But not watching from the sidelines if I have anything to do with it,' she said, a tone of defiance in her voice.

'That makes two of us,' he said.

Their eyes met and Alix felt a surge of hope. It was good to know that he felt the same as she did. Walking back to the park she found her dismay at the news turning to a new determination.

When Alix rejoined the group, Raoul looked at her suspiciously.

'Where have you been?'

'I told you. To get some aspirin.'

'It doesn't take that long to go to the pharmacy.'

She considered staying with the lie, telling him there had been a long queue, but asked herself why she needed to make excuses for a perfectly innocent conversation with a friend.

'If you must know, I went to find Steve, to make sure he had heard the news. I told him he ought to get the next boat back to America.'

He frowned at her, digesting the implications of her statement, then apparently decided to see it as positive. 'Good. Best thing he can do.'

–

Two days later, Raoul was waiting for her when she left the college. His face was grim and he had an envelope in one hand.

'It's come.'

'What?' Alix asked.

'My call-up papers.'

She caught her breath. 'Oh God! When do you have to report?'

'By six o'clock tonight.'

Abruptly, the reality of the situation came home to her. 'Oh, Raoul!' She caught hold of his hand. 'When shall I see you again?'

He shrugged. 'Who knows? I shall probably be sent straight to the front line. After all, I'm fully trained. They'll need the men who have done their military service to lead the attack. We've got to teach the Boches they can't just march into other people's countries and take over. If they think we are just going to sit behind the Maginot Line and let them do what they like in Poland, they're mistaken. They weren't reckoning on facing up to the French Army. We'll make them regret their mistake.'

She looked at him. His face was flushed, and she suddenly realised that he was excited by the prospect of battle. She put the thought aside and said only, 'I hope you're right.'

'Come back to the apartment with me, now,' he said. 'God knows when we'll have another chance.'

She went. Despite what had previously happened between them, the prospect of not seeing him, maybe ever again, brought home to her that life was changing irrevocably and everything familiar was being swept away. So, they made love with an intensity that both excited and alarmed her.

Chapter Two

London

September 4th 1939

A smartly dressed woman made her way briskly along Grosvenor Gardens, negotiating her way past squads of soldiers erecting barricades of sandbags at the entrances to buildings. From her graceful carriage and her brisk, agile walk, a casual observer might have guessed her to be quite young, in her thirties perhaps, but a closer look would have revealed that the chestnut hair under the fashionable hat was showing grey at the temples and there were fine lines around her eyes. She turned into the doorway of one of the buildings where a brass plate announced First Aid Nursing Yeomanry. Accosted by a young woman in khaki, she presented a visiting card.

'I'm here to see Captain Baxter Ellis.'

'Is she expecting you, ma'am?'

'No, but I have no doubt that she will see me,' was the reply.

She followed the younger woman up a flight of stairs to a door marked Commanding Officer. The girl tapped and put her head around it.

'There's a Countess Malkovic to see you.'

'Countess who?' was the irritable reply. 'Never heard of her. What does she want?'

Without waiting to be invited, the visitor stepped into the room.

'Don't worry, Dick. It's only me.'

A sturdily built woman in uniform rose abruptly from behind her desk. 'Good God! Leonora Malham Brown! Where have you sprung from?'

'Oh, here and there.' She extended her hand. 'How are you, old thing?'

Baxter Ellis grimaced slightly. 'As well as can be expected, I suppose, under the current circumstances.' She looked her visitor up and down. 'I must say, you're looking pretty chipper. But what's all this Countess rot?'

Leonora smiled. 'I married Count Alexander Malkovic in 1920. We went through the Serbian campaign together, so we had... well, a lot in common.'

'Oh yes, I remember now. You left the rest of us to cope with the mess in Calais and went off to join Stobart's lot in Serbia.'

'It was no picnic, I assure you.'

'No, I heard that... So, what do I call you now?'

'Let's just settle for Leo, shall we?' In FANY circles, Christian names were not regarded as acceptable, being 'unmilitary', so most members acquired a nickname, often one that could equally well belong to a man.

'Leo, it is! Look, I think this calls for a drink. Sorry, the best I can offer you is tea or coffee.'

'Coffee would be lovely. Thank you.'

Baxter Ellis pressed a button on her desk and when a voice answered, she said, 'Bingham, see if you can rustle us up some coffee, will you?' She gestured towards two easy chairs set by a low table near the window. When they were both sitting, she went on, 'Do tell me what I've missed.'

'Well, as I said, I married Sasha Malkovic, and we have a daughter, Alexandra. She's twenty-one now – oh, all right, I can see you doing the mental arithmetic. Yes, she was born before we were able to marry. But in wartime, you know, conventions like that don't seem to be important. But that's all past history now, and I had settled down to the life of the wife of a country gentleman. Until this damn war came along and upset everything.'

'So, you live in Serbia now?'

'Yugoslavia, we have to call it these days. Yes, Sasha has an estate outside Belgrade. But I still have some land over here, left to me by my grandmother. The London house is let, of course, and I have a very good estate manager, but I like to pop over from time to time to keep an eye on things.'

'Will you go back now, to Belgrade?'

'No. That's why I came to see you. There's nothing I can do to help from there and I want to "do my bit", as the saying goes.'

'Won't Yugoslavia fight with the Allies, like they did last time?'

Leo shook her head. 'The thing is, the whole concept of Yugoslavia is flawed. It's all very well to call ourselves the country of the South Slavs, but the fact is that people still think of themselves as Serbs or Croats or Bosnians or Slovenes and they are far more concerned about the issues that divide them than the ones that might unite them.'

'Such as?'

'Well, religion is the most crucial thing. The Serbs belong to the Eastern Orthodox Church and use the Cyrillic alphabet, the Croats are Roman Catholic and use the Latin alphabet, a lot of the Bosnians and the Kosovans are Muslims... and so on. The Serbs have always wanted the whole country to be Greater Serbia, and the Croats resent their attempts to dominate. In short, it's a mess. That's why I think I can be more use here than there.'

'Won't your husband want you back with him?'

Leo looked away. 'He's fully occupied trying to keep the country out of Hitler's hands.'

'You mean they might go over to the Nazis?'

'It's not impossible. Yugoslavia isn't a democracy; it's a regal dictatorship. But the last king was assassinated back in '34 and his heir, Crown Prince Peter, was only eleven, so the government has been in the hands of a regency council headed by the boy's uncle, Prince Paul. Paul's very pro-British, educated at Oxford, friends with the royal family and so on. He's very charming, but he's basically weak, and there are a lot of people in the government who want to push the country into a closer alliance with Germany. Hitler has been using a combination of flattery and veiled threats to persuade Prince Paul to agree to some kind of treaty. Sasha is desperate to stop that and keep the country neutral.'

Baxter Ellis finished her coffee. 'Look, I'd love to sit and chin-wag, but I am up to my eyes, as you can understand. I'm sure you didn't just drop in for a chat. What can I do for you?'

'Isn't that obvious? I've come to join up.'

Chapter Three

Although Raoul had left, Alix continued to join her friends in the cafe on most evenings. They were a smaller group but no less argumentative than before. The news that the government had proscribed the Communist Party shocked many of them.

'This is an imperialist war. The Party has said that we should have no part in it.'

'But what about patriotism?'

'Patriotism! Why should we feel any loyalty to a country that has banned our party? They've closed down our newspapers, and they are threatening the death penalty for anyone propagating what they call "communist propaganda"! What sort of democracy is that?'

The newspapers reported that the army had advanced into the German region of the Saar, without meeting serious opposition. It began to look as though Raoul had been right and Hitler had not reckoned on having to face the greatly superior forces of France. Then, to everyone's surprise, news came that General Gamelin had given the order for the army to retire back to the Maginot Line. It was generally accepted that this line of fortifications, with its concrete bunkers and its artillery emplacements, all connected by an underground railway, was an insuperable barrier to an invading force. There was no fighting, and the expected bombing did not materialise. By October people were beginning to talk about the *drôle de guerre*, the joke war. Raoul's letters, heavily censored, spoke of boredom and frustration.

With Raoul away, there was no reason for Alix not to talk to Steve, and when he offered to walk her back to her college through the darkened streets, she accepted gladly.

As they walked, he said, 'I don't understand why you hang out with those people. I can't believe you agree with their views. Is it just because Raoul was one of them?'

She gave him a sharp look. 'I am capable of thinking for myself, you know.'

'I'm sorry. I didn't mean to offend you. But I can't see how you can accept the Communist ideology. I get the impression that they don't want people to think for themselves. They just expect you to toe the party line.'

'I have to agree that some of the attitudes make me angry,' she confessed. 'I just think the basic ideas are right.'

'Such as?'

'That wealth should be shared out equally. That people should be regarded as equals, not subjugated by an elite. It used to make me furious when I was growing up to see how the peasants were treated. Not by my father. To do him justice, he looked after his people, set up a school for their children, built a clinic for the ones that were sick and employed a doctor to come in twice a week. But it shouldn't have been necessary. People should have those things as a right. Most of the villagers can't grow enough crops on their little bit of land to feed their families. There's no proper sanitation, no water supply, very little education. That has to be changed, and communism seems to me to be the only ideology that can do that.' It occurred to Alix that this was the first time she had actually voiced these ideas, instead of letting Raoul speak for her, and she was suddenly aware that her passion was genuine, and not just a reflection of his dogma.

Steve looked at her seriously. 'I can respect that point of view. But there are other ways. Where I come from we believe that it's up to the individual to make his own fortune. If a man is prepared to work hard, he can create a good life for himself and his family.'

'And I can respect that, too,' she responded. 'But you have to have the freedom to do that. In Serbia, the ordinary people don't have that freedom. Things have to change.'

He sighed. 'Well, maybe this war will change things – but I can't see it being for the better.' He stopped walking and turned to look into her face. 'Let's forget politics. I think we both believe in the same things at bottom.'

After that, it seemed natural for him to walk her back the next night, and when they reached the college, he took her hands and drew her towards him and she knew he was going to kiss her, and knew that she had been waiting for it to happen. It was a very different experience from being kissed by Raoul. At first, he was tentative, as if he expected her to resist. When he felt her eager response, he grew passionate, but whereas Raoul's kisses had demanded a total surrender, Steve's were always tempered with tenderness. As the days passed, she found it harder and harder to restrain herself.

One evening, he lifted his head and looked down into her eyes.

'Listen, I don't know how you'd feel about this, but I have a room of my own. It's only a garret, but I don't have to share it. Would you…?'

Every fibre of her body urged her to say 'yes', but she had a sudden memory of Raoul grasping her hair and calling her a whore. She had rejected the accusation, but it struck her that if he could see her now, he would have grounds for it. She detached herself reluctantly from Steve's embrace.

'Steve, I'm sorry. I'm really, really sorry – but I can't. Not with Raoul away in the army. It wouldn't be right – would it?'

He let her go, but she could see he was struggling for control. After a moment, he drew a deep breath and said huskily, 'No, I guess you're right. I'm sorry I suggested it.'

They were both silent for a moment, then he said, 'It would probably be best if we don't see so much of each other.'

Now she was the one struggling. It cost her an almost physical pain to say, 'Yes, I suppose you're right.'

He took her by the hand and walked her to the gate leading into the college grounds. With a formality that cut her to the heart, he wished her goodnight.

'Goodnight,' she whispered, 'And Steve, thank you! Thank you for… everything.'

He bent his head in acknowledgement and turned away.

After that, he came less often to the cafe, and she made a point of joining some other girls who also lived in the college for the walk home, but she could not rid herself of a sense of loss. Going over and over in her mind their last evenings together, she came to the conclusion that she had been foolish, that her loyalty to Raoul was a mistake.

When she faced the facts squarely, there was no denying that she was much happier in Steve's company than she had ever been in Raoul's. She missed their long, friendly chats; she missed using her native language; above all, she missed his touch and his kisses. It occurred to her that she should simply go to him and tell him she had changed her mind.

When he came into the cafe one evening and asked if he could walk her home, her heart leapt. He had missed her as much as she had missed him, and now she would have the opportunity to put it all right.

They walked in silence for a few minutes. Then he said, 'Look, I've got something to tell you.'

A cold hand seemed to grip her heart. Her first thought was that he had found someone else, someone more compliant. 'Oh?' was all she said.

'I've decided to join up.'

'Join up? Why? Where?'

'I can't sit around doing nothing. Hitler's not going to give up, so there's got to be a showdown of some sort soon. I want to be part of it.'

'So, what are you going to do? Volunteer for the army?'

'No. I'm going to England. I'm going to apply to join the RAF.'

'To England? How? When?'

'Tomorrow. I've booked a seat on the boat train to Calais.'

She stopped walking and stared up at him. A confusion of thoughts surged through her brain. Was it too late to tell him she had changed her mind? If she did, would he change his plans? With a sudden stab of guilt, she asked herself if this was all her fault.

'Don't go!' The words came unbidden. 'You might be killed.'

He shrugged. 'So might Raoul. So might hundreds of other fellows. That doesn't make it right to hold back.'

'But… but you're an American. America isn't even in this war.'

'Not yet. I can't see how we can keep out of it for long.'

She grasped at another idea. 'Nothing is happening, anyway. Maybe it never will. Why don't you wait and see?'

'If that's the way things pan out, I can come back and… well, get on with my life. But if things do hot up – as I expect they will – then at least I'll have been trained to do something useful.' He began to walk again. 'It's no good trying to change my mind. My ticket's booked, and I've given in my notice at the shop and paid up my rent on the apartment.'

She caught up with him. 'You will write? Let me know how you are getting on.'

'Do you really want me to?'

'Yes! Yes, I do. Please, Steve, promise me we'll keep in touch.'

His expression softened. 'OK. If that's what you want. I promise.'

At the college gate, he kissed her once, briefly, and turned away.

'Steve!' she called after him. 'Good luck! I'll… I'll pray for you.'

He turned and raised his hand, then walked away without looking back.

Chapter Four

November 15th 1939

My dear Alix,

Well, it's done. I am now officially Aircraftman Popovic of the RAF. It wasn't difficult to get in. I got the impression that the powers-that-be are desperate to build up manpower and attract new recruits. There is one disappointment, however. I injured my left knee playing football several years ago, and it has made it slightly less flexible than it should be. It never bothers me, but the medics decided it might make it hard for me to control a plane, so I can't train to be a pilot. Instead, I have volunteered for aircrew, which means flying in a bomber. I'm hoping to train as a navigator, which is the next most important position after the pilot.

Right now I am undergoing basic training, which means square-bashing and PT and fire-arms training, plus a lot of boring routine chores. However, I think there is a sense of urgency about pushing us through to the point where we can be useful, so I am hoping this stage won't last too long. I can't write in too much detail because of the censor, but I will try to keep you up to date with my progress as far as possible.

I miss Paris, our evenings in the cafe and all the talk and discussions. I miss walking along the banks of the Seine and my job in the bookshop – and I miss you. I hope you are keeping well and not suffering too much from the blackout and the rationing.

Take care of yourself.

Yours as ever,

Steve

Enclosed was a photograph of him in RAF uniform. It was not a very good picture, taken on a cheap camera in rather poor light, but it sent a thrill of tenderness through Alix's nerves. She pressed it to her lips and then put it carefully away, tucked inside her passport.

Chapter Five

England

December 1939

Leo was beginning to regret her decision to rejoin the
FANY. There seemed little she could do other than
interview new recruits and help out with paperwork.
The 'phoney war' dragged on without any movement on
either side and the only action was taking place far to the
north, where the Finns were waging a desperate struggle
against a Russian invasion. One morning, Baxter Ellis's
secretary announced that the Finnish ambassador's wife
wished to see the commanding officer.

An elegantly dressed woman of middle age walked into
the room.

'Moose!' The exclamation broke from Leo's and Baxter
Ellis's lips simultaneously.

Madame Gripenberg, née Diana Mosley-Williams,
held out both hands. 'My dear old things! How wonderful
to see you again after all these years.'

For a few moments, they exchanged reminiscences
of their time driving ambulances in France during the
previous war. Then the ambassador's wife said, 'I wish I
could stay and chat, but I'm here on a very important
mission. You will have heard, of course, about the war

going on in my adopted country. Our men are putting up a wonderful fight, but inevitably there are casualties, and we are in urgent need of ambulances and drivers to pick them up from the front line and get them to hospital. The Finnish Red Cross is doing a marvellous job, but they are overwhelmed, and they asked my husband if there might be any chance of help from England. Of course, as soon as I heard that, I thought of you – of us, I should say. If anyone is qualified for that kind of work, we are. What do you think?'

Baxter Ellis seated herself at her desk and drew a pad of paper towards her.

'How many do you want?'

'We were hoping perhaps for ten?'

Baxter Ellis looked at Leo. 'That means at least twenty volunteers. Can we muster that number?'

'No problem!' Leo declared. 'I'll put the word out.'

Chapter Six

Paris

January 1940

Alix shivered and huddled closer to the small radiator in her college room. The winter in Paris had been dreary enough, with the darkened streets and the food rationing, but now the temperature had suddenly dropped and a freezing rain had fallen, making the pavements into ice rinks. It all added to a deepening sense of depression which had gripped her since Christmas. There had been little traditional cheer to be found over the 'festive' season, and even in the cafe where she and her friends had been in the habit of meeting, there had been a pervasive atmosphere of gloom. They were a much smaller group now. Most of the men had been called up, and many of the girls had gone back to their families in the provinces for the holiday. Quite a few had chosen not to return.

Her mother wrote from England.

> *Darling Alix,*
>
> *Thank you for your letter. I'm sorry you had such a miserable Christmas. I wish I could have come over to see you and cheer you up, but I'm afraid there is going to be very little chance to*

travel between here and anywhere in Europe for the duration of this wretched war. I wish you would take my advice and go home to Belgrade. You would have much more fun there.

I need to warn you that I may not be able to write to you for a month or two. As I told you, I have rejoined the FANY, and we have been asked to take a convoy of ambulances to Finland to help the Finnish Red Cross cope with casualties. The Finns are fighting with amazing courage, but their losses are heavy, and they need all the help we can give them. I'm not sure yet when we shall be leaving or how long we shall be away, but I suspect that the Finnish postal service may not be able to cope with sending letters abroad under current circumstances. So please don't worry if you don't hear from me for a few weeks. I have given your address to colleagues here at HQ so they will know how to get in touch with you if anything untoward should happen – but that is only a precaution. I'm sure I shall not be in any greater danger than I might be in London, less probably, if the promised blitz materialises.

I am beginning to hope that the war with Germany is not going to result in any real fighting. It looks as though Hitler is realising that he's bitten off more than he can chew, and he is trying to find a way out without losing face. But if I'm wrong, London may not be the only city to be bombed. Alix, I beg you, leave Paris now! Go home while you still can. I've seen what war does to cities, and to people, and I do not want that to happen to you. You need not fear your father will try to force

you into a marriage you do not want. He loves you
too much for that. You will be safe there. Please,
darling, do as I say!
With much love,
Mati

Alix screwed up her eyes to stop the tears that seemed to come all too readily at the moment. '*If anything untoward should happen*'. She knew her mother well enough to recognise that she was making light of any potential danger. Their relationship had not always been untroubled, but in recent years she had come to appreciate her mother's resilience in the face of difficulties, and she relied on her more than ever since her disagreement with her father. The thought of losing her put all her other discontents into a new perspective.

Raoul came home on leave for a week just after New Year. He was simmering with suppressed anger at what he saw as the incompetence of the high command and with frustration at the war which was not a war but only an apparently endless stalemate. He seemed to expect their relationship to have remained exactly as it was before he was called up, and his sexual demands were more aggressive than ever. He even tried to take her in a dark alleyway one evening when they could not get the apartment to themselves. When she resisted, he accused her of being unfaithful and demanded to know who she was seeing. He even refused to believe that Steve was in England until she showed him one of his letters. If Alix had needed any further convincing that she was not in love with him, she had it now; but to break off their relationship when he was about to return to the Front seemed callous and somehow unpatriotic. It was a relief when his leave came to an end.

Lectures had begun again, albeit to much reduced audiences, but Alix found it hard to settle to any academic work. She had tried to find something meaningful to do, some 'war work' of her own. She had started taking classes in First Aid with a branch of the Red Cross, but she could not see any immediate use for these skills. Gloomily, she returned to classes. It was not long before she was summoned to an interview with one of her professors, who took her to task for her failure to deliver essays on time, and their perfunctory nature when they did arrive.

Alix shrugged her shoulders. 'It's hard to take an interest in the history of Europe when the whole continent is about to go up in smoke.'

The professor was a wise and kind man. 'I think you need to get a new perspective on the subject. This current situation is worrying, I know, but in the history of mankind, it is only a very small upheaval. We Europeans… we have been here before, many times. From the dawn of time, this continent has been swept by invasions and incursions from different tribes and races. Do you know the Musée de l'Homme?'

She had to confess that she did not.

'Go and have a look round. They have some amazing exhibits telling the story of the development of human societies and cultures from all over the world. The director, Paul Rivet, is a remarkable man – and a fervent anti-fascist, incidentally. I think a visit there will broaden your outlook and enable you to put our current troubles in context.'

Without any great enthusiasm, Alix made her way to the imposing Palais de Chaillot and wandered into the museum. Very soon, she was enthralled by the variety and geographical scope of the exhibits. She was absorbed in the contemplation of a crystal skull, which according to the explanatory label, probably originated in pre-Columbian South America, when a voice behind her said, 'Can I help you? Are you looking for anything in particular?'

Alix turned to see a woman of perhaps thirty years of age. She was small and dark, with a pointed chin and very bright brown eyes, and she wore a badge that identified her as one of the curators.

'Oh, no, thank you,' Alix replied. 'I'm really just browsing. I've never been in here before. There are so many fascinating exhibits I hardly know where to start.'

'Are you a visitor to Paris? I ask because your French is perfect, but I think I detect a slight accent.'

'No, I'm studying here, at the Sorbonne. But you're quite right. I'm not French. My name is Alexandra Malkovic. I'm Serbian – I should say Yugoslavian.'

'Really! I've never met anyone from there before. I'd love to hear more about your country. Oh, my name is Marie Louise Beauclerc, by the way.'

They shook hands and Marie Louise asked what she was studying. They chatted for a while until Marie Louise said she was about to go for a break and suggested that they get a coffee. Half an hour later, Alix was sure that she had found a new friend. She spent the rest of the morning touring the museum with the benefit of a knowledgeable guide, and when she left, they agreed to meet that evening at a nearby bistro called Au Bon Coin.

Alix enjoyed the evening. The conversation made a refreshing change to the stale arguments of her friends in their usual cafe. So when Marie suggested meeting again the following evening, she agreed readily. Marie was genuinely interested in everything Alix could tell her about Serbia, and in return, Alix learned a lot about life in France outside of the limited circle of the university. After that, they met frequently for coffee or a meal at the bistro. She was the first real female friend Alix had made since she came to Paris. Until then, her relationships had been restricted to the small circle of communist students to which Raoul had introduced her, and even among them, he had tended to be jealous if she showed signs of becoming too close to anyone.

One evening Marie Louise told her that her parents lived in Tours, where her father was a doctor, and she talked about a happy childhood with her two older sisters.

'How about you, Alix?' she asked. 'Where were you born?'

Alix stirred her coffee in silence for a moment. 'I'm not exactly sure, except that it was in a small village in Macedonia in the middle of a battle.'

'Good heavens! Is that where your mother lived?'

'Oh no! My mother is English. She was there working as a nurse for the Serbian army.'

'And she gave birth to you in the middle of a battle... How terrible. What happened then?'

Alix shook her head. She very rarely spoke of this to anyone, but she felt a need now to confide in her new friend. 'I don't know. All I can tell you is that for the first almost two years of my life, I was brought up by a peasant family. We were refugees from the fighting, moving from camp to camp, and I had no idea who my real parents were. Then one day, a strange man came to say he had been sent to collect me, and he took me to a grand house where a man told me he was my real father.'

'You poor child! Were you frightened?'

'Not for long. He was kind, and there was plenty of food and a comfortable bed to sleep in. I suppose when you're a child, and you've been used to being hungry and cold and frightened most of the time, such comfort was all that really mattered.'

'And your mother? Where was she?'

'He told me she was dead, that she died when I was born. That was what he had been told. Then one day, she just appeared, out of the blue. The war had only just finished then and she had been looking everywhere for me, but she thought my father was dead, too.'

'But why were you given to the peasant family in the first place?'

'I've been told that my mother was too ill to care for me, so the doctor in charge of the hospital asked this other family to take me. The woman had just lost a child so she had milk to feed me. Otherwise, I would have died.'

Marie Louise sat back and gazed at her in wonder. 'What an extraordinary story! That makes me feel that I've had a very ordinary life.'

'I feel the same.' Alix said. Her friend had touched on something that was at the back of her own mind.

'But your life has been extraordinary enough, surely?'

'Only the beginning of it. I've never done anything remarkable. My mother ran away from home to nurse soldiers in the first Balkan War when she was just eighteen. Compared to that, I've done nothing.'

Marie Louise finished her coffee and signalled for the bill. 'Well, maybe that is all about to change. We are at war now. Who knows what may happen?'

From then on, Alix saw less and less of her previous companions, and she began to feel that her life had begun a new chapter.

Chapter Seven

Leith, Scotland

February 1st 1940

Leo manoeuvred her ambulance onto the dockside and parked it at the end of a line of similar vehicles. Her co-driver, Roberta 'Robby' Vernon, was counting. 'Six, seven, eight, nine… Thank heaven, everyone has made it. There were times today when I thought we never would.'

'You and me both,' Leo agreed. 'I've heard of a baptism of fire. I reckon we've had a baptism of ice.'

Early that morning, she had driven out of the yard behind the Rubens Hotel in London, the last of ten ambulances filled to capacity with medical supplies, food, warm clothing and comforts for the Finnish troops provided by the British and the Finnish Red Cross. The weather had been bitterly cold throughout January, with record low temperatures. The Thames was frozen from Teddington to Sunbury and people had been skating on the Serpentine. Freezing rain that turned to ice as soon as it hit the ground had swept southern England, bringing down telegraph poles and freezing the birds in the trees. It had turned to snow further north, forming drifts in a strong wind. By the day the ambulances left the worst seemed to be over, but it was a nightmare journey over icy roads. As the winter darkness closed in and the snowdrifts rose higher and higher on either side of them, Leo had begun to wonder if they would reach their destination before the road became completely impassable.

She released her grip on the steering wheel and stretched fingers cramped with cold inside her gloves. 'I suppose it's just a foretaste of what we can expect when we get to Finland.'

'It can't be worse, can it?' Robby said.

'I wouldn't bank on it,' Leo responded grimly. 'Come on. We'd better join the others.'

The group of volunteers had assembled around their commander, the newly appointed Captain Mary Runciman.

'Well done, everyone!' she said. 'Now let's get to the hotel. I reckon we all deserve a hot bath and a large Scotch.'

'Will the ambulances be all right here?' someone asked.

'Of course, they will. Anyway, they are not our responsibility now. They can't come on the ship we are taking, but they will be shipped out as soon as a suitable vessel is found. Don't worry. Everything is under control. We shall see them again very soon.'

Chapter Eight

Paris

February 1940

Steve wrote to tell Alix that he had completed his basic training and had then been sent to a civilian air navigation school. He was unimpressed by what he had learned there since much of the course was delivered by men who had learned their navigation at sea. He had now been transferred to a new base, whose location he could not reveal except that '*the weather is terrible, there are mountains and more sheep than people – and those there are do not even speak English*'. (Alix smiled to herself at this. She had spent enough holidays in Britain to envisage the Welsh mountains, glorious in the summer but bleak indeed at this time of year.) Steve went on to say that he was finding this part of the training more satisfactory. He had even been up in a plane for the first time. '*It's hard work. There's a lot to learn. But I'm sticking at it. We've been told that the one who comes out top might get a commission.*'

Alix continued to meet Marie Louise at the bistro. It was a relief to share with her her worries about her mother. The news from Finland was increasingly gloomy. The Russians had sent in huge reinforcements, tanks and infantry, and there was a new man in command – General

Timoshenko. The Finns on the front line were under constant bombardment.

'I don't understand the Swedes and the Norwegians,' Marie Louise said. 'We were prepared to send in troops to help the Finns. But the Swedes and the Norwegians wouldn't let our troops pass through their territory.'

'I suppose they are too afraid of being drawn into the war. They're determined to remain neutral at all costs,' Alex said.

A week later, she was even more downhearted. 'It's as good as over. I've just heard the report on the wireless. The Russians have broken through at Summa. The Finns are retreating. It's just a matter of time now.'

Chapter Nine

Haparanda Tornio on the frontier between Sweden and Finland

March 14th 1940

'So here we are. Only six weeks too late!' Leo said bitterly.

'It's not our fault,' Robby said. 'We couldn't do anything until the ambulances arrived.'

'I'd like to know who was responsible for that mess,' Leo growled. 'Some incompetent bureaucrat in an office somewhere, I bet.'

'It might not be anybody's fault,' Robby countered. 'There is a war on.'

'But six weeks!' Leo exclaimed. 'Six weeks while we kick our heels and the war went from bad to worse for the Finns. And then, to add insult to injury, two days after the ambulances finally arrive we hear that they've signed a peace treaty.'

'Well it makes no difference to us,' Robby said. 'We've still got to deliver the ambulances to the Finnish Red Cross. And we've made it as far as the border. Hello, this looks like the reception committee.'

They were parked outside the main entrance of a hotel and two women came out to join them.

'Welcome!' the first one said. 'I'm Mrs Vereker. My husband is the British Plenipotentiary. And this is Damaris Brunow. She will act as your interpreter. Now, come along inside. I'm sure you are all tired and cold.'

Once inside, Captain Runciman began to apologise for their late arrival, but Mrs Vereker cut her short.

'Please, there is no need to apologise. We know you would have been here sooner if possible. We are just extremely grateful that you have come at all.'

'I'm afraid we are too late to be much use,' Runciman said.

'Not at all. We need you as much as ever. There are thousands of casualties to be evacuated from the battle-fields in the Karelia area. Now, the sooner we can get you to Helsinki so the Red Cross can deploy you to the places where you can be most use, the better.'

'Right!' the captain responded. 'When can we leave?'

'I've spoken to the local army commander,' Damaris said, 'and I've cleared it with him for you to travel. Here are the necessary documents and safe conducts. You can start as soon as you are ready.'

Runciman looked around the assembled group. 'Seems we are needed after all, girls, so let's make up for lost time. It's six hundred and fifty-odd miles from here to Helsinki. I suggest we drive night and day, taking it in turns with one driving while the other one sleeps. Agreed?'

Within the hour they were on the road. It was a cheerless prospect. Everywhere the Finnish flag was flying at half-mast, and they passed columns of dejected soldiers, their faces numb not just with cold but from sheer incomprehension at the defeat. The country was in the grip of the coldest winter in living memory, and the road deteriorated as they left the town, changing from the wide, well-maintained surface of the Swedish roads to a winding track, deeply rutted and coated with ice.

By evening they had reached a small town, where a hot meal had been prepared for them, but as soon as they had eaten they climbed back into the ambulances and set off again.

Leo gripped the steering wheel and peered ahead into the darkness. On either side the snow was banked up as high as the roofs of the ambulances, so the slightest skid could end in disaster, and the frozen ruts made it like driving over a ploughed field. She had been given the job, as before, of bringing up the rear, so as to ensure that no one was left behind. She could just make out the tail lights of the ambulance in front, jinking from side to side as the driver tried to find the easiest passage over the ice. Beside her, Robby had snuggled down in her greatcoat and was trying to sleep, but the chances of that were minimal with the constant jolting.

They had been driving for a couple of hours when the tail lights ahead of her came to a sudden stop. She braked gingerly and drew to a halt behind the stationary ambulance. The driver and co-driver were climbing down from the cab.

'What's up?' Leo asked.

'Don't know,' was the reply from 'Benjie' Benjafield. 'She just suddenly conked out.'

The ambulance ahead had stopped too, and looking beyond it, Leo could see that the whole convoy had come to a halt. Captain Runciman came trudging back.

'What's the problem?'

They had the bonnet up by that time, but exhaustive checks failed to reveal the fault. They tried three times to restart the engine but with no success. Eventually,

Runciman said, 'There's nothing for it. Mack, you will have to tow this one. Leo, you stay with them. The rest of us will push on and when we reach any crossroads where there might be a problem about which road to take we'll leave someone on picket duty to direct you.'

The tow rope was attached, the rest of the convoy moved on and the ailing ambulance was dragged into motion. Leo climbed back into her vehicle, thankful to turn on the engine to provide a little warmth. It was going to be slow progress from now on.

An hour later the two vehicles in front stopped again. By the time Leo reached the leading one, Jean 'Mack' McCormack had its bonnet up.

'She's over-heating,' she said. 'It's too much for the old girl.'

Luckily her co-driver was FANY Sergeant Jenny Lee, whose speciality was engines.

'Fan belt's broken,' she pronounced after a brief examination.

'Oh Lord! Can it be repaired?'

'Don't worry. There's a spare in the tool kit.'

So numbed fingers went to work again, and eventually, they were on the move once more. A short time later the leading vehicle stopped again. This time they were at a crossroads, with no indication of which was the correct route.

'I thought Runciman said she'd leave someone on picket duty,' Mack said.

'They've probably given up hope of ever seeing us,' Leo replied. 'I wonder if they left anything to tell us which way to turn.'

They gazed around at the snow-covered landscape. Each road was equally rutted by passing traffic, so there was no help there.

'Look!' Robby was pointing. At the angle where the two roads met, the snow had been flattened and on it was a pattern of fir cones forming an arrow pointing to the left.

'Well spotted, Robby!' Leo said. 'That's our way. Maybe we'll catch up with the others soon.'

A few miles further on they came to another crossroad, and this time, search as they might, there was no sign to indicate the right direction.

'God knows which is the right road,' Mack said. 'And if we pick the wrong one we could drive for miles without coming to a town of any sort. Don't know about you but my tank's pretty low already.'

Leo had a map, but it was rudimentary, giving the position of major towns but no details about the country roads. 'We should be heading south,' she said.

'But which way is south?' someone asked. 'If only the sun would come up, we could tell, but it'll be dark for hours yet.'

Leo looked up at the sky. It was studded with stars brighter than she had ever seen them before, but a memory stirred. When she was lying in the mountains of Albania, with her head on Sasha's shoulder, he had begun to teach her to recognise the constellations, to take their minds off their perilous situation. Now she gazed upwards, searching for the Plough, found it and followed the line of the two stars that made up the rear of it.

'There, see? That's the Pole Star. It's always due north. So that...' She turned and pointed, '...that must be our road.'

49

The road descended through thick forest, and here the snow seemed to lie deeper than ever on either side. As the slope became sharper, Leo began to wonder if she had made a terrible mistake. This, surely, could not be the main route to Helsinki. She could sense how little traction the tyres had on the hard-packed ice and knew that the slightest application of the brakes could cause a skid. She had cut her teeth as a driver on the unmade roads of Bulgaria with mud up to the axles way back in 1912 and had put her skills into practice in Serbia in the winter of 1915, but she had never encountered conditions as treacherous as this. She prayed that Mack, in the leading ambulance, also knew how dangerous they were.

Even as the thought crossed her mind she saw the vehicle ahead of her, the one being towed, begin to swerve from side to side. The movement was transferred to the one in front, and after veering crazily across the track for a few breathtaking minutes its offside wheels sunk into a snowdrift and the whole thing toppled over onto its side. The one being towed slewed broadside across the road and came to a standstill and for a terrible moment Leo thought she must crash into it, but she succeeded in bringing her own ambulance to a halt just feet away. The crew were already scrambling out of the cabin, and Leo, with Robby behind her, joined them. The ice was so slippery they had to clutch each other for support as they headed for the capsized ambulance and wrestled the driver's door open. Mack's head appeared, blood streaming from a cut above one eye. Leo and Benjie hauled her out and then leaned in to help Jenny Lee.

'Are you hurt?' Leo asked when she was out on the road.

'Nothing much. Just a bruised shoulder.' Lee moved her arm gingerly.

'Mack?' Leo queried.

Robby had already retrieved the first aid kit from their own vehicle and was dabbing the cut with cotton wool. 'It's nothing too serious,' she said. 'I'll put a plaster on it.'

'Mack, are you sure? How are you feeling?'

'I'm OK. Honestly. Just a bit shaken up.'

'Not surprisingly,' Leo said.

'God, I'm so sorry!' Mack went on. 'I just couldn't seem to control the thing.'

'No, it was my fault,' Benjie said. 'I felt we were going too fast and might run into the back of you, so I braked, fool that I am!'

'Never mind whose fault it was,' Leo interposed. 'What we have to do now is get this thing back on its feet.'

They gathered round and studied the recumbent vehicle without a great deal of optimism.

'Let's get the tow rope unhitched for a start,' Leo said.

That done, they all laid hold wherever they could find a grip and heaved, but to no avail.

'Maybe if we dug away some of the snow...' Robby suggested.

There were spades in the ambulances, so for a while, they all dug furiously. This enabled them to find better handholds, but still the ambulance refused to shift.

'We need to reduce the weight,' Leo said. 'We'll have to take all the equipment out.'

The rear doors proved to be jammed shut, so the only way was for someone to climb back into the cabin and try to extricate the contents by reaching back and passing them up through the window. Robby, being the slightest, volunteered for the task and she succeeded in retrieving some of the smaller items, but much of the heavier equipment was too large or too cumbersome to be removed in that way, so they had to give up. Another mighty struggle proved to be in vain.

'Could we tow it out?' Mack suggested.

'I don't see how,' Lee responded. 'The road is too narrow to get any sort of an angle on it.' Nevertheless, they tried but only succeeded in dragging the vehicle further into the snowdrift.

'Let's try the jack,' Lee suggested. All the ambulances were equipped with a jack. They dug away the snow until they could get a jack under each end of the ambulance, but the snow was too soft, and when they tried to apply leverage, the jacks just sank deeper into it.

They stood in a dejected circle. Leo looked round at them. They had all been given warm clothing, and she had never been more grateful for the unglamorous and itchy woollen underwear, but now she could feel the cold beginning to bite. She could see that some of them were already beginning to shiver. If they stood around much longer there was a danger that they might all succumb to hypothermia. She had seen men die in their hundreds from exposure on that terrible retreat through the mountains of Albania. It was Sasha who had kept her alive, holding her in his arms through the night-time frosts, and the memory brought a sudden flood of longing and regret. Their disagreement about Alix's future lingered in her mind. He was a proud man, and if they were ever to be reconciled, she would have to make the first move. But right now, she longed above everything to feel his arms around her.

She pulled herself together. 'Come on. There's nothing more we can do now. We shall have to wait until someone comes along who can take a message back to the nearest town. They must have snow ploughs and lifting equipment. Until then, let's get everyone into my ambulance. It will be a squash, but the more we huddle up together, the warmer we'll be.'

They did as she told them, squeezing in where they could. Leo fetched a bundle of spare blankets from the back, and they wrapped themselves up as well as they could.

'Can't we run the engine to give us some warmth?' Robby said.

'No,' Leo told her. 'We could suffocate ourselves. And anyway, we can't afford the petrol.' She had been nervously watching the petrol gauge for some time, hoping they would make it to the next town before they ran out.

'What time is it now?' Robby asked.

Leo looked at her watch. 'Four thirty in the morning.'

'It'll be a while before anyone comes along, then,' Mack commented.

After that, they were all silent for some time.

Leo looked around at the others, their faces palely illuminated in the moonlight reflected from the snow. It occurred to her that even the oldest of them was probably ten years younger than she was. They had joined the corps at various times in the years of peace after 1918. They had volunteered out of a sense of duty, or out of a desire for excitement. None of them had even been to war before.

'Come on,' she said. 'Let's have a sing-song. You all know this one.'

She began to sing 'It's a Long Way to Tipperary', and first one voice joined in, then the rest. After that, they sang all the old favourites they had sung round the campfire at

53

the training camps they had all attended. The windows of the ambulance misted up, enclosing them in a small world of comradeship and mutual warmth.

In a pause between songs, Mack said suddenly, 'Listen! Am I dreaming, or is that an engine?'

They all listened and heard the unmistakable sound of a heavy vehicle coming closer. Stiff from sitting, they tumbled out of the ambulance to see headlights approaching from the direction in which they were heading. There was no need to wave the driver down. The road was completely blocked. The truck stopped and three large men climbed out. They spoke no English, and the members of the FANY contingent had only a few words of Finnish between them, but the situation needed no explanation. The men smiled reassuringly and got to work as if digging ambulances out of snowdrifts was an everyday occurrence – which, Leo thought, it probably was. Planks and shovels were produced, steel ropes were attached, and a winch mounted on the rear of the truck whirred. The ambulance was dragged upright and manoeuvred by pure muscle power back onto the road. Miraculously, when Mack pressed the starter, the engine came to life.

There was still the problem of the 'dead' ambulance stuck broadside on across the road. But this presented no difficulty to their rescuers. It was manhandled into position so that the tow rope could be reattached. Now they just needed to be able to get past the truck which was blocking their way forward. The men set to with their shovels and the women joined in until a sufficient area had been levelled along the side of the road to allow the ambulances to creep past, coaxed along by encouraging gestures from the three men. With final words of thanks, which needed no interpreter, they all climbed back into their vehicles and the journey continued.

Glancing sideways at Robby, huddled in her seat with her eyes closed, Leo sent up a prayer to the God she was no longer sure she believed in. 'Let that be the last disaster, please! We've had enough – more than enough.'

Her prayer, on this occasion at least, was answered. A few miles further on, the forest ended, the road widened, and they began to pass other traffic. Then they saw lights ahead and drove into a small town – and there, miracle of miracles – was a line of seven ambulances, neatly parked outside what looked like a hotel. Inside, they received a welcome fit for the prodigal's return, but there was only time to swallow a much-needed hot breakfast and exchange a brief outline of their adventures before they were on the road again, with a revivified Robby at the wheel while Leo caught up at last on desperately needed sleep.

They reached Helsinki on the sixteenth, having been on the road for two and a half days. Leo climbed out of the ambulance and eased her aching shoulders.

'Dear God, what a journey!'

'Yes, it was pretty grim, wasn't it?' Robby agreed. 'But do you know, I wouldn't have missed it for the world!'

Leo could only shake her head and smile ruefully at the enthusiasm of youth and inexperience.

Chapter Ten

April–May 1940

The mood in Chez Michel fluctuated wildly from day to day. Michel brought a wireless set into the cafe, and the remaining customers gathered round it most evenings to listen to the news. When they heard that Germany had invaded Norway, there was a sense of excitement at the idea that something was happening, at last, coupled with a slightly shame-faced sense of relief that the enemy had turned his attentions elsewhere.

'I told you!' someone scoffed. 'Hitler dares not face up to our army, so he's gone for the soft option instead.'

They jeered when Denmark surrendered without a fight and cheered when they heard that the British had sent an expeditionary force to Norway to oppose the German attack, but the mood darkened at the news that they had been forced to retire 'with their tails between their legs'.

In the Bon Coin, the attitudes were less volatile. Marie Louise was fatalistic, seeing the German strategy as a simple clearing of decks in preparation for the main objective.

'Alix,' she said, 'you should go home while you still can. Things could get very nasty here.'

Alix shook her head. 'No, whatever happens, I'll stick it out with the rest of you. Anyway, apart from bombing us, what can Hitler do? Everyone knows he can never get beyond the Maginot Line.'

–

Steve wrote, '*I've completed the course, thank goodness. I got pretty high marks, too. No commission, unfortunately, but I have been made up to Sergeant, which is good. Now I'm just waiting to see which squadron I am posted to. It will be great to be part of an active unit – and it looks as though I may be just in time to make myself useful when the balloon goes up.*'

Alix hugged the letter to her. It was so good to hear from him in the middle of all this uncertainty, but the news meant that soon he would be in the thick of the conflict if Hitler attacked Britain.

–

It was May 11th. The trees in the Parc Montsouris were in delicate leaf, there were daffodils and crocuses under a clear blue sky, and the sun was warm on her back as Alix sat trying to compose an essay. Classes were still going on, but it all seemed increasingly futile. She became aware of excited voices a little way off and looked up to see a group of her fellow students clustered round one who was holding a newspaper. She jumped up and ran over to join them.

'Alix! Your English is better than ours. Translate this for us.'

The speaker was holding a copy of the *New York Herald Tribune*. Most of the French national papers had ceased publication, suppressed in the name of national security.

The *Tribune* was the only reliable source of information. Alix took the paper and read 'Reich Invades Low Countries, Luxembourg.'

'Oh God!' she murmured. 'The Nazis are attacking Holland and Luxembourg. Are we next?'

The answer, almost too shocking to be believed, came in the news bulletins two days later. The German tanks had advanced through what were thought to be the impenetrable forests of the Ardennes, evading the fortified Maginot Line, and taken the French army in the rear. There had been a battle at Sedan on the River Meuse, and the French had failed to hold or destroy the bridges. The Nazis were on French soil. The next day they learned that the Dutch had capitulated and then the devastating report that the entire French Ninth Army had surrendered.

Chapter Eleven

'Flight Sergeant Popo*vick*,' the Squadron Leader said.

'Popo*vitch*,' Steve corrected, then belatedly added, 'sir.'

The Squadron Leader favoured him with a stony glare. '*Vick, vitch* – whatever. What's a Yank doing in the Royal Air Force?'

'Hoping to make a contribution, sir,' Steve said.

The Squadron Leader's gaze softened slightly. 'Well, there's no question that we need every man we can get.' He looked down at Steve's documents on his desk. 'You seem to have done well in your training. Right!' He stood up and held out his hand. 'Welcome to 82 Squadron.'

Steve shook the offered hand. 'Thank you, sir.'

'Now, as you will have been told, we fly Blenheim fighter bombers here. Have you ever been up in one?'

'I'm afraid not, sir.'

'Not to worry. I'll get someone to give you the guided tour. The Blenheims have a crew of three, the pilot, navigator and a wireless operator who doubles as air gunner. You'll be with Flight Lieutenant Johnson. Come on. I'll introduce you.' He picked up a telephone and said, 'Ask

Flight Lieutenant Johnson to come to the Ops Room, please. And tell him to bring his new sparks with him.'

RAF Watton consisted of a scatter of permanent buildings interspersed with Nissen huts, and as he led Steve across the open square between them, the Squadron Leader said, 'I don't know how much you've been told, but the squadron has just got back from France where we've had a bit of a mauling. We've lost a lot of planes and far too many aircrew, so we are in the process of reforming. Crews tend to become a very close-knit team, but now those teams are having to be broken up and the gaps filled by newcomers like yourself. Men who've survived have had a rough time, so you mustn't take it to heart if your reception is – well, a bit less than rapturous.'

The Operations Room was furnished with benches and trestle tables facing a small dais backed by a curtained screen. As they entered, a young man wearing the three stripes of a Flight Lieutenant on his sleeve rose to his feet. He was slightly built with close cut dark hair, but the thing that struck Steve most forcibly was his youth. Out of uniform, Steve reckoned, he could easily have been mistaken for a schoolboy. That was before he saw the lines etched from the corners of his eyes and the shadows underneath them. At his side was a loose-limbed, sandy-haired boy wearing Sergeant's stripes, who looked, if possible, even younger.

'Johnny,' the Squadron Leader said, 'I've brought you a new navigator. Sergeant Popovic – he tells me it's pronounced Popo*vitch*. Did very well in training, apparently. Popovic, this is Flight Lieutenant Johnson.' He turned to Johnson. 'So, you've got a complete crew now. I'm sending you on a navigation exercise tomorrow morning, so you can get to know each other.'

60

'Very good, sir,' Johnson replied.

'I'll leave you to it.' The Squadron Leader went out, and Johnson turned to Steve.

'Popovic? You're a Pole, yes?'

'No, sir, American.'

'American?'

'My family come from Serbia.'

'Serbia? Where's that?'

'It's part of Yugoslavia now.'

'Oh, right.' He indicated the sandy-haired boy. 'This is Rogers – usually known as Rusty. He's our wireless operator and gunner.'

Steve offered his hand. 'Pleased to meet you.'

'Likewise, I'm sure.' There was a trace of an accent, but the words were uttered so quietly that Steve was unable to place it.

Johnson went on, 'Ever been up in a Blenheim?'

'No, sir.'

'Right. You're both new boys so the flight tomorrow will give us a chance to shake down.' He glanced at his watch. 'It's too late to do anything now. It'll be dinner in a quarter of an hour. I'll see you tomorrow, 0800 hours. OK?'

'OK – I mean yes, sir.'

'Good man.' Johnson nodded and walked out of the room.

Steve and Rusty looked at each other. 'Where are you—' They spoke in unison and stopped, grinning with embarrassment. 'You first,' Steve said.

'I'm from Aberdeen.'

'Oh, right. I thought that was a Scottish accent.'

'How about you?'

'Fairbanks, Alaska.'

'Alaska? That's right up north, isn't it?'

'About as far north as you can get without being inside the Arctic Circle.'

The boy seemed to like that. 'Well, I guess that makes us both northerners. Guess we've got something to show these soft southerners.'

Steve laughed. 'Guess we have, at that.'

'Fancy a beer in the mess?'

'Why not?'

Steve was given a friendly enough reception in the Sergeant's mess, but the mood was unsettling. The old hands who had been with the squadron in France laughed and joked just a little too exuberantly, and when he asked them what had happened there, they were unwilling to talk about it in detail. He gathered that they had been lucky to get out of France before they were captured by the Germans.

'I feel sorry for the poor bloody infantry in the Expeditionary Force,' one man said. 'What are the chances of them being evacuated before the Huns overrun them?'

When some of the men invited him to join them in the NAAFI after the evening meal, Steve made his excuses and retired to the room he shared with three others. It had been a long journey from the north of Wales, and he was tired. He intended to write to Alix but found himself yawning and decided to turn in. He wanted to be at the top of his game next morning for the navigation flight. His last thought before sleep overtook him was that he had his wish ; he would soon see active service – but for how long?

When he reported to the Operations Room in the morning, the Squadron Leader handed him a piece of paper. 'Here are the co-ordinates of your targets for today. I'll leave you to plot your course.'

In the dispersal hut, he changed into the regulation black overalls, put on his flying boots and strapped on his parachute harness, then, map in hand, he joined Flt Lt Johnson and Rusty Rogers outside the hangar, where they were standing beside a twin-engined aircraft bearing the designation PZ-K.

Johnson patted the fuselage as if it was a favourite horse and said, 'This is Katie. She's not a bad old bus. She's been through a few scrapes in her time, but she's always brought me home safe. Come on. I'll show you around.'

He opened the cockpit and pointed. 'That's your place, Popovic, beside me. The seat slides forward when you need to get to the bombsight. Rusty, you're back there in the gun turret. You won't have much to do today, but when we're operational, it's your job to watch out for enemy aircraft. Keeping your eyes skinned at all times can make the difference between life and death for all of us.'

They taxied out onto the runway, and then, preliminary checks carried out and clearance received from the control tower, Johnson opened up the engines for take-off. Steve had been used to the single-engined Anson in which he had done his training, and he found the surge of power unleashed by the two Bristol Mercury engines exhilarating. Once they were airborne he was unable to suppress an exclamation.

'Wow! She certainly goes!'

He heard Johnson laugh through the intercom attached to his flying helmet. 'She sure does. The Blenheim's the fastest plane we've got.' After a pause, he added more soberly, 'Not as fast as those bloody 109s, though. We're going to have to catch up if we're to stand a chance in the long term.'

The flight went according to plan. The 'targets' Steve had been given were all in the southeast of England, and as they flew low, he was able to look down at the green fields and hedgerows he had only seen in pictures. Black and white cattle galloped away from them as they flew over. There were fields of young wheat and patches of woodland and little villages tucked into folds in the countryside. It was so different from the wide-open plains he was used to, different even from the French countryside with its big fields and straight roads. He found himself wishing he could go down and stroll along the country lanes.

'Bit different from home, I imagine,' Johnson's voice in his earphones echoed his thoughts.

'You can say that again.'

There was no difficulty in identifying his 'targets'. The Blenheim only carried one 1,000 lb bomb, but for the purposes of the exercise, he had been given four. They could not, of course, drop a bomb on them, but the plane was equipped with cameras so that when he pressed the button that would have released the bomb, a picture was taken showing where they would have hit. Back at base, the film was developed and Johnson slapped him on the shoulder.

'Spot on, every one of them! Bloody good show.'

Steve felt a flush of pleasure, but his sense of comfortable relaxation was quickly banished. One of the other flight commanders came briskly into the room.

'We're up for an operation later today. The list's just been posted. Briefing at 1400 hours.'

Johnson looked at Steve. 'Well, I'd rather have had a bit longer for you to settle in, but it's not to be. I hope your navigation's as good under operating conditions as it was this morning.'

In the briefing room, Steve joined Johnson and the crew of five other planes as the Squadron Leader pointed out their targets for the afternoon's sortie.

'As you know, our men are being pushed back towards Dunkirk, and they are under constant fire from the enemy. Your job is to bomb the Jerries' gun emplacements. The more we can put out of action the better it will be for our chaps on the ground.'

Specific areas were allocated to each pilot, and they were told to be ready for take-off at 1700 hours.

'Right,' Johnson said as they left the room. 'We've got a couple of hours. Try and get some rest.'

It was an impossible suggestion. Back in his room, Steve tried again to write to Alix. He was painfully aware that it might be the last letter she would ever get from him, but the words would not come, and in the end, he gave up. It was a beautiful day, warm for the time of year, so he wandered outside and found a quiet spot behind one of the huts where he could sit and feel the sun on his face. Somewhere high above him a bird was singing, a constant out-pouring of song. He made a mental note to ask someone what it was when he got back. If he got back... Suddenly he had an absolute conviction that this could not be the last time he would hear it. He was coming back. This could not be the end.

In the dispersal hut, men were shrugging on their over-alls and stamping their feet into boots. Steve noticed that many of them were tucking small objects of one kind or another into their pockets – a photograph, a rabbit's foot, a small toy – while others were winding a much-worn scarf around their necks. He guessed that they were all lucky charms, and his idea was confirmed when Johnson produced a small, moth-eaten toy dog.

'This is Fido,' he said. 'He's brought me luck so far. Here's hoping he'll do the same for you.'

Walking out to the aircraft, Steve reflected on the uncertainty that had produced such superstitious reliance on luck, and it occurred to him to wonder for the first time what had happened to Johnson's previous crew. He sensed the Flight Lieutenant would be unwilling to talk about it and he did not know who else to ask. He put the thought behind him as he climbed into his seat, plugged in his intercom and fastened his harness.

Fifteen minutes later they crossed the French coast and the full impact of what was happening to the country where he had invested so many of his hopes and dreams struck him. Roofless houses, fields churned to mud by tank tracks, refugees clogging the road, some on foot pushing prams or handcarts loaded with their possessions, others in cars with mattresses strapped to the roof, and among them, columns of khaki-clad men and camouflage-painted vehicles, all struggling towards the beaches – the contrast with the peaceful countryside he had seen that morning was almost impossible to take in. Then he saw the German tanks and armoured personnel carriers surrounding the fleeing soldiers and the flashes of exploding shells landing among them.

Johnson's voice recalled him to the business in hand. 'Coming up on our target.'

Steve slid his seat forward into position so he could peer through the bombsight. They were flying low, and suddenly anti-aircraft shells were exploding all round them, but Johnson held the plane straight and level until Steve was able to press the button that released the bomb. He felt the plane shake itself as if relieved of the load and he shouted into the intercom, 'Bomb away!'

Johnson pulled the nose of the plane up and as they climbed Rusty's excited voice came through the intercom. 'We got the bastards! Direct hit! Bloody marvellous!'

'Good show!' Johnson responded. 'Let's head for home.'

As the plane banked to turn onto the heading Steve provided, Rusty's voice came again, very different in tone this time.

'109 on our tail! Coming up fast!'

Johnson pushed the steering column forward, putting the plane into a steep dive, and for the next few minutes, Steve could only hang onto his seat as Katie twisted and rolled to evade the attacker. He heard the sharp crackle of gunfire, and the plane shook, but their speed did not slacken, and below him he saw the white cliffs along the coast of England just ahead. He had heard Vera Lynn singing about the white cliffs of Dover on almost every radio broadcast, but he had not understood until that moment why it meant so much to the people who heard it.

'We've shaken him off!' Rusty's voice had a tremor in it. 'Bloody good flying, Skip!'

Back on the ground they attended the routine debriefing. This time all the aircraft had returned, but it seemed Steve had been the only one to hit the designated target, for which he was congratulated by the Squadron Leader.

As they left, Johnson said, 'Some of us go down to the pub in the village when we're off duty. Fancy joining us?'

By the time he had eaten his dinner, Steve felt worn out and he was tempted to forget the invitation, but something told him it would be a mistake. The Shady Oak was everything he had imagined an English pub to be – low-ceilinged with heavy oak beams, the floor flagged, horse brasses decorating the walls; and the publican was a jolly-looking red-faced man and the barmaid was blonde and looked as though the word 'buxom' had been invented specially for her.

Steve hesitated, looking round, unsure where to sit. Then a voice called him from a table in the corner where half a dozen aircrew were seated.

'Hey, Popeye! Over here!'

Popeye! So that would be his nickname from now on. It was not what he would have chosen, but that did not matter. It meant he was accepted. He was part of the team.

Chapter Twelve

Alix received a letter addressed in an unfamiliar hand. Her stomach turned over as she opened it. The news from the front had been so alarming, and she knew Raoul must be in the thick of the fighting. Who was writing to her now? And why?

May 14th 1940

Chère Mlle Malkovic,

I am sorry to be the bearer of bad news. Raoul Delors was killed yesterday during the fighting around Sedan. We were comrades, and he gave me your address and asked me, before we went into action, to write to you if anything happened to him. He did not ask me to pass on any special message, but I know you must have meant a great deal to him, or he would not have wanted me to write to you.

He died a hero, giving his life for France.

My condolences on your loss, chère mademoiselle,

With respectful salutations,
Pierre Beauregard

Alix read the letter through quickly, and then again more slowly. Then she folded it carefully and put it back in the envelope and sat quite still for some time. She thought she ought to weep, but no tears came to her eyes. She felt sad that the life of someone so young, so vibrantly alive and so engaged with ideas of a better future, should be ended in such an arbitrary manner, but it occurred to her that she felt no sense of personal loss. She and Raoul had been lovers, in the technical sense, but had they ever really loved each other? He had not left a personal message for her, no words of tenderness or devotion. She recalled his last leave, and his violent demands on her, and was aware that her principal feeling was one of relief that she would not have to cope with another week like that. He gave his life for France? What did that mean? How could his sacrifice make any difference to the fate of the country? His death was pointless, not heroic. The thought uppermost in her mind, she had to admit with a tremor of guilt, was that now that Raoul was dead, she was free to love Steve. That was, if he still cared about her. Her letters to him had gone unanswered, but she could not be sure that he had even received them. Perhaps he had met an English girl and forgotten all about her.

-

On May 28th, Belgium surrendered, and two days after that the French First Army also gave itself up to the invaders. Meanwhile, news bulletins were reporting that the British were attempting to evacuate thousands of their men and the remnants of the French forces from the beaches around Dunkirk.

Chapter Thirteen

RAF Watton

May 31st 1940

Steve swallowed the last of his beer and felt the tension in his shoulders relax marginally. Around him, other members of his squadron were also downing their first pints of the evening. The saloon bar of The Shady Oak was crowded, as it usually was at this time, RAF uniforms mingling with the tweed jackets of the local farmers and the flannels and blazers of what he had learned in Paris to call the '*bourgeoisie*'. There was a general buzz of conversation but, on the whole, the atmosphere was sombre. Unspoken, but at the back of everybody's mind was the threat of imminent invasion.

By the third round, the mood among the airmen had changed. To begin with they had been subdued, tired to the point of exhaustion, but now a kind of hysteria took over. Voices grew louder, jokes more hilarious, laughter less restrained.

'I can't believe it!' It was one of the grey flannels brigade, a tall man of middle age, wearing a cravat in the open collar of his shirt. 'How can you men sit here, laughing and drinking, when our boys are being slaughtered by the Huns on the other side of the Channel?

71

Why aren't you over there, doing your damnedest to help them?'

In the silence that followed his words, Johnny Johnson rose to his feet. 'Would you like me to tell you what we have been doing today?' His voice was quiet but electric with tension. 'Since dawn this morning, my crew and I have flown five sorties over the Dunkirk beaches, bombing and strafing enemy positions. The same goes for the rest of the squadron. Our ground crews have worked themselves to a standstill, refuelling and repairing damage, so we could turn round and go up again. Today, I have seen one of our aircraft go down in flames, with no possibility of anyone getting out alive, and the crew of another one baling out over the Channel – God knows where they are now. Altogether in the last five days, this squadron has lost seven aircraft to enemy action. That's twenty-one men dead or captured.' He paused for breath, his eyes on the man in the cravat. 'You remind me of what Henry V said to his troops before the battle of Agincourt. "Gentlemen in England now abed,"' he had not raised his voice, but the words were like a gun levelled at the man in front of him, '"shall hold their manhood cheap while any speaks who fought with us upon this day." Well, this may not be Agincourt, but the same sentiment sure as hell applies!' He turned to the other airmen. 'Drink up, chaps. My round, I think.'

As Johnson walked away to the bar, there was a scattered round of applause from the other customers. The man in the cravat had flushed and then gone deadly pale. He was mumbling, 'Sorry, sorry. I didn't know. I just thought…' Then he turned tail and shoved his way out of the door. The airmen looked at each other, and there was a collective exhalation as if they had all been holding their breath, and then words came again. 'Well done, that man! Bloody good show! That took the bastard down a peg or two! Serves the bugger right!'

Rusty nudged Steve's elbow. 'What was all that about Agincourt?'

'It's Shakespeare,' Steve said. 'From his play *Henry V*.'

He regarded his captain thoughtfully as he returned from the bar with a clutch of beer tankards in each hand. In the ten days since he had joined the squadron, he had had the opportunity to learn more about him. He was not quite as young as first impressions suggested. At twenty-four, he was regarded as an old hand. Posted to France, he had distinguished himself and earned promotion, but on the day the squadron was recalled to England, disaster struck. On his last sortie he was shot down by a 109. With the plane on fire, he managed to crash land in a field. His gunner was killed but he succeeded in rescuing his observer, at the cost of serious burns, and had somehow managed to get to Calais in time to be evacuated. He should, Steve's informant told him, have been sent on leave to recuperate, but after a brief stay in hospital, he had insisted on being returned to active duty.

This, then, was the man on whose skill and courage his life depended. And on top of all that, he could quote Shakespeare. Watching him hand round the tankards of beer, Steve experienced something that felt very much like hero worship.

The following morning followed the same pattern as the preceding days. They were airborne soon after dawn and within minutes they were over Dunkirk. The devastation Steve had seen on his first flight was worse. The town and its surroundings had been reduced to smouldering wreckage and the German tanks had drawn a tourniquet around the harbour and the neighbouring beaches. But it was those beaches and the sea that lapped them that held his gaze. Ships were tied up to what remained of a pier and others, dozens of them, were standing just off the beach, as close in as they could get without going aground. Between them and the beaches were dozens, no hundreds, of small boats of every description – yachts and pleasure launches and fishing boats – loaded with men to be ferried out to the waiting ships or returning for a new cargo. In the sand dunes that backed the beach, hundreds of men crouched, waiting their turn, or stood in lines until they could wade out to one of the rescue boats. Bombs threw up gouts of sand on all sides of them, but still the lines stood firm. There was no scramble for the nearest boat, no attempt, as far as he could see, to elbow others out of the way, just a disciplined, courageous endurance.

All this Steve took in in the first seconds as they flew over the scene. Then he turned his attention to the business in hand. He selected a target, a group of enemy tanks, guided Johnny onto it, sighted down the bombsight and pressed the button. 'Bomb away!' Johnson pulled the plane into a steep, banking climb, but before Steve had a chance to look down to see if he had hit the target, there was a rattle of machine gun fire and the plane shuddered with the impact. Over his intercom he heard Rusty scream. 'Oh God! He's got me!' Johnson threw the plane into a series of frantic manoeuvres, diving and twisting and climbing again. They were over the sea now, running for home, but another burst of machine gun fire rocked them, and a line of holes appeared in the fuselage close to Steve's right shoulder. Suddenly, they went into a steep dive. He recognised the tactic. If they could fly so low that they almost skimmed the waves it would be more difficult for the enemy fighter to follow them without risking ditching. But within seconds that recognition turned to alarm.

'Skip! Pull up! Pull up!' he shouted, but the dive continued.

Steve clawed his way back from his forward position by the bombsight and saw why Johnson had not pulled out of the dive. He was slumped over the controls, blood streaming from a hole above his right ear. It was his weight that was pushing the control column forward and maintaining the dive. Steve stared ahead. The sea was coming up fast. He had seconds before they hit. He undid the straps that held him in his seat and leaned forward, attempting to pull the pilot's inert body back off the controls. It was impossible. He could not get into a position that gave him sufficient leverage. They were going to hit the water, and at the angle they were going, Katie would simply plough onwards, diving still deeper. Some instinct of self-preservation made Steve slap his hand on the button that released his parachute harness and he shrugged off the straps. Then the plane hit the water. The windscreen shattered, and immediately the cockpit began to fill.

Steve just had time to catch a deep breath before he was submerged. He could feel himself being dragged deeper and deeper. Lungs bursting, he kicked off his flying boots and forced his eyes open. Somewhere above him there was a faint square of light, and he realised that the shell that had killed Johnson had made a hole in the fuselage. He kicked upwards and reached the hole. It was barely big enough for him to get through and the edges were jagged. He grabbed them, not feeling the pain as they sliced into his palms, and forced his shoulders through. Sharp edges caught on his flying suit, and for a second, it seemed he could go no further, but above his head the surface of the water was bright. Up there was air and sunlight and life! He kicked and twisted his body, and suddenly he was free, rising up until his head broke the surface.

For a minute, he floated, gasping great gulps of air. Then he turned to look around him. What had happened to Rusty? It might have been possible for him to get out through the hatch that gave access to his gun turret. Steve scanned the surface. Pieces of wreckage and a slick of oil rose to the surface, but there was no sign of a human head. For a moment, he wondered if he should dive down and try to extricate the young man, but he realised at once that it would be impossible. Katie would be deep down by now, probably on the bottom. He would never be able to hold his breath long enough to do any good – and Rusty had screamed just before the crash. He was wounded, quite possibly dead, before they hit the water. Steve could only hope that was the case.

It occurred to him that the enemy fighter might still be about somewhere, but a scan of the sky showed that it was empty. Presumably, the pilot had gone to look for another target. Steve twisted round and scanned his surroundings, discovering with relief that he was only a hundred or so yards from the beach. But which beach? It appeared to be deserted, so it was not Dunkirk. Was it possible that their flight had taken them further across the channel than he thought and that was the coast of England? He turned on his back and squinted up at the sun. When they left, it had still been low in the eastern sky and even after all that had happened it was still far from the meridian. It was creating a glittering path across the waves to his left shoulder, so he was facing south. So that was the coast of France – or possibly Belgium. He floated for a while longer, listening for the sound of approaching aircraft or boats. It was just possible that the crash had been registered on radar back at base and there might be an air-sea rescue craft heading his way, but the silence remained unbroken and he was getting cold. With a weary groan, he struck out for the shore.

He was a strong swimmer, but it seemed a long time before he was able to haul himself to his feet and wade ashore. The open beach felt dangerously exposed, so he forced himself to struggle on until he was in a valley among the dunes. There he flopped down and lay still, letting the sun warm him. For a while his mind was empty of any thought except that he was alive, then the essential corollary of that struck him. He had survived, but his two comrades had not. 'Johnny' Johnson, the man he had come to admire so greatly, was dead – and so was youthful, gently spoken Rusty Rogers. Steve turned over on the sand and buried his face in his arms while hot tears soaked into his sleeve.

At length, he recovered enough to begin to ask himself what he should do next. By his reckoning, he was east of Dunkirk but by how many miles he had only the faintest idea. He tried to calculate the speed of the plane and the length of time since he had dropped his bomb, but they had executed so many violent manoeuvres that it was impossible to come up with any meaningful answer. Nevertheless, the only chance he had of getting back to England would be if he could reach Dunkirk before the evacuation was completed, and the only way of getting there, as far as he could tell, was to walk. It was at that point that he remembered that he had kicked off his boots and had nothing on his feet except his socks. Walking was going to be a painful business – though perhaps, he thought, he could keep to the beach. Walking on the sand would be easier. That, he decided, would be the best course of action, but he felt too exhausted to start straight away. He needed a rest before he set out.

The sun was higher now, and his little nook among the sands was sheltered and cosy. He closed his eyes and let his mind drift.

A vicious kick to his ribs woke him. He twisted over and opened his eyes to see a pair of boots and above them the grey trousers of a German uniform. A desperate glance to his other side showed a second pair of boots and the barrel of a rifle pointing at his head.

'*Raus!*' a voice above him ordered. '*Hande hoch!*'

Slowly Steve dragged himself to his feet. There was no point in disobeying. He was a prisoner.

Chapter Fourteen

Paris

June 3rd 1940

Alix was having lunch with Marie Louise when the sirens sounded.

'*Mon Dieu!*' Marie Louise exclaimed. 'Are they really going to bomb the city?'

'It's probably a false alarm.' Alix said. 'We've heard the bombers overflying the outskirts for the last day or two. They are trying to intimidate us.'

The proprietor was already hustling customers out, not forgetting to hand them their bills before they left. 'You girls should get to a shelter,' he said.

'Should we, do you think?' Marie Louise asked.

'I don't know,' Alix hesitated. 'If it's going to be a real raid, I'd like to see it. They won't bomb the centre of the city, surely?'

'Me, too!' said Marie Louise. 'Let's go up on the Palais roof.'

It was the time of day when many Parisians were just returning to work after lunch, and the streets were already busy. Now there was an air of panic as men and women ran for the shelters. Alix found herself having to force her way against the current, until they entered the beautifully manicured grounds of the Palais de Chaillot. At the entrance to the Musée de l'Homme, one of the concierges was about to bolt the door.

'Mesdemoiselles!' he exclaimed. 'You should go to the shelter!'

As he spoke, the ground beneath their feet shook, and a second later, they heard a rumble like distant thunder.

'It's not a false alarm this time!' Marie Louise said.

'Come on!'

They hurried up the stairs until they came out, breathless, on the flat roof above the wing of the building where the museum was housed. A single figure was already there, a bald-headed man in his sixties with small, round eyeglasses and a winged collar whom Alix recognised as Paul Rivet, the director of the museum.

He looked at Alix and Marie Louise. 'You women should not be here. Hurry down to the shelter.'

'But what about you, M. le Directeur?' Marie Louise said. 'Shouldn't you be in the shelter too?'

'I wish to bear witness to this. If they truly intend to bomb Paris, it will prove that the Nazis have no respect for civilisation, never mind human life.'

'Forgive us, M. le Directeur,' Alix said. 'But we wish to bear witness too.'

He gave her a long, thoughtful look. 'So…' His words were cut off by another explosion and they all turned to search the horizon.

'Over there!' Marie Louise pointed. 'See?'

Alix saw a column of smoke rising from somewhere in the northern part of the city.

'Where do you think…?' she began, when a new noise drowned her voice, a detonation much closer to where they stood. It was followed by others, a barrage of sound that shook the building. Above their heads, white mushroom clouds exploded all over the sky. A whirr of wings close by made Alix duck and clasp her hands over her head; then she straightened up, shamefaced, at the realisation that it was a flock of pigeons, driven into terrified flight by the noise.

'It's the anti-aircraft guns,' Rivet shouted.

'Where are the German planes?' Alix shouted back.

They all scanned the sky, but it was impossible to see beyond the anti-aircraft barrage. Alix saw a flash over to her right, and a blast of wind almost knocked her to her knees as another explosion rocked the ground. Marie Louise screamed.

'My God! That was close!' Rivet exclaimed. 'It must be in the Bois de Boulogne.' A moment later, he went on, 'Here come our boys!' They all heard the sound of aircraft closer overhead. Alix craned her neck and stared up to see a flight of fighter planes whirling and twisting among the mushroom clouds. Far above them she glimpsed other, larger aircraft, a regular formation that broke up and scattered as the fighters got among them.

Another explosion shook the building, and a new column of smoke rose into the air from the southwest.

'I think they're going for the airfields,' Rivet said. 'Not the city itself.'

'Maybe they're just dropping blind,' Marie Louise said. 'How can they see their target from that height? The ack-ack guns are preventing them from coming lower.'

Whatever the reason and whatever the intended purpose, the barrage went on for what felt to Alix like an eternity. There was a brief lull after about twenty minutes, and they had just begun to think the worst was over when the sirens sounded again. A second wave of bombers swept across the sky, and again the anti-aircraft guns opened up. When the all-clear finally sounded and the noise of explosions ceased, they stood looking around over the city. In five different locations they could see thick columns of smoke rising from the outskirts.

'It appears the suburbs have had the worst of it,' Rivet said.

'Thank God they haven't hit any of our historic buildings,' Marie Louise responded, but Rivet shook his head.

'Don't speak too soon. My guess is this was by way of a warning. Surrender, or we will reduce your beautiful capital city to ruins.'

Alix gasped. 'Do you really think that's what they expect – for us to surrender?'

'What's the alternative? The First Army has already surrendered. The Boches are almost at the gates. We have to prepare for German occupation.' Rivet's face was grim. 'What we should be thinking about is how to resist, by all means at our disposal.'

'What could we do?' Marie Louise asked. 'We have no means of resisting, once they are in control.'

'Oh, there are means,' Rivet said, 'if there are men – and women – ready to employ them.'

Alix looked across the city at the rising smoke. Perhaps the historic centre of the city had escaped, as far as it was possible to tell, but there were men and women living and working where those bombs had fallen, children too. They would just have been assembling in their classrooms for afternoon school. How many had been killed? How many had lost mothers or fathers? And now it seemed they must succumb to the heartless monsters who had inflicted that damage. Until that moment, the war had seemed distant, something that was happening to other people, a long way away. Now it had arrived on her doorstep. The momentary relief she had felt when the bombing stopped was replaced by a slow-burning anger.

'If there is a way,' she said, 'then I will do whatever I can. You can rely on me for that.'

In the absence of newspapers, and with the wireless broadcasts heavily censored, it was difficult to find out how much damage had been done, but the American papers were still reporting, and from them, Alix learned that official figures told of two hundred casualties, eighteen of them children. Five schools and a temporary hospital had been struck and ninety-seven buildings had been destroyed or set on fire. The American ambassador had had a lucky escape when a bomb struck the building where he was meeting for a conference but failed to explode.

Next evening, Marie Louise brought a wireless set into the museum and they took it up onto the roof, where they were joined by Paul Rivet.

'I think we should be able to tune in to the English BBC,' she said. 'That's the only way we shall get truthful information. You should make notes, Alix. You are the only one of us who speaks fluent English.'

She began to twist the knobs on the set, and at first, Alix could hear nothing but the hiss of static; then suddenly an English voice came over, distorted but comprehensible. Alix crouched closer to the set, a notebook on her knee.

The Prime Minister, Winston Churchill, has described the 'miracle of deliverance' from Dunkirk and warned of an impending invasion.

His moving speech to Parliament came on the day the last allied soldier arrived home from France at the end of a 10-day operation to bring back hundreds of thousands of retreating allied troops trapped by the German Army.

'They have rescued thousands of their troops from Dunkirk,' she paraphrased. 'And Churchill is warning they might be invaded.'

Battle-weary and hungry soldiers from the retreating British Expeditionary Force, as well as French and Belgian troops, had spent many days waiting to board ships from the one remaining pier, the east mole. When those who survived the evacuation arrived exhausted in England, they were welcomed as returning heroes and offered plenty of tea and sandwiches as they boarded special trains.

'They have been welcomed back as heroes…'

'But what about the invasion?'

'Wait! … Churchill is saying it has been a military disaster, but he's thanking the RAF and the Navy… now, listen!'

He ended his speech with a defiant message to Hitler's armies.

'We shall defend our island whatever the cost may be. We shall fight on the beaches, we shall fight on the landing grounds, we shall fight in the fields and in the streets, we shall fight in the hills. We shall never surrender.'

Alix lifted her head. There were tears on her cheeks. 'Oh yes! That's the spirit! That's wonderful!'

'Translate! I didn't understand it all.'

'He said Britain would fight the Nazis anywhere if they tried to occupy the country. He said they will never surrender.'

'And we will do the same – won't we?' Marie Louise looked at Paul.

He shrugged his shoulders. 'Will we? I'm not sure.'

For the next few days, the city felt like one under siege. Trains leaving were packed to suffocation. Every road to the south was clogged with refugees, some in cars or trucks, some in horse-drawn carts or pony traps, some on foot, loaded down with their personal possessions, pushing prams and leading children by the hand. Alix watched them trudging past and recalled her mother's letter begging her to leave Paris. She had written back saying that she was determined to stay. Well, it was too late now to change her mind.

Chapter Fifteen

Somewhere in Belgium

June 5th 1940

The column of men stretched for almost a quarter of a mile along the straight, dusty road. Many carried the evidence of wounds in roughly bandaged heads and make-shift slings. Some marched with heads erect, refusing to bow under the burden of defeat. Many gazed around themselves with dulled eyes, as if unable to comprehend what had happened to them, while others kept their eyes on the road in front of them and the regular, hypnotic tramp of the boots of the man in front. On either side of the column at intervals of thirty paces marched men in German uniform, with rifles on their shoulders. Many of these were older men, others very young – the ones who could most easily be spared from the front line. At the front and the rear of the column, armoured cars carried the officers in command.

Steve marched with the rest, or rather limped. Yesterday, before they set out, someone had seen that he had nothing on his feet and had thrown him a pair of boots, but they were the wrong size. The blisters they had raised on his heels had burst long ago and he could feel the blood trickling down into what was left of his socks.

He also gazed about him as he walked, but not with the unfocused look of some of the others. He was taking in the deep ditch on either side of the road, the poplar trees that lined it at regular intervals, the manner of the guards ahead and behind him. They were relaxed, calling jokes and insults backwards and forwards to the comrade nearest to them. Sometimes one would step aside to piss into the ditch or pause to light a cigarette.

The column was made up of lines of four men, and Steve was on the outside, nearest the edge of the road. In some places there were clumps of bushes growing beside the road, and, glancing behind, he reckoned that at certain moments they would for a couple of seconds obscure him from the guard marching behind. The ditch here was full of brambles and nettles that would easily hide a man lying down. But if he was spotted as he jumped, there was a good chance he would get a bullet in the back. It was his best chance of escape, worth taking the risk, surely? He watched and waited. Finally his chance came. The guard following had stopped to piss into the bushes. The man ahead was laughing at some joke shouted to him across the column. Steve took a deep breath, stepped sideways and flung himself into the ditch.

The brambles clawed at him as he fell, but he broke through them and found himself lying in the dry bottom of the ditch. The undergrowth had closed over him making a screen of greenery. He lay still, holding his breath, expecting to hear a shout, or see the barrel of a rifle thrust down toward his chest, but nothing happened, and he heard nothing but the steady tramp of boots passing along the road above him. It was early afternoon. They had been counted when they stopped briefly to eat their rations at midday. There would not be another roll call until they reached wherever they intended to camp that night. He had perhaps four or five hours before he was missed.

After the sound of the marching feet had faded into the distance, he still lay without moving, listening. The road was not busy. All those hoping to take refuge further south had passed on days ago, and the local people who had decided to stay were keeping to their farms and cottages. Any traffic was military and infrequent. Eventually, Steve raised his head, then got to his knees. He was about to climb out of the ditch when the sound of engines approaching at speed made him duck down again. Two German despatch riders on motorcycles roared past. Again, just as he was about to stand up, he heard engines and a staff car with a motorcycle escort passed in the opposite direction. When the sound had faded into the distance, he raised himself sufficiently to turn and look across the fields that bordered the road. The flat, sparsely forested land of Flanders offered little hope of cover, but before he jumped, he had noticed a barn, about one hundred yards away, beyond a field populated by black and white cattle. It was still *le midi*, that sacred, heat-dazed couple of hours when all country folk retired to their homes to eat. There was no one visible in the fields. Steve clambered out of the ditch and ran, half doubled over, gritting his teeth against the pain of his blistered feet. Cows lumbered out of his way as he dodged among them, but he hoped that their bodies might help to obscure him from anyone watching.

Panting, he reached the barn and stopped, leaning on the wall, listening. There was no sound of voices or movement from inside. When his breathing had steadied, he edged round the corner. A rough track led from the open

88

door to a cluster of buildings a short distance away, the farm to which the barn belonged, he assumed. There was still no sign of life, so he moved quickly to the door and slipped inside. It was, as he had hoped, a hay barn. It was only partly filled by the slightly musty-smelling remains of last summer's hay-making, but there was enough there to hide him should the need arise. A ladder led up to a loft above and he hauled himself up it and made himself a nest among the hay bales. There he eased off his boots, swearing under his breath at the pain. Examining his feet, it was obvious that there was no possibility of walking much further unless he could find some way of covering the blisters and padding out the boots so that they did not rub. He lay back in the hay and considered his next move.

His captors had taken him to a temporary prison camp so close to the Dunkirk beaches that he could hear the guns and watch the aerial skirmishes taking place in the skies above them. They had walked for a day and a half since then, so they must be nearly thirty miles away. Even if he could somehow manage to walk back, the chances were that the evacuation would be finished by the time he got there, and the likelihood of being picked up by the Germans on his way was too strong to be comfortable. So, what was the answer? Perhaps if he could make his way to the coast somewhere nearer, he might find someone who would take him across the Channel on a fishing boat, but to explore that possibility he still needed boots that didn't cripple him. He would also need food and drink. That thought made him realise that he was already terribly thirsty. Maybe, he thought, when it got dark, he might be able to sneak close enough to the farm to find a well or a tap, and maybe steal an egg. He might even find some boots or shoes left outside – but there was no reason why they should fit him any better than the ones he had. A new thought struck him. He was still wearing his RAF-issue flight overalls. If he was going to have any chance of escaping he would need to steal some different clothes. He tried to imagine himself creeping into a bedroom where someone was sleeping and gathering up discarded garments. The idea was so preposterous that he dismissed it.

It was hot in the barn, and he was very tired. He decided that there was nothing he could do until it got dark so he might as well get some sleep while he could. At least that way he could forget how thirsty he was. He closed his eyes.

Sometime later he awoke with a start. There was movement below him in the barn. His first thought was that a search party had tracked him to his hiding place and he gazed around wildly, looking for a way of escape. Then the soft lowing of a cow brought him back to reality. What he was hearing was not the tramp of boots but the rustle of hooves in straw. The sound was followed by a girl's voice murmuring softly and the clank of a bucket and the hiss of liquid. It was milking time.

Steve sank back on the straw. If he kept quiet the chances were his presence would remain undetected and then, after the girl had left… then what? The light slanting through the gap under the eaves told him it was evening. Soon it would be dark. Perhaps then at least he could find something to eat and drink. He closed his eyes again.

'*Monsieur! Monsieur soldat!*' The whispered words came to him as part of a dream. '*N'ayez pas peur. Je suis ami.*'

Steve opened his eyes and jerked upright. A girl's face was visible at the top of the ladder. 'Don't be afraid,' she repeated in French. 'I will help you. I am a friend.'

'A friend?' He reverted automatically to the language he had learned during his time in Paris. 'How did you know I was here?'

'Ah, you speak French! That is good.' She climbed up the ladder to join him and he saw her properly. She had a thick mane of brown hair, held back by a scarf. Her face was brown and free of make-up, and she wore a faded blue dress. He guessed her age to be around fifteen or sixteen.

'I saw you run from the road, but I had to wait until it was time to bring the cattle in for milking. Otherwise, it would have looked suspicious. I don't know who I can trust. You are a prisoner, yes?'

'Yes. Well, I was.'

'English airman?'

'No, American.'

'American?'

'But I belong to the RAF – the British Air Force.'

'Ah. You were shot down?'

'Yes, two, no – three days ago. Please, do you have anything to drink? I am very, very thirsty.'

'Wait, please.'

She scrambled down the ladder, and he thought suddenly that this might be a trap. Perhaps she was going to call someone to arrest him, someone who would hand him back to the Germans. But a few seconds later, she reappeared carrying a jug full of warm milk.

'Drink. It is fresh, straight from the cow.'

He took a mouthful, then drained the jug. She watched him, smiling.

'Good, yes?'

'Wonderful. Thank you so much.'

'Now you can come to the house. It is quite safe. The men have gone home. There is only my mother and me.'

He shook his head. 'No. I won't put you and your mother at risk. I must move on.'

'Move on where?'

A sense of helplessness swept over him. 'I don't know. South, perhaps? Perhaps I can get back to Dunkirk. Maybe they are still evacuating men from the beaches there.'

'No.' She shook her head. 'We listen to the English wireless, the BBC. That is finished.'

'Then I don't know…' He let the sentence trail into silence.

She was practical. 'You must rest and eat. Then we will think what you might do. Come.'

He got to his feet and reached for his boots, unable to suppress an oath as pain lanced up his leg from the open sore on his foot.

'Wait!' She put a hand on his arm. 'Let me see. Oh, your poor feet! What happened?'

'These boots. They're not mine. I lost mine and these don't fit.'

'And they made you walk all this way! *Salauds!* Stay there. I will come back.'

She disappeared down the ladder again. This time he was not afraid that she might betray him, but the feeling of hopelessness had not left him. Where, indeed, might he go? He was free, but what good had it done him? The girl was back quite quickly. This time she carried a jug of water, some clean cloth and a pair of thick socks. Carefully, she bathed his feet, apologising when he winced with pain, and wrapped the clean linen over his blisters, then eased his feet into the socks.

'They were my brother's,' she explained. 'He… is not here now. So, can you stand?' He got to his feet. 'Come down the ladder. Then I will give you some shoes.'

At the bottom of the ladder, she indicated a pair of sabots, the wooden clogs that all peasants wore around their fields and farmyards. They were loose-fitting, and with the thick socks, he was able to walk in them without too much pain.

'Come,' she said. 'My mother is waiting.'

At the door leading into the farmhouse kitchen, she said, 'So, leave the sabots here. We always take them off before we come inside.'

The room was long and low, lit by an oil lamp. Hams hung from the beams that supported the ceiling, along with strings of garlic and bunches of herbs, and the smell of onions cooking brought saliva to his mouth in such quantities that he almost choked. A short, square-set woman turned from the range as he came in. She had the same thick brown hair as her daughter, but hers was streaked with grey and her face, rather than tanned, was weather-worn. Her eyes, deep-set among the wrinkles, were blue and alive with good will.

'Welcome! Come in. Sit. Don't worry; you are perfectly safe here.'

A bowlful of onion soup, a hunk of bread and a jug of red wine were set in front of him. The wine was rough and heavy with tannin but it warmed his gut, and the soup was beyond delicious. As he ate, he learned that his hostess's name was Marie Ducroix and her daughter was Jeanette.

'You are very kind to take me in, madame,' he said. 'But it is a risk for you. The Germans may be looking for me.'

'*Les sales Boches!*' she exclaimed. 'We hate them all. I lost my husband fighting them in the last war, and now my son…'

'Your son has been killed?'

'No. Taken prisoner. Maybe he, too, will find a way to escape and someone will help him. So, whatever we can do for you… Tonight you must eat and rest. In the morning we will see if we can find you some boots that fit and some other clothes. Then we will think what to do.'

The calm conviction in her voice, together with the food and the wine, lulled him into a sense of security. The two women ate and pottered around the kitchen clearing up; then Jeanette went out to shut up the hens and geese he had seen as he crossed the yard. Madame handed him a lamp.

'The privy is across the yard. To the left of the pigsty.'

He slipped his feet back into the sabots and followed her directions. When he returned, she lit a candle.

'Come, I will show you where you can sleep.'

She showed him into a small room under the eaves with a bed and a washbasin and a ewer of water on a table.

'Good night. There's no need to worry. The geese will wake us if anyone comes near the house.'

He had slept that afternoon, and now he lay awake for some time, listening to the unfamiliar sounds of the night. A horse snorted in the stable across the yard; an owl hooted and was answered by another and from time to time, and when the wind changed direction, he thought he heard thunder. In the end, he realised what he was hearing was the sound of distant gunfire. The battle for France was not over. Eventually the wine and the food had their effect and he slept heavily.

The crowing of a cock woke him, together with the need to empty his bladder. He climbed out of bed, pulled on his overalls and made his way downstairs. Madame was in the kitchen and there was a smell of bread baking. He wished her good morning, slipped his feet into the sabots on the doorstep, and headed out across the yard. He had just reached the kitchen door on his return when the geese set up a din that would have woken the heaviest sleeper. At the same instant, Jeanette hared round the corner of the house.

'Boches! At the gate! Quickly!'

He turned to run, but she grabbed his arm and pushed him into the kitchen. There, her mother was already stripping back a rug to expose a trapdoor in the floor.

'Down there! Quickly! The geese will delay them for a few minutes.'

She grabbed his arm and shoved him towards the hole the trapdoor had revealed. A ladder led down into a cellar. Clumsy in the unaccustomed sabots he clambered down, and the trapdoor was closed, leaving him in total darkness. Above his head he heard thuds, then the stamp of boots and voices.

'What do you want?' Madame Ducroix demanded. 'Is this the way to behave, marching in uninvited?'

'What do you know about an escaped prisoner of war?' The man spoke French but with a strong German accent.

'Us? What could we know? I don't know what you're talking about.' Madame Ducroix's voice was steady, faintly irritated.

'He escaped near here. Someone saw a man running across the fields. Search the house.'

More boots, moving away. Madame, sounding aggrieved, 'What right have you to search my house?'

The sound of a gun being cocked. 'This gives me the right to do whatever I want. You take orders from us now. Do you understand?'

'Oh, I understand, all right. Because you have a gun, you think that makes you a big man.' The contempt in her voice was unconcealed.

'Quiet. Keep a civil tongue in your head if you know what's good for you. You, girl. Have you seen any strangers round here?'

'Yes, plenty of them.' Jeanette's voice was as uncowed as her mother's. 'All wearing German uniforms.'

'Don't try to be clever with me or I'll make you regret it. This man would be wearing black overalls. Have you seen anyone dressed like that?'

'No.'

The second pair of boots returned. 'Nothing.'

'You searched thoroughly – under beds, in cupboards?'

'Yes, sir. There's not a lot to search. Only two rooms.'

'How many beds?'

'One large in the main room. Another single bed in the small room.'

'Both slept in?'

'Yes.'

'Who sleeps in the small room?'

'I do, of course.' Jeanette responded. 'Do you think I still sleep in my mother's bed?'

'There's a mug of coffee and a plate on the table. Who is that for?'

'Me. I hadn't had time to eat my breakfast before you came barging in.'

'I think you're lying. Come here!'

'Ow! Let go of me!'

'Tell me the truth, or I will really hurt you. Where are you hiding him?'

'I'm not! Ah!' A cry of pain.

'I could break your arm like a matchstick. Can you feel it?'

'Oh, let go! I'm not lying.'

'Let her go, you brute!' That was Madame's voice, raw with distress.

Steve had heard enough. These women had shown him kindness. He could not cower down here and let them suffer. Better to give himself up. He felt for the ladder in the darkness and hauled himself up. Putting his hand to the underside of the trapdoor, he pushed. It would not open. He pushed harder. The door was solid. He felt around for a catch but found nothing. Suddenly, he understood what the thuds he had heard meant. Something heavy had been pushed into place over the top of it.

'I could arrest you, both of you. See if you tell the same story after a few nights in the cells. We have ways of getting the truth out of people.'

For a moment Steve thought he might lose control of his bowels. If the women were taken away, no one would know he was here. He might be trapped down here in the dark for days, without food or water. He drew back his fist to pound on the underside of the trapdoor. Madame Ducroix's voice stopped him.

Her tone was excoriating. 'So this is the way Germans behave! What would your mothers say if they could see you now, trying to terrorise an old widow woman and a young girl? Would they be proud of you? Is this your honour?'

There was the noise of the door to the yard banging open and a breathless voice said in German, 'Herr Leutnant, I found these!'

'Boots! Where?'

'In the loft above the barn, Herr Leutnant.'

97

'These are British Army boots. Now tell me you know nothing about this man.'

'Oh, the rascal!' Madame exclaimed. 'So that is what happened to my sabots! He stole them.'

'What do you mean? What are you talking about?'

'I left them on the doorstep last night, as I always do ready for the morning. When I came down this morning they were gone. I have been searching all over for them. The wretch must have come in the night and stolen them.'

'And the eggs, Maman!' Jeanette joined in eagerly. 'Do you remember, when I went to collect them this morning, one of the nest boxes was empty? He must have helped himself to some eggs, too.'

'When was this?' The German officer's tone had changed.

'How should I know? We went to bed about ten o'clock, like we always do. When we woke up this morning, they were gone.'

'*Scheisse!* He could have eight hours start on us.' The boots moved towards the door. 'Come on, men. We might still catch the bastard.'

The door slammed, voices moved away, the geese cackled, and a German voice swore. Then a car started and drove away. After that, the silence drew out until Steve began to fear that they had taken the women away with them. At last he heard scraping on the floor above his head as the heavy object, whatever it was, was moved away. The trapdoor was lifted and light and air flooded in. He scrambled up the ladder and hauled himself out.

'Don't worry,' Jeanette said. 'They've gone. We checked to be sure they hadn't left someone behind to keep watch. You're quite safe.'

'Madame!' Steve stretched his hands towards her. 'You were magnificent! You both were. Such quick thinking about the sabots – and the eggs. It was genius.'

'Yes,' Jeanette giggled, 'it was, wasn't it?' And suddenly they were all laughing.

Sobering, he said, 'Did he hurt you? Are you all right?'

Jeanette wriggled her shoulder and winced slightly. 'It was nothing. I'm fine.'

'I was so afraid for you. I couldn't bear the thought that you were being made to suffer because of me. I wanted to give myself up. I tried to lift the trapdoor, but I couldn't.'

'*Mon Dieu!*' Madame exclaimed. 'It's just as well we put that chest on top of it. Don't you understand what would have happened if you had shown yourself? You would have been taken prisoner again, but we would probably have been shot for sheltering you.'

Her words struck home so hard that for a moment he was unable to speak. 'I didn't think…' he stammered eventually. 'I'm a fool! But… but I can't stay here, putting your lives in danger. I must move on.'

'You are right,' Madame agreed. 'You cannot stay much longer, but cannot just walk out of here. We must find a plan, a way you can stay safe.' She thought for a moment. 'I shall speak to the curé.'

'The curé?' Steve echoed doubtfully. 'Are you sure – I mean…'

'He can be trusted completely,' she assured him. 'He is a good man. But now…' she glanced at the clock standing on a shelf above the range, 'we must get to work. The men will be here any minute, and you must stay out of sight until they go home for their dinner.'

'The men?' Steve queried.

'You don't imagine Jeanette and I manage this farm on our own, do you? Even when my husband was alive, we employed workers.' She glanced towards the window as the geese cackled again. 'Here they come. It will be best if you stay up in your room until I call you. Jeanette, you'd better get down to the barn and get those cows milked before the men start wondering why we're so behindhand.' Jeanette hurried out and Madame thrust a mug of coffee and a plate with a hunk of bread and some butter into Steve's hand. 'Take this up with you.'

The hours of the morning stretched out interminably. Cooped up in the little room under the eaves, he listened to the sounds of the farmyard and the distant voices of the farmhands, but he dared not even look out of the window in case one of them glanced up and saw him. At last he heard the men tramp off towards the gate and Jeanette put her head round the door.

'Come down. It's the *midi*. They won't be back for a couple of hours.'

After a meal of soup and ham and more fresh bread, Madame said, 'Jeanette, take your bicycle and go to the curé's house. Ask him to call on us this evening. If anyone asks, you are going to confession.'

Another long afternoon passed until Steve was called down to supper. They had just finished eating when they heard the sound of a car.

'It's the curé,' Jeanette said. 'I'll go and open the gate for him.'

A few minutes later, she ushered in a small, round-faced man in a cassock. He greeted Madame Ducroix and then turned to Steve.

'So you are the British airman.'

'Stefan Popovic, monsieur,' Steve responded. 'Flight Lieutenant, Royal Air Force.'

'I would say welcome, but that is hardly appropriate under the circumstances.' The priest had a twinkle in his eyes that Steve found very reassuring. 'We are all indebted to you brave men who are fighting the Nazi menace.'

'Not anymore, I'm afraid,' Steve said ruefully. 'I need to get back to England, so I can get on with the job.'

The priest shook his head regretfully. 'That, I fear, will be difficult. The best we can hope to do at the moment is keep you out of enemy hands until the situation improves. I have faith that before long, the current reverses will be overcome and the Nazis will be forced out of Belgium. But until that happens you will be safer in Brussels, where a stranger can disappear among the crowds. In a small community like ours it would be very hard to hide you.'

'That makes sense,' Steve agreed. 'But how can I get there?'

'For that, I have a plan,' the priest said. 'I shall drive you there myself.'

Chapter Sixteen

Paris

June 12th 1940

'An open city! Reynaud has just declared Paris an open city!'

Alix was sitting with Marie Louise on the terrace of the Palais de Chaillot when Rivet hurried out of the building to join them.

'Open?' Alix repeated. 'Does that mean there won't be any attempt to defend the city?'

'Exactly. The Nazis will be able to walk in whenever they are ready.'

'But that's terrible! We can't just surrender. What was the point of all those sandbags in the roads if we aren't going to fight?' Alix stared out over the city, trying to envisage the streets full of German soldiers.

'What else can we do?' Marie Louis said. 'Do you want the Germans to bomb us again? This time it wouldn't just be the suburbs.'

'Marie Louise is right, I'm afraid,' Rivet said heavily. 'We can't allow the city to be devastated. What would future generations think of us if we let the Nazis destroy Notre-Dame and the Sacré-Coeur and the Arc de Triomphe?'

'What will they think of us if we just sit back and let the Fascists take over?' Alix retorted. 'It's all very well for Reynaud and the rest of the government safely tucked away in Tours. They won't have to live under enemy occupation.'

Marie Louise shuddered. 'I can't bear the thought of them strutting around our streets.'

'I'm afraid that is something we are going to have to get used to,' Rivet responded.

'When will the Boches get here, do you think?' Alix asked.

'Within the next day or two, I expect. Rumour has it that their tanks are already only hours away.'

Alix walked back to her room in the College Franco-Britannique with an oppressive sense of helplessness in the face of events. Only that morning the news had been broadcast that Italy had come into the war on the side of the Germans. It seemed they were surrounded by enemies. But she had a more immediate cause for anxiety. It was four months since she had received her mother's last letter. The Finns had been defeated back in March. It was hard to imagine what was preventing her from returning to England. Added to that, she was worried about Steve. News from the BBC told of desperate air battles over France and targets successfully destroyed, but she knew that there must have been losses on both sides. Perhaps Steve was just too busy, or too exhausted, to write. But it occurred to her that now the city was under German control it was unlikely she would receive letters from any source. It might be months, even years, before she heard from either of them again. She went to bed that night as close to tears as she had come for many months.

For twenty-four hours the city held its breath. On the morning of June 14th, Alix was jolted awake by the noise of heavy vehicles rattling her window panes. She looked at her watch. It was not quite six a.m. As she got out of bed and dragged on a dressing gown, there came a new sound – a voice on a loudspeaker, at first distant, then coming ever closer. In good French but with a German accent, it informed her that the city was now in German hands. All shops and businesses were to remain closed, and everyone was to remain inside until further notice.

Alix dressed quickly, pulling on slacks and a dark shirt. In spite of the summer sunshine, this did not feel like a day for bright colours. In the corridors, students who had remained in residence were gathering, twittering like a flock of starlings, or peering out of the windows for a first sight of the enemy. Alix did not feel like joining them. At this fateful moment she wanted to be with her friends at the Musée de l'Homme, even if it meant flouting the instructions of the occupying power. She ran down the stairs and saw that the concierge was crouched over the wireless in her office, paying no attention to the main door leading to the street. She slipped out and began to walk swiftly in the direction of the museum, keeping to the side streets, her ears straining to catch the sound of engines or marching feet. In the distance she could still hear the loud-speaker broadcasting its instructions and once she came to a sharp halt just as an armoured car accompanied by two motorcycle outriders passed the end of the road. Faces peered out from doorways and windows, but otherwise, the streets were deserted. When the Palais de Chaillot came into view, she stood in the shadow of a building watching for several minutes. The approach to the main doors was up a wide flight of steps that offered no cover, and besides, she guessed that the doors themselves would be locked. She knew of a side entrance used by members of staff and was about to make her way round the building to reach it when the main door opened and Paul Rivet appeared. He did not come down the steps but seemed to be fixing something to the door. Alix watched for a moment, then when a swift glance around the area revealed no sign of the enemy, she ran quickly up to join him.

He swung round in alarm at the sound of her footsteps. 'Ah!' It was an expression of relief as he recognised her. '*Bonjour, ma petite! Bienvenue!*'

'Good morning,' she responded. 'What are you doing?'

He stood back with a gesture towards the door, where a sheet of paper had been pinned. For a moment Alix was reminded of Martin Luther, nailing his fifteen theses to the church door – 'Here I stand, I can do no other.'

'What is it?' she asked.

'Read it. I think you will recognise it.'

She moved closer and read what he had written. 'Oh! It's a French translation of that poem by Kipling – *If* –. My mother taught it to me when I was a child.

> '*If you can keep your head when all about you*
> *Are losing theirs and blaming it on you…*'

'Yes, precisely.' Rivet smiled.

Speaking from memory she quoted the original English:

> '*If you can wait and not be tired by waiting,*

> *Or being lied about, don't deal in lies,*
> *Or being hated, don't give way to hating…* and it goes on…
> *If you can meet with Triumph and Disaster*
> *And treat those two impostors just the same…'*

Rivet took up the next verse, also in English.

> *'If you can force your heart and nerve and sinew*
> *To serve your turn long after they are gone,*
> *And so hold on when there is nothing in you*
> *Except the Will which says to them: 'Hold on!'*

Alix concluded:

> *'If you can fill the unforgiving minute*
> *With sixty seconds' worth of distance run,*
> *Yours is the earth and everything that's in it*
> *And what is more, you'll be a man, my son.'*

'Apt, don't you think?' Rivet said. 'We are, after all, the museum of man, in the sense, of course, of mankind, and I think we are going to need all the courage we can muster in the next months – and all the integrity too. But come inside. I'm glad you have chosen to join us. If we go up on the roof we may be able to see what is happening.'

Waiting on the roof were several of the museum staff including Marie Louise. Alix had met most of them during her research. Among them were Yvonne Oddon, the librarian, and another woman whom she had not met before, who was introduced as Agnès Humbert, who worked at the museum's sister institution devoted to French folk art and culture. They all, it seemed, had felt the same compulsion to be together to witness the unfolding tragedy, rather than cooped up separately in their own homes.

They did not have long to wait. The Palais de Chaillot was situated in the Place du Trocadéro at the heart of several broad boulevards, and their position on the roof gave them a clear view across the city. Distantly at first, from the northeast, they heard the roar and grinding of heavy vehicles. Soon they saw detachments of tanks and armoured cars fanning out around the city to occupy all the main intersections. Then, looking southeast, beyond the Eiffel Tower, they saw a convoy of vehicles crossing the Seine.

'They're heading for Les Invalides,' Rivet said. 'Going to accept the formal surrender from the military governor.'

'Oh, look!' Marie Louise was pointing in the other direction, her expression horrified.

Alix turned and let out a groan of distress, a reaction that was echoed by those around her as they watched a column of tanks advancing through the Arc de Triomphe. Moments later, a huge swastika flag was unfurled to hang from the top of the arch.

'I've seen enough!' Rivet said. 'Let us go downstairs.'

That afternoon the rumour went around that the Germans were planning a ceremonial march down the Champs-Élysées. Torn between the wish to show her disdain and the instinct to bear witness to a historic event, Alix finally decided to join Marie Louise in the crowd lining the street. An apparently unending parade of tanks, motorcycles and goose-stepping infantry marched along the wide boulevard, to the accompaniment of military bands and escorted by photographers and camera men. The crowd watched in sullen silence and then dispersed in obedience to the curfew which had been imposed from nine p.m. until five in the morning.

Alix's mood was more despondent than ever as she walked back to the college. She had stayed on in Paris impelled by romantic notions that she would be able to play a part in saving the city from the Nazis. Now, there was nothing she or anyone else could do.

There was little to cheer her up over the following days. On June 16th, the news broadcasts announced that the Prime Minister, Reynaud, had resigned and been replaced by Marshall Pétain. 'He won't kowtow to the Nazis!' people said.

Yet, a day later Pétain broadcast to the nation. He was seeking an armistice. France was about to surrender.

The following evening Alix found Marie Louise and several of the other museum staff grouped round a radio set in Rivet's office.

'What's going on?' she asked.

'Ssh! We're listening to the BBC.'

'Isn't that forbidden now?'

'Never mind. Listen! De Gaulle is going to broadcast.'

They heard the General say that the war was not over, that France was not alone. They had a huge empire behind them, and together with the British, they would achieve ultimate victory. He invited all French soldiers who had escaped to Britain to join him and ended, 'Whatever happens, the flame of French resistance must not be extinguished. It will not be extinguished.'

'That's what we want to hear!' Alix exclaimed. 'We should do as the British have promised to do – fight them every inch of the way.'

Next day Marie Louise sought Alix out at the college.

'Paul has called a meeting. It's a secret, just for a few of us, but he wants you to be there.'

In Paul Rivet's office at the museum, Alix found many of the same people who had watched the arrival of the Germans from the rooftop. With them was a man she had never seen before. He was, she judged, in his early thirties, with a broad forehead and intense dark eyes under heavy brows, but what struck her most forcibly was that he was extremely pale and very thin.

Marie Louise gasped and ran towards him.

'Boris! You're alive! We were so afraid that you had been killed in the fighting around Sedan.'

He took her hands and kissed her formally on both cheeks. 'Well, you see, I am not dead – not quite. I was taken prisoner and sent to a camp in the Jura Mountains, but I escaped.'

'And he walked in last night just as we were sitting down to dinner as if nothing had happened,' Rivet said, smiling. 'But you can hear his story later. Right now, we have other matters to discuss.'

When they had all managed to find somewhere to sit or perch, he looked around, focussing his gaze on each of them in turn.

'What I am about to say could be, will be, interpreted as an attack on the men who have just occupied our city. I am saying it to you because I think you feel as I do that this situation cannot be supinely accepted without some form of protest. What I am proposing will be dangerous. Even to listen to what I have to say would lay you open to a charge of treason. So, I shall understand if any of you decide to leave now. I think I can trust you never to mention what you have heard to another living soul.'

He paused and looked around again. No one moved. Then Agnès said, 'Go on, Paul. We're all with you on this.'

'These men, these Nazis, are the antithesis of everything we believe in as anthropologists. For years now we have striven to combat this pernicious idea that some races are superior to others. Now we are facing a regime that wishes to set up the so-called Aryan "race" as dominant over all others – with what terrible consequences for those they regard as inferior we can all imagine. It is our duty to combat this ideology in whatever way we can. We cannot allow ourselves to passively submit to their rule. We must resist with all means in our power.'

'What do you have in mind?' Boris asked. 'We are few and unarmed. Whatever we did, it could be no more than a pinprick against these forces.'

'I'm not advocating armed struggle,' Paul said. 'That would be futile under the circumstances. But there must be other ways.'

'We should refuse to cooperate,' Agnès said. 'The Germans can't expect to run the city themselves. They will need ordinary people to carry on as normal – to drive the buses, operate the trams, bring food in from the provinces, empty the rubbish bins – all the hundreds of jobs that need to be done to make a city somewhere people can live.'

'And you think we can persuade enough of our fellow citizens to take that line?' Yvonne said. 'There will be repercussions. The Germans won't tolerate strikes and that sort of thing.'

'Not all-out strikes perhaps. But there must be hundreds of small ways we can make life uncomfortable for the occupiers – telephone calls misdirected at the exchange, food deliveries held up, small acts of sabotage… I don't know.'

'We can't prescribe what people should do,' Rivet said. 'The important thing is to communicate to ordinary people that they don't have to let the Germans walk all over them. That we may have surrendered but we are not defeated. People are already saying that the war is over and there is no point in trying to fight.'

'We need to organise, then,' Boris said. 'There must be hundreds of others who feel as we do. Each of us must know other people who are prepared to undertake the sort of actions we have been discussing. I suggest we all reach out tentatively to our friends and acquaintances and try to build up a nucleus of resistance. The movement can grow from there.'

'Alix,' Rivet said. 'Do you think your friends in the Communist Party will join us?'

For a moment Alix could not think how to respond. She had not expected the focus of attention to turn to her. 'I… I'm not sure. Most of the hard-liners are still saying that because of the friendship pact signed between Herr Ribbentrop and Comrade Molotov, it would be a betrayal of the Party to take an anti-German position. But I know a lot of others are very unhappy about that idea. I could put out some feelers.'

'Be very careful,' Boris warned her. 'Don't make any definite suggestions until you are sure someone can be trusted.'

'Yes, of course,' Alix responded. The prospect of what she was being asked to do produced a visceral thrill that she felt in her bowels, but it was not entirely fear. It reminded her of her childhood at home in Serbia, riding her horse at a big fence, knowing she might fall but excited by the challenge.

Looking around her, she realised that the mood of the whole gathering had changed. People were beginning to chatter eagerly, exchanging ideas and suggestions. Listening to them, Alix felt her spirits lift. For too long she had been oppressed by a sense of futility. Here, at last, was something she could do. Her war was only just beginning.

As the meeting broke up Marie Louise took Alix's arm and led her over to the newcomer.

'Boris, I want you to meet Alexandra Malkovic. She's Yugoslavian, but she's studying here at the Sorbonne, and she has decided to stay in Paris and throw in her lot with us. Alix, this is Boris Vildé. He's a fellow anthropologist, specialising in Nordic cultures – but as you will have gathered he was called up at the outbreak of war and he has only just got back to us.'

Vildé took her hand with a little formal bow. '*Enchanté, mademoiselle.* When time permits, I shall be very interested to hear more about your country.'

–

On June 22nd, the now German-controlled media informed them that the armistice had been signed. The terms of the surrender were outlined. The country was to be divided into two zones. The Germans would control the whole of the north and the entire Atlantic seaboard, while Pétain's government would rule the south from their new base in Vichy.

'The terms are shameful!' Boris declared. 'Pétain has let the Boche have more than half of the country, while he had his pals sit comfortably in Vichy and pretend that part of France is "free". And they have agreed to pay the Germans' costs – to pay them for occupying us!'

'How can they do that?' Alix demanded. 'How can they just roll over and let the Germans dictate to them? We should be fighting them in the fields and the forests and the towns, like Mr Churchill promised the British would do.'

'De Gaulle would never have given in so easily,' Boris said bitterly.

'I'm worried about my family,' Marie Louise said. 'My parents live just outside Tours, and it seems as if the demarcation line between the occupied zone and the "free" zone must run very close to them. I don't know which side they are on.'

'Write to them,' Boris said. 'They must know.'

The next day another broadcast announced that everyone in the occupied zone must hand in any weapons they possessed, together with any wireless sets capable of picking up transmissions from Britain.

Alix was sitting with Marie Louise in her office in the museum, trying to draw up a list of people who might safely be approached to join a resistance organisation when they heard shouting and heavy footsteps on the marble floors. The door was flung open by a black-uniformed German soldier.

'Out!' he ordered.

'Out, where?' Marie Louis asked.

'Why?' Alix demanded.

'No questions! Out!' was the reply, accompanied by a gesture with his rifle that left no room for doubt about his meaning.

Alix felt a churning in her gut. Surely it was not possible that their plans had been betrayed before they had really begun? Who could have told the occupiers what had been discussed at that meeting? She crumpled the piece of paper with the list of names. What should she do with it? If she kept it on her and she was searched it would incriminate her and the friends she had listed. Better perhaps to leave it here, but the office might be searched too. There was a vase of roses on the desk. A quick glance showed her that the soldier was looking at something that was happening along the corridor. She thrust the paper into the water. With luck, by the time a search reached this point, it would have become illegible.

In the corridor, they joined other members of the museum staff who had also been ordered out of the rooms where they were working. They were herded by black-clad soldiers to the staircase leading down to the main entrance. Ahead of her, Alix heard Rivet expostulating indignantly.

'You have no right to drive us out of our place of work. I demand to speak to your commanding officer.'

He was silenced by a thrust from a rifle butt that would have sent him tumbling down the steps if Boris had not caught hold of his arm.

They came out of the building to see that the Place du Trocadéro was ringed by soldiers standing as if on parade. All the roads leading into it had been blocked by armoured cars, except for the Avenue du Président Wilson, which was lined by more troops.

'What on earth is going on?' Marie Louise asked, clutching Alix's arm.

'Somebody important is coming, I suppose,' Alix replied.

'You don't think…?'

'Quiet! Move!' The soldier behind them prodded them to move round the side of the building and into the formal gardens with their fountain and their view towards the Eiffel Tower. They were herded onto the path at one side, penned in by a ring of soldiers. There was a wait, long enough for Rivet to repeat his demand to speak to an officer and to be told curtly to close his mouth. Then they heard the sound of vehicles approaching down the Avenue. There were shouted commands and the stamp of boots as men came to attention. After that there was another pause, until they saw movement above them on the broad terrace that looked out along the length of the garden. Three uniformed figures appeared, the central one shorter than the others.

'My God, it is!' Marie Louise breathed. 'Hitler himself!'

'How dare he?' Alix whispered, her voice shaking. 'How dare he stand there gloating!'

The three men stood for some time, looking out towards the Eiffel Tower. Then they turned with their backs to it while a photographer took their pictures. Among the museum staff, there was a low murmur of mutual disgust, but no one dared voice their feelings aloud – except for one.

'Hubris!' Rivet said. 'And we all know how the gods punish that.'

Chapter Seventeen

Brussels

June 1940

'Please come in, Stefan.' The rector in charge of the major seminary in Brussels indicated a chair on the other side of his desk. 'Take a seat.'

Steve obeyed, with a rising sense of hope. He had been living in the seminary since the curé had brought him there a week ago, driven into the city dressed in the soutane and biretta of a Catholic priest. The curé had confidently predicted that the occupying troops would not bother to question two men of God going about their pastoral duties and he had been proved right. At the seminary, Steve had been welcomed and given sanctuary. He was grateful, but he found it hard to accept this as a long-term solution. The quiet, ordered life of the seminarians was too far removed from any life he might have chosen, and he had little in common with them, even in terms of religious faith. He had been brought up in the rites of the Eastern Orthodox Church, which the migrants from Serbia had brought with them to Alaska, and although he no longer set much store by any religion, he felt it would be inappropriate for him to take part in the daily services of the seminary, or to attend lectures intended for the instruction of catholic priests in training. He had been given unlimited use of the library and had used the time to write, starting with an account of his experiences in the RAF. He knew it was unlikely that he would be able to take his notebook with him if, or when, he left, but the exercise helped to embed the details in his memory for later use and if – God forbid – he was condemned to stay here for the rest of the war, at least he would not have entirely wasted his time. Nevertheless, he felt confined, and he had more than once begged the rector to find somewhere for him where he would, at least, have some occupation and might be able to plan his escape.

'I know,' the rector said, 'that you are finding your current situation difficult—'

'Please!' Steve broke in, 'don't think I am ungrateful. You have given me a place of safety when I could so easily have been recaptured by the Germans, and I owe you my heartfelt thanks for that. It's just that… I feel it's wrong for me to be sitting around doing nothing when… when we are in the middle of a war. And I think I am abusing your hospitality. I know how short rations are, but you are feeding me…'

The rector held up his hand to check his words. 'My son, I appreciate what you are saying. We have spoken of this more than once. Well, now I think I may have found an answer to your problem. Do you have any expertise as a mechanic?'

'A mechanic?' Steve repeated.

'Are you competent with things mechanical, with the engines of motor cars specifically?'

'Well, I used to service the car we had at home, and sometimes the delivery vans, if there was a problem. I can do basic repairs.'

The rector gave a nod of satisfaction. 'That should be sufficient. Let me explain. I heard the other day from a colleague that one of his flock is in difficulties. He owns a garage, but the occupying forces have taken it over and are demanding that he services their vehicles. The problem is that he is in poor health and finds the work too much for him. Until a few months ago his son undertook most of it, but the boy was called up at the beginning of the war, and nothing has been heard of him since. M. Lebrun is prepared to take you in and treat you as part of the family if you can help in the business.'

'But…' Steve protested, 'surely that is a terrible risk for him. Suppose the Germans suspected who I am?'

'But why should they?' the rector asked. 'As far as they are concerned, you are M. Lebrun's employee.'

'Wouldn't they wonder why I wasn't called up, too?'

'Probably you were, but you have now been demobilised.'

'What about the neighbours? They will wonder where I've sprung from.'

'Believe me,' the rector said, 'however much they wondered, they would never betray you to the Germans. I do not believe there is a man or woman in Brussels who does not hate them. Perhaps I should deplore that, as a Christian, but I cannot find it in my heart to disapprove. Anyone who gave you up to the enemy would incur such contempt from their friends that they would never be able to hold up their heads in the neighbourhood again.' He sat back and looked at Steve. 'The fact is, that if you leave here, you will be in more danger anywhere you might go.

But I do not think you can be content to wait out the war within these walls. If you prefer to stay, you are welcome, but if you truly want to take your chances outside I think this is as good a prospect as you are likely to find.'

'You are right, of course,' Steve said. 'I am just worried that I might bring danger to the people who are sheltering me.'

'They know what the situation is and they feel it is a risk worth taking. So, if you are sure that you want to take this course...'

'I am,' Steve said. He felt as if his sluggish blood was suddenly coursing with new energy through his veins.

'Then I will ask Father Marcel to take you there tomorrow.'

Father Marcel was not much older than Steve and had a warm, open smile that quickly put him at ease. The Lebrun garage was on the outskirts of the city. It was not a large concern. There was a forecourt with a couple of petrol pumps and, behind that, a workshop backing onto a small house. It looked as if nothing much had changed since it was first opened, maybe ten years ago, but it was clean and tidy. When Steve arrived, clad in working man's overalls provided by a friend of the rector and carrying a small case containing a change of clothes and basic toilet necessities, there was a civilian car on the forecourt. The bonnet was open, and a skinny figure in overalls several sizes too large was head down over the engine.

'Good morning!' the priest called as they approached.

The figure straightened up, pushing a long strand of blonde hair out of its eyes with a hand that left grease marks on a smooth cheek.

'Father Marcel! Good morning. Forgive me if I do not shake hands.' The voice dispelled any lingering confusion in Steve's mind about the sex of the speaker.

'Don't worry about that,' the priest replied. 'Look, I have brought someone to meet you. His name is Stefan, and he is willing to help out with the work in return for his keep.'

Blue eyes met and interrogated his own, and then the girl returned her attention to the priest. 'Of course, Papa told me you thought you might be able to find someone. We are very grateful. Will you come in for a glass of wine?'

'Thank you, no. I can see you are busy and I, too, have things I must do. I will leave Stefan in your care, but remember, if there are any problems I am always available to help.' He turned to Steve. 'That is true for you, too. Yvette knows where to find me.' He held out his hand. '*Bonne chance, mon fils.*'

Steve suppressed a grin at being called 'my son' by a man so near his own age and shook hands. 'Thank you. I really appreciate your help.' He would like to have said more, that he understood the risk that was being taken on his behalf, but he knew that in this situation, the least said the better.

When Father Marcel had gone, Steve found himself being studied with a slightly sceptical expression. 'You know about motor cars, then?'

'A bit.'

'This one belongs to the local doctor. He brought it in this morning because he thinks there is something wrong. I've only just started looking at it. What do you think?'

'Can we start her up?'

'Of course. But the battery is flat. You will have to crank her.'

Steve found the crank handle, and after two or three turns, the engine fired. He listened for a moment, then turned it off. 'It's certainly running a bit rough.'

'Why is that, do you think?'

Looking at the girl, Steve knew that he was being tested. She had already made up her mind what was wrong. He stuck his head under the bonnet.

'Do you have…' He realised his knowledge of French did not include the word for a plug spanner. 'A… a thing for removing…'

The requisite tool was placed in his hand as if she had been waiting for him to ask for it. He removed one of the spark plugs and held it up. 'Clean these up and it should solve the problem.'

She grinned at him. 'So, you do know.' She held out a greasy paw. 'I am Yvette Lebrun.'

He took it in one now as grimy as her own. 'Stefan—'

'No.' She stopped him with a quick squeeze of his fingers. 'You're name is Carl Lebrun. You are the son of my uncle, Georges Lebrun. You live in Ghent, but you have come to help us out.' She returned her attention to the car. 'Help me to finish this job, then I'll take you indoors to meet my father.'

As they got back to work, he said, 'I don't know many girls who can do what you're doing. Have you always helped out with the work here?'

'No. I always wanted to. I've been fascinated by engines since I was a child. But when my brother Robert was… was here… he would never let me touch anything. He said it wasn't suitable work for a woman.'

Steve remembered the newspaper stories he had read in England about women going into factories to take on the jobs of men who had been conscripted. 'I guess there are a lot of women doing unsuitable jobs these days.'

'But are they any good at them?' she asked. 'I'm good at this – as good as any man.'

He glanced sideways at her small, intense face. 'Yes. I can see you are.'

After a pause, he added, 'Your brother was killed?'

'We don't know. No one can tell us. He might be a prisoner, or badly wounded and in a hospital somewhere. The Red Cross are trying to find out, but the Nazis aren't being very helpful.'

'I'm sorry.' Steve removed the last plug. 'This is a civilian car. I was told you had been taken over and forced to repair German vehicles.'

'Because it belongs to a doctor, he is allowed to use it and get it maintained. But most of the work we do is on cars belonging to the Boches.'

'That must be… annoying…'

She shot him a sideways glance. 'Yes, it is. But sometimes…'

'Yes?'

'Sometimes the repairs don't last as long as they should. But after all, what do you expect when the job is left to a girl?'

He met her eyes and saw them widen in an expression of total innocence. He grinned and she grinned back.

When the doctor's car was running as sweetly as a new Rolls-Royce, Yvette wiped her hands on a bit of rag and said, 'Come inside. Father will be waiting to meet you.'

Lebrun *père* was a small man, and it was obvious as soon as they met why he was no longer capable of working on engines. His hands were crippled and gnarled with arthritis, and he walked with difficulty. Nevertheless, he had managed to produce a meal which, if not refined, still made the most of the limited rations available. There was an omelette, followed by a vegetable stew with carrots and potatoes. He greeted Steve warmly and thanked him for being prepared to help out.

'You've met my daughter and seen what a brave effort she is making to keep the business going, but… well, it's not right for a woman to be working like that. It takes a man to run a garage.'

Steve caught Yvette's eye, but she shrugged and grinned. 'It's not right for a man to have to cook, either, is it, Papa? But you are doing a grand job.'

Steve said, 'I should be thanking you, not the other way around. I hope you understand the risk you are running.'

'If we can do something, however small, to give the finger to the Boches anything is worth the risk,' Lebrun said. Then he glanced at his daughter. 'You didn't hear me use that expression.'

'No, Papa,' she agreed demurely.

As they sat to eat, Lebrun said, 'We need to get your story straight.'

'Yvette has already told me that I am supposed to be her cousin – your brother's son.'

'Correct. So let me fill in some of the details for you.'

Over the meal, Steve learned a good deal about the family and the background he was supposed to have come from. 'You were called up, of course,' Lebrun added, 'but you have flat feet, so you were discharged as unfit.'

'Fair enough,' Steve agreed. 'But if your neighbours see me, won't they recognise that I'm not your nephew?'

Lebrun shook his head. 'Georges and I fell out years ago. He and his family have never been to visit here.'

'There's something else. What about rations? I know they are pretty restricted. How much are you allowed?'

'Officially we get 225 grams of bread a day, and every month we get 250 grams of butter, a kilo of sugar, a kilo of meat and 15 kilos of potatoes,' Yvette told him. 'But that's a joke. There's been no butter in any of the shops for weeks, and I can't remember when I last saw any meat of any kind.'

'But that's hardly enough to live on!' Steve said. 'I can't let you feed me as well.'

'Don't worry about that,' Lebrun said. 'We have ways around that problem. Best if you don't enquire too closely.'

'Are you sure?' Steve asked doubtfully. 'I can't let you suffer, or run extra risks—'

'Enough said!' Lebrun cut him short. 'We wouldn't have agreed to Father Marcel's suggestion if we didn't think it could be managed.'

Steve would have liked to press further, but something in the older man's face told him that it would not be welcome.

'Well, all I can say is I am immensely grateful, and I'll do all I can to make sure the risk is worth your while.'

'There is just one thing,' Yvette said. 'You speak good French, but your accent still sounds American.'

'If anyone comments on that, tell them I worked in America for a year or two,' Steve suggested.

'Oh, good idea!' she agreed, then added, 'There's something else that puzzles me. Father Marcel said you could have stayed in the seminary. You would probably have been safer there. Why didn't you?'

'Because,' Steve said, 'if I had had to stay cooped up there for another month I would probably have handed myself over to the Boches out of sheer boredom!'

They laughed at that and Yvette began to clear the table. As she did so, they heard the sound of a vehicle being driven onto the forecourt and a German voice shouted for attention.

'Back to work?' Steve said.

'Back to work,' she confirmed.

A truck was standing outside with a German private leaning against it. As they approached, Steve felt himself tense. He told himself that there was no reason for the man to assume he was anything other than a local mechanic and forced himself to behave as if this was just a normal part of his daily routine. The German jerked his head at the truck.

'Brakes, caput!'

As they leaned over the engine, Steve said, 'You mentioned that the repairs don't always last as long as might be expected.'

She met his eyes. 'So?'

'So perhaps I'm not as good a mechanic as I seem to be. For instance, if I forgot to tighten this nut here...'

'The brakes might fail...'

'But not at once. The car would have done quite a lot of miles since it was serviced here – and some of these Belgian roads are not as well surfaced as they should be...'

She grinned. 'After all, it would be very easy to forget...'

He glanced across at the German driver. He was leaning against the wall a short distance away enjoying a clandestine cigarette. 'That's done, then,' he said.

The next car that came in had a passenger, an officer who stood over them impatiently tapping his foot. The fault was rectified perfectly and in record time. But the one after that, which came in with a puncture, left the garage with a wing nut on one wheel slightly loose. After that, they decided that any more 'mistakes' on the same day might occasion unwelcome attention.

While they worked, Yvette quizzed him on the cover story he had been given and filled in more details. Then, when the working day was over, she showed him to a small room under the eaves.

'There is a basin there, but you might find it easier to wash in the kitchen, where you can get hot water from the kettle on the stove. The privy is in the backyard. I'll see you in a few minutes.'

When Steve went downstairs, M. Lebrun was outside, pottering in a small garden where he could see lettuces and tomatoes growing and a few chickens scratching in the dirt. He stripped to the waist and scrubbed himself in the kitchen sink with a piece of hard soap, then went back to his room and put on a clean shirt. He was glad he had taken the trouble because when Yvette came down the contrast with her earlier appearance took him by surprise. She had put on a summer dress, and without the baggy overalls, he saw that her breasts were full and firm above a tiny waist. She had brushed out her blonde hair, and it fell in soft waves to her shoulders. He was fairly sure that she had also put on some make-up. Suddenly, it was no longer easy to accept her as 'as good as any man'.

They had just finished eating when a voice hailed them from outside and the back door opened to reveal a middle-aged woman with a lean, sharp-featured face.

'*Bon soir, monsieur. Bon soir, Yvette. Ah—*' She stopped abruptly as she saw Steve.

'Madeleine,' Yvette said smoothly, 'this is my cousin Carl. He has come from Ghent to help out in the garage.

Carl, this is our neighbour and good friend Madeleine Peeters.'

For the next half hour, Steve was very glad that he had taken in the information he had been given about Georges Lebrun and his family, as the visitor displayed an almost impolite curiosity. M. Lebrun and Yvette filled in details that he could not supply, but he was left feeling that he had undergone the sort of interrogation he might expect from the Gestapo.

Eventually, Madeleine turned her attention to Yvette. '*Cherie*, you look tired. *Pauvre petite!* It is not right that you should have to work so hard.' She reached out and stroked the golden hair with a gesture that struck Steve as unsettlingly sensuous. Then she looked at him. 'So, from now on, you do all the work. Let this little one rest.'

'Don't worry, Madeleine,' Yvette said with a laugh. 'You always treat me as if I was a china doll. I'm quite strong, you know.'

'Ah, but you must not overdo things. M. Lebrun, you must insist that now you have a man to help, our little angel can take it easy.'

Lebrun looked at her and Steve sensed a simmering hostility. 'Please be assured, madame, my daughter's welfare is my first concern.'

Madeleine looked round the room and seemed to realise that her presence was no longer welcome. She shrugged her shoulders. '*Eh bien!* You must do as you think best.' She stooped over Yvette and kissed her on the forehead. '*Bonne nuit, ma chère.*' Then with an unsmiling glance at the two men and a brief '*Bonne nuit, messieurs,*' she was gone.

Steve looked at Yvette. 'She seems very fond of you.'

'She's a busybody, always poking her nose in,' Lebrun grunted.

'Don't be too hard on her, Papa,' Yvette said. 'I think she's lonely.'

'She's not married, then?'

'No. She's had a hard life. Her father left them when she was twelve and then her mother got ill, and Madeleine had to look after her for years. When my mama passed away, she stepped in to help. She's been like another mother to me. She means well, but sometimes... well, she just can't accept that I'm grown up and can stand on my own feet.'

'She needs a man in her life, give her something else to think about,' Lebrun said. 'Not that any man in his senses is going to fall for a hard-nosed bitch like that.'

'Oh, don't be unkind, Papa,' Yvette chided him. 'She's really very kind-hearted and we're all the family she's got.'

She yawned suddenly and wriggled her shoulders. 'I'm going to bed. It's been a long day. Good night, Papa.' She kissed the top of his head and smiled across him at Steve. 'See you in the morning – Carl. It's good to have someone to share the work with.'

Chapter Eighteen

Helsinki

June 1940

'France has fallen!'

Leo looked up from the book she was reading with a start. 'What?'

'I've just spoken to Mr Vereker. He's had a signal from home. France has capitulated and signed an armistice.' The speaker was Mary Runciman, the leader of the contingent.

'Oh God!' Leo's hand went to her throat. 'When did this happen?'

'A couple of days ago, apparently.'

'Was there much fighting? Was Paris bombed?'

'No. The French government declared it an open city and just let the Huns walk in.'

'Typical!' That was Mack. 'Trust the French to place more value on their precious monuments than on loyalty to their allies.'

'I don't know,' Robby put in. 'Do you think we would feel differently if it was a question of saving St Paul's or Westminster Abbey?'

'It may not be long before we have to ask ourselves that question in reality,' Runciman said. 'It looks as though we're on our own now.'

'Isn't there any hint of the Yanks coming in?' someone said.

'It seems not.'

'Leo?' Robby's tone was concerned. 'Are you all right? You've gone a bit white.'

Leo swallowed and took a deep breath. 'I'm OK, thanks. It's just that my daughter's in Paris, studying at the Sorbonne.'

'Oh lord! I'd forgotten that. You must be worried sick.'

'Well, it could be worse. If there wasn't any bombing or street-to-street fighting, she's probably all right. I've been trying to persuade her to go home to Serbia, but last time I heard from her she was determined to stay in France. There won't be any chance of getting out now.' Leo got up and walked restlessly the length of the verandah on which they were sitting. 'If only we could get home! We'll be needed there, more than ever.'

Upon arriving in Helsinki with their ambulances in March, the contingent had been split into two groups. One had gone to Savonlinna and another to Ristiina, both towns to the northeast of the capital and nearer to the frontier with Russia. There they had been collecting sick or wounded soldiers and transporting them to and from hospital. But the war between Finland and Russia was over, and the country was demobilising, and after a few weeks, the need for their services came to an end.

At that point they had all been eager to set off for home. It was then that they understood that the route they had followed on the way out was no longer open. The Russians and the Germans between them controlled the Baltic Sea, and Sweden had closed its borders. Urgent messages had gone backwards and forwards between Mr Vereker and FANY HQ in London, and applications were made to various government departments, all of whom were willing to help, but the problem seemed to be insoluble. They took matters into their own hands with a visit to the local shipping office. There a possible route came to light. Finland had a port in the far north, at Liinakhamari, with access at this time of year to the Arctic Ocean. It might be possible to get them on a ship there that would drop them off in Iceland, where they could probably find a vessel that would take them to a British port. There was a difficulty, however. It was pointed out to them that if a body of uniformed British servicewomen fell into German hands, they would spend the rest of the war in a concentration camp. It might be possible, it was suggested, to smuggle them out in twos and threes.

Runciman called them together and told them what was suggested.

'What do you think? Try it in small groups, or stick together?'

'Stick together,' several voices chorused.

'We can't risk the last two or three being left behind to fend for themselves,' Leo said. 'They might be stuck here for the duration.'

'Agreed,' Runciman said. 'It's all or none.'

For days it seemed that was the end of the project. The FANYs lounged around Helsinki, trying to find ways to pass the time and becoming increasingly restless. With nothing else to occupy her mind, Leo was forced to think about her relationship with her husband – a topic she recognised she had been avoiding. It seemed unbelievable that there could be a real breach between her and Sasha. She knew she was as much in love with him as she had been twenty-eight years ago when she was working as a nurse in the war between Serbia and her allies and the

Ottoman Empire. Not that he had been aware of the fact then. She still vividly remembered their first encounter, when he had arrogantly dismissed her request for help in reaching the battlefield, on the grounds that the front line was no place for a woman. That was the crux of the matter. He was a proud man, wedded to concepts of honour handed down through generations of Serbian aristocrats.

For over twenty years they had worked together to keep the peace in their new, turbulent country of Yugoslavia and it was only when Alix had shown signs of wanting the same independence that her mother had enjoyed that their arguments started. Sasha had accepted Leo's need for freedom to live her life in her own way and she, in turn, had taken care never to behave in ways that would embarrass him in front of his conservative friends. But he still retained his conviction that a woman's place was in her husband's home. It might have helped, Leo knew, if she had been able to give him a son, but the traumatic birth of Alix in a snowbound mountain village in the middle of a battle had meant that she was unable to conceive again. A son would have allowed Sasha to form the sort of alliance through marriage with another aristocratic family that would have cemented his place in society and perhaps put to rest an age-old feud that had plagued both sides for generations, but in the absence of that possibility, he had transferred his hopes to Alix. And she, Leo, had forestalled him. She knew that to have disobeyed him was an almost unforgivable sin in his eyes, but she could not stand by and see her daughter denied the independence she had claimed for herself. She had told herself that in the end he would understand and forgive. She had not intended to stay away so long. Her idea had been to spend a few weeks in England, at Bramhall, the estate in Cheshire left to her by her grandmother, to give Sasha a chance to cool down. Then the war had intervened and she was not sure whether it was possible to go back – even assuming they ever got out of Finland. She had written before she left with the convoy, but he had not replied.

After weeks of waiting, a message came from the shipping office. There was a ship due to leave Liinakhamari bound for America in a few days' time. If they could get there, the captain had agreed to take them on board. The proviso was that they must travel incognito. There was a frenzy of preparation, unpacking everything but essentials, obtaining the necessary passes to allow them to travel and buying train tickets. The train would only take them as far as Rovaniemi, halfway up the country. From there they would have to rely on a bus to carry them up the Arctic Highway to the port.

At last, all dressed in civilian clothes and looking as much like refugees as possible, they boarded the train, waved off by Mr and Mrs Vereker and all the many friends they had made during their time in Finland. As the train pulled away, Leo heaved a sigh of relief. There was a long way to go yet, and there was no guarantee of success, but at last they were on the move.

At Rovaniemi, they caught the bus with ten minutes to spare, but it was the start of a seemingly interminable journey. In places, the road had been washed out, and the vehicle sank in the mud so that everyone had to get out and push, a diversion they welcomed as a chance to stretch their legs. It was raining and very cold, but there was one consolation. In midsummer this far north, it never got dark. Someone joked that the sun never sets on a FANY. It was one a.m. when they finally arrived in Liinakharmari. As the bus departed, they stood in a huddle, wondering where to go next. There seemed to be no sign of a hotel or accommodation of any sort.

'Right!' Runciman said. 'Leo, you come with me, and we'll try to find the ship. The rest of you wait here.'

Leo had always had a gift for languages. Growing up with her archaeologist father, she had learned Greek and Arabic and Turkish from the children she played with in the dust of a dig. An English education had added French, and her time with the Serbian army had taught her Serbocroat. Since they had been in Finland she had started to teach herself Finnish. Most of the group had acquired a few words of the language, but none were as fluent as she was.

They located the ship eventually, but their requests to speak to the captain were met with puzzlement. What possible reason could these strange women have to want that? It was the middle of the night. The captain was sleeping. Leo persisted, and in the end, they were allowed on board and the captain was called. He arrived bleary-eyed and obviously furious at being woken.

'We're very sorry to disturb you,' Leo said. 'But we thought you would be expecting us.'

'Expecting you? Who are you?'

'We're the party of English women you agreed to take on board as far as Iceland.'

'English women? I know nothing about that,' he said.

'The shipping office in Helsinki told us they had arranged it with you.'

'Well, it's the first I've heard of it.'

Leo tried to swallow a growing sense of despair. 'He says he's never heard of us,' she explained to Runciman.

Then, turning back to the captain, 'I'm sorry you haven't been informed. But please, will you take us? We're all desperate to get back to England. We're ambulance drivers, and we will be needed now our country is fighting for its life.'

'How many of you?' he asked.

'Seventeen,' Leo told him.

'Seventeen! Not possible,' the captain said.

'But we don't mind where we sleep. We'll fit in anywhere. Down in the hold if necessary.'

'But…' he paused, looking at them. 'I had not understood that young ladies like yourselves could be so… so brave, so capable. Are you truly prepared to sleep anywhere?'

'Anywhere!' Leo assured him.

'Even on deck?'

'Even on deck.'

'You would have to keep out of the way. I cannot have you interfering with the running of the ship.'

'Of course. Don't worry. We'll be like mice. You won't even know we're there.'

The captain's face relaxed, and for the first time Leo saw him smile. 'Then fetch your friends. You have two hours to get yourselves on board.'

Chapter Nineteen

Paris

July–August 1940

Alix paused under a lamp and looked up and down the street. The blackout was a thing of the past now that there was no danger of Paris being the target of German bombs and, unlike in other occupied cities, there was no curfew. This was because it had become the destination of choice for German soldiers and their officers on leave. She had heard that the troops had a motto: '*Jeder einmal in Paris*'. Everyone once in Paris. They had even published a guide to the 'must-see' places in the city. As a result, the Moulin Rouge and the Folies Bergère were thronged with a raucous crowd of soldiers, and the bars and cafes were full of men in uniform, too often, in Alix's opinion, accompanied by French girls, while the more sophisticated restaurants were occupied by officers and their elegantly dressed mistresses. It was not hard to see the reason for the women's behaviour. Over the last months, rations had been cut again and again. Virtually all the meat and milk produced by French farmers were being commandeered by the occupying forces or sent back to Germany. The Parisians had to manage on a weekly ration of 360 grams of meat and 100 grams of oil or fat. The bread allowance was 300 grams per day, and sugar was rationed to 500 grams a month. Fish, milk and eggs were also rationed, when they were available, and even amounts of potatoes and salt were limited. There were days when the longing for a good, tasty meal almost dominated Alix's thoughts. But in her mind that was no excuse for fraternising with the enemy.

Tonight, however, she had other things on her mind. She was carrying a satchel. In it were several innocent-looking folders containing work for her course at the university. If she were to be stopped and searched there was nothing there to arouse suspicion. But neatly folded among the pages were several long strips of paper. Alix took another look along the street. No one was paying any attention to her. Nearby there was one of the kiosks that were to be found at frequent intervals along the city streets. In the daytime it would sell newspapers and, in pre-rationing days, sweets and cigarettes, but now it was empty and shuttered. Alix fumbled in her satchel, and when she walked away, a poster was attached to the shutters. *VIVE GENERAL DE GAULLE*, it read, in bright red capitals.

The stickers had been the idea of Agnès Humbert, the art historian. She produced them at the Museum of Folk Art and had handed them out to the group assembled by Paul Rivet. It was a small gesture, perhaps, but one they all felt was important in alerting the population to the fact that there were those among them who were not prepared to buckle down passively under the occupation and that there was a leader who could give them hope of liberation.

Alix sauntered down the street and went into a bar. She ordered a glass of *vin rouge*, drank it and paid her bill, then went to the toilets at the back of the shop. There were two cubicles, one for men and one for women. Both were empty, and when she left, the slogan *VIVE GENERAL DE GAULLE* was displayed across the mirror in both of them. From there she made her way to a small patisserie where she ordered coffee and a cake. The coffee was a disgusting brew made mostly with chicory, and the cake was a hard yellow bun that tasted of bicarbonate of soda, but there was a menu on the table, and the next customer would find the same slogan neatly folded into it.

Her next stop was at the metro station Pigalle. She changed lines at Madeleine, again at Châtelet and finally alighted at Porte d'Italie. At each stop she contrived to leave at least one of her stickers where travellers on their way to work next morning could not fail to see it. From there she walked back to the College Franco Brittanique.

In her room she found three other girls awaiting her with eager expressions. Alix spread a map on the table and on it they marked all the locations where they had managed to leave stickers. There was an undercurrent of excitement that she recognised was dangerous.

'You've all done really well but remember this is not a game. If you're caught, you could be punished severely.' She looked at her watch. 'Suzanne and Paulette should be back by now.'

That burst the bubble and they looked at each other with alarm.

'I expect they had to wait around for a chance to put up their stickers,' Moira said. 'They'll be back in a minute... won't they?'

To everyone's relief, the two missing girls arrived a few minutes later, but Paulette's face was taut. 'I thought I was for it. I was just looking in my bag for a sticker to put up at Invalides metro station when I heard this voice behind me.

"What are you looking for, *Fräulein*?" I turned round and there was a German soldier. I hadn't seen him come onto the platform. I can tell you I nearly wet myself. Then he smiled at me and asked if I had lost something important – he spoke quite good French and perhaps he could help me find it. Then I realised he was trying to pick me up.'

'What did you do?' Alix asked.

'I put my hand in my bag and I felt my powder compact. So I pulled it out and put on my frostiest voice and said thank you very much but I've found what I was looking for – and just at that moment the train came so I jumped in and, thank God, he didn't try to follow me.'

'Well done!' Alix told her. 'That was quick thinking. So,' – she looked around at the others – 'we've done a good night's work. I think we deserve a drink.'

Wine was rationed, like everything else, but, like most things, it could be bought on the black market, and Alix was still able to draw on the generous allowance her mother had paid into the Crédit Agricole bank before the outbreak of war. She produced a bottle of Sauvignon Blanc and poured six glasses.

'To General de Gaulle,' she suggested, and they all drank.

Alix looked around at their faces and felt a surge of warmth. She had assembled her little group by cautious steps over the last weeks. They were an international collection. Moira was Irish and Hanna was Polish. Both, like Alix, had been trapped in Paris by the outbreak of war. She had had no hesitation in approaching either of them. Hanna was Jewish and made no attempt to conceal her hatred of the people who had invaded her country. Moira, too, had good reason to hate the enemy. Her brother had volunteered for the British Army, and she had learned, via a crackling long-distance telephone call from her mother, that he had been killed in the defence of Dunkirk. The other three were all French and Alix had approached them rather more obliquely. Talking to fellow students after classes or in the refectory it was not hard to introduce her own feelings about the occupation. Some of the girls she spoke to shrugged and remarked that there was nothing to be done about it and they would just have to make the best of it. One or two warned her against making such remarks in case they were reported back to the Germans. Some looked frightened. With these, she took the conversation no further. If she received a more encouraging response, she moved on to remarks like, 'I wish there was something we could do, just to show them we're not cowed, just some way of cocking a snook at them.' She was often met with another fatalistic shrug, but in three cases, there had been fervent agreement. She followed up with, 'If there was some group, some organisation, that was trying to do just that, would you join it?' The response had been a fervent affirmative. At that point she had told them that she was already part of such an organisation and had invited them to join her. In this way, Suzanne, Paulette and Christine had joined Hanna and Moira. Suzanne was probably the most intelligent, a girl who might have had a high-flying academic career ahead of her if things had been different. Paulette was more timid but utterly devoted to her clever friend and would follow her lead whatever the cost. Pretty, blonde Christine was the romantic who lived for poetry and music, a fervent patriot whose love for her country and its civilization fuelled her hatred of the occupiers who were trampling it underfoot.

This, then, was Alix's chosen band. She was beginning to think of them already as a sisterhood. The distribution of the stickers had been their first operation.

Alix had considered approaching some of the friends she had made through Raoul among the communist students, but her tentative comments had been met with the persisting dogma that they had been instructed by the Comintern not to take part in any anti-German activities since Russia and Germany were allies.

The day after the distribution of the stickers, she attended a scheduled meeting with Boris and Marie Louise and the others who had been present when Rivet had initiated their activities. Since then, Boris had taken over the day-to-day organisation and numbers had grown remarkably quickly. Each member had recruited others, but, as a matter of policy, no one revealed the identities of their group. Only the leaders knew their names, so in the event of a disaster, only a small number could be arrested and interrogated.

Alix had come to like Boris very much. He often joined her and Marie Louise for dinner at the bistro He had been born in St Petersburg, but he and his mother had fled at the time of the revolution. He questioned her eagerly about life in Serbia and she soon discovered, as they compared the lives of the peasants in her own country with that of the serfs in Russia, that his views on society were in tune with her own. She also found him very attractive. He was a complex, slightly enigmatic figure, with a love of poetry and literature as well as his interest in science. He even admitted that he had once had an ambition to be a writer, which brought Steve back very vividly to her mind. She remembered how he always carried a small notebook in which he would scribble hasty notes when something caught his interest. The memory brought a wistful nostalgia for their time together, but she pushed it to the back of her mind. Those days were over, and she would probably never see him again. She wondered if Boris, also, privately still employed his latent literary talent. It added to his allure, though she knew that any romantic involvement was impossible. For one thing, he was married and showed no sign of wanting anything other than friendship from her.

When each of them had reported on the activities of their own group, Boris said, 'I think the time has come to divide our efforts so they can be more systematic. There are two areas in which I think we can operate effectively – propaganda and intelligence. Yvonne and Agnès are best placed to organise the production of leaflets and posters, so I am going to put them in charge of the propaganda element. And there is a third project I will ask them to consider. We know that there are still British soldiers stranded over here who were not evacuated from Dunkirk but who have managed to evade capture by the Germans. There are also increasing numbers of airmen forced to bail out over French territory. I have heard that some of them are coming to Paris looking for some means of returning to England. I am putting out feelers around the city in the hope of making contact with groups or individuals who are prepared to assist them in this. These men will need papers if they are to survive – the papers we all have to carry now – ID cards, ration cards, tobacco vouchers, work permits or travel permits. I am asking Agnès to investigate the possibility of producing convincing facsimiles of those.'

'So what about the rest of us?' asked Anatole Lewitsky. He was another anthropologist on the staff of the museum. 'What are we supposed to do?'

'The rest of you will concentrate on gathering intelligence.'

'What sort of intelligence? And what are we supposed to do with it when we've gathered it?'

'I have a contact who is in touch with de Gaulle's people in London. What they want to know is what is the strength of the occupying force and where is it concentrated. And the British desperately need information about the disposition and numbers of troops preparing for an invasion.'

'And how are we supposed to do that?' Lewitsky demanded. 'Go up to German officers in the street and ask them where they are based and how many of them there are?'

'Obviously not,' Boris said, 'but there are other ways. For a start, we should all familiarise ourselves with the insignia of the different regiments and what they do. If we can learn that we can get a good idea of which ones are allowing their men to come here on leave. That, in itself, would suggest that they are not expecting to go into battle in the immediate future. But there are better ways of obtaining the information we want, and that is where you, Alix, and your group can be most useful. I take it they are all young women?'

'Yes,' Alix replied, puzzled.

'Good. It should not be difficult for an attractive girl to get on friendly terms with a soldier on leave, or even with an officer. That way, you could find out far more than we can do by simple observation.'

Alix stared at him in horror. 'You are not suggesting "*le collaboration horizontale*", are you?'

He returned her look, and she saw the colour rise in his cheeks. 'Horizontal collaboration' was the phrase that had been coined to describe those who prostituted themselves to the occupying troops in return for favours or extra rations.

'I hope you know me better than that!' he said. 'I would never ask you or any of your group to go to those lengths. But would it be so difficult to allow yourself to be – picked up – by a German soldier, invited for a drink, perhaps a dance? I know the idea is repugnant, but a chat over a glass of wine could reveal so much.'

'Such as?'

'Well, the sort of thing I've already mentioned for a start. Which regiment does he belong to and where is it stationed at the moment? What sort of armament does it have? Is it a tank corps or artillery or infantry? Most importantly, the British need to know how many troops are amassing along the channel coast, preparatory to invade. If, for example, you were talking to a man who is part of a tank regiment stationed at Calais and he was suddenly told his leave was cancelled and he must return to duty, that would indicate that the invasion was imminent. That sort of information would be invaluable to the defenders along the south coast of England. Do you see?'

'Yes, I see,' Alix replied. 'I don't know if I can do it. I don't know if any of the girls would be prepared to try.'

'Will you think about it?' Boris asked. 'Will you ask them?'

'Yes,' Alix agreed doubtfully. 'I'll ask.'

Chapter Twenty

Leo dumped her rucksack on the platform and stood looking around her as the train chugged away towards Birkenhead. Behind her, the little Victorian railway station hid the view of the village and the land sloping away towards the Mersey. Opposite, beyond the railway lines, the wooded hills rose sharply upwards to meet a cloudless blue sky. She took a deep breath. At last, the soft air of an English summer and in a nearby tree a blackbird was singing. She was home. The Bramhall Estate had belonged to her grandmother and had been her refuge in times of trouble since she was a teenager.

In the station yard, a smart trap drawn by a bay horse stood waiting, a stocky man in his middle years standing at the horse's head. Leo crossed to him and held out her hand.

'Jonty, it's so good to see you!'

Jonathan Wainwright gripped the outstretched hand. 'And you, too, Miss Leonora. We've been hoping to hear from you these last weeks, but no one seemed to know where you were.'

'It's a long story, Jonty,' she said with a weary smile. 'Can it wait till we get back to the hall?'

'Of course. You'll be tired after your journey. I hope you don't mind the trap, instead of the car? It's the petrol rationing, you see.'

'I quite understand – and I love going in the trap anyway.'

He took her bag and threw it into the back, then handed her up to sit beside him on the driver's seat. 'Walk on!' He clicked his tongue and the bay stepped forward.

Leo said nothing until they were out of the village and climbing the hill to the ridge behind it. Jonathan had worked on the Bramhall Estate since he was a boy and they had known each other since the days when, as a teenager, she had escaped here from London and her grandmother's strict discipline. Over the years he had progressed from stable boy to head groom, and when the couple who had managed the estate for her father had retired, it had seemed natural that he should take over. They were at ease with each other and the silence, broken only by the clop-clop of hooves, was comfortable.

At length, Leo said, 'How are things going, Jonty?'

'Not too bad, considering. We're short-handed because all the young lads have been called up, but apart from that, and the rationing, you'd hardly know there was a war on. Bit different down south, by all accounts.'

'What's happening there? I've been abroad for several months, and I haven't been able to keep up with the news.'

'We're expecting Jerry to invade any day, and when he does, it'll be on the beaches along the Channel coasts. Puzzle is, why he hasn't already tried it.'

'I saw something about a battle in the air.'

'Yes. The BBC's been reporting that the Luftwaffe are trying to put our airfields out of commission, but the RAF boys in their Spitfires and Hurricanes have seen them off.'

'Well, good for them! But will they be able to keep it up?'

He shrugged. 'Who knows? There must be losses, but of course, they don't tell us about them.'

'And what about your boys?'

'Safe enough for the time being, I think. Jack's stationed somewhere up north, guarding a battery, and Phil's training to be a fitter for the RAF. Neither of them was involved in the Dunkirk shambles, thank God.'

They turned into the drive leading to the Bramhall Estate. The big house had been let to a wealthy Liverpool businessman for the last twenty years, since Leo's marriage, but there was a cottage in the grounds which she had had modernised and furnished to her own tastes and she and Sasha, with Alix, had been in the habit of spending a month or so there every summer.

'How are the Marchants these days?' Leo asked as they approached the house.

'I wouldn't know. You remember I wrote to you a few months back to say they'd moved out?'

'Yes, of course! I'd forgotten. Why did they go?'

'Well, he only ever came at weekends, spent the week staying at his club over the water. That worked out OK while the kiddies were small, but now the daughter's married and moved away, and both the sons have been called up. Mrs M didn't fancy being left in the house all alone, so she's gone to stay with her sister in Warrington.'

'Can't blame her, I suppose. Do they still come at weekends?'

'No, he goes to the sister's place instead.'

'I wonder if they will want to keep paying the rent when the lease is up,' Leo mused. 'Well, time enough for that, but it's sad to see the place stand empty.'

'Aye, it is,' he agreed. 'Now, Jane will have a meal ready for you. Will you come straight in or shall I drop you at the cottage?'

'Give me half an hour to freshen up,' Leo said. 'Then I'll join you.'

'Right you are.' He stopped the trap outside the cottage and helped Leo down. She unlocked the door and stepped inside with a sigh of relief.

Half an hour later she knocked on the door of the estate manager's house. It was opened by Jane Wainwright, who threw up her hands in shock.

'Oh, Miss Leo! You look right done up. Whatever have you been doing to yourself? Come in, come in and sit yourself down. I'll make the tea.'

Leo seated herself at the dining table, and a moment later, Jonathan joined her, and his wife bustled in with a large brown teapot.

'Now, help yourself, do. It's not what I'd have liked to give you, what with the rationing and all, but the butter and cheese are from our own cows and the bread and jam are homemade.'

Leo took a slice of fresh bread and spread it with butter. 'It looks wonderful, Jane. I haven't seen food like this for weeks.'

'So, have you come far?' Jonathan asked.

'Quite a long way,' Leo replied, with her mouth full. 'From Finland, actually.'

'Finland!' both her hosts exclaimed in unison.

'What were you doing there?' Jonathan added.

As briefly as she could, Leo described the work the convoy had been doing and their frustration at being unable to come home when the job was done. She told them about the final dash to Liinakhamari and the disappointment when the captain of the ship had refused to take them on board.

'I think he saw that we were tougher than he imagined. So he said he'd take us if we didn't mind sleeping on deck.'

'Sleeping on deck! In those latitudes?' Jonathan said.

'Oh, it wasn't as bad as it sounds. We were all warmly kitted out because we'd started out in the depths of winter, and we had our sleeping bags. And it was high summer, and it doesn't get dark all night up there. We tucked ourselves away in any odd corners we could find, to be out of the way of the crew. I found a place in the stern where there were a lot of ropes coiled up and made myself a little nest there. It could have been a lot worse.'

'Well, it sounds awful to me,' Jane said. 'Not suitable for young ladies at all!'

Leo laughed. 'Well, we're all used to doing unsuitable things, Jane. It's what the FANY are known for.'

'So that's how you got home?' Jonathan said.

'Not quite. The idea was for us to be dropped off in Iceland in the hope that we could find a ship there to bring us back. It all seemed to be going very well until the captain casually remarked that he'd "missed" Iceland.'

'Missed it? How could he miss a big island like that?' Jonathan asked.

'Quite,' Leo agreed dryly. 'I don't think he ever intended to take us there. It was out of his way, after all. So, we had all just about made up our minds that we were going all the way to America when we had a stroke of luck. We sighted a British naval frigate and the captain signalled to it. They hove to and sent over a boat. When we explained the situation they agreed to take us on board. As it happened, they were at the end of their tour of duty and on their way home, so after three days of luxury in proper cabins, we docked at Rosyth early this morning. The rest of the troop are on their way back to London, but I thought as I was that far north it made sense to call in here on the way – and I reckoned I was owed a bit of leave. So here I am.'

'And right glad we are to see you!' said Jane. 'Now you must have a good rest. You deserve it.'

'I can't stay too long,' Leo said. 'I must get back on duty. We may have an invasion to fight off.'

'Oh, God forbid!' Jane exclaimed.

'We've another reason to be glad to see you,' Jonathan said. He fished in an inside pocket and produced an envelope. 'This came for you a couple of days ago. I've been wondering what to do with it. I didn't know where to send it on.'

Leo took the envelope. It was addressed to Countess Malkovic at Bramhall, Cheshire, and bore the crest of the Ministry of War.

'What made them think they would find me here?' she puzzled, opening it. She read it aloud:

> Dear Lady Malkovic,
>   According to our records, you are the owner of the property known as Bramhall in the village of Brandon. We are seeking your cooperation in a matter of national security. A Brigadier Colin Gubbins will call on you on July 16th to discuss matters further. He will be in touch to let you know when to expect him.

'July 16th! That's tomorrow!'

'Well, it's lucky you're here,' Jonathan said. 'I wouldn't have known what to do with him.'

'I wonder what he wants?' Jane said.

'*A matter of national security*,' Leo repeated. 'What could that have to do with Bramhall?' Then she snapped her fingers. 'I bet I can guess. They've found out somehow that it's unoccupied and they want to turn it into a convalescent home for wounded soldiers, or something like that.'

'That doesn't sound like a matter of national security to me,' Jonathan said doubtfully.

'Oh, that'll be some boffin at the ministry trying to make himself sound important,' Leo responded. She was suddenly caught by a huge yawn. 'I'm sorry. I'm going to have to go to bed. I'm dropping.'

'You go and get a good night's sleep,' Jane said.

'Do you want me to walk over with you?' her husband asked.

Leo grinned at him. 'Thanks, Jonty, but I think I'm safe to walk a hundred yards in my own land. Good night. I'll see you in the morning.'

She went out into the balmy summer dusk, breathing the scent of honeysuckle growing round the door. As she walked towards her cottage something struck her as odd. There was something missing beyond the line of elms that marked the boundary of her land. It took her a few minutes to realise that she was looking towards Liverpool, but instead of the lights of the city, there was only darkness. The whole country was under a blackout – a sharp reminder that the peaceful atmosphere of the evening was a temporary illusion.

–

Leo woke next morning with a wonderful feeling of relaxation, as if it was the first day of a holiday, then she remembered that she had this mysterious visitation to prepare for. She had made light of it yesterday, but on second thoughts, it filled her with a sense of foreboding. She got out of bed and drew the curtains. The view instantly restored her mood. Beyond the elms, the green fields sloped away to where a flicker of reflected light picked out the River Weaver. Some of the fields had been mown and the hay was drying in the sun. In others, the black and white cows grazed contentedly. She felt a sudden certainty that this timeless scene could never be swept away by the ravages of war. Jane had left milk and bread and eggs and a small packet of tea in the larder leading off the little kitchen. Leo treated herself to a leisurely breakfast and then walked over to the manager's house.

'Any word about when this Brigadier Gubbins is likely to arrive?' she asked.

'Not so far,' Jane told her.

'We shall have to invite him to dinner. Can you manage that?'

'I've got a nice capon to roast. He'll have to be satisfied with that.'

'I'm sure he will be. Perhaps we ought to ask him to stay the night. Is the bed in the spare room made up?'

'In the cottage, you mean?'

'Yes, of course.'

Jane pursed her lips. 'A single man to stay the night, and you alone. It's not fitting.'

Leo laughed. 'You're a dear old-fashioned thing! Manners have changed, you know. And I'm more than capable of defending myself against unwanted advances.'

'That's not what I meant. What would the Count say if he was here?'

Leo had to admit to herself that Sasha probably would not approve. Aloud she said, 'Well, I suppose he could stay here, if it's not too much trouble.'

Jane's face cleared. 'No trouble at all. I'll get a room ready.'

At that moment they heard the sound of bicycle wheels on the gravel outside. Leo looked out of the window. 'Telegraph boy.'

Jane's hand went to her throat and Leo felt a stab of anxiety on her behalf. 'Don't worry. It's probably to let us know when the Brigadier is arriving.'

She was right. Gubbins's telegram told them he expected to arrive that afternoon on the 2.30 train.

'There you are,' Leo said comfortingly. 'Nothing to worry about.'

'I'm sorry,' Jane said. 'It's just, when you see the boy... We're not used to telegrams. It was the same yesterday when you wired to let us know you were coming.'

'Oh gosh! I'm sorry,' Leo said. 'I didn't think. But I had to let you know and I couldn't see any other way.'

'Oh, bless you, it was only for a moment, and then we both fairly danced round the kitchen when we got the news. Now, we'd better tell Jonty. He'll need to collect the gentleman from the station.'

'No, don't bother him,' Leo said. 'I'll go. I can drive the trap.'

She puzzled for some minutes over what to wear to meet her mysterious guest. She had found an old pair of slacks and a blouse that she had left in the wardrobe on her last visit, but apart from that she had only a rather formal afternoon dress, also left behind, or her FANY uniform. In the end she opted for the uniform.

It was not hard to distinguish her visitor among the people descending from the train since he was dressed in the uniform of a Brigadier in the Royal Field Artillery. The first word that occurred to Leo as she watched him approach was 'dapper'. He was short and dark, and everything about him was immaculate, from the clipped moustache to his fine kid gloves and the silver-topped cane in his left hand; but any suggestion of the dandy was dispelled by the sight of the ribbons of the Military Cross and the Distinguished Service Order on his tunic. He was looking around, obviously expecting to be met, but she saw his slight start of surprise as he recognised her uniform. She advanced towards him and held out her hand.

'Brigadier Gubbins, I presume. I'm Leonora Malkovic.'

There was no concealing his surprise now, but he collected himself and took her hand with a small, gallant inclination of his head, 'Countess Malkovic. Forgive me. I was not aware that you were a member of the Nursing Yeomanry.' His voice was low and slightly roughened, as if he had spent too long shouting orders in inclement weather, but beneath the gravel were the soft edges of a Scots burr.

Leo laughed. 'Well, I was a FANY long before I was a countess — though I have to admit that one led to the other.'

His expression relaxed. 'I sense an interesting story there.'

'A long one,' Leo agreed, 'but perhaps not one to embark on now. I have transport waiting outside. Shall we go?'

She led him out to where the pony stood, its bridle held by a small boy who had been glad to earn sixpence. 'I hope you don't mind. We're economising on petrol.'

'Quite right, too,' he said. He slung his case into the back of the trap and climbed nimbly up to sit beside her. Leo clicked her tongue and the pony stepped forward.

He said, 'When I saw that Bramhall was owned by a Countess Malkovic, I was expecting to meet a foreign lady.'

'Understandably,' she replied. 'The title belongs to my husband. He is Count Alexander Malkovic – a Serb.'

'A Serb?' he repeated. 'How interesting. So are you and he both resident at Bramhall?'

'No, we reside for most of the time on his estate outside Belgrade. Bramhall was left to me by my grandmother, and we come over a couple of times a year to stay – at least, we used to. That's not going to be possible for the foreseeable future.'

'Quite. So is the Count with you now?'

'No. He's still in Belgrade. I happened to be in England when war was declared so I decided I had better rejoin my old unit and see if I could make myself useful.'

'Very creditable,' he said.

'As a matter of fact, you were lucky to get hold of me. I'm just grabbing a few days' leave after getting back from Finland.'

'Finland? You were there – why?'

As briefly as possible, Leo told him about the convoy and their difficulties getting home. When she finished, he said gravely, 'You are obviously a very resourceful lady.'

'Oh, well, that's the FANYs for you. Resourceful is our middle name.'

He was silent for a moment. Then he said, 'So, when you are out of the country, the house is empty?'

'No. The Hall itself has been let for many years to a Mr George Marchant. I have a cottage in the grounds for our occasional visits and the estate is in the hands of my manager, Jonathan Wainwright. You'll meet him in a few minutes. But as it happens, the Marchants are not there at the moment. Both their sons have been called up, and Mrs Marchant didn't fancy being in the Hall on her own while her husband was over in Liverpool, so she has moved out to stay with a sister.' She glanced sideways at him. 'Do you have plans for the place? Your letter spoke of a matter of national security.'

'Not for the house,' he said. 'No.' She waited for him to expand on the statement, but instead, he said, 'I presume you speak fluent Serbocroat?'

'Oh yes, of course. It's my second language these days.'

'And what can you tell me about the situation in Yugoslavia? Will it remain neutral?'

'It will if my husband has anything to do with it. His family traditionally holds a position at the royal court and he is very close to Prince Peter, the heir to the throne. He helped the poor boy through the terrible time after his father, King Alexander, was assassinated. I know he is trying very hard to use his influence to persuade the Regent, Prince Paul, not to sign any agreement with Hitler, but of course, I've been out of touch for weeks.'

'Understandably,' he agreed.

They turned into the drive and Gubbins peered around him with what seemed to Leo more than casual curiosity. He twisted in his seat to look up to their right.

'That is Frodsham Hill? I imagine the view from there must be... extensive.'

'Yes, it is. I'll take you up there if you like.'

'Later, perhaps'. He focussed on the Hall itself, the sandstone walls glowing amber in the sunshine. 'It's a fine building. How old is it?'

'There are parts that date back to the seventeenth century, but most of it is mid-Victorian.'

'Ah,' he said and left it at that.

The Wainwrights were waiting at the door of their house, alerted by the sound of wheels, and Billy the stable boy was ready to take charge of the pony. Leo handed him the reins and jumped down. The Brigadier followed and she introduced him, adding, 'I hope you'll stay to dinner?'

'Thank you, that's very kind. Oh, I should have asked you earlier. Is there a hotel in the town where I could get a room for the night?'

'There is,' Leo said, 'but I shall be glad to put you up.'

He glanced at her and for a moment she saw an echo of Jane's doubts about the propriety of the arrangement. She suppressed a laugh and said, 'That's my cottage, over there, but there is a spare room here you are welcome to use.'

He looked relieved. 'Thank you. That's very helpful.'

Jane took him up to the room, but he was down again in a few minutes. He refused her offer of tea or coffee and said, 'Well, shall we get down to business?'

Leo led him into the comfortable, if slightly shabby, living room and settled him in an armchair. Jane disappeared into the kitchen, but Jonathan hovered uncertainly by the door.

Leo said, 'Whatever your plans are, Brigadier, Jonathan will have to know about them. I shall not be here.'

Gubbins had produced a pipe and was engaged in filling it. 'Yes, yes, of course.' He indicated the pipe. 'You don't mind if I smoke?'

'Not at all. Jonty, can you find the Brigadier an ashtray?'

Jonathan produced one and took a chair nearby and they both sat looking at the visitor in expectation. When Gubbins had got his pipe drawing to his satisfaction, he returned their gaze. There was something about his sharp, dark eyes that made Leo think of a hawk. She had a feeling that under the wrong circumstances, their look could be intimidating.

'The first thing I have to say,' he began, 'is that everything you hear now is top secret. I am relying on you, as patriots, to make sure that none of it goes beyond this room. If there were to be leaks, the consequences could be severe. Do I have your assurances?'

'You do,' Leo said, and Jonathan added, 'You can rely on us, sir.'

Gubbins looked at Leo. 'I have to confess that when I saw your name as owner of this property, I wondered if it would be a mistake to go any further with this project, which is why I decided that I must come in person. But after our earlier conversation, I feel sure that I can put my trust in your loyalty.'

'I'm glad to hear it,' Leo remarked, somewhat dryly.

Gubbins proceeded. 'It may be hard to comprehend, here in this peaceful corner, that the country is facing the gravest threat it has experienced in centuries. As we speak, young men are risking their lives, and losing them far too often, over the skies of southern England, in an attempt to keep the Luftwaffe at bay. We believe that Hitler is waiting to be sure he has command in the air before launching a full-scale invasion. God willing, the RAF can prevent that from happening, but we have to be prepared for any eventuality. You will be aware of the Home Guard, of course.'

They both nodded.

'Their role, should the worst come to the worst, will be to defend their towns and villages to the last man, if necessary. But I have been commissioned by Mr Churchill to set up another organisation – we are calling them auxiliary forces – who will have a different job to do. If all else fails and the country is occupied by the Nazis, they are to form the core of a resistance operation, to collect intelligence and to carry out acts of sabotage.'

Gubbins paused to draw on his pipe, and Leo asked, 'Who will these people be?'

'Volunteers, of course. We are looking for people who know their locality and who can move around the countryside without arousing suspicion. Gamekeepers and farm workers would fit the bill very well, but there may be others.'

'Well,' Jonathan said eagerly, 'you can count me in!'

'Your alacrity does you credit. But hear me out before you make such a decision. It will, inevitably, be a dangerous job. The chances of being captured, or killed, will be high. Most crucially, those involved must maintain total secrecy. Legally, they will be under the aegis of the Home Guard, but the regular Home Guard will have no knowledge of their existence and no idea of who is involved.'

'So what do you want from us?' Leo asked.

'When the time comes these men will go underground – quite literally in many cases. They will need places where they can live, eat, and sleep, safe from detection. I have already been in touch with landowners in the south who are prepared to provide such a facility. Now I am looking in this area. We expect that the Liverpool docks would become a base for German shipping and it seems to me that it would be possible to watch the comings and goings in the Mersey estuary from the top of Frodsham Hill. Am I right?'

'Quite right,' Leo and Jonathan agreed in unison.

'So, what I am looking for is a place where these men can hide out, if necessary for days. Ideally there should be an entrance in a place where they could come and go without causing comment and another, more hidden, which would allow them to sally out after dark, or which might provide a way out if the first entrance was under surveillance or otherwise unusable. Can you think of any such place?'

Leo and Jonathan exchanged glances, remembering youthful adventures.

'I think we can,' Leo said. 'We have a series of caves on our land. They were created by men digging out the sand. They are quite well-known and something of a tourist attraction in peacetime but they are quite extensive and very few people penetrate to the innermost ones. Also – and this is not common knowledge – there are cellars under the Hall. Principally they are wine cellars, but again they are more extensive than required for that purpose. We have always thought that they must finish very near to the caves and there have always been rumours that once upon a time they were used by smugglers, who had dug a secret passage leading out into the cave.' She glanced again at Jonathan who was smiling broadly. 'We tried to find it when we were kids but never succeeded.'

'But this is wonderful!' Gubbins exclaimed. 'Even if the passage does not exist, it might be possible to make one. Can you show me?'

'Of course.'

Leo collected the keys to the main house and a pair of torches and led her guest across the farmyard and in through the back door. It was twenty years since she had set foot there, but it immediately evoked memories that made the intervening time evaporate. She pulled her thoughts back to the present and led the way to the cellar door. At the bottom of the steps, they were in a spacious area lined with shelves on which a few cobwebbed bottles remained. On another shelf, jars of long-forgotten preserves were gathering dust.

'It doesn't look as though the Marchants have used the place,' Jonathan commented.

Leo led the way past the shelves to where an archway opened into a second cellar. This was a long, narrow space stretching back beyond the foundations of the house.

'We think this may be where they dug out the sandstone to build the original hall,' Leo said. 'I imagine that it would be easy to conceal this archway with a dummy set of shelves, mounted in such a way that they could be slid aside. That way no one would suspect there was a second cellar.'

Gubbins looked at her, a glint in his eyes that was more than the reflection of the torches. 'Very good!'

The passage ended in what appeared to be a solid block of sandstone. Leo put her hand on it.

'We always thought this must be where the secret passage began, but without excavating there was no way of knowing.'

Gubbins studied the block for a few minutes. Then he said, 'Can you show me the caves?'

They made their way out into the sunshine again and walked a short distance to a field gate beyond which cattle were grazing. To one side the ground rose steeply to a gorse-covered bank, and in the bank, there were two holes large enough for a man to walk into without bending. By the light of the torches, they penetrated deeper, into a cavern where the roof was supported by a series of arches, giving it an almost church-like appearance. Gubbins caught his breath.

'What is that greenish light?'

Ahead of them the rock glittered with tiny diamond points of light. Jonathan walked over to it.

'They call it goblin's gold, but it's actually a very rare moss. See, the little flowers reflect the light, like a cat's eye.'

'Remarkable!' Gubbins examined the moss with fascination, then stood back. 'We mustn't let ourselves be distracted, however exotic this is.'

Leo led them deeper still until they came to a raised ledge of rock. 'They call this the pulpit. It's as far back as you can go. But if there ever was a secret passage it must have come out somewhere near here.'

Gubbins nodded and began to pace back towards the entrance to the cave, counting his steps. Outside, he performed the same exercise as they walked back to the Hall. Leo and Jonathan followed in respectful silence. When they stood again by the back wall, Gubbins said, 'I can't make any real judgement about the feasibility of the idea at the moment. I shall have to get a surveyor up here to map the ground out properly, but if it can be made to work it would be ideal. We can install beds and electric light in the cellar and put in a stock of tinned food, and there is access to drinking water from the kitchen. But it would mean workmen coming and going for some time to dig out the passage – or to create one if necessary.'

'We could say that while the Hall is empty, I have decided to have some renovations made,' Leo suggested. 'That would give cover to any activity.'

'Excellent idea!' Gubbins turned his eyes on her with an expression which contained, she thought, both approval and speculation. 'Now, you offered to show me the view from the top of the hill.'

At the summit, he spent some time inspecting the view over the Mersey towards Liverpool through a small pair of folding binoculars. At length, he closed them with a snap. 'Ideal! Thank you.'

'I'm glad you think it can be useful,' Leo said. 'And please feel free to use the Hall, and the land, as you see fit. I shall be glad to think it is serving a useful purpose instead of standing empty, and I know I can trust you not to do any lasting damage.'

'I think we've done all we can do for the moment,' Gubbins said. 'Shall we go down?'

They dined alone in the cottage, and as they ate, he said, 'You mentioned when we met that there was a long story to be told about how you came to meet your husband. Would you tell it to me now?'

Leo paused, ordering her thoughts. She told him as concisely as possible about her initial experiences in the First Balkan War and her meeting with Sasha Malkovic. She went on to relate how she had joined Mabel Stobart's mission to the Serbs in the Great War, how she had taken part in the terrible retreat through the Albanian mountains and then gone back with the Serbian army to fight with them from Salonika back to Belgrade.

'It's a remarkable story,' he said when she had finished, and she saw frank admiration in his eyes.

Next day he asked to be taken back to the station to catch the ten a.m. train, and as they shook hands, he said, 'You can be sure I shall be in touch very soon. It's been a most informative visit.'

After that little bit of excitement, Leo settled back to enjoy what remained of her leave, but two days later she received another letter on War Ministry paper.

Dear Lady Malkovic.

You are requested to attend for an interview at the Inter Services Research Bureau, 64 Baker Street, London on Monday, 22nd inst. at 2.30 p.m.

The signature was illegible.

'Inter Services Research Bureau? What's that when it's at home?' Leo asked, not expecting an answer. 'I suppose it must be something to do with Brigadier Gubbins's visit, but I can't see why I have to go down to London when all the answers are up here.' She stretched her arms. 'Oh well, my leave is nearly over anyway. I'd have to get back soon.'

64 Baker Street was a large, anonymous-looking building, its entrance guarded by a line of sandbags, like most other public buildings. Leo announced her name to a WAAF at the reception desk and was directed to an office on the first floor. A man she had never met was sitting behind a desk, and she was taken aback to be greeted in Serbocroat. She replied in the same language and for

the next ten minutes or so they conducted a conversation which ranged over the geography of Belgrade and its surroundings and on to the customs of the people and the tensions between the various ethnic groups which made up the newly formed state of Yugoslavia. Leo soon recognised that the interview was intended to ascertain whether her knowledge of the country was consistent with her story of marriage to a Serbian count or whether it was some kind of fabrication, but the reason for it escaped her.

Eventually, her interlocutor rose to his feet and said in English, 'Thank you, Lady Malkovic. If you wait here, someone else will be along to talk to you.'

More puzzled than ever, Leo waited and very soon the door opened to admit Colin Gubbins. As they shook hands, he said, 'I'm sorry about all that, but it was a necessary precaution. Would you like some tea?'

Leo said she would, and he touched a button on his desk and requested the girl who answered to bring tea for two. As they waited, she said, 'How are your plans for the Hall progressing?'

'Very well so far. You should get a visit from an army surveyor within the next few days.'

'Well, I shan't be there,' Leo said. 'My leave is over tomorrow. But Jonathan Wainwright will do all that's necessary.'

'I'm sure,' he agreed. 'You say your leave is coming to an end. What do you expect to be doing next?'

'I wish I knew. Waiting, I suppose, like everyone else, to see whether the invasion materialises.'

The tea arrived, and as he poured it, Gubbins said, 'You must be wondering why I have dragged you all the way down to London. It's time for me to put my cards on the table. I want you to go back to Belgrade as part of a network of people whose function is to provide information useful to His Majesty's Government.'

Leo stared at him. 'You want me to spy for you?!'

'No. That word suggests a clandestine operation. You would be there quite openly. What could be more natural than that you should return to be at your husband's side? It is simply a matter of keeping us in touch with developments. You told me that he has access to the royal court, to the councils of Prince Paul. You must know that we are very worried by rumours that the prince might sign some kind of pact with Hitler. If that were to happen, it would almost certainly allow the Germans to move troops and equipment through Yugoslavia to Thessaloniki, giving them direct access to the Mediterranean. If the Nazis can resupply their forces by a direct route like that, it would make our job in North Africa even harder than it already is.'

'I can see that,' Leo said. 'And I'm sure Sasha is as well aware of the danger as you are. But where do I come in?'

'You would provide a direct channel of communication, passing back high-level information. It will not surprise you to know that we already have agents operating in the Balkans, but none of them has access to the sort of circles in which your husband moves. And the flow would be in both directions, of course. We may be able to pass on information which he would find useful in his efforts to counteract the pro-German influences around Prince Paul.'

Leo considered. 'I could not contemplate an assignment like this unless my husband had full knowledge of what I was doing.'

'Of course,' Gubbins said. 'I would never suggest otherwise. It would rely on your mutual discretion to keep the arrangement secret from… other elements at court. But if between you you can prevent the German alliance from going ahead and even perhaps use your influence to bring the Yugoslavs over to our side, you will be doing both the country of your birth and your adopted one a great service.'

Leo was silent for a few minutes. 'I shall need to think about this. But two immediate practical questions come to mind. One, how am I supposed to get back to Belgrade now that most of Europe is under Nazi control?'

'Don't worry about that,' he assured her. 'There are ways and means. And the second question?'

'Suppose I agree. How do I get the information back to you?'

'Ah, yes. Did your FANY training include the use of radiotelegraphy?'

'I learnt the Morse Code, but I think machines for transmitting it were very much in their infancy in those days.'

'Yes, of course. But if you know Morse, it would not take long to teach you how to use a transmitter.'

Again Leo said nothing for some time. At length, she said, 'Give me twenty-four hours, and I'll let you have an answer.'

'Excellent. I can't ask for more than that.' He stood up. 'Shall we say four o'clock tomorrow, here? And if you have any more questions, I shall be happy to answer them then.'

Back at the small flat she had rented, on the assumption that she would be based in London for the duration of the war, Leo made another pot of tea and sat at the table staring at nothing and trying to think. She could understand Colin Gubbins's argument. The outcome of the machinations around Prince Paul was obviously of vital importance to the progress of the war. It would not be difficult to find out which way the balance was shifting and she could not see that she would be acting in any way contrary to her husband's interests. Morally, she decided, the assignment was acceptable.

The stumbling block was the state of her relationship with Sasha. He had still not replied to her letter, though whether that was deliberate or simply due to the collapse of the postal system, she had no way of knowing. If she went back now, it would be hypocritical to pretend that she was the contrite wife returning to beg her husband's forgiveness. But on the other hand, if she told him that she was returning at the behest of the British government, to act as their agent, it would destroy any suggestion that she genuinely wanted to be reconciled. Then there was Alix. He had been furious when she had taken their daughter away against his wishes. How much angrier he would be, and with some reason, now that Alix was trapped behind enemy lines and in who knew what sort of danger. All in all, she could not expect to be welcomed back with open arms.

Yet that was what she longed for. She wanted to go home, to feel Sasha's arms around her, to slip back into the ease and the sense of comradeship they had shared for so many years. While she was in Finland, she realised that her impulsive decision to rejoin the FANY and fight through this new war with them had been a mistake. But with Europe in turmoil and Yugoslavia surrounded on all sides by the Axis powers she could see no way of getting back – until that afternoon. Colin Gubbins had said there were 'ways and means' and she did not doubt him. If she accepted his invitation she would at least be able to face whatever fate had in store for Yugoslavia at her husband's side – and possibly she might play a small part in directing that fate. If she could help to ensure that the country did not end up as part of the Nazi war machine, that would be a better contribution to the ultimate victory than driving an ambulance in England. She lifted her head and looked around her. Her tea was stone cold, and the angle of the sun through the window showed her that evening was approaching, but she had made her decision. She would tell Sasha exactly what she had been asked to do and ask him to believe that she honestly thought it was the right thing. She would explain, also, that she had embraced the chance it had offered to return to him. She would not apologise for what she had done. Whatever the outcome, she could not have stood by and seen Alix pressured into a marriage she did not want. But she genuinely regretted the distress her action had caused him and wanted to be reconciled. If he would accept her on that basis, they might have a foundation on which to rebuild their relationship. If not… she knew he would not publicly reject her; his pride would not allow that sort of scandal. She would act out the part of a repentant spouse and get on with the job Gubbins had sent her to do.

Chapter Twenty-One

Brussels

August–September 1940

Steve straightened up and looked at Yvette across the bonnet of the car they were working on. Her hair had come loose, and she had a smear of grease on her face, but that just heightened the sudden surge of desire that took him by surprise. He tried to suppress it, reminding himself that he was only here because she and her father were prepared to take a great risk for him. It would be wrong to repay their trust by trying to seduce her. And then, there was Alix. But his memories of her, once so vivid, were beginning to fade and he told himself that she had probably completely forgotten him by now. After all, she had chosen to remain loyal to Raoul when the choice had been offered, so he was under no obligation on that count.

Yvette wiped her hands on a piece of rag and walked round the car to his side.

'I think we've done enough for one day, don't you?'

He looked into her eyes and read there an answer to his own desire. He took her in his arms and kissed her, feeling an immediate and passionate response. After a long moment, she drew back and smiled at him.

'Tonight?'

'Oh yes,' he breathed. 'Yes, please!'

When M. Lebrun had gone to bed, Steve made his way softly to Yvette's door. His heart was thumping so hard it hurt. He was not completely inexperienced. There had been a clumsy and unsatisfactory grappling with a girl-friend in the back of a car while he was at university, but he had never felt physical desire so inextricably interwoven with emotional need.

Yvette was sitting on the edge of the bed, waiting for him, and when he closed the door, she ran to him and threw her arms around him. He pressed her close, feeling the soft contours of her body melding with his own. He knew before he gave in to the urgent response of his own desire that there was one thing he had to say.

'Cherie, you understand, this can't be forever? I shall have to go away one day.'

She lifted her head and looked him in the eyes. 'I know. But this war changes everything. There's no telling where any of us may be in a year's time. We must make the most of what we have in this moment.'

He kissed her then, and there was no need for any more words.

If Yvette's father guessed what was going on, he gave no indication of it. Steve concluded that he had seen what was bound to happen and had either adopted a wilful blindness or tacitly approved the situation. His main worry was that Yvette might become pregnant, but to his relief, on the second night, she shyly handed him a packet of condoms. There were days when he began to think that perhaps it would not be a bad outcome if he was forced to stay where he was until the end of the war. They were good companions by day and passionate lovers by night. As time passed, he cared for her ever more deeply.

They continued their minor acts of sabotage. Enemy vehicles brought in for service or repair regularly left with a nail inserted into the tread of a tyre, a brake cable severely abraded or the plug for draining the oil slightly loose. It was childish, perhaps, but it gave him the feeling that he was not being entirely useless. Once or twice he was tempted to do more, but he knew that any real damage could be traced back to the garage, putting Yvette and her father in danger.

In his spare time he made notes on any scraps of paper that came to hand about conditions under German occupation and some of the personalities he met. As with what he had written while at the seminary, he knew that if the chance ever came to escape, he would not be able to take them with him, but he was determined to commit as much as possible to memory for future use.

There was one fly in the ointment of his contentment. Madeleine was a constant irritation, dropping in most evenings and sometimes hanging around on flimsy excuses while he was working with Yvette. It was plain that she was jealous of their relationship and it worried him that it might impel her to denounce him to the authorities, but he consoled himself with the thought that she could not do so without embroiling her beloved Yvette. Nevertheless, her baleful presence made him uneasy. She was always dressed in black, although he had heard Yvette teasing her about it. 'Why do you dress like a widow? You're not an old woman. You could still marry and have a family of your own.' To which Madeleine would reply, 'Marry whom, I should like to know. Anyway, the last thing I want is some man pawing me and watching my every move.'

As the weeks passed, Steve began to move about more freely. It seemed the local people had accepted him, though whether they believed in him as Carl, Yvette's cousin, or guessed his true identity but colluded in the deception out of loyalty to their neighbours, he was never sure. Whatever the case, he felt safe enough to go to local shops and occasionally to the bar on the corner of the road. He also went to church with Yvette and her father. When he expressed reluctance he was told that his absence would arouse suspicions, so he gave in. On Sunday afternoons he and Yvette went for long walks along the banks of the River Senne, though they were careful to avoid the city centre, where there was more danger of being stopped and asked to produce their papers. It disturbed him, however, that from time to time, looking back over his shoulder, he caught a glimpse of a black-clad figure disappearing round a corner or into a shop doorway. He told himself that he was being paranoid. In the current situation, there were enough women who had good reason to don widow's weeds, but he could not rid himself of the suspicion that they were being followed.

He discovered that his new habit of churchgoing had its advantages. Father Marcel suggested to him that he should come to confession and there was something in his look that told Steve he was not simply concerned about the state of his soul. He was proved right. Kneeling in the confessional, he learned that the priest was in contact with a network of others who were all working to ensure the safety of escaped POWs and downed aircrew, many of whom had managed to find their way to Brussels and, like himself, had been given sanctuary by local families. When

Steve raised the question of a possible escape route, he was told that it was the subject of much thought but as yet no definitive plan had been agreed upon.

The problem of eking out rations when he and the Lebruns had only two ration cards between the three of them was partly solved by the vegetables from the garden and the eggs from the hens, but as the summer turned to autumn, it was obvious that these supplies were going to diminish. Yvette had a bicycle, and Steve discovered at the back of the workshop a slightly dilapidated man's bike that her father had ridden until his arthritis made that impossible. An evening's work rendered it usable again, and he and Yvette formed the habit of riding out to the suburbs when they had finished work for the day. Here many of the residents had turned their gardens over to growing produce of various kinds, and a flourishing black market had grown up. There was plenty of competition for the results, and sometimes they returned with nothing in their baskets, but usually, they were able to buy potatoes or swedes and cabbages. Onions were a treasure trove indeed, and once, to Yvette's delight, they came home with a jar of honey. On Sundays, instead of their walks, they started to venture further afield, into the surrounding countryside. All farm produce was requisitioned by the occupying Germans, but farmers often managed to keep a little back and were sometimes prepared to sell milk or butter, and even cheese, though the prices were extortionate.

'You can't blame them,' Yvette said. 'If they are caught they could be fined or perhaps sent to prison.'

One Sunday in the middle of September they were about to set off when a boy, the son of a neighbour, ran into the garage forecourt.

'Mlle Yvette, Mlle Yvette! Mlle Madeleine needs you. She's very ill.'

'Ill? How?' Yvette asked.

'I don't know. She just called me out of her window and asked me to come and fetch you.'

Yvette turned to Steve. 'I'll have to go to her.'

'She's probably putting it on to get your attention,' Steve said. 'Tell her you'll look in later.'

'No, I can't do that. She may be really ill.'

'It might be something catching. I don't want you going down with it too.'

'I'll be careful. She nursed me when I had measles. I owe it to her to take care of her now.'

'What about our shopping trip?'

'You can go without me. The farmers know you now. You don't need me.'

Reluctantly, Steve yielded and watched her hurry away towards Madeleine's house. Then he mounted his bike and set off.

Evening was drawing in when he returned, feeling triumphant. In his basket, as well as a kilo of potatoes and two onions, there was the carcass of a rabbit. His mouth watered at the thought of rabbit stew, to replace the boiled vegetables with a few scraps of sausage which made up their normal diet. As he came to the street leading to the garage he stopped abruptly. A hundred yards ahead a roadblock had been set up, and soldiers of the Feldgendarmerie were searching baskets and checking everyone's papers. He swung round, intending to lose himself in the network of streets behind him, and saw to his alarm that another roadblock was in the process of being created at the other end of the street. The thought flashed through his mind that this was Madeleine's doing. She had found a way of trapping him without incriminating her beloved Yvette, taking it for granted that his sense of honour would not allow him to reveal who had harboured him all these weeks. Even as his racing brain conceived the idea he found himself wondering how long his sense of honour would withstand interrogation by the Gestapo.

All this went through his mind in parallel to more practical considerations. He forced himself to move slowly, giving no hint that the sight of the roadblocks disturbed him. A narrow alleyway led off to one side. He leaned the bicycle against the wall of the house beside it and strolled into the alley. Once out of sight, he ran to the far end, but there he stopped short and peered cautiously out into the adjoining street. That, too, was blocked. Behind him he could hear shouted orders and doors being forced open. The Germans had begun a house-to-house search and it could be seconds only before he was discovered in the alleyway. To his left, a high wall bounded what he assumed was the garden of a house. He leapt and seized the top of it, scrabbled up and flung himself over and landed in a heap on the far side.

Getting to his knees, he discovered that his arrival had been observed by a small child, a little girl of perhaps five years old, who was now regarding him with eyes like saucers. On an impulse, he put his fingers to his lips and winked conspiratorially. The small face broke at once into a grin. This was a game she recognised. Steve looked around. The garden was not large, and the only possibility of concealment seemed to be a tool shed at the end of it. He got to his feet and pointed to it, raising his eyebrows and again signalling silence with fingers to lips. The child nodded, her eyes alight with mischievous glee. It was a poor hiding place, the first place anyone would look, but he could see no alternative.

Once inside he discovered a knot hole in the door that gave him a limited view up the length of the garden. A moment later he heard voices and the sound of a door opening, and a gendarme appeared. Seeing the little girl, he at once dropped to his knees beside her and Steve heard him ask, 'Have you seen a man in here?'

She regarded him solemnly with a finger in her mouth. Then she shook her head.

He persisted. 'Did a man just jump over that wall?'

Steve held his breath. The child looked from the policeman to the wall and then back. She took her finger out of her mouth and he heard her giggle.

'Silly! Wall too high to jump over.'

The man straightened up and patted her on the head, then he turned and went back into the house and Steve heard him say something to whoever was inside. Then a voice called, and the little girl ran in. For long minutes Steve crouched in the shed, expecting to hear the gendarme returning, but the garden remained empty and silent. At last he heard boots on the cobbles, fading into the distance, and then engines starting and pulling away. It seemed the search was over.

He sat down on an upturned bucket and considered his next move. One thing was clear. He could not return to the garage. To go back would be to risk not only his own arrest but that of Yvette and her father. He felt a stab of anguish as the thought struck him that he would never see Yvette again, and there had been no chance to say goodbye. He pushed it to the back of his mind and forced himself to concentrate on what he might do next. His watch told him that it was only ten minutes before the curfew, so to go wandering about the streets would be asking for trouble. He decided reluctantly that his best solution would be to stay where he was until next morning. His stomach growled, and he had a sudden vivid memory of the rabbit and the vegetables in his bicycle basket. Who would benefit from them now? Undoubtedly someone would notice the abandoned bike and investigate. He hoped it might be the owner of the garden so that his young saviour might get some reward.

He heard the door of the house open again and put his eye to the knothole. A woman came down the garden path carrying a bucket and a pair of scissors. She bent down beside the shed and he heard her snipping away at something. The scent of thyme filtered into the shed, overpowering the pervading smell of old sacks and dust. Then a voice spoke close to the door.

'There is a door out into the alley. I shall leave it unlocked, but stay where you are till morning. I am going to put this bucket inside now.'

Steve moved back as far as the contents of the shed would let him. The door opened briefly, the bucket was deposited and the door closed again. There was something in the bucket, wrapped in a white napkin. He took it out and unwrapped a hunk of bread enclosing a slice of cheese. Underneath was a bottle of water. Breathing a blessing on the kindness of strangers he drank the water and ate the bread and cheese. Then he set to work to make himself as comfortable as possible for the night ahead. There was little he could do. Most of the space was taken up by a wheelbarrow. There was a rack of tools and a shelf of plant pots, and apart from that, there was only a small heap of old sacks. In the end, he used the sacks to line the wheelbarrow and settled himself as comfortably as possible inside it.

He managed to doze from time to time, but most of the night was spent wondering anxiously about what had happened to Yvette and her father. He was sure that Madeleine, if this was her doing – and he was certain it was – would have done nothing to incriminate them. She must have cooked up some story about people returning from the country with black market goods that would have instigated a search and the need to produce documents. How would the Lebruns have accounted for the absence of 'Carl'? Perhaps they might say he had returned to his family in Ghent… The thoughts circulated endlessly in his mind, but he knew there could be no resolution to them. He was glad when light coming through the grimy window told him that it was morning.

Stiff and aching from his cramped position he got to his feet and relieved himself into the bucket. He looked at his watch. The curfew would have been lifted by now, and people who worked shifts or had to start early for some other reason would be out in the streets. One positive thing had emerged from his cogitations overnight. He knew where he was going next. He opened the door cautiously. The garden was empty, and the blinds were still down in the windows of the house. The door in the wall was unlocked, as had been promised. He stepped through it and walked briskly down the alley. In the street he joined the early risers, knowing that the way he was dressed made him indistinguishable from any Belgian workman. A ten-minute walk brought him to his destination – Father Marcel's church.

As he expected, the church was open, and early Mass was in progress in the presence of a small congregation consisting largely of elderly women. Steve slipped into one of the rear pews and knelt down. The service was almost at an end, and when the worshippers filed out, he remained kneeling with his head devoutly bowed until he was fairly sure that everyone had departed. When he straightened up, he saw Father Marcel coming down the chancel steps. As soon as he stepped out into the aisle the priest saw him and came swiftly to grasp him by the shoulders.

'Carl! Praise God, you escaped! Yvette came to see me yesterday evening, and she told me what had happened, but we felt sure you must have been picked up.'

'It was a near thing,' Steve confessed, 'but I think my guardian angel was watching over me in the shape of a little girl.'

He told Marcel briefly about his encounter with the child and his night in the garden shed.

'Certainly God was watching over you last night,' he responded. 'Now, to be practical. You clearly cannot go back to the Lebruns. We shall have to make other arrangements. But first, you need breakfast, and perhaps a bath. Come.'

He led the way to the small house adjacent to the church where he lived with a housekeeper called Josette.

'This is Carl,' he informed her. 'He is our guest for a short while. Please see that he has a good breakfast and anything else he requires. I have to go out for an hour or two.'

Josette followed his instructions to the letter. She was a taciturn character who asked no questions and seemed not to require him to engage in conversation, for which he was grateful. Once he had eaten and bathed, he was shown to a bedroom and tried to sleep, but without success. It was a relief when he heard the priest's voice in the hallway below.

'Carl,' he said as Steve appeared on the stairs. 'I have some news for you. But first, someone is waiting for you in the church.'

Steve caught his breath. That could mean only one person.

Yvette was standing in front of the altar, a dark shawl over her head. When she saw Steve, she gave a small sob and ran into his outstretched arms. He held her tightly, and she whispered into his neck, 'I've been so afraid for you. I was sure you must have been captured.'

He drew her into one of the side pews, and they sat gripping each other's hands while he repeated again the story of his escape.

'Tell me something,' he added. 'Was Madeleine really ill?'

'She had been very sick – but I think she had swallowed something to make that happen,' Yvette told him. 'She soon got over it.'

'You know who was responsible for what happened, don't you?' he said.

She nodded and sniffed back a tear. 'You were right all along. I could tell from the way she reacted when the soldiers came that she was expecting it.'

'You mustn't tell her that I escaped.'

'No, of course not – though I wish I could. I'd like her to know that her evil scheme came to nothing. But what will you do now?'

'I'm not sure. I think Father Marcel has a plan of some sort. It means I shall have to go away. I don't want to say goodbye, but we must.'

'I know that.' She looked at him with eyes full of tears. 'But we always knew that this would happen one day. I just wish it hadn't come quite so soon.'

'So do I,' he said. 'I… I have loved being with you; and you and your father have been wonderful. I can never thank you properly.'

'We don't need thanks. You know how happy it has made me. Just promise me one thing. When this awful war is over, will you come back to see us? I don't mean to pick up where we… where we are now. Bring your wife – I'm sure you'll have a wife by then. Or do you think she will be jealous?'

'If I ever find a woman to marry, she won't be small-minded enough to be jealous of what you have done for me,' he said. There was a catch in his voice and he felt tears were not far away.

She hugged him and then drew back regretfully. 'I think you should go back to Father Marcel now. It is dangerous for you to hang around here. Someone might have seen you.'

He blinked back tears he could no longer repress. 'Yes, I should go back.'

They both rose and he took her in his arms and kissed her for the last time. 'I'm so glad I had a chance to say goodbye,' he murmured huskily. 'Take care of yourself, my darling.'

'And you!' she answered. 'Good luck, my dearest.'

He let he go, but as she turned away, he said, 'Will you go on doing… you know, what we were doing with the cars?'

Her smile flashed through her tears like sunshine through rain. 'Of course.'

'Be careful! Don't… don't overdo it.'

'I won't. Take care of yourself! I won't say *adieu*. *Au revoir*, my dear.' She turned away and walked swiftly to the door and did not look back.

Back in the house Marcel was waiting for him in his study.

'Thank you, father,' he said. 'It was distressing me that I wouldn't be able to say goodbye.'

'I understand,' the priest replied. 'But now we must think of the future. As I told you, I have been in contact for some time with people who are trying to find ways of helping men like you get back to your own country. As yet, our plans are still not finalised, but it is only a matter of weeks I feel sure. Meanwhile, we need somewhere safe for you to stay. I have spoken to the rector, and he thinks it will be best if you return to the seminary for the time being.'

'Back to the seminary!' Steve exclaimed. 'Is that really the only solution?'

Marcel smiled understandingly. 'I know that you found your stay there... well, frustrating. We are not all suited to the contemplative life. But I assure you that it will not be for long. Please be patient.'

Chapter Twenty-Two

Paris

August 1940

When Alix put Boris's idea of gathering intelligence by flirting with German soldiers to her group, it met with mixed reactions.

'Sure, why not?' Moira said. 'I'm happy to do anything to get back at these swine for what they did to my brother – and if it means they pay for my dinner into the bargain, so much the better.'

Hannah nodded. 'You can count on me.'

Suzanne needed more convincing, but once she was satisfied, Paulette followed her lead. In addition, she was able to offer another source of information.

'My sister is a nurse at the Hôtel-Dieu hospital. Sometimes German soldiers are sent there if they need specialist treatment. It would be easy for her to talk to them.'

Christine, however, shook her head. 'No, Alix! Please don't ask me to do that! I just couldn't. I couldn't pretend to be friendly with any of them. I hate them all. Just the thought of being near one makes me feel sick. I'm sorry. I don't want to let you down.'

Alix put her arm round her and murmured, 'It's all right, *cherie*. I won't ask you to do anything you feel so bad about. It's fine. You can be just as useful keeping your eyes open in the streets and making notes about uniforms and insignia.'

She had to admit to herself that she viewed the project with great misgivings, but in the event, it turned out to be less difficult than she expected. To begin with, they worked in twos or threes which gave them a sense of security, but as they gained confidence, they split up in order to cast their net as wide as possible. It was easy to catch the eye of one of the soldiers drinking at one of the pavement cafes, and it was surprising how much inform-ation could be gleaned in casual conversation, especially when it was lubricated with alcohol and encouraged with judicious amounts of flattery. After all, these men were not monsters, whatever their masters might be. Most of them were young, away from home perhaps for the first time in their lives, and had already faced dangers they had never expected to experience. Soon they might be facing the guns again, and all they wanted was an evening drinking and dancing with a pretty girl. Even the officers were happy to entertain beautiful young women like Alix or her friends, and for the most part, she had found their beha-viour correct to the point of punctiliousness. In spite of herself, there were times when she enjoyed their company and sometimes she felt guilty about accepting the meals and drinks they bought her.

There were drawbacks. She had to put up with the contemptuous looks from other women passing by as she walked arm-in-arm with one of the enemy. Once or twice she had seen someone turn away and spit. The trickiest moment was at the end of the evening. She was always escorted back to the college, and she understood very well that her companion hoped for something in return for his expenditure, even if it was only a kiss. That was a sacrifice she was not prepared to make, and she became practised in the art of a rapid exit.

A time came, however, when her plan misfired. As she turned away to pass through the college gateway, a hand grabbed her arm, and she was shoved back against the brick gate post.

'Oh no!' Her companion for the evening, a large man who wore the black tunic and breeches of the Panzer troops, was breathing heavily. 'I know what you're up to, you little whore! Chatting away, all friendly concern – so interested in everything I do. It's all a sham! You think I haven't seen through it? You think I'm stupid, eh?'

Pinned painfully against the post, Alix could only whimper. How had he guessed her purpose? Had she been so obvious? She struggled to think of some excuse, some explanation that would satisfy him but words escaped her.

'I know your type,' he went on, his breath hot on her face, smelling of the garlic sausage he had eaten, 'all you want is a nice evening out and a good meal, but you don't want to pay for it. Well, you don't get away with it with me. Now it's payback time!'

He shifted the grip of one hand and thrust it inside her dress, grabbing her breast. He pressed himself against her and she could feel his erection. Using his weight to hold her trapped against the gate post and covering her mouth with his own he shifted his other hand, and unbuttoned himself, and pulled up her skirt. Struggle as she might, she could not free herself. Desperately she sought some weapon with which to fight him off and just in time, inspiration came to her. She had taken off her high-heeled shoes on the walk back because her feet were hurting and she was carrying them in her right hand. As he panted and tried to thrust himself inside her she dropped one and gripped the other tightly round its middle, then drew it back and rammed the heel as hard as she could between his buttocks. He jerked back with a yelp and an oath, and she tore herself free.

'You'll pay for this, you little whore,' he gasped. 'Striking a German officer. You'll face a firing squad.'

She turned to look back. He was doubled up, clutching himself, unable to pursue her. She bent to pick up her shoes.

'You're going to bring a charge against me, are you?' she taunted him. 'Going to show your war wound? That'll give your mates a good laugh!'

She left him cursing and went quickly inside. Once she reached her room her bravado deserted her, and she collapsed on her bed, shaking and sobbing. It was a long time before she was calm enough to get undressed and try to sleep.

Next day she went to make a routine report to Boris Vildé. She considered telling him what had happened the previous evening, but decided against it. He was pleased with the information she was able to pass on to him. The other girls had also done their job well, and it enabled him to piece together a fairly comprehensive picture of which units were located where and how long they expected to remain there. At first, some of the men had told them they were only allowed forty-eight hours' leave as they expected the invasion of Britain to be launched any day. As the weeks passed this sense of urgency evaporated and was replaced with impatience as the invasion was delayed. How useful all this was to the authorities in Britain, or exactly how it was relayed to them, Alix did not know. Every evening, before she set out on her regular trawl of the cafes, she and Marie Louise, Boris and Paul Rivet huddled round the wireless set that Boris kept hidden in the vaults of the museum, hoping to pick up a news bulletin from Radio Londres, the BBC station that opened every programme with its slogan, "*Ici Londres! Les Français parlent aux Français…*" It was strictly forbidden for anyone to listen to the broadcasts, but very few people were deterred by that.

That evening the bulletin relayed news that brought gasps and profanities from the listeners. The Germans had switched from bombing airfields to bombing London and other major cities, including Liverpool. The newsreader described scenes of devastation. The docks were on fire and whole streets of houses were reduced to rubble.

'*Merde!*' Boris exclaimed. '*Cochons!* Bombing civilians! That is unforgivable.'

'It makes me ashamed,' Marie Louise said. 'To think what they are enduring. And we declared Paris an open city and let them walk in because we didn't want them to damage our beautiful monuments.'

A sob silenced their exclamations. Alix was struggling to hold back tears.

Marie Louise put her arm around the shaking shoulders. 'I'm sorry, *ma chère*, of course, it's much worse for you. I keep forgetting that you are half-English. You must know London well.'

'It's not that,' Alix choked out. 'My mother's there! At least, I think she is. I haven't heard from her for such a long time, and I don't know where she is now. But she was living in London.'

'Oh, my dear!' Marie Louise murmured. 'No wonder you are upset. But they have shelters. It said so on the wireless. She will probably be safe enough.'

'But it's my fault!' Alix wept. 'She left my father in Belgrade to bring me here, and then she went to England because she knew he would be angry with her. If I'd stayed at home, as he wanted, she would still be safe there. So… if she is killed it will all be my fault!'

She hid her face in her hands and sobbed inconsolably, and Marie Louise could only hold her and murmur, '*Pauvre petite! Pauvre petite!*'

'I'm sorry! I'm sorry,' Alix repeated when she was able to speak. 'It's just that this has come on top of something else. I'm feeling a bit… fragile.'

'What else has happened?' Boris asked.

Shakily, she told them about her encounter with the Panzer officer the previous night.

'*Mon Dieu!*' Marie Louise exclaimed. 'How could we put you in such a terrible situation?'

Boris said, 'This will have to stop. It was a mistake and I apologise. Don't go out this evening – and tell the others not to.'

Alix drew a long, shuddering breath, sniffed and rubbed her hands across her face. 'No, I'll be all right. I'd rather be doing something.'

Marie Louise tried to persuade her to stay with them, but she washed her face, applied the few remnants of make-up she had left and set off. Her mind was still full of images of burning buildings, and she felt more strongly than ever that she should be doing something more to damage the enemy, if only a chance presented itself. As she walked, she saw a German staff car parked outside one of the hotels. Tonight, in her bag she carried a penknife. In peacetime it had served to sharpen her pencils, which was how she would explain it if she was searched, but earlier that day she had persuaded one of the technicians who worked on the restoration of artefacts at the museum to put a razor-like edge on it. It gave her a little comfort to think that now she had some means of defending herself if there was a repetition of what happened the previous evening. She paused beside the car. On a wall opposite was a poster, one of many that had appeared around the city in recent days. It was signed by General Otto von Stülpnagel, the military commander of the city, and proclaimed that in future anyone carrying out sabotage would be shot. Alix looked at it. Then she dropped her bag on the pavement, knelt and drove the blade of the knife into the sidewall of one of the tyres. It deflated with a satisfying hiss. Alix straightened up and walked on.

Chapter Twenty-Three

Yugoslavia

August 1940

Leo walked down the gangplank in Dubrovnik harbour and experienced a sense of homecoming. She and Sasha had spent some enjoyable holidays here over the years, but she wondered if circumstances would ever allow them such uncomplicated pleasures again. As she paused, looking around, a young man in the uniform of the Royal Navy Volunteer Reserve stepped forward to meet her.

'Lady Malkovic?'

'Yes.'

'My name is Glen, Alexander. Most people call me Sandy. I've been asked to meet you and escort you back to Belgrade.'

Leo's stomach contracted in a spasm of fear. Why was this man here and not Sasha?

'Asked? By whom?'

'By our lords and masters back in London, actually.'

'How did you know I was coming?'

'Oh, we have our channels of communication. Is this all your luggage?'

'Yes… yes. Does my husband know I'm coming back? I wrote, but I haven't had a reply.'

'I'm afraid the postal services are rather unreliable at the moment. But yes. I called on him yesterday to tell him. He's waiting for you.'

That was some comfort. At least Sasha was all right. But he had not come himself and that was a bad sign.

Glen picked up her two suitcases. 'My goodness, this one's heavy! What are you carrying, gold bars?' Then he caught her eyes and his expression changed. 'Shall we go? I've booked seats on the flight leaving in forty minutes.'

As they boarded the Aeroput de Havilland monoplane, Glen kept up an innocuous chatter, asking about her journey, enquiring how she had found things in England, and passing on small items of local gossip. She replied automatically, still trying to collect her thoughts.

The last month had passed in a blur of mingled anticipation and frustration. In a small, airless room in the basement of 64 Baker Street, she had spent hours with a gloomy-faced young man being drilled in the use of a Morse code transmitter and receiver. Throughout that time she had been wondering how, if she ever completed the course, she was supposed to get back to Belgrade.

A day came at last when she was told to present herself at Northolt aerodrome. Colin Gubbins was waiting for her there.

'So, you're off at last. Sorry it's been such a long wait, but there's a lot of competition for transport these days. Anyway, everything is arranged now, so I've just come to wish you luck.'

They shook hands, and she climbed into the little Lysander plane that was waiting on the tarmac. At Southampton she was transferred to a flying boat. They stopped off at Malta to refuel and then flew on to Cairo. Here she had to wait again, but eventually, she had been put aboard what appeared to be a small freighter, which, she discovered, was crewed by Navy personnel in civilian clothes. 'We call them Q-ships,' the captain explained. 'Basically, we're bait for Hun submarines, but if they surface, they'll get more than they bargained for.' She was tempted to enquire further but guessed that her curiosity would not be welcome.

Now, here she was, being escorted to Belgrade by this young man whose function she did not understand. His reference to 'lords and masters' in London suggested that he had at least more than one string to his bow.

'Forgive me,' she said. 'What, exactly, is your position in Belgrade?'

'I'm naval attaché to the Yugoslav army command. I'm sorry, I should have introduced myself properly.'

'I see. And how do you know my husband?'

'Oh, we've met socially.'

'How is he? Is he well?'

'Yes, as far as I know, he's fine.'

It was a short flight, but the ship had not docked till mid-afternoon, so it was late by the time they reached Belgrade. Glen drove her straight to the substantial house in Knez Mihailova Street which had been the city home for the Malkovic family for several generations. As he handed her out of the car, Glen said, 'I won't come in. You've had a long day, and you'll be wanting some quiet time with your husband.'

She thanked him for fetching her and wished him goodnight, trying to conceal the fact that her legs were trembling in anticipation of the meeting ahead of her. The front door was opened by Ivo, the butler, who welcomed her gravely and took her cases, then tactfully disappeared.

Sasha was standing in the middle of the high-ceiling hall with its elegantly curving staircase. She saw at once that he had lost weight. His face was thinner and sharper, making his large, dark eyes beneath his arched brows seem more imperious than ever; there was more grey in his hair, and she found herself noticing, almost as if she had forgotten about it during their separation, the empty cuff of his left sleeve where his hand should be.

He said, 'So you've come home. You must be tired. There's a room ready for you upstairs.' His voice was level, unemotional.

She had imagined this moment so often in the last weeks. Sometimes she had seen herself rushing to him, throwing herself at his feet to sob out her apology; sometimes she had seen him opening his arms, with tears of welcome running down his cheeks; sometimes she had heard his voice angrily upbraiding her. Nothing had prepared her for this cold formality and for a moment it left her speechless.

She found her voice. 'No, I don't want to go up until we've talked.'

'Very well.'

Her knees were shaking more than ever, and she suddenly felt as if she might collapse where she stood. 'Sasha, please can we sit down?'

He moved to the door of the drawing room and held it open for her. She walked in and was suddenly overcome by another memory. This was the room in which she had been welcomed, nearly thirty years ago, by Sasha's mother and sister, who had then thoughtfully withdrawn. She was nineteen years old, and she had been sure that Sasha was about to propose to her, but instead he had told her, in broken tones, that they could never marry, that he was already betrothed to the daughter of a rival family and to break the engagement would be to reignite a feud that might destroy them all. She had thought then that every possible chance of happiness had been torn away from her. She put her hand to her throat, feeling the locket she always wore there, a locket he had given her that day containing a lock of his hair, and which now held three interwoven strands, black and auburn and red-gold. She swayed on her feet and felt his hand grip her elbow.

'What's wrong? Are you ill?'

'No. No, I was just… remembering.'

'Ah.' His hand dropped away. 'We have forded a lot of rivers since that day.'

Sensing a softening in his mood, she sank into a chair. 'We certainly have.' He sat opposite her, and she went on, 'Sasha, I am so, so sorry that things have come to this between us.'

His eyes were accusatory. 'It was your doing.'

'I know. And I can't regret what I did, only the effect it has had on us.'

'You took our daughter and placed her where she is now in imminent danger.'

'How could I know that would happen? Back then it still seemed that war could be avoided. And who could have foretold that France would collapse as it did? They told us the Maginot Line was impregnable. When the war started, I begged her to come home, but she refused. She wanted to stand by her friends. She thought it would be cowardly to run away.'

'Huh,' he grunted. 'That shows that the Malkovic blood still runs in her veins, at least.'

'Yes,' she pressed on. 'But truly, I don't believe she is in real danger now. Since Paris was declared an open city there hasn't been any bombing, and the fighting has passed them by. She is probably safer there, certainly safer than she would be in England.'

'She would be safer here,' he said.

'Do you really think so? Do you really imagine that we can stay out of this war?'

'That is beside the point. You took her away against my wishes and by a deception. That was a betrayal of trust.'

Leo hung her head. 'I know it seems that way to you. But I would have betrayed her if I had done nothing and let her be pressured into a marriage she did not want.'

'You do not understand! You have never understood how things are here. Family is all. Loyalty to the family and its interests is vital. We needed that alliance.'

'And you would have committed your daughter to a life of misery to achieve it?'

'Don't exaggerate. The boy was good-looking, well brought up. He could offer her a good position in society, a good life. She would have come to care for him in the end.'

'Would she?' Leo looked at him. 'Nearly thirty years ago you stood in this very room and told me we could not marry because you were committed to a marriage you did not want. Did you ever come to care for Anastasia? Did that marriage fulfil your needs?'

'You know it did not. Anastasia was a sick woman – and besides, I was already in love with you.'

'And you would deprive our daughter of the chance to marry a man of her own choosing, a man she loved, as you loved me?'

He looked startled. 'Are you telling me she's in love with someone else?'

'No, not as far as I know. But it will happen one day. Would you take that chance away from her?'

He was silent for a long moment and for the first time she saw the deep sadness in his eyes. Then he changed tack. 'So how does it happen that you have returned like this... your journey arranged by some mysterious agency in England, your arrival communicated to Alexander Glen rather than to me. Have you been sent to spy on us?'

'No!' She sat forward in her chair, spreading her hands towards him. 'Sasha, I would never agree to do that. I have been approached by a British Brigadier who belongs to some secret organisation, but I am here quite openly. I have nothing to hide from you.'

'Then what does this Brigadier want from you?'

'The British government is desperately worried that Paul is going to sign the Tripartite Pact with Germany and give Hitler access to a direct route to the Mediterranean.'

'That's no secret.'

'I know, but they just want to understand the situation here better.'

'They have their agents here already who can tell them all there is to tell. My guess is Glen is one of them.'

'I think you're right. The point is, I... *we* can offer them something none of their agents can – direct access to the thinking of the people around Prince Peter. And perhaps the chance to influence them. You know Yugoslavia will never be allowed to remain neutral. We are surrounded by enemies – Austria, Hungary, Bulgaria, now Italy... Surely we need to cast in our lot with Britain. If we could push the men in the regency council in that direction, I think help would be forthcoming from Britain to support them.' She sought his gaze and held it. 'Sasha, I will do nothing without your full knowledge and assent.

But think about it! Working together, we may be able to influence the fate of our country – influence it for the better. What do you say?'

He stared back at her, and she could see him struggling to reconcile his hurt pride with his passionate love for his country – and, more importantly, for her. At length, he said, with weary sadness, 'So that is why you are here?'

'No. That is how I am able to be here.' She leaned towards him and took his hands. 'My darling, for months now I have regretted the impulse that prompted me to commit myself to stay in England and rejoining the FANY. At the time I thought it was the right thing, that I owed it to my homeland to defend it. But since then I have realised that I have a far greater duty. My duty to you, and to the country I have fought for in the past and lived in since. But I could see no way to get back here. When the Brigadier asked me to work for him, he promised that he could get me home. That was why I agreed. I have longed and longed to be here. To see you, and ask you to forgive me. I know I hurt you deeply and all I ask is a chance to make up for it, to put things right between us. Please, Sasha. Will you give me the chance to do that?'

She left her chair and went to kneel beside him. Tears were on her cheeks, and suddenly she saw that there were tears in his eyes, also. For a moment he resisted, then he pulled her to him and they clung together, both weeping. At length, he gasped out, 'Oh, my dear girl! I have been so alone, so bereft, without you. Thank God you have come back to me!'

He held her close until their sobs had subsided. Then he drew back and pushed the damp hair off her forehead. 'Enough for tonight. We can talk more in the morning. Is there anything you need before we go to bed?'

'No, no thank you. I have everything I could possibly want.'

'I meant food, drink…'

'I know. There's nothing.'

He got up and drew her to her feet. 'Let's go up, then.'

She hesitated. 'You said something about a room being ready for me…'

He smiled at her, suddenly twenty years younger. 'Oh, forget about that. You know the way to our room – or do you need me to show you?'

Before she could respond, he picked her up and carried her up the stairs.

—

Next morning, over a late breakfast, he brought her up to date with the political situation.

'Paul is in a terrible state. You know he has always been prone to wild swings of mood but now he seems to be in the grip of complete despair. I can understand why. The pro-Axis lobby don't give him a minute's peace.' He put down his coffee cup and leaned towards her. 'If only the British government could give us some evidence of their support. We desperately need basic supplies for the army. Simple things like tyres, and aviation fuel. I know Ronald Campbell, the Minister, has repeatedly put in requests, but nothing has been forthcoming.'

Leo sighed. 'I can see why that makes Paul feel abandoned, but the situation in Britain is so dire at the moment I'm not surprised.'

'The British have even threatened a boycott of trade, in case some of the supplies are siphoned off by the Germans.'

'What a mess! I've been told that the government is very keen to bring Yugoslavia into the war on our side, but it sounds as if the various ministries can't agree among themselves about how to do it.'

'You say you've been told.'

'I was briefed before I left England.'

'By whom? By this Brigadier you mentioned?'

'Brigadier Gubbins, yes.'

'How did you come to meet him?'

'Ah, now that's an interesting story.' She told him about the Brigadier's visit to Bramhall and the plans to create a secret hideout in the cellars.

'My God!' he said when she had finished. 'So it's that bad? They really think the country could be overrun?'

'He told me that they think Hitler is only waiting for the Luftwaffe to put the RAF out of action before he mounts an invasion.'

'And is that likely?'

'I don't know. Only that there is a terrific battle going on in the skies between the German fighters and ours.' A sudden thought struck her. 'Oh, Sasha. Can you pick up the BBC still? I'd really like to find out how things are going.'

'We can try,' he said, 'but reception is terrible. There are only three possible wavelengths, and the Nazis are jamming two of them.'

After several frustrating attempts, Sasha succeeded in tuning in to the BBC in time to catch a news bulletin. Listening through the hiss of static they heard that the German Air Force had mounted another bomb attack on airfields in the south of England, but every time the runways were put out of action they were repaired overnight. Meanwhile, the British pilots continued to fight off the enemy planes, inflicting many losses. The broadcast ended by quoting Winston Churchill's speech in Parliament: '*Never in the field of human conflict was so much owed by so many to so few.*'

Sasha switched off the set and Leo found herself wiping tears from her cheeks. He put his arm round her.

'I didn't realise it was so desperate. It makes our problems here seem rather insignificant.'

'No, that's not true,' she said, 'but we must do everything we can to make sure Yugoslavia doesn't have to face the same terrible threat.' She thought for a moment. 'How is Prince Peter?'

'He's well enough, physically. But like all of us he is worried that his uncle will commit us to an alliance with the Nazis.'

'If Paul is the problem, is there any chance of... well, I don't know... side-lining him and putting Peter in his place?'

He looked at her for a moment, a sharp, assessing gaze. 'You are talking about a palace coup.'

'I suppose I am. Is it a possibility?'

'It's been... spoken of, in certain circles. General Simovic floated the idea a month or two back but it never came to anything.' He paused. 'Do you have any means of contacting this Brigadier Gubbins?'

She smiled. 'What do you think was in that very heavy case I brought with me?'

Chapter Twenty-Four

Paris

October 5th 1940

One morning, Alix set out for the museum as usual. She had long ago given up going to lectures or writing essays. It was raining hard and the weather had turned unseasonably cold, so she was glad to get inside. She entered as usual through the door used by the staff and made her way through the galleries, heading for Marie Louise's office. The museum had been allowed to remain open, though they had very few visitors. Occasionally one or two of the occupying soldiers would come in and wander round the exhibits. They did not usually stay long.

As she walked through one of the galleries Alix was puzzled by a strange vibration that seemed to come from one of the display cases. There was no one else visible, so she went over to investigate. Crouched behind the case, she saw a young man in RAF blue. He was soaked to the skin and shivering so violently that the movement was causing the whole case to rattle.

Alix bent down and said in English, 'Don't be afraid. I won't give you away. You are English, yes?'

He shook his head. '*Polski.*'

She had read that a number of Polish airmen had escaped with their planes during the invasion and gone to England, where they now formed a separate unit in the RAF.

Alix stretched out her hand. 'Come with me. You need help.'

He hesitated briefly, then got to his feet, but he seemed unsteady, and she had to take him by the arm to support him. His hand was icy and his face was almost without colour. With difficulty she got him to the end of the gallery and up the stairs to Marie Louise's office.

'Look what I've found.'

Marie Louise looked up from her desk and caught her breath. '*Mon Dieu!* He looks half-dead. Sit him down here.'

'He's a Polish airman,' Alix said. There was no need to explain further.

'He needs a hot drink. You put the kettle on and I'll call Boris.' She picked up the house telephone and dialled a number.

Alix made a mug of what passed for coffee. It was a disgusting concoction, but at least it was hot.

'Give him some of my sugar,' Marie Louise instructed, and Alix added a generous spoonful, knowing that she and her friend would have to take their drinks unsweetened until the next week when they could use their new ration coupons.

The warm drink brought a touch of colour back to the pale face. Alix said, 'You're soaked. Let me take your jacket.' She helped him out of it and hung it on the back of a chair. 'Did you crash, or did you have to bail out?'

'Bail out – four, no five days ago. Shot down, north of here. Walked. Walked a long way.'

'What is he saying?' Marie Louise asked.

203

Alix translated for her benefit. 'Do you speak French?' she asked him. He shook his head.

Boris arrived, carrying a blanket. Alix repeated what the airman had told her.

'We need to get him out of those wet clothes,' Boris said. 'If you ladies wouldn't mind waiting outside for a few minutes…'

When they were allowed to return, the airman was wrapped in the blanket, and his wet clothes were in a heap on the floor. He was eating half a baguette filled with salami, which Alix guessed was Boris's lunch.

'What are we going to do with him?' Marie Louise asked.

'He needs a bed and some hot food.' Boris said. 'I'd take him back to my place, but I can't guarantee that one of the children won't say something to give the game away – not deliberately, of course, but they're too young to understand.'

'Of course they are,' Marie Louise said. 'You mustn't dream of putting them in that situation. He can come to my flat.'

'Are you sure? It's a risk for you, too.'

'Never mind that. The only problem is getting him there. He doesn't look as if he's capable of walking that far.'

'I still have a little petrol in my car,' Boris said. 'I'll drive you. But we'll have to find him something else to wear, in case we are stopped.'

Alix thought quickly. 'There's a boy, Benoit. He lives in the college, and we've talked a few times. I think he can be trusted. I'm sure he would lend some clothes.'

'If you're convinced he's reliable…'

'Yes. I'm certain of that. I'll go now. It shouldn't take long.'

Half an hour later she was back with some underwear, a pair of grey flannels, a shirt and a sweater. 'Benoit says he can keep these if they fit.'

The young airman had stopped shivering and was looking better. His name, he told them, was Dominik. The clothes fitted quite well, except that the trousers were slightly too long, and with the addition of Boris's overcoat, he looked respectable enough not to cause suspicion. They got him into Boris's little Citroën and soon had him tucked up in Marie Louise's spare bed. She warmed up some soup for him and as soon as he had drunk it he fell into a deep sleep.

'What are we going to do with him?' Alix asked.

'I think I know someone who can help with that,' Boris returned. 'We'll discuss it tomorrow. Meanwhile, you two had better stay here with him.'

–

Unwilling to leave Marie Louise alone with their Polish airman, Alix offered to stay the night. Next morning they left Dominik in the flat, with strict instructions to stay away from the windows and not to answer the door to anyone, and set off back to the museum. In Boris's room, they found a stranger, an attractive young woman with dark, curly hair.

Boris introduced her as Germaine Tillon. 'She's a fellow anthropologist, just back from North Africa where she had been studying the Berbers. She's very keen to join us, and she has brought us some useful connections – particularly in view of our new guest. How is he, by the way?'

'Much recovered,' Marie Louise told him. 'But he's asking if we can help him get back to England.'

'That's where Germaine comes in,' Boris told them.

'I was devastated when I got back from Africa, just in time to hear about the surrender and the armistice,' Germaine said. 'I was actually physically sick when I heard the news. I've been in the south, in the unoccupied zone, for a while, and I met a really interesting man called Paul Hauet. He's a retired brigadier who works with the UNCC, the national union for retired colonial soldiers. He has built up a network of people prepared to help men who have fallen on hard times, and he says the same people are willing to help escaping prisoners of war – or downed airmen in your case. But, as I say, he is operating south of the demarcation line. We should need to get your man across into the so-called "free" zone first.'

'I've been thinking about that,' Marie Louise said. 'My parents live outside Tours, just this side of the line, but my father is a doctor and I know he has patients on both sides. And the hospital he is associated with is in the unoccupied zone. My mother has told me that he can go backwards and forwards quite freely. I think they would take Dominik in and get him over the line.'

'Are you sure about this?' Boris asked. 'You would be asking them to take a great risk.'

'I know,' she replied, 'but they feel as bad about Pétain and the armistice as we all do. I'm sure they will want to help.'

'Then let us think of the best way to go about this,' Boris said.

'The first thing he will need is papers,' Germaine said. 'Identity card, ration voucher, tobacco voucher, a travel permit…'

'We have been working on that,' Boris told her. 'Agnès, one of our colleagues, has shown quite a talent for forgery. We should be able to provide him with all he needs in that area.'

'There's a problem,' Alix put in. 'He doesn't speak or understand French. If he was challenged he would give himself away immediately.'

'Then you must go with him,' Boris said. 'I'm sorry to ask you, but you are the only person who can communicate with him. None of us speaks Polish, and English is the only other language he understands.'

Alix felt a shiver run through her nerves, though whether of excitement or fear she could not determine. 'Yes, of course. I can do that.'

'It doesn't solve the problem that he can't answer if anyone asks him something,' Marie Louise pointed out.

'I have an idea,' Germaine said. 'His face could be bandaged. Suppose he was one of our soldiers, wounded perhaps in the early fighting. If he had a head wound, a really serious one, it might have deprived him of the ability to speak.'

'So where has he been since then?' Boris asked. 'There has been no fighting since the spring.'

'In a hospital somewhere north of here. We would need to forge a discharge note. But as one of our own wounded, he would attract a lot of sympathy.'

'This could work out well,' Marie Louise exclaimed. 'If he's recovering from serious wounds it would look reasonable for him to be in the care of my father. Perhaps he is being taken home, somewhere on the other side of the line.'

'And I could be a nurse, looking after him on the journey,' Alix said. The churning in her gut was definitely excitement now.

'Can we borrow a nurse's uniform somewhere?'

'Yes, and I know where. One of my group has a sister who is a nurse. I'm sure she could find me something suitable.'

'Right,' Boris said. 'Marie Louise, I think you need a few days off, to go home to your family. There shouldn't be any difficulty getting a travel permit for that. I'll speak to Agnès and make arrangements there. He will need to have his photograph taken. Alix, you had better stay with our friend and keep him calm. When Agnès is ready for him, I'll let you know.'

For Alix, the following day was an uncomfortable mixture of boredom and nervous anticipation. Confined to Marie Louise's flat, it was hard to keep Dominik occupied. Then she remembered that Hannah was Polish and left Dominik alone long enough to find her and bring her back to the flat. It was a tearful meeting, both bewailing the fate of their country under the Nazis, but soon they were deep in conversation, glad to speak their own language. Alix took the chance to slip out again to meet with Paulette, whose sister worked as a nurse, and ask for her help. That evening she returned to the college to find Paulette and her sister Jeanne waiting for her.

'I've brought you as much as I could get hold of,' Jeanne said. 'I'm afraid the laundry is going to be short of a collar and cuffs, and I managed to borrow a cap. The cape is mine, so I'd like it back before the weather gets any colder. Do you have a suitable dress?'

'I have something that would do,' Paulette offered. 'It's dark blue, and we're about the same size.'

'Did you manage to get me a bandage?' Alix asked.

'Oh yes, here. I pinched it from the store. I hope no one will notice it's missing.'

Alix thanked them both and carried her disguise back to the flat. While she was in the kitchen preparing a meal, Hannah came in and closed the door behind her. Looking at her face, Alix could tell that something was wrong.

'What is it, Hannah?' she asked. 'Is it something Dominik has said?'

'We've been talking about what is going on in Poland. There are rumours of terrible things happening to the Jewish community.'

'What sort of things?'

'Synagogues have been blown up and all Jews have been forced to register and have the word "*Jude*" stamped on their identity documents.'

Alix gave her a hug. 'That's terrible, as you say. But surely it can't happen here.'

'Can't it?' Hannah said dismally. 'You haven't seen today's paper. The governor has published an "ordinance of Aryanisation". All Jewish-owned businesses are to be transferred to non-Jewish ownership and Jews are forbidden to practise in any of the professions, like law or medicine. It's starting, Alix. Where will it end?'

'But you're safe enough, aren't you?' Alix asked. 'The ordinance hasn't mentioned students?'

'Not so far.'

Alix hugged her again. 'Try not to worry. I'm sure it will be all right. We'll look after you.'

Chapter Twenty-Five

Brussels

October 4th 1940

'Stefan, I have a possible course of action I should like you to consider.'

Steve sat forward eagerly. It was not the first conversation he had had with the rector since his return to the seminary, but this sounded more hopeful than any of the previous ones.

The rector went on. 'I must emphasise that what I am suggesting will be risky… But I can say with a good deal of certainty that we can get you into France, and hopefully as far as the demarcation line between the occupied sector and the so-called free sector. After that it will be up to you.'

'Then I'll take that chance,' Steve said. 'How do I get that far?'

'The men who work the railways are cooperating with us. The *cheminots* hate the Nazis as much as we do and will do what they can to help. I have contacted one of them, and he is prepared to take you as far as Lille, and he thinks that there he will be able to hand you on to a colleague who will take you further.' He sat back and spread his hands. 'It's a very sketchy plan, I'm afraid, but it's the best I can offer.'

'It sounds excellent!' Steve exclaimed. 'And I am enormously grateful. When do I start?'

'Tonight. At six o'clock you must go to the main station. Go to the news stand and buy a copy of *De Film*. A man will approach you and say, "Are you a fan of Rita Hayworth?" and you must reply, "No, I prefer Bette Davis." He will then show you where you should go.'

Later that day, as the streets began to be busy with men and women going home after work, Steve said goodbye to the rector and made his way to the station. He bought the magazine and stood, pretending to read and trying to quell the sensation of a loosening of his bowels. Then he heard the prescribed question and looked up to find a man in the uniform of a railway guard. He gave the answer, and the man grinned cheerfully, apparently quite at ease.

'Shall we go, then?'

He led Steve across the tracks to where a train stood in a siding and slid open the door of the guard's van.

'Hop in here. No one is likely to bother you, but just to be on the safe side, I'll slide the bolt. The train leaves in half an hour.'

Once again Steve found himself with nothing to do but wait, but then he remembered the magazine in his hand. He was trying to interest himself in the latest films when there was a jolt and the sound of couplings rattling, and the train began to move. It travelled a short distance and then reversed, and he realised it was being shunted into the platform. Very soon he heard voices and feet passing by as the passengers boarded. He understood why he had been secreted here so much in advance. The men and women boarding the train now would have had to show their papers at the barrier.

Steve tensed as the door rattled, but it was the guard again. He climbed aboard and remarked cheerily, 'Off we go! All stations to Lille.' He leaned out and waved his flag, there was an answering whistle from the engine and the train chugged into motion.

The guard was apparently happy to have someone to talk to, though he tactfully avoided any questions about Steve's identity or his recent history. Instead, they spoke generally about the war.

'The Brits are still holding out, thank God,' the guard said. 'But it can't be for much longer. They're taking a real pasting from the Luftwaffe.'

'The RAF will see them off,' Steve said, though without much conviction.

'What I don't understand is how the Yanks can stand by and watch it happening and do nothing. Seems like they're happy to let Hitler take over the whole of Europe as long as they can cover their own arses.'

That struck home with uncomfortable force. Steve felt shamed by his own country's lack of response.

They continued to chat for a while, but the steady rhythm of the wheels was soporific, and Steve found his eyelids drooping.

He came to with a start as the train jolted to a stop, and there was a noise of doors banging open and loud voices. The guard slid the door of the van back and peered out.

'Christ! The Boches are checking everyone's papers. What the hell made them decide to do that on this trip of all trips? Normally we have no trouble crossing the border. It's all part of the same *zone militaire*.'

'Where are we?' Steve asked.

'Lille – but they've stopped us outside the station. They're making everyone get out.' The guard was still watching what was happening outside. Abruptly he drew back. He crossed to the far side of the van and slid open the opposite door. 'Sorry, mate. You're going to have to bail out, or we're both for the high jump.'

Steve moved to the door and peered out. Night had fallen. With blackout restrictions in force, the whole area was shrouded in darkness, but by the light of a quarter moon he made out a second rail track running parallel to their own and on the far side of that a high wall.

'Jump!' the guard's tone was panicky. 'They're almost here.'

Steve glanced back over his shoulder. 'Thanks, chum. Good luck.' Then he turned and gripped the edge of the doorway ready to jump down. He was about to launch himself into mid-air when he heard the rails beneath him singing with the vibration of an approaching train, and an engine appeared out of the darkness heading straight for him.

Clinging to the doorway, he watched it pass. It was going very slowly and behind it was a line of goods trucks. Most of them were covered with tarpaulin, but as they rolled past, he made out one where the cover had come loose and flapped back. Behind him he heard the guard protesting to one of the Germans and the rough response '*Raus!*' Steve poised himself, drew a breath and jumped.

–

Steve opened his eyes and groaned. He was bruised all over from the impact of his leap into the goods truck, and he had lain all night on the coal it was carrying. All through the hours of darkness the train had rattled and clanked slowly on its journey. There had been times when it came to a standstill and others when it was shunted backwards into a siding and he heard another train steam pass. He tried to make out from the stars which way they were heading, but the sky was overcast, and he gave up in the end and let his eyes close. He had dozed on and off and finally fallen into a deeper sleep, from which he had woken to realise that they were no longer moving, and he could hear men's voices calling to one another. It was light, and his watch told him it was 6.30 a.m. He raised his head cautiously and peered over the edge of the truck. He was in a large marshalling yard, and railway workers were moving around, calling morning greetings and exchanging jokes. He had grown used to hearing Belgian accents, but this sounded more like the French he was used to hearing in Paris. He looked around, but there was nothing to tell him where he was.

He remembered that the rector had told him that the *cheminots* were solidly anti-Nazi and willing to do anything they could to help escapers. He had to hope that this applied here as it had in Brussels. He climbed stiffly out of the truck and lowered himself to the ground. There were buildings of some sort a short way off, and as he headed towards them, a man came across the tracks and barred his way.

'*Merde alors!* You look as though you've had a rough night.' The speaker was grinning, and Steve sensed that he had nothing to fear.

'Yes, I have,' he agreed. 'Where am I?'

'You don't know? You're in Paris, *mon ami.*'

Paris! Then somehow in the course of the night, the goods train had carried him across the border. Steve felt a surge of hope. Perhaps he could stay here, slip back into his old life as if he had never been away. Perhaps he could see Alix again. But even as the thought occurred to him, he knew it was impossible. He was still unable to prove his identity or his nationalit, and as far as the Gestapo were concerned, he was still an escaped POW. Besides, what of his recent determination to get back to England and carry on the fight?

His new companion was speaking. 'You look as if you could do with a hot drink and a bit of a wash. Come on. I'll show you where to go.' Then, seeing Steve hesitate, he added, 'You needn't worry. We're all friends here. My name's Gaston, by the way.'

For an instant, Steve hesitated. Then he said, 'Carl,' and offered his hand.

Gaston took it with a lift of his eyebrows that conveyed both the fact that he knew this was a pseudonym and understood the reason for it. He led Steve along the track to a building which revealed itself to be a workers' canteen. A number of men were sitting at tables, eating breakfast before starting work. After the early morning chill, the air struck Steve with a welcome blast of heat and humidity. Gaston directed him to a table and went to a counter on one side of the room, then returned with two steaming mugs and two pieces of a baguette. Before sitting down, he beckoned to a young man heading for the door.

'Jacques, run back to my place and get my sister, will you? Tell her I have a parcel to deliver. She will know what I mean.'

'OK, boss,' the boy said, and left.

'You are the foreman, I guess,' Steve said, and Gaston nodded.

'POW?' he asked.

'Yes.'

'Left behind at Dunkirk?'

'No. I'm an airman,' Steve responded.

'Ah. Bravo, the RAF! You crashed?'

'Shot down. Some time ago now.'

The boy was back very quickly, bringing with him a girl of around twenty, wearing the sort of overalls common to shop assistants.

'What is it, Gaston? I'll be late for work if I don't hurry.'

'Annette, this is Carl. He needs somewhere to stay for a day or two. Show him the way back to the apartment and ask Maman to look after him.'

The girl looked at Steve for the first time, and he saw that she understood the situation. 'Very good. Come with me, please.'

Gaston smiled at him. 'Go with Annette. I'll see you this evening.'

Steve did as he said. In a way he could not quite explain, he knew he could trust these people.

At a flat near the station, they were greeted by a small, round-faced woman who seemed surprised but not put out by Steve's sudden appearance.

'Maman, this is Carl,' Annette said. 'I must fly. See you later, Carl.'

The little woman looked him up and down. '*Merde alors!* Where have you come from? Down the chimney? Here, take this, and I'll show you where you can wash.'

She handed him a towel and a kettle of warm water and showed him into the bathroom. He stripped and washed himself and was looking with distaste at his grimy clothes when she tapped on the door.

'M'sieu, I have left a robe for you outside the door. Leave your clothes on the floor. I will deal with them.'

Wrapped in a woollen dressing gown, he returned to the kitchen. Madame looked at him with her head on one side. 'That's better. You're a good-looking young fellow when it's possible to see through the grime. But you look tired. When did you last sleep?'

'Night before last, really. I only caught a short nap last night.'

'Well, sit down and eat. Then you can rest.'

She placed an omelette on the table, and in spite of his protestations that she should not be giving him her family's rations, she insisted that he eat it. Then she showed him to a room with two single beds.

'That one is Gaston's,' she said, pointing.

'And the other?'

She looked at him, a look of bleak resignation. 'My other son, Pierre. He is a prisoner, we think. He disappeared after Sedan. The Red Cross are trying to trace him.'

Steve lay down on the bed, intending just to rest for a few minutes. When he woke again, it was to the sound of voices. Gaston and his sister had returned for the midday meal. As before, his doubts about eating their rations were swept aside, though the meal consisted only of a soup of turnips and cabbage, enlivened by a few scraps of lamb.

As they ate, Gaston said, 'Now, do you know where you are trying to get to?'

'Over the demarcation line, for a start. After that… who knows.'

'Very well. I think I know someone who can help you get that far. I shall go and see her this evening.'

Steve spent the afternoon making rather stilted conversation with his hostess. He discovered that she had washed the shirt and trousers he had been wearing, and as they talked, she ironed them as carefully as if they had been

Sunday best. His jacket she had sponged and brushed until almost all traces of soot had been removed. He was glad to be able to discard the dressing gown and dress properly again. At five thirty, Jeanne returned, looking pleased with herself. She opened her coat and revealed a length of andouillette sausage.

'The patron let me have it, off the ration, when I told him we had a guest.'

The coarse, garlic-flavoured sausage was not something Steve would normally have chosen to eat, but he had learned during his time in Brussels to be grateful for any kind of protein. Gaston did not appear, so a portion was put aside for him. He returned just as they finished eating, carrying a carpet bag, which he set down in the middle of the floor.

'Here are some better clothes for you.'

He pulled out two pairs of grey trousers, a white shirt, two jackets and a tie – definitely not the kind of working men's clothes Steve had been used to wearing.

'I brought two in the hope that one of them will fit,' he said. 'I hope I have guessed right.'

'Where have those come from?' Steve asked.

'A week or two ago a lady spoke to a friend of mine who is a ticket inspector. She asked him if he ever came across men who were trying to smuggle themselves across the line. He said not so far, but she told him that if he ever did, he should send them to her, because she knew how to help.'

'That was taking a big risk, wasn't it?' Steve said. 'Talking to a stranger about something like that.'

'Perhaps,' Gaston conceded, 'but not that great. She knew she could trust the *cheminots*. I've just been to see her and she gave me these. She is an English woman, married to a French nobleman, the Comte de Milleville. She owns a property in Sauveterre-de-Béarn which straddles the border with the unoccupied area. She is willing to escort you there.'

'She must be a very brave lady,' Steve murmured.

'Yes, indeed. But she tells me she served as a nurse in the last war and was awarded the Legion d'Honneur, so she's not a stranger to danger.'

'So, what is the plan, exactly?'

'You are to go south with her and her family in the guise of tutor to her son, Octave. He is about fourteen, I think. Hence the respectable clothes. But you will need papers. I am to take you to the Museum of Folk Art, where they have the facilities to produce the documents you need.'

'The Museum of Folk Art?' Steve repeated incredulously.

Gaston grinned. 'I know it sounds unlikely, but Madame de Milleville assures me that there are people there who are working for the same ends as we are, and they have the necessary skills and equipment for the job. So, are you happy to go along with that?'

'Yes,' Steve said. 'Yes, of course. It all sounds... I don't know... a bit far-fetched, but if you are convinced that this lady knows what she is doing...'

'Wait till you meet her,' Gaston said. 'This is no airy-fairy romantic. She is a formidable lady.'

Chapter Twenty-Six

Paris

October 7th 1940

Tired of 'babysitting' her Polish airman, Alix was relieved when Boris called in to tell her that Agnès was ready for them. Alix had already explained their plan to Dominik, so he submitted without complaint as she wound the bandage around his head until only his eyes were visible. When he was ready, she put on her nurse's uniform and took him by the arm for the short walk to the Museum of Folk Art. In spite of their precautions, she could not quell the feeling of 'butterflies in her stomach', to use the expression she had learned from English friends. Until Dominik had the necessary papers, they could both be arrested if they were stopped. But Boris had been correct in one thing. Passers-by stepped aside with murmurs of sympathy, especially when Alix murmured '*blessé pour La France*' to anyone who seemed curious.

At the museum, Agnès and a colleague were waiting for them. The bandage was unwound and Dominik was photographed.

'Come back tomorrow, when we have had a chance to develop the film,' Agnes said. 'We'll have the papers ready for you then.'

Having committed himself to the plan Gaston had outlined, Steve was eager to get on. He had tried on his new clothes. Gaston's guess about his size had been quite accurate so it only took Madame a few minutes with her needle and thread to make them serviceable. So he and Gaston set off for the museum. They were greeted by a young woman.

'Good morning. My name is Agnès. If you come this way, my colleague has everything set up ready for you.'

They chatted casually while the photographer went about his business, and when he was satisfied, Agnès said, 'I won't ask too many questions, but I can't help being curious. You speak very good French, but I detect an accent. I thought perhaps English, but that doesn't seem quite right.'

Steve smiled. 'That's because I'm American.'

'American? So how does it come about that you are – well, in this predicament?'

'I guess I've only got myself to blame. I volunteered.'

'I see. Then we need to give you a legend… a story, that will account for that.'

For several minutes they discussed possible options until they arrived at a backstory that Steve felt comfortable with.

'Come back tomorrow, and we shall have everything ready for you,' she told him.

–

When Alix and Dominik arrived at the museum next morning, Alix asked, 'Are we your only customers?'

'Not quite. One of the *cheminots* came in yesterday with an escaped POW.'

'Oh, one of the soldiers left behind after Dunkirk?'

'No. He was an airman, like our friend here, but in bombers, I think. The funny thing is, he was an American, though what an American was doing flying a bomber for the British I never discovered...'

For a moment Alix was unable to speak. She forced herself to take a deep breath and said, 'Did you take his photograph?'

'Yes, of course. What's the matter?'

'It's just — it could possibly be someone I know. Did you keep a copy?'

'No, I'm afraid not. It would be too incriminating if we were ever to be searched.'

'Of course it would. Sorry. What did he look like?'

'Not the way I imagine Americans to look. Quite dark, prominent cheekbones. As an anthropologist, I would have put him down as a Slav. But then, I suppose there are all sorts of racial types in America.' She stopped and looked at Alix. 'Are you all right? You've gone a bit pale.'

'No, no. I'm OK. It's just — I think from your description it is a man I met last year.'

'No, really? You just missed him. He came back an hour ago to collect his papers.'

'An hour ago? Did you... did he say where he was planning to go next?'

'No, and I didn't ask. The less any of us know, the better.'

'Yes, of course.' She realised that Dominik was looking from face to face, puzzled and slightly worried by the intensity of the conversation. She reverted to English. 'It's all right. Nothing to worry about. We'd better get that bandage back on so you're ready to go home.'

As they walked back to the flat, Alix tried to calm her thoughts. Steve had been in the same place, only an hour ago. She had no doubt that it was him. How he had come to be there, she could only guess. The important thing was he was being helped to escape; he was perhaps following the same route that she would be taking in a day or two. What chance was there that she might catch him up? She told herself that she was being foolish. He would be in disguise and there must be a dozen possible ways he could travel. But she could not suppress a hope – a fantasy perhaps – that they might come across each other. The most important thing, she reminded herself, was that at least she knew he was still alive.

That evening Boris brought an envelope containing all the necessary documents, and Alix was impressed, and greatly reassured, by how convincing they looked. Dominik was now Laurent Fabrice who had been seriously wounded at Sedan and recently discharged from a hospital in Amiens after a long period of convalescence.

–

Marie Louise returned from Tours. Her parents had readily agreed to their part of the plan and would be ready to receive Alix and her 'patient' as soon as they could make the journey.

'Papa had an idea. He suggests he can take you and Dominik to the hospital and whoever is going to take him on further, could pick him up there.'

When the plan was put to Germaine, she agreed at once. 'I am meeting Brigadier Hauet tomorrow. He uses his work with the UNCC to give him a reason for crossing the line. I'll make arrangements with him and let you know what to expect.'

Two days later, Alix and Dominik set out. Boris had bought the train tickets for them, single for Dominik, return for her, and insisted on giving her a substantial amount of money – in case of emergencies. The journey was smoother than Alix had imagined it could be. Dominik's bandaged state worked in their favour again, and they even got seats on the train. Marie Louise had managed to put a telephone call through to her father, asking him to meet 'some friends' at the station. The gendarme at the ticket barrier merely glanced at their papers and waved them through, and a tall, greying man stepped forward with a smile to say, 'This is my patient, I assume.'

At the home where Marie Louise had grown up, her mother greeted them like old friends, and Dominik was able to shed his bandages.

As they sat over glasses of brandy after dinner, Dr Beauclerc asked, 'Have you arranged what is to happen to our friend here after I deliver him to the hospital?'

'Yes. Someone will come and say he is to take Laurent home.' Alix had been translating for Dominik's benefit all evening, and she saw now that he was trying to follow the conversation and repeated what she had just said in English.

He shook his head with a look of panic. 'But I shall not understand him. Will he speak English? And what about the other people on the way? How am I going to manage?'

Alix felt her heartbeat quicken. Somehow none of them had thought about this. She could see how frightened Dominik was, understandably so. She reached across and pressed his hand. 'Don't worry. I'll come with you.'

'All the way?'

'Yes, all the way.'

Chapter Twenty-Seven

Belgrade

October 10th 1940

Leo and Sasha were invited to dine with Alexander Glen and his beautiful wife, Baroness Zorica Collaerts. They were not the only guests. Julian Amery was there. He had been a war correspondent during the Spanish Civil War and was now an attaché at the British Foreign Office in Belgrade. Also present was an intense-looking young man wearing heavy-rimmed spectacles whom Glen introduced as Peter Boughey.

At the end of the meal the baroness rose and Leo, accustomed to the convention that required ladies to withdraw at this point – a convention that she had frequently and furiously challenged.

The baroness raised her hand, 'No, my dear Leonora, tonight I am told that you should be regarded as an honorary gentleman. Please stay where you are.'

As the decanter of port went round the table, Glen said, 'I've invited you here tonight because we have come to the conclusion that we should share certain information with you. I need not emphasise how vital it is that it does not go beyond this room. I think Leo may have already guessed that we are working for the same organisation. It used to be known as Section D, but it now comes under the umbrella of a relatively new outfit, the Special Operations Executive.'

Leo glanced at Sasha, but he was apparently unsurprised.

Glen went on, 'Sasha, I know you are close to young Prince Peter. How would he react to the idea of taking his proper place on the throne?'

'He would relish the opportunity,' Sasha replied. 'He is strongly pro-British and as worried as the rest of us about the possibility of his uncle signing a pact with Hitler. Are we talking about a coup?'

'It is... under consideration. What would your attitude be if we were to pursue the idea?'

'I'm in favour, provided it does not involve shedding the blood of Prince Paul or any of his family. And Peter must be kept out of it. Any suggestion that he was involved could cause untold problems in the future.'

'Yes, of course. And as to bloodshed, none of us would contemplate that.'

'But do you have any realistic prospect of organising such a thing?'

'We have put out feelers in one or two directions, particularly the Party. They have seats in the National Assembly and the leader, Tupajanin, is prepared to cooperate with us. Narodna Odbrana are in favour...'

'Narodna Odbrana?' Leo interjected. 'Isn't that a new version of the Black Hand?'

'They are called the National Defence League,' Glen said. 'But they certainly developed from the Black Hand.'

Leo shook her head sadly. 'That brings back some very unhappy memories. You are all too young to remember, but it was the Black Hand that was behind the assassination of the Arch Duke Franz Ferdinand in 1914.'

'We know the history,' Amery put in somewhat impatiently.

'Yes, of course,' Leo responded. 'Sorry, I didn't mean to lecture. It's just my brother and my then fiancé, Tom, were almost caught up in those events and the stories Tom brought back… Are we really going to have to work with those people again?'

'If assassination is what they have in mind this time, I refuse to be involved,' Sasha said.

'No, I told you,' Glen said. 'We will not contemplate anything like that. Narodna Odbrana have petitioned Prince Paul a number of times asking him not to conclude any agreement with Hitler, and their leader, Voivodja Trifunovic-Bircanin, is an influential figure. We can't afford to ignore them.'

'The church leaders are in favour, too,' Amery said. 'They won't countenance bloodshed.'

'Very well,' Sasha said. 'Where do we go from here?'

'If we want the Serbian Peasants Party and Narodna Odbrana to play an active role, we need to fund them,' Boughey spoke for the first time.

'Peter's our money man,' Glen explained. 'He handles all that side of things.'

'So you want our government to provide those funds?' Leo asked.

'Ideally, yes. But persuading them won't be easy. They still seem to trust Prince Paul. He's referred to as "our friend" in official communiqués. I'm told King George has written to him personally, asking him to resist pressure from Hitler.'

'We'd make more progress if we had a bit more cooperation from the mandarins in Whitehall,' Amery said bitterly. 'I sometimes feel we are fighting on two fronts – against the Nazis on one side and against our own people on the other.'

'How do you mean?' Sasha asked.

'Well, for example, we had a useful project going to block traffic on the Danube by blowing up locks and sinking concrete-filled barges in the channel. The idea was to prevent Germany from importing oil from the Romanian oil fields by that route. We'd made a few attempts and been quite successful…'

'To be honest,' Glen put in, 'each one only lasted a matter of weeks before the Germans cleared the channel again.'

'But we were learning,' Amery said. 'We would have become more effective given the chance.'

'So, what happened?' Leo enquired.

'Our much respected (I don't think) Minister Plenipotentiary for His Majesty's Government put a stop to it.'

'Ronald Campbell did?' Sasha queried. 'On what grounds?'

'That it might have a bad effect on military opinion, as it would cut off this country's only outlet to the sea. And that might make them less likely to come in as our allies.'

'Mr Campbell is a very cautious man and a stickler for correct protocols,' Glen said. 'He hates our guts. I hear he refers to us as a group of bomb-happy amateurs.'

'It seems to me that all this is very Serbian-centred,' Sasha said. 'What about the rest of the country? What about the Croats and the Bosnians and the Slovenians?'

'We are hoping to place men in those areas too,' Glen told him. 'There's Alec Lawrenson already working in Slovenia…'

'That man is an accident waiting to happen,' Amery exclaimed. 'He has no idea of security. Half Ljubljana knows what he's up to.'

'But he has made some useful contacts,' Glen said.

'We are planning to spread our net wider,' Amery said. 'I think the Bulgarian Peasant's Party might be interested in staging a similar coup there, with a view to forming a pan-Slav alliance to oppose Hitler. I'm planning to take a trip over there in the next day or two to sound them out.'

'Assuming this coup goes ahead,' Sasha said, 'who's going to head it up?'

'We are sounding out General Simovic. As head of the Air Force he's well placed, but so far he hasn't committed himself.'

'Well, his name has been associated with earlier attempts,' Sasha said. 'He's probably the right man for the job.' He finished his port and put the glass aside. 'So what do you want from us?'

'You know what is going on at court, who is pushing Paul to sign an agreement with Hitler and who is trying to stop him. Who might be likely to favour a coup, or at least accept one if it happened. That sort of intelligence will be very valuable if we are definitely going ahead with the idea.'

'Very well. I can do that. But it goes both ways. I rely on you to keep us in touch with any developments on your side.'

'Of course. We're very glad to have you and Leo on board, and between us, perhaps we can put a stop to

Adolf's little plan to drag this country into the Axis alliance.'

The meeting broke up soon after this. On their way home, Sasha remarked, 'I can't believe Sandy really thought I didn't know what he and his little gang are up to.'

'But you approve?' Leo said.

'In principle, yes. But if they succeed, I wonder what the unintended consequences might be. It's a dangerous game we are playing.'

'I'll let Gubbins know what we've discussed and see how he reacts,' Leo said.

A couple of weeks passed without further incident and then one evening Alexander Glen called on them. His face told them at once that all was not well.

'Two setbacks, I'm afraid,' he said. 'Campbell found out about Julian's little jaunt to Bulgaria. He's absolutely incandescent with rage, and Julian has been recalled to London. They are sending out someone else, but I suspect whoever it is will be given the responsibility of keeping the rest of us in order. London absolutely refuses to countenance a coup.'

'Does that mean we have to forget about the idea?' Leo asked.

'I've no intention of doing so,' Glen replied. 'But we may have to move very carefully until we see just what the new chap's brief is.'

'You said two setbacks,' Sasha reminded him.

'Yes. This doesn't directly concern us, but it is a rather worrying incident. You remember we mentioned Alec Lawrenson in Slovenia? He managed to get himself accredited as vice-consul, and he was given an assistant, a chap called Frodsham. Well, the other day, Frodsham was found dead in his flat, gassed, apparently. The police have put it down as suicide, but Lawrenson says there's no reason for him to do such a thing. He believes he was killed by German Intelligence.'

'That is worrying, as you say,' Sasha said. 'Do you believe any of us is in immediate danger?'

'I suppose we are, and always have been. Not you, Sasha, or Leo. As Yugoslav nationals and respected members of society, I doubt if you would be targeted. The rest of us will just have to be extra careful from now on.'

Chapter Twenty-Eight

Sauveterre-de-Béarn, France

October 10th 1940

On his return to the Museum of Folk Art, Steve had been given a wallet in which were all the documents he needed. He had chosen to keep the name he had got used to in Belgium, but now Carl Lebrun had been born to French parents in the USA, where his father was a visiting professor at the University of Minnesota. He had a degree in French literature from the same university and had returned to France the previous year to pursue his studies. Because of the disruption to transatlantic shipping due to the war, he had been unable to return home, so he had now taken up a post as tutor to the son of Madame de Milleville as a way of earning a living. Respectably dressed and, on paper at least, suitably qualified, he was taken to meet his new employer.

–

Two days later Steve woke in a spacious, beautifully furnished room. He was lying on a feather bed and the sheets were of crisp, white linen. Sunshine was streaming through a small gap in the brocade curtains. It took him a second or two to work out where he was. This was the Comtesse de Milleville's chateau. They had arrived the day before after an easy train journey. It seemed that even in occupied France an aristocratic lady and her entourage could travel without being too closely questioned. Madame herself had proved a pleasant travelling companion and her three children had lively minds and perfect manners. Steve had taken to Octave, Oky as he was known in the family, at once. He had an impish sense of humour which was particularly exercised by the notion that Steve was supposed to be his tutor.

Steve was reluctant to leave the most comfortable bed he had slept in for a very long while, but a sense that he must not allow himself to be seduced into forgetting his real purpose propelled him to his feet. He opened the curtains and looked out over the landscape of wooded hills rising gently to the distant outline of the Pyrenees. Below him he could see the ancient buildings of the village, crowned by its medieval castle, and the sunlight reflecting off the river, the Gave d'Oloron. He sighed, wishing he had spent more time exploring places like this instead of staying in Paris. It was too late now. He dressed and went downstairs.

Breakfast over, the three children disappeared to follow various interests and Madame took Steve on a walk through the farm, where the stubble left after the harvest was turned golden by the sun, still comfortingly warm this far south. He glanced sideways at her, curious to understand what had impelled her to undertake this mission. She was, he guessed, in her early fifties. Her dark hair was streaked with occasional strands of silver, but her skin was smooth, and she had that indefinable, well-cared-for look that only French women of a certain class seemed to be able to achieve. *Soigné*, that was the word for it. But her blue eyes hinted at something else. There was something imperious in her look that suggested whatever obstacles life might throw in her way would be overcome, or simply swept aside.

As they strolled along, she said, 'There's no need for you to keep calling me *Madame* when we are alone. I'm not really your employer. I was born Mary Lindell. You can call me Mary.'

They crossed a bridge over a small stream, and she said, 'Now you are in the unoccupied zone.'

'Really?' He scanned the woods and fields around them. There were no barriers, no guards.

'It is all very well to draw a line on a map,' Mary said. 'But France is a big country. To police every hundred metres is impossible. But do not think that because you are standing in what is called "free" France you are out of danger. Part of the armistice agreement signed by Pétain states that his government will surrender on demand anyone required by the authorities in the area under Nazi control. That would include escaped POWs.'

'But would the ordinary people give someone like that up?' he asked.

Her expression grew grim. 'Some would, I am afraid. Already I am hearing of people who are prepared to denounce their neighbours in order to curry favour with the enemy. There's this new organisation calling itself Service d'Ordre Légionnaire, the SOL, whose raison d'etre seems to be to collaborate with the Nazis in the expectation that they will win the war and establish a fascist regime. They are dangerous.'

Steve frowned. 'I had no idea. I assumed that everyone here would hate the Nazis as much as… well, as much as we do.'

'Oh no,' Mary said sadly. 'There are plenty of *pétainistes*, people who idolise Pétain because of the stand he made at Verdun in the last war and agree with him that our best course is to cooperate with the Nazis. So you must be on your guard.'

'I was thinking,' Steve said. 'There must be an American consulate somewhere near here. If I can get there, I presume I can rely on them to get me out of the country.'

Mary pursed her lips. 'There's a consulate in Bordeaux but I wouldn't recommend you to try it.'

'Why not?'

'Because the entrance will be guarded – and quite possibly watched by someone from the SOL – and if you can't produce a very good reason for wanting to go in you will be turned away, and possibly arrested.'

'But as an American citizen…' Steve began.

'Can you prove that?'

Steve felt a sinking feeling in his gut. 'No, I can't.'

'Even if you could,' Mary went on, 'I'm not sure they would be able to get you out of the country. To say the regulations are Kafkaesque would be an understatement. Also, rumour has it that the Vichy authorities share applications for exit visas with the Gestapo, so they can check if it is someone they want.'

Steve looked at her hopelessly. 'So, what do I do?'

'I'm afraid you have a long haul ahead of you. I know a man, a retired British Major, called William Higgins. He lives just south of here, and he is willing to put you in touch with someone who will guide you across the Pyrenees into Spain. Once there, you should be able to contact the American consul in Barcelona, or you could make your way to Portugal and, Portugal being neutral, find a ship from Lisbon either to the States or back to Britain.'

'That is where I want to go,' Steve said. 'I need to get back to my squadron. Lisbon sounds like a good bet.'

'It's not an easy journey,' she warned him. 'And you need to go soon before the winter snows make it impossible.'

Steve looked around at the peaceful landscape. It had crossed his mind that it would be pleasant to stay on here for a while. He even found the idea of tutoring Oky quite attractive.

He took a long breath and sighed. 'Well, the sooner the better then.'

Chapter Twenty-Nine

Lyon, France

October 10th 1940

The train rattled through the suburbs of Lyon, and Alix peered through the window to see the great sweep of the River Rhône at its confluence with the Saône. Closer to the centre she caught glimpses of tiled roofs glowing in the autumn sun and tall, classically elegant buildings fronting the river. Away on a hilltop, she could make out the towers and cupolas of a great church. She glanced at Dominik. Swathed in his bandages, it was hard to tell if he was awake or dozing.

'Nearly there,' she said.

So far their journey had gone according to plan – though whose plan it was and where it led next was only revealed bit by bit. Dr Beauclerc had driven them as he promised to the hospital on the other side of the demarcation line. No one had queried their presence, and they had sat in a waiting room until a man in clerical dress came in and told one of the nurses he had come to collect one of his parishioners who had been wounded in the fighting. The priest drove them to a farm just outside the village of Loches, where they spent the night. From there they were taken by the local vet to the Hotel de la Gare in the little village of Bruère-Allichamps. Folded inside the menu, she found instructions for the next part of the journey. After two changes of train they had finally arrived in Lyon. Alix sighed with relief. It had been a long day. She took Dominik's arm to guide him down the steps, and as she did so, she experienced a sudden shock. At the barrier, a gendarme was checking everyone's papers and another man in a uniform she did not recognise with an armband bearing the letters SOL was standing beside him.

'What is it?' Dominik whispered, sensing her hesitation.

'Hush! It's nothing. They are just checking papers. Nothing to worry about.'

As they approached the barrier, she held out her own ID card together with the one Agnès had forged for Dominic. The gendarme looked at them and then showed them to his companion.

'Wait!' he said.

'Why?' Alix asked. 'Our papers are in order, and we have friends waiting for us.'

'Wait!' the gendarme repeated, with a jerk of his head. 'Over there.'

There was nothing they could do but obey. When all the other passengers had left the platform, the man with the SOL armband opened the door to a small office.

'In here.'

'I don't understand,' Alix protested. 'Why are you detaining us?'

The man looked at Dominik. 'Take off his bandages.'

Alix caught her breath. 'No, I can't. It... It's not possible.'

'Why not?'

'Infection!' she improvised wildly. 'The wounds are still open. If I uncover them they might get infected.'

'Not in just a few minutes. Take them off.'

'But why?'

'How can I know if this is the man in this photograph if I can't see his face?' he said. 'Come along. We are wasting time.'

He made a move as if to pull the bandages off himself and Dominik, realising what was about to happen, jerked his head away, producing an incoherent moan of protest. It gave Alix an idea. She laid her hand on the gendarme's sleeve and tugged him to one side.

'Please!' she said, lowering her voice. 'Can't you see how the prospect distresses him? He is so terribly disfigured. He cannot bear anyone to look at him. You would not recognise him from the photograph anyway. His own mother wouldn't know him. Hasn't he suffered enough?' The gendarme was looking uneasy, and she pressed her argument home. 'Truly, I think you would find it distressing too.'

He hesitated a moment longer, then he pushed the documents back into her hand. 'Go on then. Get along with you.'

As they hurried out of the room and through the barrier, Alix could hear the gendarme and the other man arguing. Afraid that they might still be called back, she anxiously scanned the station forecourt, and as she did so, a young woman ran forward and threw her arms around the stunned Dominik.

'Ah! *Mon cousin!* I am so happy to see you. Come, Papa is waiting for us.'

The vehicle to which the girl led them came as a surprise. It was a baker's van. A tall man with a slight stoop

240

and horn-rimmed glasses was standing by it, smoking a cigarette. As they approached, he stubbed it out with a look of relief and stepped forward.

'Good afternoon. I am Marcel Pasquier. Welcome to Lyon.'

Alix introduced herself and they shook hands. 'And this,' she said, 'is Laurent.'

'This is my daughter, Florence,' Pasquier went on. 'Now, I must apologise for this unconventional mode of transport, but it is completely impossible to obtain petrol for private cars. It is only available for essential services. Fortunately, my friend Jean Claude the baker, is happy to help. Shall we go?'

Alix and Dominik squeezed into the front seat of the van, and Florence sat on the floor in the back between the empty shelves.

As they drove, Pasquier said, 'Our friend does not speak French?'

'No, I'm afraid he doesn't.'

'Hence the bandages?'

'Yes.'

'Then let us speak English.'

He told them that he was a professor at the university, where he taught English literature, and his wife was an English teacher at the local lycée. Alix could hear in Dominik's responses his relief at being able, for once, to understand what was being said around him.

Their route took them along the Quai Jules Courmont, with the River Rhône on their right-hand side. Looking around her, Alix suddenly caught sight of the American flag flying in front of one of the buildings.

'I didn't expect to see the Stars and Stripes being flown here,' she exclaimed.

'That is the American consulate,' their host explained.

'So the Americans still have diplomatic relations with the Vichy government?' Alix queried.

'Why not? America is still neutral. I believe they have taken over responsibility for British affairs since the British consul was expelled.'

They arrived at a house in a pleasant suburb and were welcomed by Madame Pasquier. They were treated with all the courtesy a guest could expect, shown to comfortable bedrooms and later offered a dinner that Alix appreciated had stretched their limited rations to the utmost. But at the same time, she was aware of the undercurrent of tension in the air. These people were risking their liberty and perhaps their lives to help Dominik to escape the country, and it would only require a nosy neighbour to mention something in the wrong quarter for them to be arrested.

Since both their host and hostess spoke fluent English, Dominik was able to shed his bandages and join in the conversation. The main topic was, of course, the progress of the war and the likelihood of America coming to their rescue.

'But you are not French,' Mme Pasquier said to Alix. 'Your country is still neutral, too. Why are you doing what you are doing?'

Alix explained that she was half-English. 'It says Yugoslavian on my ID card, of course. Otherwise, I would probably have been interned months ago.'

'You have had no problems on the journey?' Pasquier asked.

'Not till we got to Lyon,' she told him and recounted their close shave at the station.

'Ah, these SOL types!' Pasquier exclaimed. 'They are nothing more than Nazis in sheep's clothing.'

'Where do they come from?' Alex asked. 'We didn't see any further north.'

'They originated from some military unit in the Alpes-Maritimes, I think,' he said. 'But they seem to be spreading out over the country. They are going to be very dangerous if someone doesn't put a stop to them.'

'Can't the government in Vichy control them?'

'Why should they try? They embody exactly what Pétain and his cronies want. They are convinced Germany is going to win the war, and they are desperate to curry favour with Hitler.'

When the meal was finished, Pasquier said, 'Now, plans for tomorrow. In the morning, Jean Claude will take you in his van to a different railway station, so there is no danger of you encountering the men who questioned you this afternoon. You will buy tickets to Marseilles, and when you get there, you go to this address. It is the surgery of a Dr Rodocanachi. I know nothing of him except that he is part of the *reseau*, the escape line that has come into being. He will take care of Dominik and arrange for his onward journey. With the bandages, it will not seem strange for him to seek a consultation with a doctor. You must wait in the waiting room with the other patients, but when you are called into the consulting room, tell him who you are and what you want. I am sure that you can trust him absolutely.'

Alix understood that they were being passed along a chain in which each separate link knew only the identity of the next one. So far it had worked, and she had no reason to believe that it would not continue to do so. Nevertheless, as the train approached Marseilles, she was unable to suppress a nervous tension that made it hard to stop her hands from fidgeting. As they descended, she scanned the platform ahead, searching for the ticket barrier, afraid to see a man in the uniform of the SOL checking papers. The train had been crowded, and there was a throng of people pressing towards the barrier, and as they drew closer, she saw to her relief that the guards there were merely glancing at the documents held up for them to check. Some people, it seemed, were not even bothering to show them.

As they approached the barrier, Alix took out their ID papers and their tickets and steered Dominik into the centre of the crowd. The pressure of people behind them propelled them forwards, and she waved the papers in the direction of one of the guards and then they were through and out into the station yard. Alix felt herself breathe more easily, but the next problem was to find their way to the address she had memorised before leaving the Pasquiers' house. A short distance away she saw a kiosk selling papers and magazines and there she was able to buy a street map of the city. They found a bench outside the station, and Alix studied the map. Rue Roux de Brignoles was some distance away on the other side of the old port. She looked around in the hope of finding a taxi but none was visible. She nudged Dominik and pointed out the route on the map.

'Looks like we are going to have a walk,' she whispered, and he nodded.

The streets were crowded with a motley throng of people. Some moved purposefully, even urgently, while others seemed to drift, as if for no other reason than that it was easier to walk than to stand still. There was the usual mixture of characters that might be found on any city street – housewives shopping, businessmen in suits, working men carrying the tools of their trade – but there were others, some smartly dressed, others shabby and worn-looking, many carrying bags or suitcases and leading children by the hand, who seemed to have no immediate purpose and who looked around them with anxious, searching eyes. Suddenly Dominik gripped her arm and pointed ahead, and Alix gasped. Coming towards them were two men in the uniform of British Army officers. They strolled along, making no attempt to conceal themselves, apparently completely at their ease. Alix and Dominik exchanged looks. They did not dare to voice the questions that came to both their minds, but as the two officers approached, Alix had to wrestle with the impulse to accost them and ask how it was possible for them to walk freely in this city of enemies. She quashed the idea and they passed on. A little further on they saw three more officers, all in uniform but bearing the insignia of different regiments, sitting at a table in one of the pavement cafes. When they came upon two men in Air Force blue chatting to a couple of young women, she felt Dominik start towards them, but she caught his arm and shook her head. Whatever was going on here, they could not take the risk of revealing themselves.

Rue Roux de Brignoles was lined with tall, grey houses, many exhibiting the brass plates of doctors or notaries, and one such, number 21, advertised Dr G. Rodocanachi, with a list of surgery opening times. The next was due to begin in half an hour, so Alix and Dominik found a cafe at the corner of the street and ordered two beers, one with a straw to enable Dominik to suck it up without removing his bandages. As they waited, Alix watched people arriving at the doctor's door. When several had gone in, she paid the bill and led Dominik to the door. They were ushered into a waiting room where there were already three patients – an elderly woman with a swollen leg wrapped in bandages, a mother with a grizzling baby and a man with a chesty cough. Alix and Dominik found seat,s and she picked up a magazine from a small table and pretended to flick through it.

An inner door opened and a woman wearing a nurse's cap called, '*Au suivant, s'il vous plait,*' and the woman with the baby went into the surgery.

The waiting seemed endless. The other patients went in and came out and at last the call '*Au suivant, s'il vous plait*' came again. Alix touched Dominik's arm and they made their way into the surgery.

A solidly built man with a luxuriant moustache and dark hair liberally streaked with grey looked up from behind his desk. The nurse disappeared through an inner door.

'Good afternoon,' the doctor said. 'How can I help you?'

Alix took a deep breath. 'Dr Rodocanachi, we have been sent here by... by a friend in Lyon who said you would be able to help my... my companion.'

'I see,' the doctor said. 'And what is your companion's name?'

This was the crucial moment. Alix touched Dominik's arm. 'Tell the doctor your name.'

'My name,' he said in English, 'is Dominik Kominski.'

'Ah,' the doctor said. 'So you are Polish?'

Alix felt her heartbeat steady. He was neither shocked nor alarmed by the revelation. 'He does not understand French,' she explained. 'But he knows English.'

The doctor smiled broadly. 'Then let us speak English.' His speech was without accent, the speech of the educated middle-class Englishman. 'So,' he went on, 'you are Polish. A refugee from your poor, occupied country?'

'No!' Dominik replied. 'I left my country before it fell to the Nazis. I am a pilot with the British Royal Air Force.'

'Ah, now I understand. You were shot down, perhaps?'

'Yes.'

'And now you want to return to England?'

'Yes.'

'And you, mademoiselle?' The doctor turned his gaze to Alix.

'My name is Alexandra Malkovic. I am a Serb – I should say, Yugoslav.'

'Indeed? But your country is not at war. Why do you need my help?'

'I am not here for that reason. I came to help Dominik because he does not speak French, as I told you.'

'Tell me, is that the reason for the bandages?'

'Yes, it seemed the best way to explain why he does not speak.'

'Then perhaps now we can remove them?'

After a brief hesitation, Alix unwound the bandages, and the doctor leaned forward. 'Ah ha. So, there is no damage. Now we can speak face to face.'

'Please,' Dominik said, 'can you help me to get back to England?'

'Personally, no. But I can put you in touch with those who can. First, however, there is someone you need to talk to. We have to be sure that you are who you claim to be. You will understand that.'

'I can prove—' Dominik began, but the doctor raised his hand.

'Not to me. As I said, it is someone else you have to convince.' He touched a bell on his desk and the nurse reappeared. 'Please take this lady and gentleman into the next room.'

Alix and Dominik got up. She caught his eye and knew that the same thoughts were going through his mind. Was this a trap? Who was waiting for them in the next room? For an instant, she considered grabbing his arm and making a run for it. But the doctor was smiling reassuringly, and the nurse was holding the door open. It was Dominik who took the initiative, striding eagerly towards her. Alix followed, feeling her knees begin to shake again.

The next room was furnished as an office, with a filing cabinet and a desk on which stood a telephone and a typewriter. A man rose from behind it and came forward to greet them, and Alix thought for a moment that some terrible prank was being played on them. The man was dressed in the uniform of one of the Scottish regiments, complete with kilt.

He extended his hand to Alix. He was smiling, but the grey eyes were coolly assessing. 'My name is Garrow, Ian Garrow. I am a captain in the Seaforth Highlanders.' The Scottish accent was unmistakable. 'And you are?'

Alix introduced herself and went on. 'I'm not the one asking for help. It's… my friend here.'

'I was assuming that,' Garrow said, with a glint of humour. 'So?'

Dominik came to attention. 'Sergeant Pilot Dominik Kominski. RAF.'

'Very good. Shall we sit down?' They took the chairs he indicated, and he went on, 'Miss Malkovic, can I ask why you are here?'

Alix explained, and Garrow said, 'The questions I am going to ask are not your concern. If you prefer to wait in another room?'

'I'd rather stay, if that's all right.'

'Then I must ask you not to speak. Sergeant Kominski must answer for himself.'

'Of course,' Alix agreed.

'So,' he turned to Dominik, 'let's start with the basics. Name and rank you have stated. Serial number?' Dominik supplied it. 'Do you have any proof of this?'

Dominik opened his jacket and pulled at a loose thread in the lining. A small packet fell into his hand and he tipped the contents onto the table. Alix knew what they were, because she had watched Marie Louise stitch them into place before they left. They were the dog tags that every serviceman wore round his neck under his uniform. Garrow scrutinised them carefully and nodded.

'OK. Which squadron were you in?'

'303.'

'Stationed where?'

'RAF Leconfield.'

'Where and when were you shot down?'

The questioning went on for some time and eventually Garrow sat back and smiled.

'OK. I'm satisfied.'

'So, you can get me back to England?' Dominik asked eagerly.

'Probably. But it isn't going to be a stroll in the park. The Spanish have closed the border, so the only way is either over the Pyrenees or by sea. We are trying out the second method. You will have to wait until we receive a message from Gibraltar and then a small group of you will be taken to a place on the coast, probably by Dr

Rodocanachi's son. If all goes according to plan a dinghy will take you out to a felucca, a small fishing boat, which will carry you down the Spanish coast to Gib and from there you will be flown back to the UK. But I have to emphasise that it will be risky. German submarines are active in the area, and while we hope that they will not be interested in a simple fishing boat, if you were challenged, it might be hard to convince them. There is also, of course, the matter of the weather. If you were forced to put in to shore, you would probably be arrested and interned by the Spanish Guardia Civil. It's not perfect, but if it works, it will be quicker and easier than going over the mountains.'

'Well, then, that is how I would like to go,' Dominik said.

Garrow smiled. 'There will be an added bonus for you. I'm told most of the crews of these boats are Polish.'

'No! Really? Then that is definitely the way I want to travel.'

'Good. As I said, it won't happen immediately. You will be told when and where to assemble. Do you have anywhere to stay?'

'No, I don't.'

'There's a man called Donald Caskie; he's a minister in the Scottish Kirk. He's reopened the old Seaman's Mission down by the port to accommodate servicemen who have found their way here. He'll give you a bed and look after you until we're ready to move you on. I'll take you down there in a few minutes.'

'Can I ask something now?' Alix put in.

'Yes, of course. I'm sorry I had to tell you to keep quiet, but I had to be sure you weren't prompting Sergeant Kominski.'

'I quite understand,' Alix said. 'There's something that is puzzling me. We've seen British officers walking the streets here, apparently quite openly. How can that be?'

'It's because we are all on parole. Officially, we are incarcerated in the old Fort St Jean, but we are allowed to come into the city provided we return for roll call and to pick up our ration cards. Of course, most of the men you've seen are waiting for a chance to get out of the country, like Kominski here.'

'But not you?' Alix asked.

'No. I reckon I've got a more important job to do here.'

'There's one other thing. Have you by any chance come across an American also trying to get back to Britain?'

'An American? What would an American be doing here?'

'He's joined the RAF, Bomber Command. I met him in Paris before the war, but I happen to know that he was given false documents by the same people who provided Dominik's. So he must have been shot down, too, and be trying to get back. I wondered if he'd arrived here.'

'No, sorry. I haven't come across any Yanks.'

Alix shook her head, disappointed. It had crossed her mind for a moment that Steve might be waiting in Marseilles for the same boat as Dominik and she had had a brief vision of a reunion and his amazement if she suddenly presented herself. 'Is there an American consulate here?'

'Yes, for now. Maybe not for long.'

'Do you think he might have gone there?'

'It's possible, I suppose.'

'Perhaps I should try asking them.'

Garrow screwed up his face. 'Well, I wish you luck trying to get to speak to anyone. The consulate is besieged by people, mostly Jews, desperate to get out of France before the Germans take over the whole country.'

'Do you think that will happen?'

'I should say it's inevitable, sooner or later.'

'One more thing. How is it that Dr Rodoconachi speaks such perfect English?'

'Oh yes, that comes as a surprise to everyone. From the name, you would guess he is Greek, no? His parents were Greek, but he was born in Liverpool. He studied in Paris and is now a naturalised Frenchman.' He stood up. 'What are your plans now?'

'I shall go back to Paris.'

'Do you plan to be a regular courier, bringing men down the line?'

'Oh.' The question took her by surprise. 'I don't know. I hadn't thought about it. We just happened to find Dominik – but I suppose there must be others.'

'I'm sure there will be. So perhaps we shall meet again?'

Alix felt a surge of pride. She had done it once. She could do it again. Here was something really meaningful she could do. She smiled at the Scotsman. 'Yes, perhaps we will.'

'Do you have anywhere to stay tonight?'

'No. I shall have to find a hotel.'

'We may be able to do better than that. Hang on a minute.'

He left the room, and Alix turned to look at Dominik.

He said, 'You can go back to your friends. I shall be all right now that I'm with people who can speak English.'

'Yes, of course, you will.'

He reached out and took her hand, suddenly shy. 'I shall never be able to thank you properly for what you have done for me.'

'You don't need to thank me.' she said, with a sudden lump in her throat. They had been such close companions over the last few days that the thought of saying goodbye came as a sudden shock. She had come to admire his quiet courage. He had endured the discomfort of having his face bandaged without complaint, and although he must have been as frightened as she was, he had never given himself away. 'Do you remember the address, where you stayed in Paris?'

'No, I don't think so.'

'Then write to me, care of the Musée de l'Homme.'

'I can try. But will letters get through?'

'Oh, I suppose not. I wasn't thinking. I hate the thought of not knowing if you got back safely or not. Perhaps you could get someone to send a message back to Captain Garrow. Maybe the consul in Gibraltar? He must know what's going on.'

'I can try. But whatever happens, when the war is over, I will write to the museum. Perhaps I'll even come and visit you there.'

'Yes.' She had to swallow hard. 'Yes, you must do that.'

There were tears in his eyes, too, and when the door opened to admit Garrow, they both had to blink them away. He was accompanied by a plump, grey-haired woman.

'Miss Malkovic, this is Mrs Rodoconachi. She's happy to put you up for the night. You might find it hard to get a room in a hotel as things are.'

'That's terribly kind of you,' Alix said.

The woman took her hand. 'You are very welcome, my dear.'

'Come along, Kominski,' Garrow said. 'I'll take you down to the port and introduce you to Donald Caskie.'

Dominik turned to Alix and held out his hand. 'Goodbye. And thank you again, for everything.'

Impulsively, she reached up and kissed his cheek. 'Goodbye – and good luck! Take care of yourself.'

He nodded, pressed her hand and turned to Garrow. Mrs Rodoconachi took Alix's arm and led her out of the room.

Next morning Alix went to catch the train north. At the station in Marseilles, she bought a newspaper from the kiosk on the forecourt, hoping to find news here that was less heavily censored than in Paris. She unfolded it and saw a photograph on the front page.

'*Jebiga!*' In shock, she reverted to her own language. The picture showed Marshal Pétain shaking hands with Adolf Hitler. The text beneath it told her that the two leaders had met in a railway carriage outside a small town not far from the Spanish border 'to discuss future co-operation'. Alix stared, almost unable to believe what she was reading. The hero of Verdun, shaking hands with the man who had humiliated his country. It was the ultimate betrayal.

Chapter Thirty

The Pyrenees

October 1940

Steve slid his rucksack off his shoulders and bent double, his hands on his knees, drawing in great gulps of air. His companion looked at him quizzically.

'The air is thin up here, yes. But you are an airman. You are used to this.'

'In an aeroplane we have oxygen,' Steve panted.

'Well, breathe deeply now. Tomorrow we go higher.'

They were standing outside a small, stone-built hut perched on the grassy shoulder of a hill, surrounded by towering peaks. The guide led the way inside and Steve followed thankfully. Until that day he had thought he was reasonably fit, but this had shown him that the months in Brussels had done nothing to strengthen the muscles in his legs.

On the previous day, he had said goodbye to the Comtesse de Millevilles and crossed the little stream that marked the boundary between occupied France and the 'free' zone. At the far side of the next field was a road and there a car waited for him, driven by an elderly man who introduced himself as Major Higgins. They had driven to a house on the outskirts of Saint-Girons, and later that day, there was a knock on the door. A wiry, dark-eyed man with skin like tanned leather was admitted.

'Carl, this is Bolivar,' Higgins said. 'He is one of the most successful smugglers in the Ariège. Bolivar, this is Carl. He's an airman in the RAF, and he needs to get back to Britain.'

Steve offered his hand and winced at the strength of the other man's grip. It occurred to him that his false identity had served its purpose and if this man was prepared to risk his life to get him back to England, the least he owed him was honesty.

'It says "Carl" on my ID papers, but my real name is Stefan Popovic. Please call me Steve.'

Bolivar shrugged. 'Carl, Stefan, it's all the same to me. You have some other clothes, something more suitable?'

'I can kit him out,' Higgins said. 'Don't worry about that. Can you get him over the mountains?'

Bolivar glanced out of the window. 'It's late in the season. God willing, we shall make it. Be ready at six tomorrow morning.'

It was still dark when Bolivar tapped on the window. Higgins had provided Steve with a thick sweater, a knitted cap, gloves and a waterproof coat and over-trousers, and he had chosen, among a selection of boots, the ones that pinched and rubbed less than the others. He shook hands with the Major and stepped out into the pre-dawn chill.

'We go quietly,' Bolivar warned him.

In silence, they made their way through the still-sleeping town until they came to the River Salat. There was only one bridge, and Steve's heart sank as he saw that it was guarded by an armed gendarme.

'Wait here,' Bolivar said, and went forward to meet the man. Steve saw a package of cigarettes change hands and then Bolivar waved him forward. The gendarme turned his back to gaze downstream as Steve slipped past. After that, they were soon on a trail that led upwards through woodland and along the edge of pastures where goats grazed. The incline grew steeper and the path narrower as they progressed, until they were in among the mountains that had initially been only a backdrop to the scenery. After an hour, Steve's calf muscles were crying out for respite and he was panting for breath, but Bolivar pressed on remorselessly, halting only once to pass Steve a flask of water. In this way, they had made it to the refuge where they were to spend the night. Estimating by the time they had taken and the speed they had walked, Steve reckoned they had covered a good fifteen miles.

The hut was empty except for four straw-filled palliasses on the stone floor, but there was dry wood in the fireplace, and Bolivar soon had a good blaze going. As Steve crouched in front of it, stretching his hands to the flames, Bolivar fetched water from a well outside and set a pannikin to heat. When it was boiling, he drew out of his rucksack a paper packet and tipped the contents into the pan. He handed a mugful to Steve, whose nostrils flared at an almost forgotten aroma.

'This smells like real coffee!'

Bolivar shrugged and gave a rare smile. 'What is the point of being a smuggler if you cannot allow yourself an occasional treat?' He pulled another flask from his pocket and tipped a generous slug into each mug. 'This is not smuggled, however. This my father makes from the fruit in our orchard.'

It was plum brandy and lent a satisfying hint of sweetness to the coffee. As the warm drink reached his stomach Steve felt his cramped muscles begin to relax.

Bolivar produced bread and sausage from his rucksack and they chewed in silence. Then Bolivar said, 'Sleep now. Tomorrow will be harder.'

As he stretched out on the palliasse, Steve thought longingly of the luxurious bed he had occupied at Sauveterre-de-Béarn, but any regret was rapidly extinguished by sleep.

Very soon, it seemed, he was roused by the sound of movement and he jerked into full wakefulness, afraid that they had somehow been followed and discovered. It was just getting light, and he realised with relief that the noise he had heard was Bolivar building up the fire and setting a pan of water to boil. He dragged himself to his feet, his aching muscles protesting, and stumbled out of the hut to relieve himself. Once outside he was arrested in mid-stride by the panorama stretching before him. All around, jagged, snow-covered peaks reached thousands of feet towards a sky of duck-egg blue. To the east, the sun was just rising in a fiery halo of cloud, and the peaks on the west were stained pink by the reflection. The air was sharp and crisp as the first bite of a fresh apple. For a moment Steve had the illusion that he was back home in Alaska. Bolivar, joining him, was less impressed.

'Not good,' he declared, jerking his head to the scarlet ribbons of cloud to the east. 'We must move fast to get to the next refuge before the snow comes.'

Steve relieved himself and splashed his face with icy water from the well, then went back inside to the cup of scalding coffee and the hunk of bread Bolivar had prepared. Within minutes they were on the path again. As the day progressed, Steve realised that this was the hardest thing he had ever done. To begin with there was a little relief as the exercise eased his stiffened muscles, but from the start, the path was much steeper than yesterday. They climbed to a col, then dropped down only to climb again even higher. Every breath was a struggle to draw in enough oxygen from the thin air. By midday it was obvious that Bolivar's pessimism was well founded. The clouds spread across the sky, blocking out the sunlight, and an hour or so later the first snowflakes began to fall. The path grew steeper still, and the rocks under foot were glazed with ice while icicles hung from ledges on either side. It took every ounce of Steve's determination to keep climbing until, at last, Bolivar paused briefly and allowed him to catch up. It was snowing more heavily now, and the view was obscured by a curtain of falling flakes.

Steve managed to find enough breath to ask, 'How high are we?'

'Around two and half thousand metres,' Bolivar replied. 'Come. We still have far to go.'

They began to descend, but soon the snow was up to the laces of Steve's boots. It collected on his shoulders and the hood of his coat and clung to his eyebrows. His toes were numb and so were his hands. He had trekked in the mountains of Alaska, though he had never done any serious mountaineering, and even then, he had had good boots and clothing designed for extreme weather. He knew the dangers of conditions like these and that unless they reached shelter before nightfall, they would probably not survive. For a while he allowed himself to believe that at least they had passed the highest point, but soon the path began to climb again. From then on, he was conscious only of the effort required to place each foot in the footprints left by his guide. The snow grew deeper, until it was up to his calves. He no longer looked around him. Only the sight of Bolivar's boots, plodding steadily upwards, kept him moving.

At last, they began to descend, and Bolivar looked over his shoulder to call, 'We've made it. The refuge is just ahead.'

Steve stepped inside the hut, and for a moment, all he could do was stand stock still, feeling the accumulated snow slipping from his shoulders and experiencing the relief of being sheltered from the wind. Bolivar quickly set a match to the dry kindling in the fireplace. Then he came to Steve and, with surprising gentleness, eased the rucksack from his shoulders.

'Get your coat off and come to the fire.' he said. 'You did well today.'

Steve did as he was told, feeling a small glow of warmth that was not only due to the heat of the flames. The pleasure was shot through with pain as circulation returned to his numbed hands and feet, but another mug of hot coffee, well-infused with plum brandy, did much to alleviate that. He was almost too exhausted to eat the bread and sausage that seemed to be Bolivar's staple diet, but when he had managed to swallow most of it, Bolivar handed him a small package.

'Here. Something to restore your strength.'

Steve opened the package. 'Chocolate! I haven't eaten chocolate for months.'

Bolivar gave one of his rare grins. 'As I said, what's the use of being a smuggler…?'

As soon as he had eaten the chocolate, Steve stretched out on a palliasse in front of the fire and fell instantly asleep.

Waking next morning, his first thought was of the route ahead. He was not at all sure that he could manage another day like yesterday.

Bolivar was already busy with the fire and the morning coffee. Seeing Steve drag himself into a sitting position, he said, 'No more snow today. By tonight we shall be in Spain.'

Steve's faint hope that there was no more climbing ahead of them was soon extinguished. They descended at first, but soon the track rose steeply again, but, today at least, the sun was shining, and after he had walked off his initial stiffness he found the ascent less of a struggle than he expected. They descended briefly to pass a lake, where the morning mist hung between the shoulders of the hills. After that, it was a long hard slog up to another mountain pass, which Bolivar told him was the Col de Claouère.

'Look down,' he said. 'That is Spain.'

'Praise God!' Steve responded with feeling.

'Do not run away with the idea that once there you are safe,' Bolivar said. 'If the Spanish Guardia Civil catch us they will send us back to Vichy France, who will hand us over to the Germans, where I shall probably be shot and you will be returned to a prison camp.'

'But why would they do that?' Steve exclaimed.

'Because Franco is a friend of Hitler. Spain is neutral, but that does not mean they do not care who wins this war. We must go carefully.'

If Steve had thought that the long descent would be easy, he soon learned otherwise. Going down he found muscles and joints in his anatomy of which he had previously been unaware. The only consolation was that breathing grew easier. By the time they reached the River Noguera Pallaresa, he was so tired that he was, in his own terms, on 'automatic pilot', plodding along with his head down, thinking of nothing except how much he wanted to sit down. Bolivar's grip on his arm jolted him out of his stupor.

'Down! Here, quick!'

He was half dragged, half thrown onto the ground close to a gap in the low stone wall that bordered the road. He lifted his head and saw that they were approaching a bridge over the river. From the far side came the noise of engines. Bolivar was crawling through the gap so that he was hidden from the road by the wall. Steve followed just in time as two motorcycles ridden by men in the uniform of the Guardia Civil came over the hump of the bridge. If Bolivar had not been alert, they would have walked straight into them.

Instead of coming on over the bridge and past the place where Steve and Bolivar were hiding, the two men stopped their bikes. Steve's heart was pounding. Had they been spotted after all? The prospect of being arrested and returned to France, after all he had gone through to get here, was intolerable. Frantically his mind sought for a way out. There was no way he could pass himself off as Spanish. Would it help to tell them he was American and demand to be taken to the American consulate? But how could he prove it – and what reason could he give for his presence? And what about Bolivar? His mind turned to the possibility of bribery. Major Higgins had furnished him with some Spanish pesetas but hardly sufficient to tempt two officers.

All this flashed through his mind as he lay prostrate in the mud. Above his head, he could hear the two men talking. Their voices sounded relaxed, but without knowing the language it was hard to tell. Then he heard the sound of a match being struck and risked raising his head a fraction. The two men were leaning on the parapet of the bridge, smoking. His first reaction was relief. They had not seen him, or Bolivar. Then he realised that it only needed for one of the guards to glance in their direction to spot them where they lay. The wall hid them from the road, but from the top of the bridge they could be seen easily, and there was no cover to be had in the field. Ahead of him, the ground sloped down to the riverbank where there were some leafless bushes, but any movement might attract attention.

He saw that Bolivar was inching forward, flat to the ground, propelling himself with his elbows. Above them, one of the guards had turned to lean his back on the parapet, obscuring the other's line of vision. Steve took the chance to wriggle forwards in his turn, keeping as close to the wall as he could. Bolivar had progressed nearer to the riverbank. A few feet further and the structure of the bridge itself would hide them, unless someone was leaning right over the parapet. The second man straightened up and said something and they both laughed. A cigarette butt hissed as it hit the water. By now, both Steve and Bolivar were almost at the river's edge, pressing themselves against the bridge. Words were exchanged above them and a stream of liquid pattered down onto the sparse bushes a few feet away. *Great!* Steve thought. *You would have to choose this spot for a piss!* Then, to his immense relief, he heard the bikes' engines start up and the noise passed above their heads and slowly faded into the distance. It was not until the only sound was the splashing of the water in the river and the rustle of the wind through the grass that he and Bolivar hauled themselves back up the bank and got to their feet.

Bolivar was grinning. 'Close!' he said. 'But not close enough to win a cigar!'

'If you hadn't had your wits about you they'd have got both of us,' Steve said.

'Ah, I'm an old hand at this game,' Bolivar responded. 'Come, not far to go now.'

They walked on along a track that followed the river until they came to a small village.

'Don't worry,' Bolivar said. 'I have friends here. They will give us a bed for the night.'

He knocked on the door of a small, stone-built house on the outskirts, and it was opened by a tiny, wizened woman who greeted him like a long-lost son. She seemed unsurprised by Steve's appearance and quickly set out bowls of mutton broth and chunks of bread for them. Before long two men came in, the woman's husband and son, as far as Steve was able to deduce, and they, too, accepted his presence without question. An open staircase led to an upper room, roughly divided by a curtain. On one side was the bed where the husband and wife slept; on the other one, a large bed accommodated the son, with Bolivar and Steve. It was a strange sensation to bed down so close to a complete stranger, but nothing would have kept him awake for long that night.

In the morning Bolivar said, 'There is a bus that will take you as far as Sort. Don't be alarmed. No one will question why you are on it. But when you get to Sort you must be careful. Sometimes the Guardia keep a watch there. There is another, bigger bus that goes to Barcelona. Do you have money?'

'Yes. Major Higgins gave me some.'

'Good. You can buy a bus ticket from the newsagent near the bus station. When you have it, find a place where you can wait without being obvious until just before the bus leaves. Then, if no one is checking papers, you can board it. It is a risk, but it is the only way you will get to Barcelona.'

'Then that's what I shall have to do,' Steve said. 'And you? What will you do?'

'Oh, I have business here. Then, if the weather holds, I shall go back.'

'Back the way we came?'

'There is no other.'

Steve shivered inwardly at the thought of anyone enduring that crossing twice, and of their own free will. 'You're a brave man, Bolivar.'

Bolivar shrugged. 'It's a living. But you, you are going back to risk your life in a war. That is brave. Now, we should go. You don't want to miss the bus.'

Steve asked if he should offer his hostess some money, but Bolivar assured him that would be seen as an insult. 'Don't worry. They will not be out of pocket. I shall see to that.'

He walked Steve to a spot on the road where four women were waiting with baskets on their arms. They nodded to him in recognition and glanced incuriously at Steve, then returned to their conversation.

Bolivar held out his hand. 'Goodbye. Good luck.'

Steve gripped it. 'Good luck to you, too, on those mountains. And thank you. I shall never forget what you have done. Maybe, when the war is over, I can come back to visit.'

'Maybe,' Bolivar agreed. 'But for now, *vaya con Dios* as they say here. Go with God.'

Their eyes met and spoke more than words could convey. Then Bolivar turned and strode back along the street. In the distance, Steve heard the sound of the approaching bus.

Chapter Thirty-One

Julian Avery's replacement was a man called Tom Masterson. An unlikely-looking secret agent, Leo thought, with his tousled hair and glasses. However, he soon made it clear that he had a good grasp of the situation in Yugoslavia and intended to call his 'bomb-happy amateurs' to order. On October 28th, news had come that Italy had invaded Greece from its bases in Albania. Leo and Sasha were called to meet Masterson at Glen's house, together with the rest of the group.

'This Italian invasion requires us to re-think our priorities,' Masterson said. 'The Greeks are holding firm at the moment. I hear they have got the Italians pinned down in the mountains. So far, so good. With winter coming, both sides might settle for the stalemate for the time being. But in the spring the Italians are bound to make another push. Now, suppose the Greek line holds firm and the Italians can't make any headway. What is Hitler going to do?'

'You think he will feel it necessary to come to Mussolini's aid?' Peter Boughey asked.

'I would say he doesn't have any choice. He can't let his principal ally be defeated. And if he decides to do that, how is he going to get his troops there?'

'Straight through Serbia,' Sasha said. 'Don't worry. The possibility has not been lost on the royal council.'

'With what effect?' Masterson asked.

'The pro-German faction are pressing Paul harder than ever to come to some accommodation with Hitler, on the basis that when the war is over – and they are convinced Hitler is going to win – he'll leave us alone and allow us to retain our independence.'

'Do they really believe that?' Masterson asked. 'I can't see Hitler passing up the chance of incorporating Yugoslavia into Greater Germany, can you?'

'I've put that point as forcefully as I can,' Sasha said. 'But Paul is simply too terrified to think straight.'

'Which is why we need to get rid of him and put young Peter in his place, with Simovic as head of government,' Alexander Glen said.

'Unfortunately, they don't see it like that in Whitehall,' Masterson told him. 'Our lords and masters are firmly convinced that Paul will behave like an English gentleman who would never welch on his friends. And they have this vision of "brave little Serbia" standing up to Germany just like they did in the last war.'

'At what a terrible cost!' Leo spoke with feeling.

'And if Paul could be persuaded to resist, would the British government send troops and equipment to help?' Sasha asked.

Masterson spread his hands regretfully. 'We're hanging on by our eyelashes as it is. The chance of any substantial support is virtually nil, I'm afraid.'

'Then how can we expect Paul to listen to our arguments?'

'That's why we need to replace him,' Glen pressed his argument.

'The view in London is that losing his potential ally might just prompt Hitler to invade.'

'So we are damned if we do and damned if we don't,' Sasha said heavily. 'We have the choice of allying ourselves with the Nazis or standing alone against them.'

'And if that happened – I mean if Hitler invades – will the Yugoslav army fight?'

'Yes, for as long as they can hold out.'

'You seem to be implying that that would not be for very long.'

'The army is in desperate need of modernisation. Much of the equipment dates from the last war. Some has been imported more recently, largely from Czechoslovakia, but also from Italy. As a result, there are problems with servicing and spare parts. There are mechanised units, but there is far too much reliance on horse-drawn transport. Altogether, we can muster around one hundred tanks, some of which also date from the last war. Supplies of ammunition are limited, to say the least. Quite frankly, if there was a general mobilisation, I doubt if we could provide enough boots for everyone.'

There was a heavy silence. At length, Masterson said, 'Things are worse than I realised.'

'There is another factor to consider, too,' Sasha said. 'We talk about the Royal Yugoslav Army, as if we were truly one united country. But we are not. I have some doubts as to whether the Croatian units, or the Slovenian ones, would be prepared to fight to protect what they see as a Serb-dominated Yugoslavia.'

'Sasha's right there,' Alexander Glen put in. 'My contacts in Croatia have suggested as much to me.'

'Well,' Masterson said, 'that gives even greater weight to what I was going to propose. We have to prepare for the fact that the country may be overrun. Our job, as I see it, is to set up and prepare a robust resistance movement. To that end, I have got the agreement of Baker Street to supply certain "toys and chocolates" which we can store and distribute where we think they can do most good.'

Baker Street was the head office of the SOE, so it was clear to everyone present that the initiative came from there and not from the Ministry of War or any other government department.

'Does Campbell know about this?' Glen asked.

Masterson patted the side of his nose. 'Let's say, what the eye doesn't see, the heart will not grieve over. But the equipment will have to come in under cover of the diplomatic bag, so he can't be completely in the dark.'

The new direction of their efforts was agreed upon, and over the next months, supplies of rifles, grenades, explosives, fuses and detonators arrived by courier and were hidden in the basement of Masterson's office in the Legation annexe, to be distributed according to the various contacts that had been established by Glen and his colleagues. Ronald Campbell, the minister, remained deeply unhappy about the situation as the scheme was being carried out without the knowledge of Prince Paul and the legitimate government, and as a result, SOE was given a separate office, not connected to the Legation, although Masterson remained under diplomatic cover.

Leo and Sasha were only tangentially involved since neither of them was officially a member of SOE. Their remit was to continue to provide insight into the machinations of the courtiers around Prince Paul. In the years since their marriage, they had become known for hosting dinner parties where an eclectic mixture of guests might meet and mingle, and under cover of these, they continued to sound out opinion and build up a coalition among influential academics and the higher ranks of the army and the Air Force in favour of a coup.

There was one bright hope amid the growing chaos and that was the young Crown Prince. Sasha had for a long time been one of Peter's closest friends and advisers, and he and Leo were often at the palace. Usually they met Peter in what was known as the Thatched House in the Royal Compound. It was built in the style of traditional Serbian homes and had served as a schoolroom for Peter and his younger brothers until they were sent away to school in England. Leo liked the young prince very much. He was a strikingly good-looking boy, with the long, straight nose typical of his people and thick dark hair and his eyes were always sparkling with enthusiasm for whatever his latest interest might be. At that time it was motor cars, as he had just learned to drive. He had enjoyed his schooldays in England and was very pro-British and frequently expressed his vehement wish that his country and Britain could be allies. The prospect of signing any agreement with Hitler was equally vehemently rejected, but at the same time, he showed a surprising degree of maturity with regard to the dilemma faced by the Regent.

'I feel sorry for Uncle Paul,' he said one day. 'I know he never wanted to be regent. All he has ever wanted is a quiet life.'

'That is why your father nominated him to take that role if anything should happen to him,' Sasha said. 'He knew he would never be tempted to oust you and set up his own dynasty.'

'I understand that,' Peter responded. 'But he seems to think that means he has to keep everything exactly as my father left it, to hand it on to me. And that's impossible as things are now. Don't you agree?'

'I do,' Sasha said gravely.

'If only my eighteenth birthday were closer!' the boy exclaimed. 'Then we could start to change things.'

Sasha and Leo exchanged looks, but he said only, 'Be patient. It's only a few months away.'

The situation took a turn for the worse with the news that Hitler had forced Hungary and Romania to sign the 'Tripartite Pact', a treaty of mutual aid signed originally between Germany, Italy and Japan. This produced an atmosphere of panic in the Yugoslav governing council. Milan Nedic, the Minister for the Army and Navy, immediately began to press Prince Paul to sign as well, in the hope that Germany would then protect them from 'greedy neighbours'.

For a while, Paul vacillated, then to the relief of all the British agents and of Leo and Sasha, he dismissed Nedic and replaced him with the ageing General Pesic. For the time being, the talk of a *coup d'etat* was relegated to some unspecified future date.

Chapter Thirty-Two

Paris

November 1940

Back in Paris, after an uneventful journey, Alix noticed a change of mood among her communist friends. Until then, the only relaxation of the pro-German stance prescribed by the Comintern had been to prohibit expressions of support for the occupying forces; but the photograph of Pétain shaking hands with Hitler had provoked outrage and an upsurge of patriotic feeling. Alix made a point of calling in at Chez Michel regularly, to gauge opinion and look out for new recruits, and now she found that talk was turning to the possibility of some form of action to demonstrate their refusal to collaborate. What it should be and when it should happen was the main topic of discussion.

There was general agreement that Armistice Day, November 11th, would be perfect. Especially if they could stage a demonstration at a large remembrance ceremony. But two days later posters appeared on walls and notice-boards around the city signed by General von Stülpnagel banning all forms of remembrance ceremonies or processions. November 11th was to be a normal working day; schools and factories were to open as usual. The mood among the patrons of Chez Michel darkened.

'We won't let them stop us!' was the assertion heard everywhere.

One of the leaders was a young man called Jacques Brunel, who had been a close friend of Raoul's, 'We have to publicise what we are going to do,' he said. 'We need to let all the high schools and colleges know what we are planning.'

'I think I can help there,' Alix said. 'I can get leaflets printed, and I know people who will go round and deliver them.'

'It will be risky,' he said. 'If anyone is caught...'

'Yes, we know that,' she replied. It was on the tip of her tongue to tell him that she and her friends were already used to this kind of subversive activity, but she kept silent. In the event, when the leaflets were produced, there was no lack of volunteers to distribute them.

Crowded round the clandestine radio in the museum on November 10th, Alix and her friends were delighted to hear the demonstration announced on the BBC. She and her little group had been busy all day creating a wreath to lay at the Tomb of the Unknown Soldier. Fresh flowers were hard to come by, but Moira had managed to find some red crêpe paper in one of the shops that used to supply artists' materials and they had made dozens of artificial poppies and attached them to some evergreen branches purloined from the Jardin des Plantes.

The next morning they set out at ten o'clock to be in good time to reach the Place de l'Étoile for eleven, but when they reached the Champs-Élysèes, they found it already thronged with people. There were school groups in uniform where ages ranged as far as Alix could guess from as young as twelve to eighteen, and students from various institutions all over the city, all carrying wreaths or posies of flowers, many of them in the colours of the tricolour, red, white and blue. The mood was respectful, as befitted a day of remembrance, but there was an underlying feeling of defiance.

Hanna pressed Alix's arm. 'Isn't this wonderful? So many people showing they are prepared to stand up against the occupation.'

Alix was less euphoric. 'The Nazis can't just ignore a demonstration like this. I don't know how they will react.'

'What can they do? They can't arrest this many people.'

'No, I suppose not,' Alix agreed as they wormed their way into the crowd. She knew she should be thrilled by the success of the appeals they had sent out, but she was oppressed by a sense of responsibility. If the occupying troops were to take action and any of these children were hurt she knew it would be partly her fault.

Her mood lightened as they walked on. Shopkeepers and their customers came to their doors and called out words of encouragement. A line of women waiting to collect their rations gave them a cheer. There seemed to be no sign of police or soldiers. It took a long time to reach the Place de l'Étoile and by the time they got there a huge crowd surrounded the Arc de Triomphe, but it was an orderly crowd. Group after group moved forward to lay their tributes at the Tomb of the Unknown Soldier, which was soon invisible behind the surrounding bank of flowers. When they had laid their wreaths, each group moved back to allow others to take their place, but no one seemed to want to go home. They milled around, chatting among themselves or with others in the crowd. There was a rumour going around. The night before, the story ran, a party of young Frenchmen had encountered a group of German soldiers. An argument had broken out and punches had been thrown. Someone had been arrested but nobody knew who.

Looking about her, Alix saw that there were small parties of gendarmes gathering at the junctions where the various streets opened out into the Place, but so far they seemed content to watch. Then, around midday, there was a stir in the crowd, and all attention turned to a new group making its way towards the tomb. It was a party of young men whom Alix recognised from the gatherings at Chez Michel, and they were carrying their own floral tribute. It was this that was causing the stir. It was in the shape of a Cross of Lorraine, the chosen symbol of de Gaulle and the Free French movement he had established. This was too much for the authorities to tolerate. A troop of gendarmes forced their way through the crowd, seized the cross, broke it up and drove the men carrying it back out of the square.

The mood of the crowd began to change after that. Someone began to sing the Marseillaise and hundreds of voices took it up. The policemen returned to their positions, but there were more of them now, and soon Alix saw they had been joined by German soldiers carrying rifles. Some of the school groups began to filter out of the square, heading for home, but many of the older children and most of the students stayed on. Alix asked her little group what they wanted to do and they all insisted on staying. No one knew what they were waiting for, but there was a general sense that the drama of the day had not yet played out. The November dusk settled around them. By now they were reduced to a hardcore, gathered closely around the Arc. Someone raised a chant of '*Vive la France*', and it was taken up by the whole crowd. To that was added '*Vive l'Angleterre*' and, occasionally, '*Vive de Gaulle'*. It was not long before a voice over a loud hailer ordered everyone to leave the area, on pain of being arrested.

Some of the protestors did slip away, but the rest stayed, Alix with them. By now it had become a point of honour to resist the threat. It was cold, and a thin rain had started to fall. Alix looked at her companions.

'If any of you want to head for home…'

'Are you staying?'

'Yes.'

'Then we stay with you.'

Several boys who belonged to the other cells set up by Boris and Anatole Lewitsky were also there. Officially, Alix was not supposed to know their identities, but she had seen some of them around the museum, and they obviously recognised her. The two groups drew together for mutual support.

'*Merde!* Look.' It was Hanna.

Alix followed her gaze. All around the Place, in the gathering darkness, there was now a ring of armed soldiers. Beyond them, she could see others stopping traffic on all the adjoining streets. Three boys who had started to leave came scurrying back.

'They've closed the metro stations. There's no way out.'

The ring of soldiers advanced, and at an order, Alix saw to her horror, that they were fixing bayonets. Then there was another order, the rifles were raised and shots rang out. Alix clasped Hanna and Moira to her.

'It's all right! They are firing into the air.'

It was too much for some of the remaining protestors. There was a general charge, and some of them succeeded in slipping through the phalanx of soldiers. The rest of them were forced back until they were shoulder to shoulder with their backs to the base of the Arc and still the soldiers advanced, bayonets levelled. Alix shrank back, but there was no way to retreat.

Hands gripped her arm, she was dragged away from her friends, held between two men, her feet dragging on the pavement. They came to a van, a door was opened and she was thrown bodily inside and the door slammed shut. In the darkness, she became aware of others, crammed in beside her, boys and girls.

'Hanna?' she called.

'I'm here,' said a small voice.

'Moira?'

There was no reply.

'Suzanne? Christine? Paulette?'

Still no response.

One of the boys swore. 'Bastards! Nazi bastards! They have no right...'

'They don't need one,' someone else responded. 'They've got guns.'

The van swerved, heading through the streets at top speed, siren blaring. Alix found herself repeatedly thrown against the side and then back to collide with another body. Eventually, the van stopped and the rear doors were opened.

'Out!' said a German voice.

Dazed and shaken, she scrambled out with the others. They were in a yard surrounded by high walls and lit by searchlights. She looked around and found Hanna and they clutched each other for support.

'Over there!' came the order, and they were all pushed to stand in a line along one of the walls.

Alix looked along the line and found Suzanne and Paulette, who had been beside her when the soldiers moved in. Christine was a little further along. Another van drove in, and Alix did not know whether to be relieved or not when she saw Moira pulled out. She had a handkerchief pressed to her head, and when she got closer, Alix saw that it was soaked with blood. The newcomers were also ordered to line up by the wall and in the general shuffling Alix managed to grab Moira's arm.

'What happened?'

'I fell when one of them was dragging me away and I cracked my head on the paving.'

Alix put her arm around her and drew her to where Hanna stood. They huddled together, shivering.

Next, the boys were separated from the girls and sent to stand along the opposite wall. A German officer took up a position in front of the girls. He looked along the line, and Alix saw him smirk.

'Take off your clothes.'

'What?'

'You heard me. Strip!'

Anger welled up in Alix's throat. 'You can't make us do that!'

'Can't I? Come here.'

A soldier grabbed Alix's arm and thrust her forward.

'Take her coat off.'

The coat was pulled off her. The officer reached out and grabbed the front of her shirt. With a jerk he tore it down to her waist.

Alix lifted her chin. 'Is this German honour? I thought you were a civilised race.'

The remark earned her a slap that sent her staggering. 'Now, either you do as you are told, or I shall do it for you. Get back in line.'

She was shoved back into place, and the officer shouted. 'All of you. You see what happens if you disobey. Strip!'

Alix straightened her back and looked along the line. 'Come on, ladies. If this pervert gets his kicks out of watching girls undress, let's show him we are not ashamed. It is the honour of Germany that is tarnished, not ours.'

She pulled off the torn shirt and stepped out of her skirt. Along the line the other girls followed her example, throwing off their clothes with gestures of contempt and refusing to let the men see that they were embarrassed. Alix looked at the ordinary soldiers guarding them and saw that while some were grinning, there was an expression of unease on many faces. When the women were down to their underwear, the officer said abruptly, 'Enough!' and walked away.

For some minutes they all stood still, afraid to put their clothes back on. Then Alix reached down and found the coat Moira had discarded. Slowly she picked it up, expecting to be ordered to drop it, but no order came. She placed the coat around Moira's shoulders and she huddled into it. Along the line, other girls were tentatively reaching for some covering and they were not stopped. Alix found her own coat and put it on. It was only a light one and the rain had already soaked it, but it was better than nothing.

Orders were being shouted on the other side of the yard and the boys were told to strip too. One or two who refused were beaten by the guards. Then a dozen boys were picked out of the line and marched away. A few minutes later there was the sound of rifle fire.

Moira cried out, 'Oh, God have mercy!' There were screams and similar cries all along the line.

After that, nothing happened. The guards stood impassively, their faces now blank. Alix called out to them, 'How long do we have to stand here? Why can't we go home?' There was no response. The women stood shivering in the rain and the hours passed painfully slowly. One or two fell to their knees with exhaustion and were ordered back to their feet by the guards. Alix and her friends huddled together for warmth. Along the line, others were doing the same thing, the stronger supporting the weaker girls. At last, the sky above the walls grew lighter. The guards watching them were relieved, and the new men stared at them as if they were exhibits in a zoo. Finally, another officer appeared.

'Right. You've learned your lesson, I hope. You can go.'

Dazed and exhausted, hardly able to believe the ordeal was over, they gathered up the rest of their clothes and stumbled towards the gate. A small cheer from the boys drew Alix's attention, and to her great relief, she saw that the ones who had been marched away were returning, apparently unharmed. In the street, she looked back, curious to know where it was that they had been held. A sign above the gate told her it was La Santé, one of the most notorious prisons in France.

A voice called her name and she looked round to see Boris Vildé and Marie Louise hurrying towards her.

'Oh, thank God! Thank God!' Marie Louise cried out, throwing her arms around Alix. 'We have been so worried!'

'But what have they done to you?' Boris demanded. 'What has happened to your clothes?'

Alix told him what had happened as briefly as she could.

'*Cochons!* Swine!' he exclaimed. 'To treat children like this!'

Alix felt she ought to protest at being called a child, but just then her need for the protection of a father figure trumped pride.

The rest of her group had gathered around them.

'Are these your people?' Boris asked.

'Yes.'

'Quickly, all of you! I've managed to find a taxi. He's waiting over there.'

Taxis were very rare beasts indeed in these days of petrol rationing, and Alix wondered how much it had cost Boris to bribe the driver to wait for them. It was a tight fit but they all squeezed in somehow, and Alix felt tears of relief running down her cheeks. The taxi was unheated, but at least she was out of the rain – and, more importantly, safe from the sadistic power of the Nazis.

Boris leaned in through the window and touched her arm. 'Have a good rest. Then, when you feel up to it, come to the museum.'

Back at the College Franco Britannique, Alix and her friends separated with few words and hurried up to their rooms. Alix longed above everything for a hot shower but such luxuries were a thing of the past. With supplies of coal for the boiler almost unobtainable, the only source of hot water was her electric kettle. She washed herself and pulled on some dry clothes. Breakfast was just being served to the remaining students in residence, and she was torn between the desire to crawl into bed and sleep and the need for food. In the end, hunger won. It was a meagre affair – ersatz coffee and gritty bread, with nothing to spread on it but margarine that for some reason always tasted of fish – but Alix found herself cramming the food into her mouth as if afraid it would be taken away from her. It seemed a very long time since she had last eaten. When she had finished, she went back to her room and got into bed, spreading her dressing gown over the top of her blankets for extra warmth, but in spite of that, she found she could not stop shivering. It was a long time before she felt warm enough to fall asleep.

She was woken a few hours later by the concierge hammering on her door.

'Get up! You have to get your things together. The College is closing down.'

'What do you mean, closing down?' Alix asked, still only half awake.

'Orders from the military governor. He's shutting down the Sorbonne and all the student accommodation belonging to it. Now, get on with it. You have to be out by tonight.'

In the corridor, students were milling around with their suitcases.

'This is all your fault!' a girl said. 'You were one of the ones on the demo, weren't you? That's why we're being shut down.'

'What does it matter?' someone else asked. 'The lectures have virtually stopped anyway.'

'It's all very well for you! You can go home to your family. Mine are in the free zone. How am I expected to get there? Where are we supposed to sleep tonight?'

Alix sought out the girls in her group. Suzanne's parents lived in Paris, and she had already invited Paulette to stay with them, and Christine's family were not far away in Chartres, but for Hanna and Moira, things were very different.

'There's nothing for it. I shall have to go home to Ireland,' Moira said. 'I'm going to the embassy now. At least, as Ireland is neutral, I shouldn't have any difficulty getting out. But I hate leaving the rest of you.'

'It can't be helped,' Alix said. 'Our little group is breaking up anyway. We shall have to think of different ways to resist from now on.'

'I don't know what I'm going to do,' Hanna said tearfully. 'I can't go home, like the rest of you.'

'Come with me,' Alix said. 'Boris and Marie Louise will help out.'

They all exchanged addresses and promised to meet up again 'when the war is over and the Germans have been beaten'. Then Alix said goodbye to all of them except Hanna, and they set off for the museum.

Boris shook his head wearily. 'I should have foreseen this.'

'The demo wasn't your idea,' Alix pointed out. 'You can't blame yourself.'

'What matters is finding somewhere for you two girls to stay,' Marie Louise said, always practical. 'Alix, you can come and live with me. But I'm afraid there really isn't room for Hanna as well.'

'That's not a problem,' Boris said at once. 'Hanna can stay with us.'

So it was arranged – and a new act in the drama began.

Chapter Thirty-Three

December 1940

'Ye gods and little fishes! If it isn't Popeye the Sailor Man!'

The sergeants' mess fell silent and all eyes turned to the man who stood just inside the door. The speaker jumped to his feet and ran over to him.

'We thought you'd bought it, along with Johnny Johnson and young Rusty Rogers. Where the hell have you been all this time?'

'Oh, here and there,' Steve said vaguely. He didn't feel like embarking on the story of his escape immediately. He looked around the room. There were some familiar faces, but a lot of new ones, too – younger than ever, it seemed to him. Friendly hands drew him to sit at a table and a pint of beer appeared in front of him. 'So, what have you guys been up to while I've been away?' he asked.

There was a brief silence. Steve was aware of quick glances being exchanged while some of the men lowered their eyes as if unwilling to speak.

The man who had first greeted him was Sam Henderson, who had been in charge of the ground crew responsible for the Blenheim bomber in which Steve had flown. He said, 'Oh, this and that.'

'It's been bad, huh?'

'Pretty bad, yes.'

Steve recognised that if he was to be told what had happened he would first have to be more forthcoming about his own experiences. He looked around. 'Well, it's good to be back. Sorry I haven't been around to help out.'

'So, what happened? Where have you been?'

As briefly as possible Steve told the story of the crash and his escape, his time in Brussels and his journey through France and his crossing of the Pyrenees. 'After that, it was more or less plain sailing,' he added. 'I got a local bus to the nearest town, a place called Sort. No one seemed to take any notice of me, but I had a couple of nasty moments in Sort itself. I saw two Guardia Civil – Spanish policemen – giving another young guy a hard time. I couldn't tell what was going on, but I think they arrested him. He might have been trying to escape, like me, but I don't know. I managed to hide in a little side street until the bus to Barcelona was about to leave, then I jumped aboard – and that was it. When I got there, I went to the British consulate, and the Consul got me into Gibraltar in the boot of an embassy car. And from there they flew me back to the good old UK.'

By the time he finished all conversation in the mess had stopped and he was surrounded by intent young faces. There was a moment's silence, then Henderson clapped him on the shoulder.

'Well, that's certainly some story! You're one lucky so-and-so.'

'I guess I am,' Steve agreed. 'Now, your turn. What's been going on here?'

It was a dispiriting account. He learnt for the first time that in the operation in which he had been shot down, twelve planes had been lost. Eight aircrew had been killed, twelve were listed as 'missing in action', and three had been taken prisoner. The squadron had almost been destroyed, and only the determination of the Wing Commander had seen it rebuilt. The tally went on; one aircraft lost here, two more there. The simple fact was that the Blenheim was not fast enough to compete with the German 109s. No wonder, Steve reflected, that he could see so few familiar faces.

Later that night he lay in bed feeling strangely empty. For more than six months his whole focus had been on getting back to England to rejoin his comrades. Even in the almost peaceful interlude, working with Yvette in the garage, it had never been far from his mind. Now he was here he found himself among strangers – or so it felt. Apart from Sam Henderson and a few of the ground crew, there was no one he remembered in the sergeants' mess. After dinner, he had wandered along to the Shady Oak. There was a little group of RAF officers sitting in the corner where he had sat with Johnny Johnson and the other pilots, but he did not recognise any of them, and no one waved him over to join them. He left and went back to the base. It would be different in a few days, he told himself. Tomorrow he would be given a new plane with a new pilot and radio operator. They would be a team, just like before. But for how long? Given the record of losses over the past months he did not give much for his chances of staying alive for more than a few weeks – and he could not expect to be as lucky as he had been in the event of another crash.

It occurred to him that he could have gone to the US consulate instead of the British one in Barcelona and asked to be repatriated. He could be back in Fairbanks with his family by now. The RAF would never know the difference. He would continue to be listed as 'missing in action'. The trouble was, he would know. He would know that he had taken the coward's way out – and his family would know that too. He had written home as soon as he reached England, to let them know that he was alive and safe – for the moment at least. He knew it would be a relief to them to have him home, but what was he supposed to do then? Go back to studying at the university? Wait for his own country to declare war, as it must surely do sooner or later, and then start all over again? He was unable to imagine such a prospect.

He had been back in the UK for over a week now. He had expected to be sent straight back to his squadron, but instead, he had been sent to Bomber Command HQ in High Wycombe to be debriefed. Then he was sent a few miles away to a grand house set in a large park just outside Beaconsfield. Here he had been interrogated in great detail about his escape by an army officer who introduced himself as Langley. He was also asked to provide information about life behind enemy lines, both in Belgium and in France. What was the general attitude of the civilian population? Who was in charge of law and order, local police or the occupying forces? The questions went on until Steve felt his whole brain had been dredged for details. When the questioning was over he was sent back to High Wycombe, where he was offered two weeks' leave. He turned it down, saying he would rather get back to his squadron. Now he was beginning to regret the decision.

Next day, as expected, he was assigned to a new crew. The pilot was a boy called Laurence Glynn, and he was just nineteen. The radio operator's name was Ben Whittle, and he was the same age. At twenty-two, Steve felt like an old man. The very next day they were sent to bomb German shipping in the Channel. They had dropped their bomb without scoring a hit and were turning for home when the 109s found them. Glynn threw the plane around the sky with impressive dexterity. He even seemed to be enjoying himself. Then came a yell of triumph from Whittle in the gun turret. 'Got the bugger!' The 109 spiralled away with black smoke streaming from the engine, and they saw it hit the water. Another Blenheim in the flight saw it too and was able to confirm it, so they could claim their first 'kill'.

Over the next weeks, the atmosphere in the mess became more optimistic. Steve discovered that one great advantage of being back in the UK was being able to listen to the news reports on the BBC without huddling round a secret radio set to pick up Radio Londres. Britain was on the offensive at last, fighting the Italians in North Africa, and the RAF was carrying the war to German cities. A cheer went up when news came in of a bombing raid on the city of Mannheim and of a British victory at Sidi Birani in Egypt.

Steve and his crew completed several more missions without casualties and he began to believe that his luck would hold. Then one morning he was summoned to the CO's office.

'I've had a signal from some outfit in London. It seems they want to talk to you.'

'I've already been debriefed pretty thoroughly, sir,' Steve responded. 'I don't know what else they want me for.'

'Ours not to reason why,' the CO said. 'You are to report to the Inter-Services Research Bureau in Baker

Street ASAP. Get the office to issue you with a rail warrant.'

During his time in Brussels and in France Steve had heard reports on Radio Londres of bombing raids on London and his new comrades had referred from time to time to the destruction they had wrought as justification for the bombing of German cities, but he had never been to London and had been unable to visualise the scope of the damage. As the train rattled slowly through the suburbs, he began to get some idea of what the people had suffered. He had a view of the backs of small houses, each with a garden reaching down to the railway track. He began to see gaps in these rows, like missing teeth, where only piles of rubble remained. The closer they came to the centre, the more frequent these gaps became. Sometimes he could see the wall of a house remaining, shreds of wallpaper hanging off it, sometimes a cupboard or a mirror still precariously in place. Once there was a child's cot suspended at a crazy angle in a corner. Yet as far as he could tell, people were going about their daily business. Buses crawled along streets littered with debris, bicycles wound their way around the obstacles, women queued for rations just as he had seen in Brussels.

At Liverpool Street station he managed to find a taxi to take him to Baker Street. The journey took him across the centre of the city and here he was able to get a more comprehensive picture. Again and again the taxi had to turn back because the road ahead was blocked. The flanks of three and four-storey buildings were left exposed where the adjacent building had been sheered away. Once, Steve saw a London bus half buried where a crater had opened in the middle of a road. And everywhere gangs of men and women were scrabbling away at the ruins, heaving aside blocks of masonry in a search for… what? Lost belongings, or the bodies of friends and family?

His taxi driver provided a running commentary. From him, Steve learned that the majority of the population now spent their nights in underground shelters or in Tube stations. The driver himself doubled as an air raid warden at night-time, and he spoke of digging out survivors and carrying casualties to hospital.

'But my missus takes the kids down to the underground every evening,' he said. 'She takes blankets and pillows and a thermos of tea and puts the kids to sleep. She says it's quite jolly. Someone brings a squeeze box – you know, an accordion – and they have a right old sing-song. Anyway,' he added, 'we're not the only ones. Liverpool's had a right pasting, so I hear, and Coventry and Manchester.'

'Don't you ever wonder if it's worth it?' Steve asked. 'The French signed an armistice to prevent this sort of destruction.'

'Give up? Surrender to old Adolf? Never in a million years!' was the response. 'Might be all right for the Frogs, but we Brits don't give up that easy.'

As they reached their destination, Steve pulled out his wallet. 'What do I owe you?'

'Nah, you're all right,' the driver said with a nod and smile. 'We owe a lot to you boys in blue. Least I can do is give you a free ride.'

There was nothing to single the Inter-Services Research Bureau out from the other buildings in the street. Men and women in a variety of uniforms were going in and out. Steve presented himself at the reception desk and was directed to the third floor. There he was asked to wait in a corridor. He sat there feeling irritated. Why couldn't they simply share the information he had already given the people in Beaconsfield and let him get on with doing something to pay the Huns back for the damage he had just witnessed?

A secretary in a uniform he did not recognise with a flash on her shoulder that read FANY came out of a room and told him to go in. A man in civilian dress rose from behind a desk and greeted him – in Serbocroat. For a moment Steve was too taken aback to respond. Then he answered in the same language.

For the next ten minutes, he was grilled about his American origins, his family, his time in Paris and what had happened to him since. Finally, his inquisitor seemed satisfied.

'Wait here. Someone will be in to see you soon.'

A few minutes later a man wearing the uniform of a Brigadier came into the room. Steve stood up and saluted.

'As you were,' came the response, in a soft Scottish accent.

The Brigadier seated himself behind the desk and regarded Steve with sharp, assessing eyes. 'My colleague tells me that you speak fluent Serbocroat.'

'Well, I guess I'm a bit rusty,' Steve said. 'I haven't had much opportunity to use it since I left the States. But it will soon come back.'

'Very good.' The Brigadier opened a folder and took out a sheet of paper. 'You will have guessed already that this is a bit more than a routine debriefing, but before I can tell you any more I must ask you to sign this.'

'What is it?' Steve asked.

'It's a copy of the Official Secrets Act. Once you have signed it, it means that if you were to reveal any part of what I am about to tell you, you could be put up against a wall and shot. So, are you prepared to sign?'

Steve felt his pulse quicken. He sensed that he stood on the cusp of a completely new adventure. It might be risky, but it could hardly be more dangerous than flying repeated missions in a Blenheim. 'Where do I sign?' he asked.

He glanced through the document, which basically repeated in legalistic language what the Brigadier had already told him, and wrote his name at the bottom. The Brigadier took it from him and sat back in his chair.

'So, we've established that you speak the language, but you have never actually lived in Yugoslavia. Do you know anything about the situation there?'

'You mean the political situation?'

'We can start with that.'

'I know Prince Paul is being pressured to sign a pact with Hitler.'

'Indeed? How do you come to know that?'

'I don't know if the other guy – the gentleman who interviewed me before – told you I spent some time in Paris before the war.'

'Yes.'

'I met a girl there, a Serbian girl. She told me a bit about what was going on.'

The Brigadier leaned forward. 'A Serbian girl?'

'She was studying at the Sorbonne.'

'Do you happen to remember her name?'

'Yes. It was Alix, I mean Alexandra Malkovic. Her father is a Serbian count, she told me.'

For a moment the Brigadier paused, as if the inform-ation had jogged a memory. Then he went on, 'Did she tell you anything else about the situation in Yugoslavia?'

'Only that there really isn't any such place. She reckoned there was no such thing as a united kingdom of the Southern Serbs, only Serbs and Croats and Bosnians and Slovenes and Montenegrins, who all have different priorities, different religions – and the Croats and the rest hate the Serbs.'

'Hmm,' the Brigadier said. 'That seems like a reasonable summing up of the position. Given that Italy is now fighting on the side of the Axis powers, what would you say were the chances of Yugoslavia remaining neutral?'

'Pretty slim, I should think. Looks like they're between a rock and a hard place.'

'Quite. That is my assessment of the situation too. And if Hitler decides to invade, I don't believe the Serbian army will be able to withstand him. And that brings me to the point of this conversation.' He leaned forward, resting his arms on the desk. 'I belong to an organisation whose objective is to encourage and support resistance movements in countries occupied by the Nazis. Currently, I am concerned with establishing an underground network ready to do that in Yugoslavia, if it were to be overrun. To that end, I am looking for fluent Serbocroat speakers who can pass as natives and who can be embedded in the country, ready to carry out acts of sabotage and promote resistance if required. You have shown yourself to be resourceful and not lacking in courage and determination. I believe you are eminently qualified for that task.' He raised an eyebrow. 'I won't hide from you that it will be extremely dangerous… What do you say? Are you prepared to undertake it?'

Steve looked at him. His throat had gone dry. After everything that had happened, he was not sure he could face another challenge. He thought of the men and women who had helped him to escape. Their courage had to be met with courage of his own. And he thought of Alix. Was it possible that she might have gone home, and if so, what were the chances of meeting her again? He swallowed. 'I... yes, if you believe I'm the right man for the job.'

'You will not be alone. We already have people established out there. I just need to know if you are ready to join them.'

'All right. When do I leave?'

The Brigadier smiled. 'Not for a while yet. We have established a pretty exhaustive training programme. We are preparing young men like you for missions to other countries – France, Poland to mention only two. You will join them, and if you come through the training, you will then be deployed where we feel you can be most useful. Now,' he stood up, 'you can return to your squadron for the time being, but very soon you will receive notification that you are being posted elsewhere. Meanwhile, you must, of course, keep all this to yourself.'

'What should I say to my commanding officer?'

'He will be told that you are needed for special duties and that he needn't enquire further than that.' He held out his hand. 'Welcome to the Special Operations Executive. My name is Gubbins, by the way. We shall meet again in due course. Oh, and one more thing – there will be a commission for you in this. Congratulations, Pilot Officer Popovic.'

Steve passed the next few days in a kind of daze. He was informed that from now on he was confined to ground duties. It made sense. Presumably, Brigadier Gubbins didn't want to risk losing his new recruit in a bombing raid over Germany. The excuse given was that he was suffering some kind of delayed ill effects from his escape over the mountains – frost-bitten toes were suggested – but that did not stop him being the recipient of some strange looks, especially when his new commission came through and he found himself transferred to the officers' mess.

Christmas was approaching and decorations were put up in the mess. Men received cards and gifts from home. Steve had a letter from his parents. They had been praying daily for him and thanked God that he was safe. They were proud of him but wished he would come home. There were messages from the rest of his family and snippets of news, but it all seemed strangely distant. On Christmas Day there was a service led by the padre and a celebration dinner in the mess. The cooks had pulled out all the stops. There was no turkey, but there was roast beef and chicken and Christmas pudding – something Steve had never encountered before. The beer flowed freely, and there was an extra ration of rum. By the end of the evening the mood had gone from raucous to sentimental, and they finished with a sing-song, ending with the song Vera Lynn had made famous: 'We'll Meet Again'.

Two days later, the CO sent for him and told him he was being posted to a place called Wanborough Manor, somewhere in Surrey. He was to report there on January 1st.

Chapter Thirty-Four

Boris called a meeting at the museum. The usual people gathered in his office, but there was a stranger among them. Boris introduced him as Albert Gaveau.

'Albert is a mechanic, so he can offer us some very useful skills, particularly in the area of sabotage. He is prepared to put those skills to use in defeating our enemies.' He smiled at Gaveau, who grinned back, showing yellowing teeth that reminded Alix of an old dog her father had once owned.

'Now,' Boris went on, 'to business. Paul and I have decided it is time we produced our own newspaper. We have the facilities here to produce it, but we shall need all of you and your teams to distribute it. I do not have to tell you that it will be dangerous, but I am sure you can all find ways of getting it into the hands of as many people as possible. We have chosen a title for it. It will be called simply *Resistance*.'

On December 5th, the news broke that Jacques Bonsergent, the young man who had been involved in the brawl with the German soldiers, had been convicted of 'insulting the Wehrmacht' and sentenced to death. It seemed unclear whether he was, in fact, the one who had thrown the punch but he resolutely refused to name his friends and insisted on taking full responsibility. At his trial, he maintained that he wanted to show the French what sort of people the Germans really were.

Posters appeared in the city proclaiming that anyone who challenged the authority of the Reich would suffer the same fate. Alix saw little knots of men and women gazing at them in numbed silence. For the first time, the ordinary people were realising that the apparently formal and correct behaviour of their conquerors was no more than a façade. That night Alix and her friends went round the streets, tearing down as many of the posters as they could find. By the next day, it was obvious that their reaction had been shared by the rest of the population. Posters were either torn down or defaced. A favourite method was to chalk the letter V all over them. Winston Churchill had adopted the obscene two-fingered sign and made it acceptable by turning his hand palm outwards so that the fingers formed the letter V, and 'V for Victory' had become the slogan of all those opposed to the Nazis. The letter was already appearing all over Paris, scrawled on public notices and painted on walls and gateways. The posters were replaced at once and as quickly torn down or vandalised again. General Otto von Stülpnagel issued an edict declaring that damaging them was an act of sabotage and anyone guilty of it would incur the death penalty. The posters continued to disappear. In the end, the General was forced to station policemen to guard them.

The first issue of *Resistance* was produced on December 15th, and the first page was written by Paul Rivet himself. Under the heading 'National Committee for Public Safety', he proclaimed:

Resist! It is the cry which rises from your hearts in the distress in which you have been left by the disaster to our country. It is the cry of all of you who will not resign yourselves, all of you who wish to do your duty.

He went on to exhort readers to act, to do something positive and useful. He recognised that many of them felt isolated but assured them that there were many others like them, an army of them in Paris alone, and all that was needed were leaders, method and discipline.

Alix's little band of helpers had been broken up by the closure of the university, leaving only herself and Hanna, but there was still a small core of young men and a few women who congregated at Chez Michel, and since the communists' change of heart she felt emboldened to approach some of them. She quickly recruited six: four men and two women. The next problem was where to meet, but that was solved by two of the boys. They were sharing a small apartment, a garret much like the one where Raoul had lived, and assured Alix that the concierge never came in or asked questions about the friends who came to visit. Just the same, it was decided that there should be some cover for their meetings. Raymonde, one of the girls, suggested they should say it was a writers' group, arranged to share their work and give mutual support and criticism. The meetings were scheduled to take place twice weekly, but it was agreed that if something urgent arose, Alix would come to the cafe and say that she was struggling with her new novel and needed their help. It was on this pretext that she carried a sheaf of the Roneoed newspapers, concealed in her briefcase among pages of manuscript, up to the garret.

The paper was greeted with great excitement and read with general approval. Alix looked at the eager faces.

'So how do we go about distributing them?' Pierre, one of her new recruits, asked.

'You need to leave them where people can come across them, apparently by accident,' Alix said. 'Hanna and I have had some experience with leaflets, but the papers are a bit more bulky. You can leave them in public toilets, or on cafe tables, or on the Metro, as long as you make sure no one sees you. Any other ideas?'

'People hang their coats up in cafes and restaurants,' Raymonde said. 'It might be possible while you are hanging your own coat to slip copies into other people's pockets.'

'We could leave them on our seats in the cinema,' someone else said.

'We could slip them between the legitimate newspapers on a newspaper stand.'

'Or tuck them among the books in a bookshop.'

They had all taken part in the Armistice Day demonstration, so they were under no illusions about the attitude of the authorities to any expression of dissent, but Alix felt it necessary to reinforce the need for secrecy and caution.

'Remember, the penalty for distributing anti-German propaganda is death. So don't take unnecessary risks.'

Each of them took a dozen copies and secreted them about their persons, tucking them inside their shirts or down their trousers or hiding them under books in baskets or briefcases. Alix wished them good luck and they left in twos and threes.

Next morning Alix set out to perform her share of the task. She dressed smartly, putting on a coat with a fur collar that her father had given her the Christmas before last. The feel of it brought back the memory of that day, and of him, with painful sharpness. Was it possible that nearly two years had passed? What was he doing now – and was her mother with him? The inability to communicate with either of them haunted her on sleepless nights. She pushed the thought to the back of her mind and headed for the Ritz Hotel. Most of the best hotels in Paris had been requisitioned by the Germans, but Alix knew that some rooms at the Ritz were still open to other people, and there were bound to be civilians coming and going as well as officers in uniform. She walked in without looking around her, as if she was quite at home there, and found the ladies' room. In a cubicle, she extracted a copy of the paper from an inner pocket in the coat and stuck it to the inside of the door with a piece of sticky tape. There was nobody around, so she went into a second cubicle and did the same thing. Encouraged by the fact that no one had questioned her right to be there, she headed for the Hotel d'Angleterre and then the Hotel Bristol, where she performed the same routine.

After that she bought a Metro ticket and changed trains several times, leaving a copy of the paper on her seat each time. She was leaving the Trocadéro station, on her way back to Marie Louise's flat, when someone touched her arm.

'*Entschuldigen sie, Fraülein.*'

She swung round and found herself facing a German soldier. He was holding a rolled-up copy of *Resistance*. Alix felt the blood drain out of her face.

'I think…' He was obviously struggling with French. 'You leave… this.'

She looked at his face. He was very young – pale hair, pale blue eyes, and the scars of a recent bout of acne.

He held out the paper, smiling, and tried again. 'This...
yours?'

She almost laughed with relief. This was not an arrest.
It was an attempted pick up.

'Oh, no. It's just something I picked up to read on
the train.' It occurred to her that she should not leave the
paper in his possession. She held out her hand. 'Thank
you.'

He gave it to her and smiled again. 'You want cup
coffee? Go to eat, perhaps?'

The universal currency of seduction – the promise of a
good meal, off the ration, at a restaurant reserved for the
occupying forces. It was an offer she had accepted more
than once in her intelligence-gathering mode. But not
today.

She smiled back and shook her head. 'No, thank you.
I have to go.' She pointed to her watch to indicate that she
had an appointment to keep. 'Meeting friend,' she ampli-
fied. He looked crest-fallen but stepped back. 'Sorry,'
she said and indicated the paper. 'Thank you.' Then she
turned away and walked briskly out of the station.

At the corner of the street, she looked back. He was
standing on the pavement watching her, but he made no
attempt to follow. Just the same, she made a detour instead
of going straight to the flat, doubled back a couple of times
and then waited in a shop doorway to see if he came along.
When there was no sign of him, she allowed herself to
head for home. As she closed the door of the flat behind
her, she realised that her knees were shaking. If he had
looked at the paper, if he had understood enough French
to read it... She had had a lucky escape, but how long
would her luck hold?

On December 23rd, new posters appeared announcing that Jacques Bonsergent had been executed by firing squad.

The approach of Christmas brought little cheer. It was becoming more and more difficult to obtain even the meagre amount of food allowed by the ration. Luxuries were obtainable on the black market for those who had money, and somehow, by some miracle, the allowance that her mother had set up for Alix with a French bank continued to be paid. Marie Louise also had her salary from the museum, so they were better off than many people. They discussed the morality of buying on the black market while others less fortunate were starving and took the problem to Boris and ultimately to Paul Rivet. It was decided that they would pool their resources and use most of what they could buy to make up gift boxes for the children of museum employees while reserving a few small luxuries to share among themselves. The rest of the group who formed the core of the resistance movement agreed to join in, so on Christmas Day, Alix and Marie Louise were able to look forward to a glass of champagne and a small portion of paté de foie gras.

Alix's first thoughts when she awoke were of home. She had fond memories of Christmas at Kuca Magnolija, the big house on her father's estate although Serbians, being members of the Orthodox church, celebrated Christmas later, in January... For a few minutes, she lay still, allowing herself to imagine the scene, but that brought thoughts of her parents. Were they together? And were they missing her as much as she missed them? Such questions were too painful to dwell on, and she forced herself to get up and look for whatever joy she could find in her present situation.

It was a bright, cold morning so she and Marie Louise decided to go for a walk. On the first street corner they were brought to a standstill by a small crowd gazing at one of the posters announcing the death of Jacques Bonsergent. Overnight it had become a shrine, with dozens of flowers pinned to it, some fresh, most of them artificial, and amongst them were small flags, the tricolour of France and the Union Flag of Great Britain. Walking further, they came upon another poster that had been decorated in the same way, then a third and a fourth. As far as they could ascertain, every one in the city had been treated like this. It seemed that during the course of one night, the population of Paris had finally awoken to the true nature of the oppressors and was determined to express their defiance by whatever means came to hand.

Chapter Thirty-Five

Belgrade

December/January 1941

'No! I won't hear of it. It's too risky.' Sasha slammed his hand down on his desk.

'It's not. Think about it, Sasha. Somehow all these "toys and chocolates", as Tom likes to call them, have got to be distributed. It would be risky for him or any of the chaps on the embassy staff. Someone might wonder why they are roaming around the countryside to remote villages. But I have the perfect cover.' Leo put her arms around her husband's neck. 'I've done this sort of thing before. You know that.'

'You were a young girl then.'

'Oh, so you think I'm past it, do you?'

'You know that's not what I mean.'

'Well, then. Let's at least put the idea to the rest of the team. You know it makes sense.'

Sasha sighed. 'Very well. Knowing you as I do, you'll probably go ahead and do it anyway, so we might as well at least have the sanction of Tom and the others.'

They had formed the habit of inviting Tom Masterson and Sandy Glen to dinner once a week so that they could keep in touch without arousing suspicion. That night was one of the regular occasions, so when the meal was finished and the servants had withdrawn, Sasha said, 'Leo and I have a proposition to put to you.'

'Go ahead,' Masterson said.

'You tell them, Leo. It's your idea – but I should put on record now that I don't approve.'

'Oh dear,' Glen said with a grin, 'that sounds ominous.'

'Take no notice,' Leo said. 'He's just being an old man.' She paused to gather her thoughts. 'Tom, Sandy here knows a bit about my history, but you don't so I'd better bring you up to date for a start. In 1915, I came out to Serbia to join Mabel Stobart's Sick and Wounded Convoy. We set up a field hospital outside Kragujevac, but for the first month or two there was no fighting going on, so we started going out to the surrounding villages, offering basic medical services. And since I've been married to Sasha, I've continued doing the same sort of thing. The point is, I am known in the villages, and I can go there with a truck full of supplies without anyone finding it suspicious. So, if there happened to be, say, a box of grenades hidden under a stack of bandages – or rifles in a case containing splints...' She saw from his face that he had grasped her point. 'You need someone to distribute your "toys and chocolates". I'm offering to do it.'

'Leo has a point,' Glen said. 'We have to get this stuff out somehow and she does seem to have the perfect cover.'

Tom Masterson rubbed his chin. 'It could work. But it's down to you, Sasha. If you really don't want this...'

'Oh, it's no good putting it on my shoulders,' Sasha said with a wry grin. 'Leo has always done what she thinks is right, whatever I say. I found that out when I forbade her to head for the front line back in 1912.'

'Then that's settled,' Leo said. 'All I need now is a list of the villages where you have contacts with the Serbian Peasants Party and the names of the head man in each one.'

'I make one proviso,' Sasha put in. 'You can't do this alone. You must take a man with you. It's likely that the men running the branches of the SPP won't be happy dealing with a woman. The idea of female emancipation hasn't made much impact in this country.'

'It's time things changed,' Leo interjected.

'Nevertheless, in the sort of traditional society that exists in the villages, no man in authority will accept instructions from a strange woman.'

'Why don't you go?' Glen asked.

Sasha shook his head. 'I have my duties here, at court, as you know. People will think it's very odd if I suddenly start traipsing around the countryside delivering medical supplies.'

'Sasha is right,' Leo said. 'And he's right about taking a man with me – even if it's only to change the wheel if we have a puncture.'

'You're perfectly capable of doing that yourself,' Sasha put in dryly. 'But go on.'

'I thought I might take Drago with me.'

'Good idea! Yes, he's the right man for the job,' Sasha agreed.

'Who is he?' Tom Masterson asked. 'It must be someone we can trust absolutely.'

'Don't worry,' Sasha said. 'He grew up on my estate so I've known him all his life. He's utterly loyal, and he's intelligent, physically strong and he can drive. If Leo is intent on doing this, I can't think of anyone else I'd rather she had with her.'

After a little more discussion the plan was agreed, and the next day Leo and Sasha drove out to his country house. Drago, whose full name was Dragomir, was summoned to Sasha's study. He was in his early thirties, tall and with brown eyes and hair the colour of old straw. He had been educated at the school Sasha had set up, and he was currently second-in-command to the seneschal who looked after the agricultural side of the estate. For a man born of peasant stock he had done very well for himself, and he was well aware that it was Sasha Malkovic's enlightened attitudes that he had to thank. More importantly, he adored Leo. Everyone on the estate knew the story of how she had fought through the last war with the Serbian army, and since her marriage, she had devoted all her energy to improving the well-being of her husband's tenants. Like many men before him, he would have declared, if asked, that he was ready to lay down his life to protect her.

When the proposed scheme was explained to him he listened carefully, asked a few pertinent questions and then nodded. 'If the army cannot protect us against the Germans then it will be up to us to do it. I will help in any way I can.'

A year or two ago, on a visit to England, Leo had purchased a Dodge four-wheel-drive truck which she used for her visits to villages around the area. With Drago at her side, she drove it around Belgrade, loading up with medical supplies. Then they drove to the annexe of the British Legation where Tom Masterson had his base. Here, under cover of darkness, Tom and Sandy Glen added a consignment of grenades, rifles and ammunition, concealing them in boxes of bandages or under cases of antiseptics and vaccines.

Leo and Drago set off the following morning. Initially, they concentrated on villages in the Sumadija, the wooded heartland of Serbia. The villages here were prosperous, thriving on the fertile soil, with vineyards and orchards of fruit trees. In each village Leo was welcomed as an old friend and suitable space was found for her to set up her equipment. Sometimes it was a village hall, often, it was in the main room of the most prosperous family. The truck was parked at the back of the building, and while Leo started vaccinating children against smallpox and diphtheria, Drago sought out the leader of the local Peasant's Party and presented a note from Alexander Glen, who was well-known all around the area, explaining his purpose. As the local women queued with their children at the front of the house, Drago and the men offloaded the arms and equipment, which were carried away to be buried or securely hidden until they were needed.

Couriers continued to arrive from London with more 'toys and chocolates' and, since most of the villages in the Sumadija had now been supplied, Leo and Drago began to travel further afield. They headed up the valley of the Kolubara River to the mountainous area around Valjevo. Here the soil was less fertile and the villagers scratched a meagre living from their crops. Tradition was all-powerful and they clung to the old ways of doing things, distrusting any form of mechanisation. Modern conveniences such as indoor sanitation and piped water were non-existent, and Leo was driven to despair by the lack of hygiene. Roads were often hardly more than tracks, and mules and donkeys were the only form of transport. In this area the snow was already lying thick and the surfaces were icy. As she negotiated the treacherous conditions, Leo found herself vividly reminded of her adventures in Finland. It seemed hardly possible that nine months had passed since then, and here she was again, wrestling a vehicle over a snow-bound track.

They came one day to the village of Divcibare, perched on a plateau above Valjevo. It was popular in peacetime with residents of the city as a place for holidays, but now in the depths of winter the population had dwindled to a few hundred hardy souls. She carried out her usual programme of vaccinations and treated a few minor ailments while Drago and the men removed the armaments, and by the time they set off for home the short winter day was drawing to a close. As the road wound down towards the valley, Leo was forced to brake sharply to avoid running into a group of men blocking the way. They skidded to a stop and Drago muttered one word: 'Bandits!'

'We don't know that,' Leo said, but as the group advanced into the headlights it seemed a reasonable deduction. They were a wild-looking lot, wrapped in a motley collection of sheepskins and the fur of various animals, their faces half hidden by caps pulled low over their brows and beards frosted with ice – and they all carried rifles.

'They must have heard about the guns,' Drago whispered. They had not handed over all the weapons, intending the remainder for a village lower down.

'Well, we mustn't let them take them,' Leo responded grimly, though she had to admit to herself that if these men decided to search the truck there would be little she could do to stop them. 'It may be money they're after.'

A man stepped forward to stand by her door and pulled at the handle. The door was locked, but Leo lowered the window. 'What do you want, friend?'

'Open!' he demanded.

'Why? What is it you want?'

'Open!' The word was accompanied by a threatening gesture with his rifle.

'Drive on!' Drago whispered. 'Mow them down if they won't get out of the way.'

'And have them shoot the tyres out?' Leo asked. She looked out at the man beside her. 'If it's money you want...'

'Open!' he repeated, levelling the rifle at her head.

She unlocked the door and he leaned in. 'You,' indicating Drago, 'out!'

'No!' Leo said. 'We will do what you want, but he stays.'

For a moment the man hesitated. Then he climbed up into the cab. 'Move!' He elbowed Drago out of the way and inserted himself behind them, the muzzle of his rifle touching Leo's neck. 'Drive.'

'Drive? Where?'

'I'll show you. Go.'

The men who had been blocking the road moved aside. Some of them climbed on the running boards, others seized hold of any projecting parts of the vehicle and trotted beside them as Leo let in the clutch and the truck moved forwards. A short distance further on, a narrow track led off to the left, hemmed in by pine trees.

'Turn here,' the man commanded.

'Down there? I'm not sure—'

'Turn!'

Leo turned into the track. It was just wide enough for the vehicle to pass, though lower branches of the pines swept the roof. They were being hijacked, but Leo, uncomfortably aware of the rifle nuzzling her neck, could see no other course than to obey. After skidding and bumping on the icy surface for what felt like a long time, the trees opened out into a clearing where a small collection of huts stood around a blazing fire.

Leo stopped, and the man behind her said, 'Get out. You are needed here.'

'Needed?' Leo queried. 'What for?'

'To help,' was the reply.

As Leo climbed down from the cab, a woman came running across from one of the huts. 'Praise God! You are here! Come, come!' She grasped one of Leo's hands and pulled her across the open space and into the hut.

Inside, the light was so poor that for a moment Leo could see nothing. Then she heard a groan, the sound of a woman in great pain. As her eyes became accustomed to the dimness, she saw a woman lying on a low bed, with two others leaning over her. The one who had brought her into the hut pushed her forwards. 'Help her, please. It is my daughter. The child will not come.'

Suddenly Leo understood why they had been forced to come here. It was nothing to do with the hidden armaments. It was her medical knowledge that was wanted. With that thought came another, less reassuring. She had attended a good many births in her visits to the villages over the years, but she knew enough to understand that there were conditions that she was helpless to alleviate. If she failed here, there was no knowing what the reaction of her captors might be.

A scream from the woman on the bed banished all such speculation. Leo turned to the mother. 'Go to the truck. Tell the man with me to bring my medical bag.'

'Not here,' the woman protested. 'No men in here.'

'He can bring the bag and then go away,' Leo said.

As the mother went to do as she was bidden, Leo turned to the bed. 'How long has she been in labour?'

'Two days,' came the answer.

Leo knelt down and laid her hand on the woman's forehead. 'Don't be afraid. I will help if I can.' Large eyes ringed with dark circles gazed up at her trustingly, and then closed in agony as another convulsion came.

'I need hot water,' Leo said. 'Plenty of it, quickly.'

Someone moved to obey, and a moment later, her medical bag was set down beside her. She found her supply of soap and antiseptic and washed her hands in the bowl of water, then bent to examine the girl on the bed. It quickly became clear that this was a breech birth. A memory came back to her of a similar occasion fifteen years previously, when she had been a young, inexperienced nurse working with Mabel Stobart's convoy. That time an older woman had been with her, and she recalled her saying that unless the baby could be turned, in the absence of any possibility of a caesarean delivery, the only option to save the life of the mother was to dismember the child. On that occasion, they had been successful in turning the baby, but the prospect sent a chill through Leo's blood. If it came to it, could she bring herself to perform such an operation? And what might be the reaction of the people around her?

She pushed the thought away and bent to her task. In her bag, she carried a small amount of chloroform. She placed a mask over the girl's mouth and put a layer of lint over it. The girl rolled her eyes and jerked her head to one side and her mother caught hold of Leo's wrist.

'What are you doing?'

'Don't worry. She will sleep for a while, until the child is delivered. Then she will wake – I promise you.'

The hand on her wrist relaxed, and she took up the bottle of chloroform, only to discover that her own hand was shaking uncontrollably. For a few seconds, time seemed to have rolled back on itself. It was 1917, winter in the mountains of Macedonia, in the middle of a battle. It was she herself who lay there, crying out in pain, on a cold, hard floor, with strange faces peering down at her and the one thought repeating itself over and over in her head. 'Sasha is dead! Sasha is dead!'

The moment passed. She took a deep breath and opened the bottle, dripping the contents carefully onto the mask. The sunken eyes closed and the writhing body stilled. Leo gritted her teeth and thrust her hand into the girl's vagina. She could feel the baby's buttocks and its legs folded up so that its feet were beside its head. It was too late to attempt to turn it. She pushed her other hand in and grasped the tiny body, and with the next contraction, she pulled gently. The lower part of the body appeared. She waited, and on the next contraction the shoulders came free. Moments later, the baby slithered out in a surge of blood and mucus and Leo was dimly aware of a chorus of relief and jubilation from the watchers around her. She cleaned the tiny mouth and nose and turned the child over to pat its back and was rewarded with a cry.

'It's a boy. Take him. Keep him warm.'

The grandmother lifted the baby from her hands, sobbing with joy, and Leo turned back to the girl on the bed. There was a good deal of stitching to be done, and before she had finished, the girl was stirring and moaning, but by the time she was fully conscious, the work was finished. Leo looked round.

'Let her hold the child.'

The baby was placed on its mother's breast and the girl gazed up at Leo. 'Thank you! Thank you!'

Leo found she was shaking again. In a daze, she cleared up, cleaned her hands and packed away her equipment, while around her there was a buzz of voices, crooning over mother and child and marvelling at her delivery. Outside the hut, Drago was sitting round the fire with the men of the village. The man who had held the rifle to her head jumped up and ran to her.

'The child? The child is born?'

'Are you the father?'

'Yes! Yes!'

'Then you have a son.'

'And my wife?'

'Will survive if she is given the right care.'

There were more cries of joy, more expressions of gratitude, and someone put a mug of something into her hand. It was fiery but she swallowed it gratefully and looked at her watch. It was almost midnight. There was no question of continuing their journey.

'Sorry, Drago. It looks as though we are here for the night.'

Someone led her to a place by the fire where a sheep-skin was laid over the frosty ground and she sank down onto it gratefully. Another mug was placed in her hand; she drank and let herself sink into a reclining position. After that, she knew nothing until she became aware of people moving around her and sunlight filtering through the branches of the pine trees. Someone had covered her with a warm rug. She pushed it aside and sat up. Drago was squatting nearby.

'You are awake! Are you all right?'

'I'm fine – I think.' She put her hand over her eyes. 'What was it we were drinking last night?'

He chuckled. 'Their homemade slivovitz. Powerful stuff, wasn't it?'

'It certainly was!'

It took some time before they were allowed to continue their journey. Leo checked over the new mother and the child, and both seemed to be doing well. Food was pressed upon them – newly baked flat bread and goat's cheese – and eventually, she persuaded her hosts that they must leave. The drive along the narrow track was less formidable in daylight, but she was relieved when they eventually got back onto a proper road, even though here, the hard-packed snow had frozen and conditions were treacherous.

As they drove, Drago said suddenly, 'It's not right, is it?'

'What's not right?'

'The way those people are living.'

'Did you find out why they are stuck out there, in those primitive conditions?'

'They told me a bit. The top man, the father of the baby, had a job in the bauxite mine. His village couldn't grow enough to feed all the people, so he had to find other work. He tried to start a trade union to campaign for better conditions, so he was sacked. One of the others worked with him, but he got into a fight with the foreman, so he got the sack too. Another one borrowed money from a money lender, and when he couldn't pay it back, the lender threatened to burn his house down and then every other house in the village until he got his money. The head man of the zadruga paid off the debt, but he kicked the man out.'

Leo was familiar with the term zadruga. It meant an extended family, or a clan, which often occupied a whole village. It was a patriarchal system where the oldest man controlled everything that happened.

'It's not just those people,' Drago went on. 'I didn't realise until we started visiting some of these villages how hard life is for some people. Most of them have never slept in a proper bed, just the whole family on sacks on the hard floor. Women having to walk long distances to the nearest supply of fresh water. No wonder they're dirty. And half of them can't even write their own name, let alone read.'

Leo glanced sideways at him. 'It's been a bit of an eye-opener for you, hasn't it? It's not a surprise to me.'

'I never understood until now how lucky I am to have been brought up on the Count's estate,' he said. 'But can't something be done to help?'

Leo sighed. 'The Count and I have been trying to push for changes for years, but there are too many vested interests, too much in-fighting.'

'I heard some of the men last night talking about the communists, saying life would be better if they were in charge.'

'I can understand why,' Leo said. 'But from what I hear the ordinary people are not much better off in Russia under communism than they are here.'

'Will things be better when Prince Peter becomes king?' he asked.

'Perhaps. His heart is in the right place, but it will be an uphill struggle. We can only hope.' She reached across and patted his hand. 'We're doing our best. That's all we can do.'

It was mid-morning before they reached Belgrade.

Sasha was pacing the hallway when she entered the house. His hair was standing on end and his clothes were rumpled and he had not shaved. She knew at once that he had not been to bed.

'Where the hell have you been?' he demanded. 'I've had men scouring the countryside for you. What happened?' Then, with a change of tone, 'Are you alright?'

Drago tactfully slipped away to the servants' quarters, and Leo put her arms around her husband's neck.

'I'm so sorry, my darling. I know how worried you must have been.'

'Worried? I've been frantic. I knew I should never have agreed to this crazy scheme.'

'Well, it isn't actually anything to do with that that kept me away,' she said.

'Then what? Where have you been all night?'

She took his hand and drew him towards the drawing room. 'Come and sit down and I'll tell you all about it.' Ivo, the butler, was hovering in the hall. 'Ivo, would you bring us some coffee, please? And some pastries for the Count.'

They sat facing each other across a small table, their hands clasped, and she told him the story of the previous evening. As she spoke his face relaxed but his dark eyes were still shadowed.

'Good God! He forced you to drive, at gunpoint?'

'The poor man was desperate. I suppose he was afraid that if he just asked politely I might refuse to help. I would not have done, of course, but he wasn't to know that.'

'And the child survived?'

'Yes, thank God. I don't know how they might have reacted if it hadn't.'

He shuddered. 'I can't bear to think about it. Leo, I don't want you to go on doing this. They could have been bandits. They might have stolen the truck and left you and Drago for dead.'

'I think it is time I stopped anyway,' Leo said. 'The roads to those remote villages are going to be impassable for the rest of the winter, and I've shifted most of Tom's toys and chocolates. Whatever is left will have to wait till spring.'

'That is the best news I've heard for days,' Sasha responded with relief.

The coffee arrived together with a plate of *vanilice*, his favourite walnut and vanilla cookies. They ate in silence for a while, until Leo said suddenly, 'What is the date today?'

'Date? I'm not sure. I've had other things on my mind. The 23rd, perhaps? No, the 24th.'

'The 24th? Sasha, don't you realise what that means? It's Christmas Eve.'

'No, it isn't. Christmas is January 7th,' he said, but he was smiling, teasing her.

'Only for you stick-in-the-muds who refuse to recognise the Gregorian calendar.'

'It's you western Europeans who decided to cut eleven days out of the year, so Christmas comes on the wrong date.'

'It's the right date! The old calendar simply didn't work.' She grew serious. 'All right. Christmas here isn't till January 7th. I'm just wondering how they are celebrating it in England – and in Paris.'

'Of course.' He reached for her hand again. 'I hate to think of Alix all alone at this time. I don't suppose there is a great deal of Christmas cheer there.'

'She won't be all alone,' Leo said. 'The last letter I have from her spoke of finding some new friends, something to do with one of the museums.'

'I can't see Alix being interested in a lot of old fossils, or whatever they have in the museum,' he said.

'Well, what matters is she seems to have found a more sensible crowd to be with. Better than those communists she was knocking around with before. And at least she isn't in London, living through the Blitz.'

'True. Paris seems quiet under the occupation. It's ironic, really. I accused you of putting her in danger, but the way things are going here I fancy she may be safer where she is than she would be at home. Paris might be as good a place as any to sit out the war.'

'Hmm,' Leo said. 'The trouble with that is, sitting around isn't Alix's style.'

'I can't see that she's got much choice. Her war is over. Let's hope her museum friends will make sure she doesn't do anything silly.'

–

The days leading up to the Orthodox Christmas festival passed quietly. There were no dinner parties now since the Church required the forty days of Advent to be days of fasting. Leo and Sasha moved back to his country estate and took a welcome break from the machinations of their SOE colleagues. On January 6th Sasha and Drago and the men of the household went out into the forest. Sasha had previously selected an oak tree which he now blessed by throwing a handful of grain at it and greeting it with the words, 'Happy Christmas Eve to you.' He then made the sign of the cross, kissed the tree and made the first cut with his axe, on the eastern side so that the tree would fall to the east. The trunk was then trimmed and cut to a length that a man could carry on his shoulder. This was the *badnjak*, the yule log. Other logs were cut by the men, and they were all carried back and piled up in the open square in front of the main house. At midnight the bonfire was lit, and a pig's carcass was set to roast over it.

In the kitchen, Leo superintended the making of the round, unleavened loaf which would be shared with the household and the preparation of the Christmas Eve feast, which in keeping with the fast, contained no meat but was nonetheless copious and varied, with dishes of fish and beans, walnuts and honey.

Christmas morning began with a visit to church for the morning liturgy. Leo had long ago lost her belief in the dogma of any Christian denomination, but Sasha was quite devout, and it would have been a scandal if the master and mistress had not attended. Leo found the ancient ritual, with the singing and the scent of incense, comforting in the midst of unsettled times, and she was happy to greet friends with the traditional '*Hristos se rodi*', 'Christ is Born', and receive the response '*Vaistinu se rodi*', 'Truly He is born.'

At midday, the household gathered round the big table in the hall. Another loaf, the *cesnica*, was ceremonially broken so that each person present received a share and then they sat down to feast on the roast pork. Looking around the table, Leo was saddened as she always was by the fact that there was no son to take his place in the family rituals; and this year her regret was sharpened by the absence of her only child. She banished the thoughts and made herself smile. Next year things would be different – though in what way she could not guess. She could only take what comfort she could find in the present moment.

Chapter Thirty-Six

Paris

February 1941

Boris was continuing to spread his web of connections around both occupied and Vichy France. One result of this was that a network of safe houses had grown up to the north of Paris where downed airmen could be sheltered and ultimately moved on to Paris, where they were instructed to report to the museum. Since Christmas, Alix had made three further trips south, escorting escapers to Marseilles, and she was about to make another one. Two RAF pilots had arrived at the museum two days earlier and were awaiting the false papers provided for them by Agnès and her assistants. Alix was horrified by how young they were, one just twenty and the other still only nineteen. They had been lucky. Both had bailed out and landed without injury and had been collected quickly by sympathisers and hidden before being passed on down the line. They had arrived in very good spirits and seemed to regard the whole business as a great adventure.

Alix was at the flat, packing for the journey, when Hanna arrived, obviously distressed. Marie Louise was out, combing the shops for anything that could be found to eat, on or off the ration, so Alix took Hanna into the sitting room and sat beside her on the couch.

'What is it? What's happened to upset you?'

Hanna grasped her hand. 'Oh, Alix, I am afraid, so afraid.'

'Afraid of what?'

'I heard today that a family I know, a Jewish family from Poland, have been arrested.'

'Arrested? What for?'

'For nothing. There are rumours that all Jews of foreign nationality are being arrested and sent away to camps somewhere.' She looked at Alix, a look of desperation. 'It was bad enough last October when the Nazis bombed those synagogues and handed over all Jewish businesses to "Aryan" owners. It's been getting worse all the time. I passed a children's playground the other day and there was a barrier with a notice saying that it was forbidden for Jewish children to enter.' She shivered. 'I've heard terrible rumours about what is happening to Jews in my own country. Now it is beginning to happen here.'

Alix squeezed her hand. '*Cherie*, I think it is time that you left France.'

'Left? How? Where would I go?'

'I'm not sure. I just know that there are organisations in Marseilles helping Jews to escape. I think you need to come with me, tomorrow, before it's too late. Have you spoken to Boris about this?'

'No. I feel such a coward. I didn't like to bother him.'

'We'll go and see him now. I'm sure he will agree with me. And you're not a coward. We've all heard the rumours and we should have done something much sooner. Getting out is the only sensible thing for you to do.'

Boris did not hesitate. Hanna had to go with Alix the next morning. The only problem was getting the right papers for her.

'Can't I risk using my own?' she suggested. 'After all, once I'm in Vichy France I should be out of danger.'

'You can't rely on that,' Boris told her. 'Pétain is desperate to curry favour with Hitler and this new militia group, whatever it calls itself, would be happy to denounce you.'

The plan was that Alix was to masquerade as the wife of one of the pilots, the older boy whose name was Roger. The younger one, Clive, was supposed to be his brother and their excuse for travelling was that they had been to visit a sick mother in Dr Beauclerc's hospital outside Tours and were returning to their home at an address outside Marseilles. The obvious solution was for Hanna to be married to Clive. A message to Agnès brought her back to the Museum of Folk Art, and by midnight, the necessary papers were in order.

A room in the basement of the Musée de l'Homme had been converted into a room for escapers waiting to embark on the next stage of their journey. Next morning Alix took Hanna there to explain the new plan. Clive's eyes sparkled with mischief.

'Good show! I didn't see why I shouldn't have a blushing bride on my arm like Rog. Delighted to meet you, my dear.'

He made a show of kissing her hand and Hanna blushed and drew back. Alix said, with some asperity, 'Hanna speaks very little English, and you have to remember to speak French all the time. One word out of place and you could give the whole show away.'

He gave her a look of injured innocence. 'Don't worry. I know what we are doing. It was just a bit of fun.'

Both men spoke reasonable French, though Roger's was better than his friend's. He had stayed with a French pen friend before the war. Clive had had only schoolboy French when he parachuted in, but a week or two living with the family that had sheltered him had brought it up to a passable level, though his accent was not perfect. To compensate, it had been decided that he should pretend to be extremely shy and almost tongue-tied in company. He had made a pantomime of this when it was first suggested, and Alix was afraid that he would continue to play it up when he was required to be serious. She had had several conversations with both men, pointing out the dangers of what they were doing, but she still doubted that they fully appreciated them.

The first part of the journey went according to plan. Marie Louise's parents were now an essential link in a complex chain, and they accepted the associated risk with grace. The two boys were made welcome and behaved with good manners, as they would have done when invited to stay with an English family. It was when they checked into the hotel in Bruère-Allichamps that the trouble started. Alix booked two double rooms, and when they reached them, Clive seized Hanna's hand and tried to pull her inside, exclaiming, 'Alone at last!'

'Don't be a fool!' Alix said tersely. 'You and Roger will share this room and Hannah and I will be in the other one. But in the morning, before the servants are up, Hanna will come to you and Roger will come to my room so that it will look to the staff as if we are married couples.'

'You mean to tell me I am not to have even one night of bliss with this lovely lady?' Clive asked, pouting.

'This is not a joke,' she reminded him. 'This evening you will have to play your parts convincingly. There may be other guests in the dining room.'

The evening passed without incident, but as they were getting ready for bed, Alix and Hanna heard voices from the next room. The two boys were laughing and joking – in English!

Alix strode into the room without knocking. Both boys were in their underwear and they turned looks of indignation on her.

'I say,' Roger remarked, 'you might knock.'

'And I might be the Gestapo come to arrest you.' She spoke with suppressed fury. 'Don't you realise that the whole hotel can hear you? Didn't you know you were speaking English?'

'But I thought these people were in on the act,' Roger protested. 'They know who we are, don't they?'

'The proprietor does, and most of the staff can probably guess, but they rely on us behaving reasonably. You have no idea who else might be within hearing. There are plenty of people who are prepared to denounce their neighbours in order to get extra rations or privileges.'

'Oh, I say...' Clive muttered.

'The less you say, the better!' she told him. 'Do you not understand that Hanna and I are risking our lives to get you out of the country? If we are betrayed, or discovered, you two will just be sent back to a prisoner-of-war camp. Hanna and I will probably be shot. Has that not occurred to you?'

'Look,' Roger said awkwardly, 'we were out of order. I'm sorry. We'll be more careful in future.'

'You had better be,' she said. 'I give you warning now. One more display like tonight's and Hanna and I will leave you to find your own way to Marseilles. Do I make myself clear?'

They hung their heads like schoolboys and agreed.

After that, they were models of discretion and they all reached Marseilles safely. At Dr Rodocanachi's surgery the two airmen went through the usual routine of an interview with Ian Garrow. When he was satisfied, he told them that they would have to stay in the city for some time, as the weather was now too bad to attempt the crossing of the Pyrenees or the sea voyage by felucca. They would be accommodated at the Seaman's Mission until arrangements could be made to move them on. Hanna presented a different problem.

'There's a man called Varian Fry, an American, working here to get Jews out of the country. I know he's already sent hundreds over the Pyrenees and ultimately to Lisbon to take ships to America. He has also got them onto ships leaving for Martinique, from where they can get a passage to the States. If you want, I can take you to meet him.'

'America?' Hanna looked from him to Alix. 'I don't know anyone in America – and I don't speak English.'

'There are committees set up over there, I understand, to help resettle refugees. And you would not travel alone. I'm sure you would find friends on the journey.'

'You would be safe there,' Alix said, encouragingly. 'You could find a new life.'

There were tears in Hanna's eyes. 'I shall miss you – and Paris.'

'And I shall miss you,' Alix replied, her throat closing on the words. 'We've worked so well together and you've been a good friend. But you cannot stay in France. You must take this opportunity while it's offered.'

Hannah swallowed back her tears. 'Yes, you are right. And perhaps, when the war is over, I shall be able to go back to Poland and try to find my family. I shall hope for that.' She turned to Garrow. 'Please, if you will introduce me to this American gentleman, I shall be very grateful.'

As Garrow prepared to leave with his three charges, there was an emotional farewell.

Roger took her hand. 'We behaved like idiots, and you were a saint to put up with us. We can never thank you properly.'

'Just get back to England and drive the Luftwaffe out of the skies,' she replied. 'That's the best thanks I could have.'

She kissed both men on the cheek and embraced Hanna.

'Good luck! Write to me if you can. Maybe we'll meet again when this awful war is over.'

Chapter Thirty-Seven

Beaulieu Manor, Hampshire, England

March 1941

Steve stood at the mullioned window of the grand Victorian house and gazed across the shining surface of the mill pond to the formal gardens, where a riot of daffodils was just coming into bloom. He had read about the great houses of England and thought vaguely that one day he would like to visit one. He had never imagined that for a while he would actually live in one. So many such places had been requisitioned by the secret services that among his colleagues the joke was that SOE stood for 'Stately 'Omes of England'. Beyond the gardens, the horizon was framed by the trees of the New Forest, and beyond that, he knew now, was the Solent and the English Channel. He remembered looking down from the Blenheim on that first flight and wishing he could explore the countryside below him. Well, he had had plenty of opportunity to do that over the last couple of months, not just here but around Wanborough Manor and then up in the Highlands of Scotland. Looking at the peaceful scene in front of him, it was hard to make it fit with the techniques he had been taught in its woods and lanes and the streets of the towns beyond.

At Wanborough, his physical and mental health had been tested by early morning runs and assault courses, by written tests and interviews with men he assumed were psychiatrists. He had learned how to handle small arms and how to follow a trail across broken country. In Scotland, he had found himself scrambling up sheer cliffs and then abseiling down them. He had forded icy rivers and had learned unarmed combat and how to pick a lock. There had been tests of endurance and of his ability to work in a team. Here in Beaulieu, he had learned to lay a booby trap for a passing vehicle, how to handle plastic explosives and how to tell if he was being tailed and to shake off his follower. He had learned to use various forms of code, how to set up a 'dead letter' drop and how to operate a short-wave radio. He had also, most frighteningly, been subjected to mock interrogations under the threat of torture.

On this spring morning, he was waiting to be summoned for an interview – he was not sure who with – but he sensed that it might mark a new development in this strange career he had somehow fallen into. The door opened and one of the upper-class women in FANY uniform who seemed to run the establishment said, 'Would you like to come through now, sir?'

It was no great surprise that the man who came forward to shake his hand was Brigadier Gubbins. They exchanged the usual pleasantries and he was offered a seat in front of a large mahogany desk.

'So,' Gubbins said, 'I have nothing but good reports of your progress. It's been a rather hectic couple of months, I know, but we feel that time is of the essence. How do you feel about starting your work in Yugoslavia?'

'I'm ready, sir,' Steve said. He had felt for some days that he had learned all he was going to learn here.

'Good. Well, this is the plan. We're sending you to Bosnia. You are being posted to the Royal Yugoslav Second Army as a liaison officer. You will go in uniform, as a Flight Lieutenant, RAF, and your assignment, officially, will be to assess their preparedness should the country be invaded, with special reference to shortages of equipment and manpower. You can let the commanders think that this is so that any shortfall can be made up, in part at least, by HM government. It won't be, of course. We need every tank and every shell we can produce ourselves, but the hint that some stuff may be forthcoming will make you very welcome and should facilitate your real purpose.'

'Which is?'

'In part exactly what I've just outlined. We need to know what the chances are of the Yugoslavs being able to hold out against an invasion from the Axis powers. Rumour has it that the army has been starved of funds and is extremely ill-equipped for modern warfare. We want to know if that's true. But more importantly, we want to know about morale – particularly among troops belonging to the ethnic minorities. We know that the Croats and the Bosnians resent the hegemony exercised by the Serbs. We have people in place in Slovenia and in Zagreb, but not in Bosnia. You will be our eyes and ears on the ground there. Most important of all, you need to lay the groundwork for setting up resistance cells if the worst comes to the worst and the country is overrun. This will entail selecting individuals who might form the core of such an enterprise and potential leaders, as well as establishing means of communication between us and them.'

'I understand, sir,' Steve responded.

'Good. Now to practicalities.' Gubbins withdrew some papers from a buff folder on the desk. 'The second army's HQ is near Sarajevo. The C-in-C is General Dragoslav Miljkovic; his chief of staff is Brigadier General Bogdan Maglic, and under him is Brigadier Draza Mihailovic.' He rubbed a hand over his face with a wry grin. 'These Serbian names! I hope they don't confuse you as much as they confuse me!'

Steve grinned back. 'I know what you mean, sir. Even Popovic is too much for some people.'

'This last man, Mihailovic, is of particular interest. He's had a somewhat chequered career. He did well in the last war, serving in the Salonika campaign and being decorated several times. He studied at the military academy in Belgrade and then in Paris at Saint-Cyr, rising to the rank of brigadier. But he seems to have had a knack for making himself unpopular with the authorities. Last year he attended a meeting that was highly anti-Nazi in tone, resulting in a protest from the German ambassador. He was confined to barracks and threatened with demotion, but he was saved when Minister for the Armed Forces Nedic was replaced by Pesic, and instead, he was sent to join the second army. Now, it seems to me that this is a man who is prepared to go against conventional thinking, someone who might be happy to strike out on his own. I'm told that he is a fervent royalist and very patriotic. In short, I think he would take to guerrilla warfare very well and might make a leader around whom a resistance movement could be built. I want you to try to get close to him, gain his confidence. Is all that clear?'

'Yes, sir. Thank you, sir.'

'I've put together some briefing notes for you to study – strictly confidential, of course.'

'Of course.'

'You will take a radio so you can keep in touch. The wavelength and the codes to be used are all in the documents. Is there anything else?'

'If I can ask, sir, when am I likely to be deployed?'

'Very soon. It's just a question of arranging transport.' Gubbins studied him for a moment. 'You're one of the lucky ones; I hope you realise. Most of the chaps here are going to be dropped by parachute into enemy territory, where if they are caught they could be shot as spies. You are going in uniform to a friendly country where if things go wrong you will be covered by the Geneva Convention.'

The same thought had been formulating itself in Steve's mind. 'I know, sir. And I'm grateful.'

'Mind you, if the Germans do come in, things could get pretty sticky. There's no guarantee we'll be able to get you out in a hurry.'

'I understand that, sir.'

'Good. I think that's all. Oh, one more thing. Keep an eye open for good targets for sabotage, if the crunch comes. You know the sort of thing – mines, rail terminals, electrical supply facilities.'

'Very good, sir.'

Gubbins rose, and Steve got up too. 'There's just one thing, sir, if I may...?'

'Yes?'

'You said something about going in as a Flight Lieutenant...'

'Ah, yes.' Gubbins smiled. 'A promotion seemed justified. You'll have a bit more status than as a lowly Pilot Officer. Congratulations.' He held out his hand. 'And good luck.'

Chapter Thirty-Eight

Belgrade

March 1941

Alexander Glen arrived unexpectedly at Sasha's door just as he and Leo were finishing dinner. Just a few days before, they had heard that Bulgaria had signed the Tripartite Pact with Germany, which allowed Hitler to position forces right on the Yugoslav border. It was common knowledge that he was bringing greater and greater pressure to bear on Prince Paul and his advisors to sign the Pact as well.

'What's happened?' Sasha asked.

'I've just learned that Paul is in Germany. Yesterday he had a meeting with Hitler at his place in Berchtesgaden.'

'With what result?'

'That I don't know, but he must be on the verge of signing; otherwise, why would he agree to go?'

'So what do we do now?'

'We have to be ready. If he does sign, there will be an outburst of hostility, demonstrations in the streets and so on. That will be the moment for the coup.'

Leo felt a tightening of the muscles in her gut. If the coup failed, Glen and the others would be able to claim diplomatic immunity. Not so herself and Sasha, although her British passport would provide her with some security. For Sasha, it could mean a sentence of death, or, at best, exile from his beloved country. But if the coup succeeded… She knew she was at the heart of events that could change the progress of the war.

'What do you want me to do?' Sasha asked.

'We have already sounded out a number of senior officers, mainly in the Air Force. You have contacts among the people around Prince Peter, and in the Church. We need to bring the key people together to make a definite plan. If I give you the names, can you invite them to dinner?'

'Of course. When?'

'As soon as possible, but there needs to be an excuse, a reason for such a gathering.'

Leo and Sasha exchanged looks. She said, 'It's my birthday next week. We were thinking of having a party.'

'Excellent! Invite all the people you would normally invite, so it doesn't look suspicious, plus the names on my list and anyone else you think needs to be involved. You'll be able to give us a room where we can talk confidentially?'

'Of course.'

'Good. Let me know the date, and I'll prepare my list.'

The date chosen was Saturday the 15th, and Leo immersed herself in preparations. Sasha always entertained on a grand scale, and his staff were used to it, so a well-oiled machine swung into action. It had to look like a real birthday celebration, so there was the menu to be decided with the cook; extra help and provisions to be summoned from the estate; flowers to be ordered; table settings and seating plans to be arranged. Together they drew up the guest list, including the names Glen had given them, and invitations were sent out.

On the evening of the fifteenth, the cream of Belgrade society, high-ranking military officers and members of the clergy converged on Knez Mihailova Street.

After dinner there was dancing in the ballroom. Leo knew, to her profound irritation, that it was necessary for her to remain there in her role as hostess while Sasha made the rounds tactfully murmuring in selected ears that the gentlemen concerned might find the entertainment in the billiard room more to their taste. There, a few of the men took up billiard cues as cover while the rest settled themselves in front of the fire with glasses of brandy. Among them were Slobodan Jovanovic, president of the Serbian Culture Club. Also, there were the British Air Attaché, Captain A.H. McDonald and his deputy T.G. Mapplebeck together with General Dusan Simovic, commander of the Yugoslav Royal Air Force, and Brigadier General Borivoje Mirkovic, his deputy. By the time the meeting broke up, a plan had been agreed, and only the date remained to be decided.

Four days later Glenn arrived at the house again. This time he looked triumphant.

'At last! We've got Campbell to see sense. We had a meeting this afternoon, and he has agreed that if Paul signs the Pact, the only course of action will be to implement the coup. He doesn't like it because he still hangs onto the hope that Paul will renege on the agreement and pull back from the brink, but he sees that we have to act. He's going to send a message to Anthony Eden in London to that effect.'

'It's really going to happen then,' Sasha said, his face clouded. 'It still feels like an act of treachery.'

'A necessary act to preserve the integrity of the country,' Glen said. 'After all, all we are proposing to do is put the rightful king on the throne, just a few months earlier than would happen anyway.'

'True,' Sasha agreed. 'Do you want me to warn Peter?'

'Better not. If anything goes wrong, he has to be completely innocent of any involvement.'

'So, how long do you think we have?' Leo asked.

Glen lifted his shoulders. 'It's hard to say. The pressure on Paul is growing. I don't think he'll be able to hold out much longer.'

'The sooner, the better,' Sasha said. 'Before someone blabs and gives the game away.'

Almost a week passed.

On the 25th, Sasha turned on the wireless to listen to the news and they heard the announcer say, 'Prime Minister Cvetkovic and the German Foreign Minister Herr von Ribbentrop have signed the Tripartite Pact in Vienna. Herr Hitler has agreed that the Axis Powers will respect Yugoslavia's sovereignty and will not request any military assistance or permission to transport troops through Yugoslav territory.'

Sasha turned off the set. 'Hah! Only a fool would put his faith in that promise!'

In the streets of Belgrade, the reaction was unequivocal. Mobs gathered chanting, 'Better a grave than a slave; better a war than the Pact.'

Masterson convened a meeting at his office.

'This is it, chaps! Paul is out of the country, supposedly on the way to a holiday in Brno. McDonald is meeting with Simovic, and Mapplebeck is speaking to Mirkovic. They are going to tell them it's got to happen within the next forty-eight hours. It's all in the hands of those Air

338

Force officers from now on. We must just hold ourselves in readiness to deal with the outcome – particularly you, Sasha. Peter is going to need all the support you can give him.'

Chapter Thirty-Nine

Paris

March 26th 1941

Alix was returning from another trip south, this time escorting two airmen and one escaped POW. One of the airmen was a Squadron Leader, some years older than the pilots she had escorted before, and his presence had had a sobering effect on the other two, so there had been no major difficulties. Alix herself now had a new identity. After several journeys there was the possibility that her face might be recognised by a guard or a ticket collector, so now she wore a dark wig and carried identity papers in the name of Monique Gaultier.

Having successfully handed the men over to Ian Garrow to be prepared for the long trek over the Pyrenees, she arrived back in Paris feeling quite pleased with herself. All the arrangements with the various links in the chain were working smoothly and she saw no reason why they should not continue to do so. Leaving the train, she was surprised to see Marie Louise waiting for her at the ticket barrier. When she got closer she saw that her friend's face was pale and tense, her eyes circled with dark shadows.

'Marie Louise? What's wrong? Has something happened?'

Her friend gripped her arm, her fingers digging in like talons. 'Not here. Come with me.'

Outside the station, Marie Louise pulled her into the shadow of a shop doorway. It was evening and a light rain was falling. Soon it would be dark.

'Tell me!' Alix begged.

'Boris has been arrested. And Yvonne and Anatole and Agnès.'

Alix felt as if the ground under her feet had melted away. She grasped the handle of the shop door for support. 'My God! When? How?'

'This afternoon. The Abwehr came and searched the museum. They took them away.'

'How did they know? Someone must have denounced us.'

'That little swine Gaveau. He was with them, telling them who to arrest.'

'They didn't take you…'

'I was not in the museum at the time. I went out to try to buy some coffee on the black market. I was on my way back when one of the gallery attendants stopped me. He'd heard what was going on and slipped away to catch me before I got back. But I can't go home, in case they are watching the flat – and you mustn't go there either. That's why I came to meet you.'

'My God!' Alix said again. 'I can't believe it. But thank God you are safe, at least. Where are we going to stay tonight?'

'With Germaine. I went to her place to warn her. There was no sign of anyone watching it, so I took the chance. We think the Abwehr don't know about her – or perhaps they didn't know her address. She never had much to do with Gaveau. But we've moved to a safe house

341

anyway, one she set up to accommodate escapers. I'll take you there now.'

'Yes… yes, OK.' Alix felt too stunned to ask any more questions. She picked up her case and followed Marie Louise through the darkening streets. She tried to work through the implications of what she had heard, but her brain seemed incapable of coherent thought. The same words went round and round in her head. '*Boris has been arrested…*' They arrived at length in an area of the city she had never visited, a rundown neighbourhood of shabby apartment blocks and small shops. Marie Louise led her up a flight of stairs and tapped on a door, and a moment later, Germaine Tillon opened it.

'You found her. Thank God for that. Come in, quickly.'

Inside, Alix sank down on a chair and pulled off her wig, running her fingers through her hair. 'I can't believe it. Gaveau? Are you sure?'

'The man who stopped me going back there said he had seen him, with the Germans, telling them where to find people,' Marie Louise said.

'The little shit! And Boris trusted him!'

'He knew how to make himself useful.'

'Do you think he was working for the Abwehr all along?' Alex was still struggling to make sense of what had happened.

'I think he must have been.'

'Where have they taken them?'

Germaine came in from the kitchen with mugs of coffee. 'I presume they've got them in the Hotel Lutetia. They've taken that over as their HQ.'

'Is there any chance of getting them out?' Alix asked.

'Don't be silly. It would take an army to get into that place.'

'Yes, of course.' She rubbed her hand across her face. 'So, what do we do now?'

'Lie low and wait. This place is safe enough for the time being. We need to know who else has been picked up. I've got agents in place around the city. They will report to me as soon as they know anything.'

'Can I stay here?'

'Of course. You must both stay until we know better what the situation is.'

'So, the network is finished?'

'Not necessarily. It may be possible to rebuild it, after a while.'

Alix caught her breath in a gasp. 'Oh, my God! What about all the people we've recruited? What about my team – and yours, Marie Louise?'

'Have you given their names to anyone else?' Germaine asked.

'No. Boris said each of us should only know our own group.'

'Now you see why. As long as we can keep you two out of the Abwehr's hands, then your people are safe.'

'What about Paul ? Have they arrested him?' Alex asked.

'No, it seems not. My guess is that he has such an international reputation as a scholar and a humanitarian that to arrest him would put the Nazis in a very bad light. And he hasn't been actively involved in the day-to-day organisation. He left all that to Boris.'

'And the others? There were a lot of us, in the end.'

'Who knows?' Germaine shrugged. 'There are rumours of several other arrests, but I don't know any details. Have you eaten?'

'Eaten? No.' Alex shook her head.

'I'll make an omelette.'

'No, please!' Marie Louise begged. 'I couldn't eat anything.'

'Yes you can. We all need to keep strong and alert. Starving ourselves is not going to help.'

As soon as they had eaten, Germaine said, 'You both look exhausted. Get some sleep. We'll talk again in the morning.'

Chapter Forty

Belgrade

March 26th–27th 1941

On the evening of the 26th, the SOE agents, together with Leo and Sasha, collected at Tom Masterson's office in the Legation annexe. The atmosphere was tense.

Masterson said, 'I've heard back from McDonald. Everything is in hand for tonight. This is the plan. Officers from the Air Force base at Zemun have been assigned to take control of various key buildings and locations, including the base itself, the bridges over the Sava between there and here, the Police Directorate and the radio stations, the HQ of the General Staff, the main Post Office and the barracks of the Royal Guard, and the palace complex. A colleague who is an inspector of post, telegraph and telephone will cut all communication between Belgrade and the rest of the country. Simovic will be at the War Office, and a detachment has been tasked with arresting Prime Minister Cvetkovic and taking him there. Zero hour is two a.m. Sasha, the officer in charge of guarding the royal court, is a Brigadier Zdravkovic. I suggest that when the time comes, you join him.'

'How will we know if the coup has been successful?' Sasha asked.

'They are keeping a phone line open from Simovic to us. He will call when there is any news.'

'And how will the rest of the country find out?'

'There will be a radio broadcast. They have got someone who will impersonate Peter and inform the populace that he is now king.'

Sasha shot up in his seat. 'Impersonate him! That can't be allowed.'

Masterson raised a placatory hand. 'I understand your objection, but consider this. The people need to be reassured that the king is backing us. That is what gives the coup its legitimacy.'

'Then Peter should tell them so himself.'

'And he will, in due course. But think about it. How can we wake him up at some ungodly hour in the morning, tell him he is now king and expect him to make a broadcast before he has had a chance to assimilate the news? It would be inhuman. After all, he is only seventeen.'

Sasha relaxed but shook his head. 'I can see the necessity, but I wish there was some other way.'

'It isn't our decision in the final analysis,' Masterson pointed out. 'This isn't our show.'

After that, there was nothing to do but wait. Someone suggested a game of bridge to pass the time, but no one was able to concentrate and they soon gave up. Leo found herself wishing she had brought a book to read. P.G. Wodehouse would be her choice, to help to pass the time and lighten the mood. Sasha smoked and paced the floor.

A long silence was broken by Glenn. 'For God's sake, Sasha, sit down, will you? You're like a cat on hot bricks.'

Sasha came to a standstill in front of him. 'You don't understand. How could you? This whole situation has very unhappy memories for me.'

'How so?'

'Back in 1903 there was another coup, when King Alexander Obrenovic and his wife were assassinated.'

'I know all about that,' Glen said irritably.

'What you do not know is that my father was captain of the Royal Guard at that time. He knew as well as anyone that Alexander and his wife were unfit to rule, but he also knew his duty. He tried to stop the assassins and was cut to pieces in the palace courtyard.'

There was a moment of stunned silence. Then Glen said, 'I'm so sorry, Sasha. I had no idea.'

Leo saw her husband take a deep breath and move his shoulders to relieve the tension. 'No. How could you?'

Masterson said, 'I can see that the association is uncomfortable for you, Sasha. But there is no question this time of assassination. All we are looking for is a peaceful transition of power.'

'If for a moment I had thought otherwise, I should not be here now,' Sasha said.

The silence that followed was broken by Alexander Glen. 'Listen!'

Masterson opened a window and they all heard the rumble of tanks coming closer.

'Our people?' Sasha asked.

'Let's hope so,' Masterson replied with a grim smile. 'What time is it?'

'Just after two,' Glen said.

Twenty minutes later the phone rang. Masterson picked it up.

347

'Yes? … Yes? … Good! And the tanks? … Yes, of course. Thank you for letting me know.' He turned to the others. 'Cvetkovic is in custody at the War Office.'

Another tense wait followed and then the phone rang again. Masterson listened and turned to the others. 'Mirkovic's men are in control of the streets and of the area around the palace. The city is quiet and there is no sign of opposition.'

'Then we've done it!' Glenn exclaimed triumphantly.

'*They've* done it,' Masterson corrected. 'We must remember that. If it became known that we have had any part in it, it could cause a major diplomatic incident. HMG does not go around unseating the rulers of allied countries.'

'Yes, of course,' Glen responded more soberly. 'But all the same, I think we might allow ourselves a moment of private rejoicing, don't you?'

'I think we might,' Masterson agreed. 'I've been saving this for a special occasion.' He produced a bottle of Glen-fiddich whisky from a cupboard and poured them all a generous tot. Raising his glass, he said, 'To the future of Yugoslavia and ever closer alliance with Britain.'

After they had drunk the toast there was a sense of anti-climax while they waited for morning and the next act in the drama. Eventually, Sasha looked at his watch. It was almost five a.m. 'When is that broadcast scheduled to go out?'

'At six o'clock.'

'Just over an hour. I'm going to join Zdravkovic at the palace. I don't want anyone giving Peter the news until I'm there.'

'Take this.' Masterson opened a drawer and took out a sheet of paper. 'It's a safe conduct signed by Simovic. I thought we might need something to let us move around the city until things are quieter.'

The palace was situated in the area of the city known as Dedinje, the most affluent neighbourhood, and was quite close to the diplomatic quarter, so Leo and Sasha decided to walk there. It was just beginning to get light as they walked down Prince Alexander Karadjordjevic Boulevard towards the hill on which the palace stood. They were stopped where two tanks were drawn up across the road, but the safe conduct saw them through without further query. The city was uncannily quiet. The only sound was the first tentative chirruping of the birds in the park surrounding the palace compound, but glancing around her, Leo was aware of faces peering out between the slits of closed curtains. The sight of armed sentries at every road junction was enough to deter anyone from venturing out.

At the gates of the park, they found two armoured cars and a small group of officers in the uniform of the Royal Yugoslav Air Force. Sasha approached a man wearing the insignia of a brigadier.

'Brigadier Zdravkovic? I am Count Alexander Malkovic.'

'Ah, Count!' Zdravkovic seemed relieved to see them. 'I was told to expect you. They know you in the palace. That will make things much easier when we go in.'

'What about the Royal Guards?' Sasha asked.

'Those on duty out here have been returned to their barracks and replaced by my own men. The palace is surrounded but so far we have made no attempt to enter. I did not wish to disturb His Highness – I mean His Majesty – until it was necessary.'

'Very good,' Sasha said. 'We will wait a little longer.'

Zdravkovic was regarding Leo somewhat doubtfully. Sasha took her arm. 'May I introduce my wife?'

'Ah, Countess,' the officer bowed slightly. 'Forgive me. I did not recognise you.'

'There is no reason why you should,' Leo said.

Sasha went on, 'The young king knows my wife well. I think he will find her presence reassuring.'

'Of course, of course,' Zdravkovic said.

A distant clock struck five-thirty. Sasha said, 'I suggest we wait another ten minutes. Then we will move in.'

At the end of that time, he and Leo joined Zdravkovic in one of the armoured cars and, followed by two others full of armed men, they drove up the long slope to where the palace buildings clustered on top of the hill. Looking ahead, Leo was glad that their destination was the New Palace, not the old one. It had been built in the 1920s, so was not the one where Sasha's father had been struck down, distancing it from his youthful memories. As they approached the white stucco façade with its neo-classical pillars, she saw one of the guards on duty at the foot of the steps leading up to the main door turn and shout something. Seconds later the doors opened and half a dozen men in the uniform of the Royal Guard clattered down, readying their rifles as they came.

'Stop. Let me deal with this,' Sasha commanded.

He got out of the car and approached the sergeant in charge. Recognising him, the man lowered his weapon and came to attention.

'You know me, Vassili,' Sasha said. 'You know I am a friend of Prince Peter and I mean no harm to him or anyone else here. I am here to tell you that there has been a change of government. Prince Paul has been deposed and Peter is about to become king. I am here to break the news to him and support him in any way I can. If you are in any doubt, there will be a broadcast on the wireless in a few minutes announcing the change to the general public.'

The sergeant looked from Sasha to the armed men behind him with a worried frown. 'I need to clear this with my commanding officer.'

'Of course,' Sasha agreed. 'We will wait here.'

There was a pause and then Leo's attention was drawn by movement further along the terrace and murmurs of surprise from the men behind her. Turning, she caught her husband's sleeve.

'Sasha! Look!'

Coming towards them, in dressing gown and pyjamas, was Peter. Seeing them, he broke into a run.

'Sasha! Thank God you're here. I don't know what is going on. There's been someone on the radio pretending to be me and saying I've been proclaimed king. My guards wouldn't let me go down to find out what's happened, so I climbed down the drainpipe.'

Sasha bowed deeply. 'Your Majesty.'

Peter stopped short and stared at him. 'You mean…?'

'The government has changed. You have been declared of age and proclaimed king.'

'Changed? How?'

'Overnight, Prime Minister Cvetkovic has been arrested and a new government has taken the place of the old one.'

'And my uncle…?'

'Prince Paul is in Zagreb at the moment, I understand. Rest assured, he will not be harmed.'

Peter straightened his shoulders and ran a hand through his tousled hair. In that moment Leo saw him take on his new role, the role for which Sasha had helped to prepare him.

'So, who is my new Prime Minister?'

'General Simovic, sire.'

Boots clattered on the stone steps and they looked round to see the captain of the Royal Guard with a company of his men behind him. It was obvious that he had been roused from sleep. He was bare-headed and his tunic was only half-buttoned, but in his hand he brandished a revolver.

'What do you want?' he demanded. 'Why are you here?'

Behind her, Leo sensed movement as Zdravkovic's men reacted by reaching for their weapons.

'The first man to raise a rifle gets a bullet in the head!' the captain shouted. 'Put down your weapons. This is treason!'

Sasha stepped forward. 'Captain,' he said calmly, 'I think you are under some misapprehension. There is no treason here. His Majesty King Peter is among friends. You were wrong to try to detain him.'

He moved aside to reveal the pyjama-clad figure behind him.

Peter stepped forward in his turn. 'Please tell your men to stand down, Captain. As you see, I am perfectly safe.'

'Your Highness— Your Majesty— sir,' the captain babbled. 'Forgive me. I heard the broadcast. I thought it was a hoax.'

Peter smiled. 'So did I, Captain. But it seems not. Please don't worry. I appreciate that your intentions were to keep me safe.'

As they spoke, a car drew up to the steps and Simovic stepped out. He looked around at the assembled company until his eyes alighted on Peter. Approaching him, he said, 'Your Majesty, I salute you as King of Yugoslavia. From this moment you will exercise your full sovereign power.'

'Thank you, General.' Peter extended his hand and Simovic bowed over it.

'This is because of the signing of the pact?' Peter asked.

'Yes, Your Majesty.'

'Good! Now we can repudiate it. Do the people know?'

'Only those who have heard the broadcast at the moment.'

'Ah, yes. The broadcast. You had no right to allow someone to imitate me.'

Simovic bent his head. 'Forgive me, sire. But we felt it would be… inappropriate to ask you to speak yourself with so little notice.'

Peter regarded him for a moment with compressed lips. Then he said, 'Yes, I can see that. What about the people who have not heard the broadcast?'

'Leaflets explaining the situation are being dropped from aircraft over all the major cities as we speak.'

'That's all very well, but the people must see me in person. Otherwise, they cannot be assured that I am a party to this new regime. Some will guess that that was not my voice on the radio and they may think that… well, in short, that you have done away with me.'

'Your Majesty—' Simovic protested, and the young man smiled suddenly.

'It's all right. I know you would never countenance such a thing. But others may not be so sure.'

'His Majesty is making a good point,' Sasha said.

'Yes, yes,' Simovic replied. 'We have already thought of it. I suggest a motorcade through the streets this afternoon, if that is agreeable.'

'Excellent idea!' The young king's face brightened. 'I shall drive my new car. Now,' he looked around the assembled company, 'have any of you had breakfast?'

There was a general murmur of denial.

'Nor have I and I'm starving!' He turned to his major-domo who was hovering at the door. 'Bogdan, ask them to prepare some food for me and my friends here.'

The major-domo bowed. 'Breakfast is already waiting in the dining room, sir.'

'Good! Gentlemen, shall we?' He looked around and his gaze lighted on Leo, standing quietly in the background. He moved towards her and offered his arm. 'Countess?'

Leo curtsied and took his arm and they led the rest of the group into the palace.

When the meal was over Leo and Sasha begged to be excused to go home and snatch a few hours of sleep, a request that was granted on condition that they return in time to join the motorcade. The tanks had disappeared, and as they walked back, crowds were beginning to gather, many of them waving copies of the leaflets that had showered down from the sky less than an hour earlier. The mood was one of happy excitement.

Leo squeezed her husband's hand. 'This is what you've been hoping for. Well done, my darling.'

'I hope it is,' he answered, 'but we are far from out of the woods yet. We don't know what Paul will do. He's in Croatia at the moment, and there are elements there who would be happy to foment trouble in Serbia. It's not impossible that they might try to persuade him to make a counter-coup backed by Croatian units in the army.'

That afternoon, however, was given over to rejoicing. The Holy Assembly of Bishops convened to welcome the coup and the Orthodox Patriarch, Gavrilo V, broadcast supporting it. Peter insisted on driving himself in the parade through the city with the hood down on his car and without bodyguards, and the streets were lined with cheering crowds. Many of them waved Yugoslav flags, but amongst those, there was a generous sprinkling of Union Jacks and the shouts of 'Long Live the King' and 'Long Live Yugoslavia' were joined by cries of 'Long Live the United Kingdom'. Then someone started the chant they had all heard after the news came out of the signing of the pact with Germany: 'Better a war than the Pact, better a grave than a slave!' Following the procession in their own car, Leo felt a lump in her throat and reached for Sasha's hand again.

The question remained of what should happen to Prince Paul. His wife and children had remained in Belgrade, and his train was rerouted back to the city that evening. He was met by Simovic and taken to the War Office, where he and his two co-regents relinquished power. The same train then carried Paul and his family to Athens, en route to exile.

'Frankly,' Sasha said when they heard the news, 'I don't think he'll be sorry. He never wanted the regency. He will be happier living as a private gentleman.'

Next day the new king was inaugurated in the presence of the Patriarch.

'So, it's done,' Leo said as they left St Mark's Church after the ceremony.

'Yes,' Sasha agreed, 'but have we done what is really in the country's best interests? Everything now depends on how Hitler reacts.'

Chapter Forty-One

Paris

March 27th 1941

Alix woke with a sense of foreboding that she could not immediately understand. Then she remembered the arrests of the previous day. In the kitchen she found Marie Louise, pale and red-eyed, toying with a crust of bread. Germaine put a jug of coffee on the table, then she went to a cupboard and pulled out a wireless set.

'Let's see if we can get Radio Londres and find out what's going on in the rest of the world.'

After twiddling the knobs for a few moments, she succeeded in finding the right frequency, in time to hear the announcement that was their only lifeline to the outside world. '*Ici Londres. Les Français parlent aux Français.*' They huddled over the set, keeping the volume as low as possible. There was no guarantee that some other resident of the block would not denounce them to the authorities if they heard.

'There has been a coup d'etat in Yugoslavia,' the newsreader said. 'The Regent, Prince Paul, has been ousted and Peter, the seventeen-year-old son of the assassinated King Alexander, has been declared King.'

Alix put down her cup. 'Oh, my God! Oh, my God!'

'Hush a moment,' Germaine said.

The newsreader went on, 'The news has been welcomed in England. Prime Minister Winston Churchill declared that Yugoslavia has "found its soul". In Belgrade, the king was greeted by ecstatic crowds chanting pro-British slogans, and there were demonstrations in favour of the new regime in several other cities.'

Germaine switched off the radio and looked at Alix. 'I know you have family in Belgrade. How will this affect them?'

Alix ran her hands through her hair. 'My father must have been involved. He is very close to Prince Peter – King Peter. I hope he is safe. Was there any fighting?'

'The news didn't mention any. But I presume Hitler will not welcome the change. Doesn't this mean there is a danger that he might invade?'

'I thought,' Marie Louise put in, 'that the Yugoslav government had signed a pact with Germany. The newspapers here were announcing it as a great success only the other day.'

'That will be what triggered the coup,' Alix said. 'My God, they must have been planning this for months!'

'But if Hitler invades, will they be able to stand up to him?' Germaine asked.

Alix shook her head. 'I don't know. I'm so out of touch. I should have guessed this would happen…' She raised her head with sudden decision. 'I have to go home! Germaine, Marie Louise, I'm sorry to leave you in the lurch at such a terrible moment, but I must go back. I need to find out what has happened to my family. And whatever is going to happen next, I want to be part of it.'

'You are right,' Germaine said decisively. 'There will not be much you can do here anyway. Your cover may be blown and you could be in danger. You should go while you still can.'

'But how will you get there?' Marie Louise asked.

'I shall go south, down the line we have set up. They all know me now. It should be easy.'

'But even if you get to Marseilles,' Germaine said, 'how will that help? German submarines are patrolling the Mediterranean. There is hardly any shipping moving.'

'I can go over the mountains into Spain.'

'Then what?'

'The escapers are told to go to the British consul in Barcelona. I could do that.'

'You have a British passport as well as a Yugoslav one, don't you?' Marie Louise said.

'No, damn! I destroyed it when they walked into Paris. I didn't want to risk being interned as an enemy alien. But even if I can convince the consul that I have British nationality and get him to send me back there, what good would it do? I can't take the *Orient Express* across Europe to Belgrade, like we used to do. And it's not possible to fly direct. I can't see the British government putting themselves out to get me home.' She shook her head in frustration. 'There must be a way.'

'You need to go to Switzerland, not Spain,' Germaine said. 'They really are neutral and as long as Yugoslavia remains so, I can't see why there should not be flights from Geneva to Belgrade.'

'Of course!' Alix exclaimed. 'That's the answer.'

'If you can get to Switzerland…' Marie Louise said.

Alix was thinking hard. 'Lyon is not so far from the border. The family we stay with when I'm taking the escapers south are very helpful. I'm sure they would let me stay for a while and maybe M—' She stopped herself, remembering that no one else was supposed to know the name. 'He might have some ideas about how I could cross.'

'There will be smugglers going back and forth with black market goods,' Germaine said. 'If you can get close to the border you might find someone who can put you in touch with one of them. Do you have money?'

'I always carry some for emergencies. I don't know if it will be enough. I shall have to hope.'

'It seems the best chance you have,' Germaine said. 'You had better travel as Monique Gaultier until you cross the border, in case the Abwehr are looking for you under your real name. And if Hitler declares war on your country, as a Yugoslav you could be arrested and interned.'

'But I shall need my Yugoslav passport if I make it as far as Geneva,' Alix pointed out.

'Then hide it securely in case you are searched before you get there.'

'Don't worry. I've got it sewn into the lining of my coat.'

'So, when will you go?' Marie Louise asked.

'Straight away, I suppose.' She reached across the table and grasped her friend's hand. 'I'm sorry. I hate to leave you.'

'Wait,' Germaine said. 'I think you should go too, Marie Louise. If you can get across the demarcation line, you would be safer in Vichy France. Your parents are there, aren't they?'

'No, they are just this side, but my father crosses regularly to a hospital. That's how we've been getting the escapers across – in an ambulance.'

Germaine jerked up in her seat. 'Dear God! I'd forgotten! Who else knows about this?'

'Well, Boris, of course…' Marie Louise's voice faded. 'You think they are in danger?' she whispered.

'Boris is tough, and brave. He will hold out for as long as he can. But everyone gives in, in the end.' Germaine leaned closer and put her hand on Marie Louise's shoulder. 'You must go with Alix today. Tell your parents they must go into hiding, at least temporarily. We don't know if the Abwehr are aware of the escape line. Boris had a lot of other irons in the fire. Did Gaveau know?'

'No, I'm pretty sure he didn't,' Alix said. 'Boris was very good at… at compartmentalising things, and he made a point of not telling anyone anything they didn't need to know. The sabotage work, the intelligence gathering, the escape line – they were all kept separate.'

'Yes, you are right there,' Germaine agreed. 'But we can't risk the possibility that the Nazis won't find out about the escape line. You must warn your parents, Marie Louise.'

'Yes, of course,' she said. 'I pray it won't be too late.'

'What about the rest of the line?' Alix asked.

'All that was arranged by Brigadier Hauet through his contacts. You remember? I told you about him. The man who works with the retired colonial soldiers. Boris didn't know anything about them. And no one in the chain knew anything except the name of the next person, so if we can take Marie Louise's parents out of the picture, the rest should be safe.'

As soon as they could gather their things together, Alix and Marie Louise embraced Germaine and left the flat. The streets were busy with early workers so they quickly lost themselves in the crowd. At the station Alix bought the tickets while Marie Louise skulked outside, keeping her head down. These were dangerous moments.

In her disguise as Monique Gaultier there was little chance of Alix being picked up by the Abwehr, but they both knew that there might be an arrest warrant out for her companion. As they approached the ticket barrier, Alix's heart was beating fast.

Marie Louise touched her arm. 'If they stop me, you must go on. I need you to get through to warn my parents.'

Alix hesitated a moment. It seemed like treachery to leave her friend in danger, but she knew there would be nothing she could do to help. She nodded. 'I understand.'

As they had planned, the station was busy with people on their way to work. The north of France might be occupied, but the normal commercial activity had to continue. People still needed to earn a living. They joined the line waiting to go through the barrier to board the train to Tours. People were holding out their tickets and their documents to be checked, but the train was due to leave in a few moments and everyone was in a hurry. The guard was only glancing at the papers and waving people through. Alix held out her own and passed onto the platform. She turned to wait for Marie Louise and her heart seemed to stop for a moment. She could not see her. Surely, she could not have been arrested and taken away in those few seconds! Then her friend appeared. She had been shouldered aside by two large men in their hurry to catch the train.

Alix grabbed her hand. 'Thank God! Quick, or we'll miss it.'

They scrambled aboard and found seats. Alix leant back with a sigh of relief. That was the first hurdle cleared. Her mood was quickly changed, however, by the sight of her friend's pale, set face and restless hands. It was not hard to imagine the torment of anxiety she was suffering.

As they got off the train at Tours, Alix's heart sank. Papers were being checked more thoroughly here. Marie Louise touched her arm. 'This way. I know another way out.'

She led Alix along the platform to where a small kiosk selling papers and magazines stood. Just behind it there was a small gate leading out to a back street.

'This is where they deliver the papers in the morning,' Marie Louise said. 'It's supposed to be kept locked but it never is.'

She pushed the gate and it opened and they made their way at a brisk walk down the side street to the main road.

'How did you know about that?' Alix asked.

Marie Louise grinned briefly. 'I had a friend who lived in Amboise. We used to go backwards and forwards to each other's houses, and if we were short of money, we used to nip onto the train without paying. We found this way out to avoid the ticket collector.'

There had been no chance to contact Marie Louise's father, so there was no one to meet them, and Alix was glad to be with someone who knew her way around. The Beauclerc family lived in the Quartier Saint-Symphorien in a tall, narrow house on a tree-lined boulevard. As they approached it, Alix stopped suddenly and drew Marie Louise into an alleyway.

'I think you should wait here and let me go in first – just to be sure… well, you know.' They both understood that she meant – in case the Abwehr were already there.

'But what will you say if…'

'I shall just pretend to be a patient expecting to attend the surgery. Don't worry. I'm sure it will be all right. I won't be long.'

Leaving Marie Louise out of sight, Alix walked as casually as she could manage up to the house. There was a separate door to one side that led directly to the doctor's waiting room and surgery and as she approached she was relieved to see a woman come out, holding a small boy by the hand. An elderly man leaning on a stick went in as she came out. It seemed that the surgery was operating normally, but to be sure, Alix went down the side of the house to where a door gave access to the kitchen. She waited for a moment, listening and peering through the glass panes. Someone was moving inside, but without haste, and humming softly. Alix tapped on the door and went in.

Madame Beauclerc was standing at the stove, stirring a saucepan. She swung round as Alix entered. 'Alix? We were not expecting you.' Her expression grew taut. 'Is something wrong?'

'We do have a problem,' Alix said, trying to speak as calmly as possible. 'You have not had any... unwelcome visitors?'

'Visitors?' Madame's tone was sharp with alarm. 'Should we expect them?'

'I'll explain in a moment. Marie Louise is waiting outside. Let me fetch her.'

She ran back into the street and saw Marie Louise peering anxiously from her hiding place in the alley. She waved to her, and in a moment, she was at her side.

'Is everything all right?'

'Yes, so far. But I'm afraid I've worried your Mama. She's in the kitchen.'

Marie Louise brushed past her and ran into the house, throwing herself into her mother's arms.

'Oh, *Maman*, *Maman*! Thank God you're safe. I've been out of my mind with worry.'

Madame Beauclerc stroked her daughter's hair and murmured a few consoling words, then looked across her head to Alix.

'What has happened?' Her voice was strained but she had herself under control.

'The group has been betrayed and some of us arrested,' Alix said. 'We don't know yet how far it has gone but it is possible that your connection may be revealed.'

Madame put her daughter gently away from her and said, 'You father needs to know about this. Wait until I fetch him.'

She left the room and Marie Louise sank into a chair with her head in her hands. Dr Beauclerc came in, glancing swiftly from her to Alix.

'Tell me.'

Alix explained as briefly as possible. 'Boris Vildé knows about your part in the escape line,' she concluded. 'He will do his best not to betray you but...'

'You need say no more,' the doctor said. 'We need to leave here.'

'Yes, I'm sorry, but I think you must.'

'Fortunately, we have anticipated this possibility. We have bought a little gîte in the hills of the Auvergne and it is provisioned for an extended stay. No one else knows about it. We shall simply take a holiday.' He smiled tenderly at his daughter. 'Dry your eyes, *Cherie*. We shall all enjoy a little break from routine.'

'I will pack,' Madame said. 'It will not take long. Marie Louise, pull yourself together and make us a coffee and then put together some food for the journey. Alix will help you.'

'We shouldn't wait!' Marie Louise exclaimed. 'We should go now!'

Dr Beauclerc put his hand on her head. 'I have two patients still to see. It will cause suspicion if I leave without completing my surgery. By the time I have finished, we shall be ready to go.'

Both he and his wife left the room and Alix said admiringly, 'Your parents are brave people. They have taken this so calmly. Now we must do the same. Show me where the coffee things are.'

As the doctor had predicted, by the time he returned, the coffee was waiting, a basket of food had been packed and his wife had brought down a suitcase.

'We have left plenty of clothes at the cottage,' she said. 'This is only last-minute essentials.'

As they drank the coffee, Dr Beauclerc outlined their plans. 'We shall take the ambulance. You two will be patients in urgent need of treatment. Your mother often comes with me when we have an emergency, so the police at the crossing point will not find it unusual. Alix, are you joining us at our little country bolt-hole? You are more than welcome.'

Alix smiled at him. 'I'm grateful for the offer, but I plan to make my way to Switzerland. You will have heard the news from Belgrade. I'm trying to get home. But I shall be glad to come with you across the demarcation line.'

'Good. Then let us go.'

He led them out to the garage at the back of the house where the ambulance was kept. The suitcase and the food were stowed away in lockers and Alix and Marie Louise pulled off their outer clothes and lay down on the two stretchers, covering themselves with blankets.

'If we are stopped, you are both suffering from a high fever,' the doctor said. 'So act accordingly.'

As the ambulance started, Alix had an idea. She pulled her handbag out from where she had hidden it under the blanket and found her lipstick. It was the work of minutes to adorn her face with red spots. Then she handed the lipstick across to Marie Louise. They had just finished when the ambulance came to a standstill and they heard the border guard questioning Dr Beauclerc. Then he walked around to the rear of the ambulance.

'If I were you, I'd keep well clear,' they heard the doctor say. 'Those patients are highly infectious.'

The rear doors were opened and a face peered in. Alix let out a groan and mumbled incoherently and the doors were closed again. Moments later the ambulance rocked as they passed through the barrier and into Vichy France. Dr Beauclerc parked at the back of the hospital and laughed aloud at the sight of their faces as they scrambled out. Madame produced a jar of some kind of salve and some cotton wool from the first aid kit for them to clean off the lipstick, and while they were doing that, the doctor disappeared into the hospital.

When he came back, he said, 'I have just telephoned Father Dumont and told him one of his parishioners needs to be picked up from the hospital, Alix. He knows you well by now, so there shouldn't be any difficulty there. Now, we should get on our way.'

'How?' Alix looked around, 'You're not going all the way in the ambulance, are you?'

'No. I bought a second-hand car and left it here,' he said. 'No one else knows about it, so it should be hard for the police to trace – if they even try. We are in the free zone now, after all.'

'Don't let down your guard,' Alix warned him. 'And watch out for anyone wearing the uniform of the SOL.'

'What is that?'

'They are a pro-Nazi militia. Nasty types.'

'Well, I don't suppose we shall come across them where we are going,' he said.

Alix turned to Marie Louise. 'You must go. I'm so sorry we have to part.'

Her friend hugged her tightly. 'So am I. Shall we ever meet again, do you think?'

'Of course we shall, when the war is over and France is free again. Just take care of yourself till then.'

She shook hands with Dr and Mrs Beauclerc and thanked them again for their help. Then she kissed Marie Louise on both cheeks and watched them get into the old car. As they drove away, she felt a wrench at her heart. It seemed the last threads of her old life in Paris were being torn away.

Chapter Forty-Two

Srebrenica

March 27th 1941

Steve was encoding a report for his handlers in Baker Street.

> *The news of the coup in Belgrade has met with a varied response here. The commanding officers, who are all Serbs, have reacted with delight, seeing it as reinforcing the anti-Axis approach they favour. However, some of the NCOs and ordinary soldiers, many of whom are Croats or Bosnians, see it very differently, as an attempt to strengthen the Serbian control over the country. I am concerned that if Hitler decides to attack there may be mass desertions or fifth column activities carried out by the Croat and Slovene elements in the army.*
>
> *With regard to the preparedness or otherwise of the army to meet any such attack, I have to report that the situation offers little reason for optimism. There is a serious lack of equipment in all areas. Tanks and field guns, where they exist at all, are so old as to be virtually obsolete and there is an acute*

lack of mobility. Many units still rely on draught animals to move equipment, and even those are in short supply and of poor quality.

On a personal level, I have been well received at HQ, largely because I am seen as a possible conduit for deliveries of arms and equipment from the UK. I have not formed a very high opinion of the commanding officers, who seem to lack any real sense of the urgency of the situation. The exception to this is Brigadier Draza Mihailovic, who has a very good grasp of the problems and is fervently anti-Nazi. In the event of an attack and defeat by Axis forces, I think he is our best hope of creating a credible guerrilla force to resist German occupation.

Steve transmitted his report and locked his radio set away. Getting up and stretching his arms, he wandered over to the door of his office and looked out across the parade ground. On the far side, a team of oxen was struggling to extricate a field gun. It had been a wet spring, and as a result, the cart tracks that passed for roads had been turned into a trampled quagmire of fetlock-deep mud. He shook his head in disbelief. The second army was supposed to be deployed to defend the eastern sector of the border with Hungary along a front that stretched from the River Drava to the River Danube, but at the moment most of the force was encamped well behind that line, and he could see that in the event of an attack, it would take days, if not weeks, to bring them into position.

A gleam of sunshine broke through the clouds, and Steve lifted his gaze to the forest-covered mountains surrounding the town. The trees were coming into leaf, and he knew from his expeditions around the area that the forest floor was now covered by a delicate carpet of wild blue crocuses. It was beautiful, but his imagination overlayed the scene with images he had seen of the landscape of France ravaged by the First World War, a desolation of mud with the skeletal remains of a few trees. It was almost unbearable to think that the beauty before him now could be reduced to the same condition. He took a deep breath and returned his attention to the immediate prospect in front of him. Brigadier Mihailovic was crossing the parade ground and he went to join him. He had made a point of building up a good relationship with him. He was not the easiest man to work with, short-tempered and autocratic, but he was capable of making quick decisions, and Steve had noticed that the lower-ranking officers had more respect for him than for the other men in command. He had encouraged him to talk about his part in the heroic Serbian struggle to free their homeland in the last war, and in return Mihailovic had pressed him for details of his escape from occupied France. As a result Steve felt they had built up a mutual respect, and he had made up his mind that if, or when, the German attack materialised, Mihailovic was the man he wanted to follow.

Chapter Forty-Three

Lyon, France

March 27th 1941

The links in the escape line set up by Brigadier Hauet were still intact and Alix reached her destination without incident. She was met as usual by Marcel Pasquier with the baker's van.

'You are alone?' he said in surprise. 'No... parcels to convey?'

'Today I am the parcel, myself,' she told him. 'But, if you will forgive me, I will explain when we get to your home so I don't have to repeat it all to Madame and Florence.'

As they drove, she saw once again the American flag flying outside the consulate.

'So the Americans are still here.'

'Why would they leave?' Pasquier said with a shrug. 'Their country still refuses to come to the aid of the Allies.'

'At least they have passed the Lend–Lease bill, so we can buy arms from them.'

'True. But the news is bad. The British Army is in retreat in North Africa. They can't stand up to Rommel's Africa Corps. And the bombing of the British cities continues. I foresee that soon Britain will be forced to surrender, before their country is reduced to rubble.'

Alix sighed and said no more.

At the Pasquier's home, she explained her situation to the family. 'I am afraid that the Abwehr may have put out a warrant for my arrest, so I need to get out of the country and also I need to find out what is happening to my family after the coup.'

'Will your parents be affected by the change of regime?' Madame asked.

'I know my father will, but my mother—' She left the sentence unfinished as a sob caught her throat. 'I don't actually know where my mother is. The last time I heard, she was in England, but that was months ago. I am praying she has returned to Belgrade, but I am very afraid that she may have been caught in the Blitz in London.'

Madame Pasquier reached out and patted her hand. '*Pauvre petite!* That must be so hard for you. We had no idea.'

'How could you have?' Alix swallowed and forced herself to concentrate on the matter in hand. 'I need to find a flight back, and the best chance seems to be from Geneva. So I want to get to Switzerland. Can you help me?'

'Switzerland?' Pasquier shook his head. 'I'm sorry. We have no connections in that direction.'

Alix's hopes sank. She had hoped for some form of concrete suggestion. 'Do you know how things are at the border?'

'I believe the Swiss are determined not to compromise their neutrality by accepting fugitives. But perhaps as you are a national of another neutral state…?'

Alix shook her head. 'I dare not use my real name or my Yugoslav passport in case the Vichy authorities are looking for me.'

There was a silence, and the germ of an idea that had come to Alix on the journey from the station began to take root. 'I'm wondering if the American consulate might help me. I presume they have been asked to take care of British interests, and after all, I am half English.'

'Of course!' Madame said. 'That must be the answer.'

'I'll go there tomorrow and ask,' Alix said with renewed optimism.

Pasquier pursed his lips. 'It won't be that easy. The Vichy police and the SOL are watching the embassy and questioning everyone who wants to go in. I've seen it happening as I drive past.'

'But how can they prevent people from entering a neutral embassy?'

'I suppose they cannot in the end, but they can demand to know who you are and what your business is. I think they are obsessed with the idea that the Americans might be smuggling fugitives out of the country. To get in, you would need to have a very convincing story. You say you cannot use your real identity. But what business could Monique Gaultier have with the US Consul??'

Alix sank back in her chair and ran her hand over her eyes.

'Just a moment,' Madame said. 'I think I may have an idea. Jean Claude, the baker, delivers bread every day to the consulate. I know, because he gets a special allowance of flour, so the Americans can have good bread. We know he is sympathetic. Might he not agree to hide Alix in the back of his van and get her in that way? Once she is technically on American soil, the police can't touch her.'

'That's brilliant!' Alix exclaimed. 'Do you think he would agree?'

'I think it is worth asking him,' Pasquier said. 'But there is one difficulty. How do we account for your presence here? He cannot be told about the escape line. He lends his van when I need transport, but he never asks why and I have never told him.'

'Could we not simply tell him that Alix needs to get home? If we say she is British, but she got trapped in France when the Germans took over? An English woman would have every reason not to turn up at the gate of the consulate and be forced to reveal her identity.'

'So how did she get here? How do we know her?'

'I know!' Florence spoke for the first time. 'Say we met when I went on that youth hostelling holiday the last summer before the war. There were lots of English people there. I met Alix and we became friends and I gave her my address, so she has come to us for help.'

'I think that could work,' Pasquier said. 'Why don't you take Alix to see Jean Claude now?'

The baker was prepared to cooperate and suggested that Alix should spend the night at his house in order to be ready when he left on his early morning rounds.

As they parted, Alix took Madame Pasquier's hands. 'I don't know if I'll be back tomorrow or not. If the Consul turns me down, I'll have to find another way. If that happens, can I stay on with you for a day or two?'

Madame kissed her on both cheeks. 'Of course, *ma petite*. But we shall pray that the Consul can help.'

'If I don't come back… I haven't said goodbye properly to Monsieur, or Florence. Will you tell them I'm grateful for all their help?'

'Of course. Now, I must go, before the curfew. *Bonne chance, cherie*. I hope you find your parents both safe and well.'

Alix was woken at the crack of dawn by the smell of freshly baked bread and the sound of the baker and his wife moving around downstairs.

'Ah, good!' Jean Claude said when she appeared in the kitchen. 'I shall be ready to leave in a couple of minutes. There's coffee in the pot. Help yourself to a piece of baguette.'

It was the best bread Alix had tasted for a long time, but she was careful not to take too much. She realised that the baker and his family were probably able to keep a little more than they were strictly allowed, but even so, they, like everyone else, must be surviving on around thirteen hundred calories a day, which was all that the meagre rations provided. As soon as she had finished, the baker ushered her out of the back of the house. The rear doors of the van were open and she climbed in and settled herself between the racks of loaves. The smell brought saliva to her mouth and she had to shove her hands into her pockets to stop herself reaching out and pinching small pieces of crust from the nearest ones.

A few minutes later, those thoughts were banished as the van came to a stop, and she heard the baker exchanging some banter with someone outside. From what she could hear, he was speaking to the guards at the consulate gates. She tensed and shrank back in the space, drawing her knees up to her chest in an attempt to make herself as small as possible. To her horror, the rear doors opened and the baker's face appeared. For a second she wondered if he was not, after all, sympathetic to the resistance. There would probably be advantages to him in handing her over to the police. Then he leaned in, pulled a baguette off the nearest shelf and shut the doors again, and she heard him tell the guard to keep it under his cloak and not tell anyone else how he came by it. There was some further cheerful chatter and then the van moved forward and she heard a gate clang shut behind them. She knew that she was now, technically, on American soil and she let herself relax.

She was reminded as she climbed down that the baker still needed to retain his cover. He dumped a tray of rolls into her arms and said, 'Carry those in for me.'

She did as he told her and found herself in a huge kitchen. A man in white overalls took the tray and called over his shoulder, 'Got yourself a new assistant, Jean Claude?'

'Only temporary,' was the reply. 'Come out to the van for a moment. I've got something that might interest you.'

As the man moved away, the baker caught Alix's eye and jerked his head towards the rear of the room, where double swing doors must lead, she recognised to the rest of the building. Without hesitating, she pushed them open and found herself in a large dining room. How the baker was going to explain her disappearance, she had no idea, but that was up to him. On the far side of the dining room another double door led out to a hallway. A woman in a smart suit was coming down the stairs. She stopped short and stared at Alix.

'Who are you? What do you want?'

Alix drew a deep breath. 'I'm a British subject and I need to see the Consul.'

'How did you get in here?'

'I came in the baker's van. Please, I need help. Where can I find the Consul?'

'He is not here at the moment.' The woman looked at her and seemed to come to a decision. 'My name is Constance Harvey and I am the Vice-consul. Come with me.'

Alix followed her up the stairs and into a large room furnished with a desk and several easy chairs. The Vice-consul seated herself behind the desk and indicated a chair in front of it.

'Sit down, please. Now, tell me who you are and why you need my help.'

Alix swallowed, trying to bring some moisture to a mouth that had suddenly gone dry. 'My name is Alexandra Malkovic. My mother is British, but my father is Serbian – I mean Yugoslavian. I have come to ask for your help to get across the border into Switzerland so I can get a flight back to Belgrade.'

'I see. Do you have any documentation to prove this?'

'Yes. Please, can you lend me some scissors?' Alix slid off her coat, causing a dusting of flour to fall on the carpet. The Vice-consul, seemingly unsurprised by the request, opened a drawer, handed her a pair of scissors and watched as she slit the stitching along the seam in the lining and extracted her Yugoslavian passport. Constance Harvey studied it carefully and then raised her eyes to Alix.

'So what is preventing you from simply taking a train and presenting this at the border?'

'I'm afraid the Vichy police may have a warrant for my arrest.'

If she had expected to see shock on the other woman's face she was mistaken. She merely lifted her eyebrows.

'Would you like to tell me why?'

Alix hesitated for a moment. She was so conditioned to secrecy that it seemed wrong to explain to this stranger.

But she reminded herself that this was a foreign diplomat, and an American, whose sympathies must lie with the Allied cause. If she could trust anyone, she must be able to trust her. So she launched into an account of her work for the Musèe de l'Homme resistance group, finishing with the arrests of Boris and the others. 'I was out of Paris when it happened, which is why I wasn't picked up with the rest.'

Harvey listened without comment until Alix fell silent. Then she said, 'So why here? What brings you to Lyon?'

'I came down the line – the *réseau* – we set up to bring escaped POWs and downed airmen south to Marseilles. I thought this was the closest point to the Swiss border.'

'And this is what you have been doing – bringing escapers down from Paris?'

'Yes. I've brought nine, no, ten men down so far.'

Constance Harvey folded her hands on her desk and leaned forward. 'You won't mind if I say you are probably the most remarkable young woman I've ever met?'

Alix felt herself blush. 'I'm not the only one. There are lots more like me.'

'That doesn't make your contribution any less courageous. So, let's get back to the reason you are here.' She paused in deep thought, tapping her fingers on the desk. 'I'm trying to see a way to get you across the border. But you understand I can't be seen to be aiding someone evading capture.'

'Of course. I understand that.' Alex's hopes began to fade.

The Vice-consul seemed to come to a decision. 'I'm thinking that there may be a way I can help.'

Alix caught her breath. 'Oh, if you can, I should be so grateful.'

'It's not without risk, and it won't be comfortable, but it should work.'

'I don't mind discomfort. Please go on.'

'Until I took up this post, I was based in Switzerland. I still have a small chalet over there and I often go there for the weekend. The border guards are used to seeing me go backwards and forwards, and I have diplomatic immunity, so they don't bother me too much. But that won't extend to letting me take a passenger without producing the correct papers. So what I suggest is, I shut you in the boot when we get close to the border. The boot has a separate lock, not on the same ring as the ignition keys. I shall lock it and put the key down my bra. If the guards should take into their heads to search, I shall tell them that I have lost the key. They cannot search me, and if they were to try to force the boot open, they would be damaging American property. What do you think?'

'I think it's a wonderful plan!' Alix said, and her voice shook. Suddenly the tension of the last days was catching up with her.

'Well, today is Friday and I was planning to take the weekend off anyway, so we have a deal.' Harvey smiled at her.

'I can't tell you how grateful I am.'

'No need. You look as though you're due for a lucky break.'

The telephone on the Consul's desk rang and she picked it up. 'Yes? … Yes, of course. … Look, can I call you back in five minutes? … Yes, fine. Speak to you soon.'

She put the phone down and looked at Alix. 'I'm going to have to ask you to excuse me for an hour or two. But of course you're welcome to stay here in the consulate. Have you had breakfast?'

'Yes – well, sort of.'

'Right.' Harvey touched a bell push on her desk and a young woman put her head round the door of a side room. 'Betty, I want you to take Alexandra up to the library. Make sure she has all the newspapers and get the kitchen to send up some breakfast for her, will you?'

As she left the room, Alix found she was trembling. It was a relief when the secretary showed her into a large room lined with bookshelves on the next floor and left her to sink into a leather armchair. Shortly, a waiter appeared with a tray.

'I wasn't sure what you'd want for breakfast, ma'am. If there's anything else I can get for you, please tell me.'

The tray bore a pot of real coffee – the smell was unmistakable – milk, a boiled egg, some white bread, a croissant, butter and honey. Alix looked at it and back at the waiter, wondering if he had any conception of how rich and rare his offering was. She managed to say, quite casually, 'Oh, no thank you. This will do very well.'

When she had devoured every crumb and drained the coffee pot, she wiped her sticky fingers on the fine linen napkin and looked around her. On a circular table in the middle of the room there was a selection of newspapers – the *New York Times*, the *Washington Post*, several others. Alix fell upon them with almost as much delight as she had fallen on the food. It was the first time in over a year that she had been able to read news that had not been censored or twisted for propaganda purposes. The main item in all the papers was the coup in Yugoslavia, and she read avidly, searching for any reference to her father, but his name was not mentioned, and after a while, she turned her attention to other news. The photographs of London and other British cities hit by the Blitz brought her close to tears. Even Buckingham Palace had been hit, she read, but the king and queen refused to leave the capital. The pictures brought to her mind more vividly than ever the possibility that her mother was there, in the middle of that devastation, perhaps injured, maybe even killed. She turned the page to hide the images.

Over lunch, the main topic of conversation between her and Constance Harvey was the situation in Yugoslavia, and Alix found herself being interrogated about the reasons behind the coup. Then Harvey said, 'So, I plan to leave around four o'clock. Can you amuse yourself until then?'

Alix returned to the library, but now it was hard to concentrate on the newspapers. Her stomach was in a tight knot of anticipation. The Vice-consul's plan sounded watertight, but she could not help imagining what would happen if the border guards somehow forced her to produce the key to the boot. At four o'clock, she went down to Constance Harvey's office and found her locking some papers into her desk.

'Right,' she said. 'Ready?'

Alix nodded, not trusting her voice.

Harvey's Renault Suprastella car was parked in the consulate garage.

'Better get down on the back seat till we're out of the city,' Harvey said. 'I don't want to have to explain you to the goons watching the entrance.'

Alix did as she was bidden, tucking her bag down beside her, and Harvey threw a rug over her. Alix heard the gates opened and Harvey's cheery 'Just off for the weekend,' and the car swung out onto the road. They drove for a few minutes and then Harvey stopped the car and leaned over to lift the rug.

'So far, so good. You can ride up front with me for the next bit.'

They kept to the minor roads, and Alix had a chance to enjoy the scenery as they climbed into the hills. They crossed the River Rhône at the pretty town of Seyssel, and shortly after that, Harvey pulled off the road into a small copse of trees.

'I'm afraid it's time for you to hide yourself.' She opened the boot lid and spread the rug on the floor and threw in a cushion. 'Make yourself as comfortable as you can.'

Alix climbed in and curled up. She hated confined spaces and had been dreading this part of the journey.

'I'm going to lock you in, as we agreed,' Harvey said. 'Don't worry. I'll let you out as soon as it's safe.'

The boot lid clanged shut and Alix found herself in darkness. She heard the key turn in the lock and swallowed down a feeling of panic. Was there going to be enough air for her to breathe? Suppose something happened? What if there was a crash? If Constance was killed, or injured and taken to hospital, no one would know she was in here, and even if she made herself known, they would not have the key to the boot. She forced herself to banish the images that crowded her mind and breathe slowly. The engine started, and the car jolted as it drove back onto the road, then she felt it accelerate. How far to the border? She wished she had asked before she was shut in.

Sooner than she had expected, she felt the car slow to a halt, then the driver's door slammed and she heard footsteps moving away. Where was Constance going? There was a long pause, then the steps returned, doors were opened and shut again. Then someone rattled the handle of the boot and she heard Constance's voice: 'I'm sorry.

It's locked, and I simply cannot think what I've done with the key.'

A man's voice responded and the handle rattled again. 'Will the ignition key not open it?'

'No, it won't. I suppose I should keep the boot key on the same ring, but I don't often need it and having both keys makes it rather cumbersome.'

'I have a Renault myself. Perhaps my key would work.'

Constance chuckled. 'Oh, I doubt it. After all, what would be the point of locking it if anybody with the same make of car could open it?'

The man sounded unhappy. 'I'm supposed to check, you know.'

Constance's voice took on an edge of irritation. 'Look, you do know who I am? I have diplomatic immunity, and you really have no right to check anything.' From somewhere behind them came the sound of a horn. 'I think we are holding up the traffic. I come through here most weekends and I've never been stopped before. I really think you should either call your superior, who won't be happy when he gets a complaint from my ambassador, or let me get on.'

'I'm just trying to do my job,' the man mumbled. 'All right, on your way.'

'About time!' Alix heard her move to the front of the car. 'I shall be reporting this to the relevant authorities. You won't have heard the last of it, I promise you.'

The engine started and the car moved off. They drove on for long enough for Alix to wonder if Constance had forgotten her, but at last, they stopped and the boot lid was lifted. Alix unfolded her cramped limbs and climbed shakily to the ground.

'Are you all right?' Constance asked. 'I'm sorry about the little hold-up at the border. That wretched little man! Give some people a badge and a uniform and they can't resist wielding whatever petty power they think it gives them. But that shouldn't surprise us now we've seen how the Nazis behave. Here…' she handed Alix a bottle of mineral water. 'I expect you're thirsty.'

Alix drank and looked around her. 'Where are we?'

'In Switzerland, obviously, so you're quite safe. The next town is Confignon. You can get a bus from there into the centre of Geneva. Do you have money?'

'Yes, but it's in French francs. I'll need to find a bank to change them.'

'Hmm. The banks are shut now.' Constance thought a moment, then smiled at her. 'You'd better spend the night at my place.'

'Oh, I can't expect you to do that!' Alix exclaimed. 'You've been so good to me already.'

'So I'm not going to leave you destitute without a roof over your head, am I?' Constance said. 'Come on, get in. It's not far.'

Alix slept better that night, in Constance's cosy little chalet, than she had done for a long time. Waking next morning, she stretched luxuriously. She was safe! No more pretending to be someone else. No more shivering with alarm at the sight of a German uniform. Today, or tomorrow perhaps, she would find a flight to Belgrade. She pictured the house where she had grown up and imagined her father waiting there. How would he receive her? Would she be forgiven at last for defying him? She thought of her mother. Would she be there, or would there at least be news of her? Her mind went back to the time she had spent in Paris and the friends she had made there, and she wondered if she would ever see any of them again. Then another image came into her mind. A young man with unruly dark hair and deep-set eyes. She felt in her coat lining and pulled out the photograph he had sent her. Steve! What had happened to him since the day that picture was taken? Would they ever meet again?

She sat up in bed. All those questions would have to wait for another day. All that mattered now was that she was going home.

Epilogue

Berlin

March 28th 1941

In a large, ornately appointed room in the Reich Chancellery in Berlin, a group of high-ranking German officers exchanged uneasy glances as the tirade flowed over them. Adolf Hitler was incandescent with fury.

'These degenerate Slavs have reneged on the treaty! I was wrong ever to think they were capable of keeping their word. Well, they will come to regret it.'

'Perhaps, Mein Führer, they may yet come to see the error of their ways,' one of his braver generals suggested tentatively.

'It is too late for that. We shall act without waiting for possible declarations of loyalty from the new government. I am issuing Directive 25. The Second Army is to prepare to attack at once with the First Panzer Division and Luftwaffe support.'

'But, Mein Führer,' another general exclaimed, 'what about Operation Barbarossa? That is due to be put into operation on May 15th.'

Hitler dismissed the argument with a sweeping gesture. 'By then the Slavs will have been crushed. If not, the Russian campaign will have to wait. I am determined to destroy Yugoslavia militarily and as a state – and to do it with pitiless harshness. The tornado is going to burst upon Yugoslavia with breathtaking suddenness.'

A letter from Holly

Many thanks for choosing to read *A Call to Courage*. This is the first book in a three-book series following the adventures of Alix and Steve and Leo and Sasha through World War ll and is a sequel to my earlier Frontline Nurses trilogy.

Like all my historical novels, this one is based on extensive research and all the major events described in it really happened. While the main characters are fictional many of the subsidiary ones were real people.

The FANY expedition to Finland. I was privileged to be given copies of the actual reports produced by members of the expedition when they returned to England, for which I am grateful to Lynette Beardwood, herself an ex-FANY. Madame Gripenberg, née Diana Mosley-Williams, was the wife of the Finnish ambassador and an ex-FANY and she did in fact request her colleagues' help in providing ambulances during the 'winter war' between Finland and Russia in 1939. My account of that expedition is closely based on those reports.

The Paris Resistance. Paul Rivet was the director of the Musée de l'Homme and was the first person to initiate any resistance to the German occupation. He really did nail a translation of Kipling's poem 'If' to the doors of the museum on the day that the German army entered the city. Boris Vildé, Anatole Lewitsky, Yvonne Oddon and

Agnès Humbert were colleagues of his who took part in the resistance activities. They were all arrested after the group was betrayed. The men were shot and the women were sent to concentration camps.

As early in the war as 1940/41 the established escape *reseaus*, like the Comete line, which were responsible for bringing so many escaped POWs and downed airmen out of France, had not been setup with their safe houses and couriers, so Steve and Alix's activities were on an ad hoc basis, but there were already men and women who were prepared to take great risks to help escapers. Germaine Tillion, another anthropologist, and Paul Hauet were instrumental in setting up and running one of the first such lines. Mary, Comtesse de Milleville, worked as a nurse in World War 1 and used to help escapers to cross from occupied France into the 'free' zone via her estate at Sauveterre de Bearn. Dr Rodocanachi used his surgery in Marseilles as a base for assisting escaping servicemen.

Constance Harvey was the American vice consul in Lyon and she did, indeed, carry secret documents across the frontier, though there is no record of her transporting escaping personel.

Special Operations Executive Brigadier Colin Gubbins was the man in charge of training agents to be dropped into occupied territories and later became the head of the organisation. It is likely that he was the inspiration for Ian Fleming's 'M' in the Bond stories.

Yugoslavia. The coup described in the book really did take place and the British agents who feature in the book were the actual men involved. The Serbian officers and politicians mentioned are also historical figures.

RAF Watton was the home of 82 Squadron flying Blenheim fighter bombers and their exploits and losses were as outlined in the book.

If you've enjoyed reading *A Call to Courage*, please mention it to your friends and family, as a word-of-mouth recommendation can really help make a book. And do please leave a review – it can be as long or as short as you like. I'd be very grateful.

I love hearing from readers, so feel free to get in touch, via my website: hilary@hilarygreen.co.uk. I am also on Facebook at Hilary Green Author.

Acknowledgements

As stated above I am indebted to Lynette Beardwood for all her input regarding the exploits of the FANY.

I want to say a big thank you to Dan O'Brien and Keshini Naidoo and Jennie Ayres for all their invaluable help and to all at Hera and Canelo for allowing this book to find you, the reader.

I hope you will stay with me for the rest of the story.